BITTER IS
THE HEART

Also available by Mina Hardy

Like a Mother
We Knew All Along
After All I've Done

BITTER IS THE HEART

A NOVEL

MINA HARDY

CROOKED
LANE

NEW YORK

Copyright © 2024 by Megan Hart

Published in the United States by Crooked Lane Books, an imprint of The Quick Brown Fox & Company LLC.

Crooked Lane Books and its logo are trademarks of The Quick Brown Fox & Company LLC.

Library of Congress Catalog-in-Publication data available upon request.

ISBN (hardcover): 978-1-63910-863-3
ISBN (ebook): 978-1-63910-864-0

Cover design by Heather VenHuizen

Printed in the United States.

www.crookedlanebooks.com

Crooked Lane Books
34 West 27th St., 10th Floor
New York, NY 10001

First Edition: September 2024

10 9 8 7 6 5 4 3 2 1

For Rob: What should we watch on Shudder tonight?

CHAPTER

1

Someone was standing at the foot of her bed.

In that first moment, alerted by the creak of the floorboards and then the low and soughing sigh, Tamar Glass assumed she was dreaming of her childhood and the many nights she would wake from dreams, terrified that something was coming to get her. As she'd done in childhood, Tamar closed her eyes tight and gripped her pillow with shaking hands as she carefully and slowly retracted the foot that had been foolish enough to wander from beneath the blankets. She took a few careful breaths, counting them, one at a time until she reached the tenth. That one, she held.

She could open her eyes now, roll her body just enough to get a view of the foot of the bed. She could search the shadows for the lumpy shapes that would reveal themselves to be dirty laundry and not a person. Not a monster or a ghost, either. She would open her eyes and find herself, as she'd been every night for the past four years, alone.

A breath.

A creak.

The soft whiff of something rotten tickled her nostrils.

Tamar opened her eyes. A face loomed inches from hers. Dark holes for the eyes. A gaping maw of a mouth, rampant with teeth. Hissing.

She screamed, flailing. It was back, oh, it was back and she wasn't dreaming, this was *real* and she wasn't a child anymore, why was it *here*—

The figure retreated. Tamar grappled for the bedside table and the lamp, managing to switch it on a scant second before she knocked it over. The bulb flickered, casting wild shadows all over the room, but it didn't go out. Shaking, she looked into the corner of the bedroom, convinced it would be empty.

It was not.

The light stopped flickering. Tamar froze in place, uncertain. Was she still sleeping? Dreaming? Slowly, she pinched the soft flesh of her inner thigh, exposed below the edge of the boxer shorts she'd stolen from Garrett before she left him for good.

The woman facing the bedroom corner wore a long flannel nightgown patterned with flowers. High neck. Long sleeves. Ruffled hem. Her gray hair hung to the small of her back. Once it had flowed in thick sheaves of platinum, but it was thin now. Straggly. Her shoulders hunched and shook. It sounded like she was weeping.

She might have been laughing.

Tamar tried to call out, but the words stuck in her throat. She didn't want the figure to turn around. She didn't want it to look at her the way it used to.

The soft patter of liquid hitting the hardwood floor caught her ear. She smelled urine. Her body unlocked—she swung her legs over the bed. No longer terrified, only confused.

"Mom," she said. "How did you get here?"

CHAPTER

2

TAMAR HAD NOT called her mother "Mom" in years. She referred to her by her first name, if she had to address her at all, which Tamar did as infrequently as possible. Yet when faced with terror, the name she'd used during childhood and into her teen years had come out first. She didn't want to dwell on why.

It took an hour to clean her mother up. Ruth Kahan made no protest when Tamar took her by the hand and into the primary bathroom. She didn't struggle at the noise of water spattering in the large, walk-in shower, made no protest when Tamar pulled her nightgown off over her head to reveal her nakedness. As though she were the child, Ruth let herself be gently pushed under the warm spray. She allowed her body to be washed, then her hair. Tamar held the washcloth over the elderly woman's eyes to protect them as she rinsed away the shampoo, the way her mother had done for her when Tamar was a child.

"Oh, Ruth. What happened to your feet?" Tamar knelt outside the shower to wash away the filth that had collected between her mother's toes. The nails were thick and yellowed beneath the chipped crimson polish, but they were trimmed neatly. The feet themselves were swollen and crisscrossed with blue veins and red scratches, some of them deep, with puffy edges. Tamar didn't dare lift them even one at a time, too

aware of how unsteady her mother seemed to be and how likely she was
to topple over. It was clear by the condition of Ruth's feet that she'd
walked with them bare.

All the way from Somerset House? That seemed impossible. The
independent living home where her mother had been a resident for the
past six years was a twenty-minute car ride from Tamar's house—much
longer than that on foot. Even if it was possible that her seventy-seven-
year-old mother had left the place on her own and walked the entire way
without shoes and wearing only a nightgown with nobody stopping her,
nobody noticing she was gone, it was impossible that she could be *here*,
because Tamar's mother had never been to her house.

"Let's get you dried off." Tamar guided Ruth carefully out of the
shower. Using a soft towel, she dried her mother's naked body and
wrapped another around her hair.

Ruth complied, docile and pliable. She'd closed her mouth, which
was a relief. The slack-jawed look had fully disconcerted Tamar almost
as much as finding her mother standing over her bed in the first place.
Tamar guided her back to the bed.

"Sit here. Let me comb out your hair."

Her mother sat without argument. Tamar used the towel to squeeze
out the water from the long gray strands. Ruth's hair had gotten so thin
on top that Tamar could clearly see the pink of her scalp as she carefully
moved the wide-toothed comb through it. Her mother's hair was too
long, too ratty. It had always been such a point of pride for her, a blond
crown she'd spent hours of time and thousands of dollars to maintain.
Now it lay limp and colorless in Tamar's palm, so fragile it tore as she
detangled it.

"There we go." Tamar winced at her tone. She hadn't meant to
address her mother the way she would a toddler or a pet.

Ruth didn't seem to care. She stared straight ahead without speaking or moving, even when Tamar's comb caught a knot. She shivered
every now and then. Her teeth chattered. Tamar kept the house cold to
combat her hot flashes, and now she shivered too.

"Are you cold?" Tamar leaned to look at her mother's face. "C'mon,
let's get you into something warmer. And I'll make you some tea. We
can talk about how you got here."

Tamar expected to have a hard time getting the clothes on her, but her mother took each garment she was handed and put it on by herself without fuss or even much fumbling. She moved slowly but competently. Not as frail as she looked, then. Tamar was not surprised. Her mother had always been very, very good at presenting herself as she wanted to be seen, not necessarily how she really was.

At last, dressed in a long-sleeved flannel nightgown Tamar hadn't worn in years, a soft gray cardigan, and knee socks in a bright rainbow pattern, Ruth followed her daughter down the stairs. She took them one at a time, holding on to the railing with Tamar gripping her other arm. Ruth was slow but steady enough, and by the time she reached the bottom she no longer seemed even to need Tamar's support.

In the kitchen, Ruth sat at the table without being told. Tamar filled the electric kettle and got out her tea chest. Instead of the delicate cups and saucers she normally used, she took two plain crockery mugs from the cupboard. The mugs had come in a box of matching dishes from the discount store and could be replaced, but the teacups were one-of-a-kind thrift store bargains.

Tamar did not trust her mother with anything she held as precious.

The thought stabbed into her, spreading guilt like poison. Tamar focused on the hot water getting ready to boil. Her abrupt awakening had flashed her back to childhood horrors, but her mother had changed since then. So had she. The nightmares of years ago were only dreams, nothing to fear now.

The kettle boiled. She filled the mugs with hot water and added chamomile teabags. After a thought, she dropped a few ice cubes in her mother's mug before putting it in front of her.

Ruth didn't take it. She sat without moving, as quiet as she'd been this entire time. When Tamar took the seat across from her, her mother finally looked up. Her gaze was cloudy. Distant, but not distressed. Without the full face of makeup Tamar was used to seeing on her, her mother looked . . . old.

It had been weeks since Tamar had visited her. No. To be fair, it had been months. She no longer had any excuses for it—the social distancing and lockdown restrictions had been lifted, and although it was always possible a new surge or outbreak would put them back in place, she'd had no valid reason for some time now other than she simply didn't want to. She waited for an accusation, even if it was only in her mother's eyes and not voiced aloud, but she could see none. Honestly, it seemed like her mother barely recognized her.

"Here." She pushed the mug a little closer and waited for the older woman to lift it. She watched for the liquid to slop, but she'd been careful not to overfill it. Ruth's hand steadied after a moment.

Her mother sipped, slowly at first. Then greedily, slurping and slopping, until the cooled tea ran down her chin and dripped onto the front of her borrowed nightgown. Tamar took a paper napkin from the holder on the table and leaned across to dab at her mother's chin.

Ruth slapped her hand away.

Tamar sat back. "Sorry. You were dripping."

Her mother drank again. She held the mug in both hands and looked at Tamar over the rim of it. She held that gaze deliberately as she slurped, then put the mug down. This time, nothing dripped.

"How did you get here?" Tamar hadn't sipped her own tea, but the warmth of the mug in her hands had spread all through her. She put it down and pulled at the neck of her T-shirt to cool herself, readying for a hot flash.

Her mother said nothing.

"Ruth," Tamar said with an edge in her tone, "it's the middle of the night. You don't have a car. How did you get here? Did someone drive you?"

That had to be true—her mother's bare, dirty, and lacerated feet aside, there was no way, none, that her almost eighty-year-old mother could have walked from Somerset House to here. It was at least fifteen miles away, far off on the other side of town, along highways that forbade pedestrian use.

"Did someone bring you here?"

Her mother nodded.

Tamar sat back in her chair hard enough to rock it a little on the back legs. "Who was it? Someone from Somerset House?"

Ruth replied by sipping tea. She didn't look at Tamar this time, but was that a hint of a smile hidden behind the mug? Too hard to see, too hard to catch.

Her mother had always been good at getting what she wanted. Was it so hard for Tamar to believe that Ruth, if she had so desired, could have convinced someone to drive her to Tamar's house in the middle of the night? The vision of gnarled toes covered in filth and thin stripes of blood tried to take over, and again, Tamar shoved it away. It was impossible to believe that her mother had walked here. She might as well imagine her mother with leathery black wings sprouting from her shoulder blades, hovering inches above the ground, toe tips dragging along gravel and asphalt as she flew.

Ruth's gaze snapped up. Her body straightened, shoulders squaring. Both hands went flat to the tabletop with a slap. She jabbed a bent finger in Tamar's direction. Ruth had always sported immaculate manicures, but now, like her toenails, her fingernails were in bad shape. The polish had chipped away, the nails yellowed and ridged. The one on her pointing index finger had cracked and broken, leaving a ragged edge.

"Shh," Ruth hushed.

"I'm calling Somerset," Tamar said. "Stay here. I'll be right back."

Her phone was still upstairs. As she walked out of the kitchen, she heard what sounded like the faintest of low chuckles, but she didn't turn around.

run run up the stairs don't look back it's waiting underneath to grab your ankles and trip you and if it trips you it will grab you

and if it grabs you it will eat you

run run up the stairs

Tamar gasped at the force of those childhood memories sweeping over her and gripped the railing. The basement stairs in her childhood home had been open slats, but in this house, risers would prevent anyone from reaching through to grab at her as she climbed them.

Anyone . . . or any *thing*.

She took each stair deliberately, slowly, one step at a time, for as long as she could stand it. She hated the way her heart pounded. Her throat tightened. Her hand gripped the railing tight enough to squeak as she ran her palm along it. Halfway up, she heard a noise from behind her at the foot of the stairs. She did not look behind her.

She ran.

CHAPTER

3

TAMAR DIDN'T ASK again how or why Ruth had ended up there in the first place. It was clear her mother was either not capable of answering or refusing to. She seemed fine now, though. She stared out the window as they drove, every now and then humming different tunes under her breath. Nothing recognizable. By the time they pulled into the parking lot, the sky had grown light enough that Tamar could see every line on her mother's face. Ruth's vanity had always been a huge part of her personality. What did she think when she looked in the mirror now?

"We're here," Tamar said.

"Thanks for driving me home, honey." The endearment sounded natural, even if after all these years it still felt weird to hear. Ruth patted Tamar's arm. "I don't need you to go in with me. I'll be fine. You just go on and get back to doing what you need to be doing."

"I'm going to walk you in."

The front doors were locked, but Ruth had the code for the keypad. Her fingers fumbled a bit as she punched it in, and she whispered something that sounded angry as the keypad flashed red. She tried again, this time gaining entry. The door automatically swung slowly open. Tamar followed her mother inside.

The lobby desk was empty this early in the morning, although there was a sign that requested visitors to sign in. Ruth ignored it as she moved with purpose beyond the lobby and down the hall, through another set of doors and into a different wing. Her earlier frailness had vanished entirely. Tamar actually needed to take a few skipping steps to catch up to her.

Soft lighting and art on the walls gave the hallway an upscale hotel feeling, contrasting with the cold tile floor and lineup of doors decorated with residents' names. Cork or whiteboards hung for leaving messages that reminded Tamar of her college dorm, even to the way a couple of the doors were left cracked open, inviting visitors despite the early hour.

One door opened as Ruth passed it, but whoever was inside swiftly stepped back out of sight. When Tamar passed it, she saw the glint of a gaze watching through the crack. The door opened again when Ruth reached the corner of the hall, and when Tamar looked over her shoulder, the woman watching from her doorway once more ducked back.

The doors to the individual apartments were also accessed with keypads, but Ruth didn't fumble this time. She had her door open and was through it by the time Tamar got there. She went into the bathroom, shutting the door behind her as Tamar stepped inside.

The independent living spaces here at Somerset House were advertised as "apartments," but they were studio spaces at best, and more like long-term hotel suites. The tiny kitchenette featured a half-sized fridge, and there was a microwave on the counter but no stove. The living room was large enough for a loveseat and a recliner, both facing a flat-screen TV set up on a dresser that had come from her mother's house, and beyond that was a wall separating the bedroom space and the bathroom.

Six years ago, Ruth had sold the home on Spring Hill Drive that she'd lived in for almost five decades to move into Somerset House. Tamar had still been living in New York with Garrett. She had not been back to Kettering or even Ohio since moving in with her Aunt Naomi in Syracuse days before she turned eighteen.

Four years ago, after the divorce, Tamar had come back to her hometown. She'd wanted to spend more time with her sister Lovey, her husband Mark, and their brood of six kids. Tamar didn't have children of her own, and her nieces and nephews were as close as she was ever likely to get. If that meant putting on a neutral face when faced with Ruth at birthday parties and other celebrations, Tamar had been willing to do it.

For Lovey's and everyone else's sakes, Tamar had done her best to avoid animosity. For Ruth, this had always seemed perfectly fine. They circled around each other at the same distance, each pretending the other was no more than an acquaintance. It all worked until two years ago, when Mark was offered a dream job in California, and Tamar had been the one left behind to deal with their mother.

Without Lovey to take care of her, Ruth had turned back to her older daughter with an arrogant confidence that Tamar would pick where her sister had left off. And what had Tamar done? Accepted the responsibility. Not for Ruth's sake, but for Lovey's. So she wouldn't fret.

Tamar was no substitute for her younger sister, not even a poor one. But once every few months, Ruth would ask Tamar to take her to lunch or to run some errands, and Tamar would agree so she'd have an answer for Lovey the next time she asked, "How's Mom doing? Is she okay?" Ruth most often met her in the lobby, and Tamar had not personally been inside her mother's apartment since Lovey moved away.

She looked around now, noticing the bits and pieces of her childhood that Ruth had used to decorate the space. A battered Raggedy Ann doll, homemade, her embroidered heart visible through the worn fabric of her gown. Once there'd been a matching Andy, but he was nowhere in sight—it felt like an analogy for something Tamar didn't want to explore.

Framed portraits hung on one wall. Photos of a young Tamar and Lovey, clad in matching dresses. Lovey's blond ringlets dangled past her shoulders, while Tamar's dark, choppy bangs left too much of her high forehead exposed. Her mother had paid the man on the phone selling Olan Mills picture packages for the biggest package he offered. Versions of this photo had hung all over the house, and in every size, for years. It touched her, surprisingly, that her mother had put up these reminders of days long gone. It had probably been Lovey's doing. She'd been the one to oversee the sale of the old house, the packing up of everything inside it, the moving into Somerset House. She would have made sure Ruth had photos of them both whether or not their mother gave a damn one way or another.

Ruth was still in the bathroom. Tamar paused in front of the coffee table, strewn with open Sudoku tablets and other notebooks with pages covered in line after line of thick, dark writing. She picked up one, flipping through it, to see more gibberish, along with black-and-white drawings done with such a heavy hand each line was a scar on the paper.

At a sound from the bathroom, Tamar put the notebook back and wiped her hands on her shirt. Her fingertips felt oddly sticky. She went to the small kitchenette to wash them.

Her mother had not come out. Tamar knocked on the door. Ruth didn't answer. Tamar knocked again.

This time, when only silence came as a reply, she turned the knob. She'd expected it to be locked, but it turned easily under her palm. Inside the bathroom, Ruth stared into the mirror, her mouth opened wide and head tilted back, as though she was looking at her tonsils. She snapped her head down and mouth closed when Tamar came in.

Ruth covered her throat with one hand. "Yes?"

"Are you okay?"

"I'm fine."

The hand covering her throat moved like a raft on a lake, up and down, then went still.

A faint odor of sewage wafted. Tamar left the bathroom without looking back. In the kitchenette, she pulled out two mugs. She found instant coffee. Dry creamer.

"You don't need to do any of that. The food court opens in ten minutes. I'll get my breakfast there. Tammy," her mother said sharply. "I don't need you to do this for me."

"Do you just want me to leave, then?" The words came out as bitter as tea brewed too long, but there was hopefulness in them too.

"I assumed you'd *want* to leave, Tammy. I'm trying to be considerate." Ruth had changed out of the borrowed nightgown and into a flashy track suit, coordinating top and bottom, and a pair of athletic shoes fancier than any Tamar had ever owned.

"I've asked you not to call me that."

Her mother's eyebrows rose, and Tamar noticed that in the time she'd been alone in the bathroom, she'd used a pencil to draw them in. She'd also added mascara. Foundation, blush, a hint of lipstick, although not the bright crimson that Tamar remembered her sporting in the eighties. None of her mother's efforts should have made her feel dowdy, disheveled, or unkempt. She'd been woken in the middle of the night to find her nearly catatonic mother pissing in the corner of her bedroom. Never mind how she'd gotten there, Ruth had not been living her best life in that moment for sure. So why, now, did Tamar feel grungy, grimy, as though she ought to be ashamed of her appearance?

"It's your name," her mother said after a pause. "Your father gave it to you."

"He named me Tamar. Not Tamara. Not Tammy. I'd like you to call me Tamar."

Her mother's lips pressed together, but the tremble was still evident. She nodded rigidly. "Whatever you want. It's not about what I like."

"Well," Tamar said stiffly, "you don't have to *like* it. You just have to use it."

"Of course," Ruth said, her voice softening. "Of course, I'll call you whatever you like best."

Tamar sighed. The beginnings of a headache brewed between her eyes. She needed more caffeine and a few more hours of sleep. "Are you going to be okay? Do I need to talk to anyone?"

"About what?" her mother asked with what seemed like genuine surprise.

"About . . . how you ended up at my house in the middle of the night?"

"I guess I just really wanted to see my girl." Ruth shrugged again. Smiled again. Her tone didn't shift or change or dip. It stayed soft and sweet, charming. Disarming. She was nothing but a sweet-tempered little old lady who'd certainly never, never screamed so fiercely in her daughter's face that her own eyes had burst some blood vessels.

It was how Ruth spoke to and about Lovey, not Tamar, but in that moment, a longing hit her so hard right in the heart that she took a step back. What would it have been like to have a mother who'd treated her that way? What would her life have been like if her mother had loved her the way Ruth had always loved her sister?

Tamar's calf nudged the coffee table, and the unstable pile of notebooks teetered. A few fell onto the floor, and she picked them up. The one that fell open in her hand was full of more of that heavy-handed inkwork. Hebrew letters, but so messy she couldn't really read any of it, not that she was fluent in written Hebrew anyway.

"What's this?"

Ruth shrugged without giving the notebooks so much as a curious glance. "I don't know."

I don't know either means you weren't paying attention, or you're too lazy to bother.

"You always hated when I'd say that to you," Tamar said.

Her mother simply shrugged again and gave Tamar a beatific smile. "I don't remember that."

Of course she didn't. Whatever had happened in the past, whatever Ruth had done or said, or how she'd behaved, it was all supposed to be forgotten. Forgiven.

Looking at her mother now, it was impossible to tell if Ruth was sweeping it under the rug or if she truly had no recollection of the arguments they'd had when Tamar was younger. It was possible she'd been so drunk back then that she really didn't. Tamar would have a talk with the Somerset House director and see about getting Ruth assessed for possible mental decline. Right now, she wanted to get home and take a shower before she logged in to start her day.

"You're more than welcome to stay and have breakfast with me. I have some guest passes. Today's pancake day." Her mother's pink-painted lips spread back, revealing grayish teeth.

Had they always been so crooked? Tamar pressed a hand to her own mouth, recalling the torture of braces, headgear, a retainer she'd "lost" in the school cafeteria trash can. In adulthood, she'd given herself the gift of invisible aligners to make up for the years of not taking care of her teeth. She didn't recall her mother's mouth being in such bad shape.

Ruth's grin widened. Flecks of spittle foam had collected in the corners of her mouth. It too had a pinkish tinge to it. Her breath, when it wafted toward Tamar's face, was thickly redolent with the stink of something strong, like onions or garlic, or both.

Tamar stepped back again, but the smell followed her. She coughed as politely as she could but stopped herself from covering her mouth and nose. She shook her head.

"No, I have to get to work."

Ruth's shrug seemed to have become her default gesture for everything. "Suit yourself. You know you're always welcome here, Tammy. It's up to you."

This time, Tamar didn't correct her about the name. She could not bring herself to offer her mother any sort of embrace, both because of the smell of her breath and because she had not voluntarily hugged her since . . . well, it had been a long, long time. Instead, Tamar gave her a sharp nod and a smile that felt false, and she let herself out the door without looking back.

Her sigh, when the door closed behind her, came up inside her from a hundred miles deep.

Quick steps took her down the hall and around the corner to the next, heading for the lobby. More doors were open now. Music or voices drifted from inside them. A few stood wide open, the residents leaning in the doorways and chatting across the hall.

The door she'd passed earlier, the one from which the woman had peeked out but just as quickly gone back inside, was open. Tamar hesitated as she got to it. The room was a mirror image of Ruth's. A woman in a flowered housecoat watered plants in pots set up on a pyramid-shaped wooden rack near the window. She looked up as Tamar's shadow fell across the doorway.

Tamar meant to keep moving, but the woman bustled forward. She waved the small watering can in Tamar's direction. She gestured with her other hand too.

Tamar paused. "Hello?"

"Are you her daughter? Ruth's, I mean."

"I'm one of her daughters, yes."

"You're the one who ran off on her?"

Tamar frowned at what sounded like an accusation, although the woman's expression was neutral. "I lived away for a while, but I moved back here a couple of years ago. My sister and her family moved to California for her husband's job. Neither of us ran off on her."

"Oh, you're Tammy then. She talks about you," the woman said, then lowered her voice. "I saw her leaving last night."

"You did?" Tamar moved closer. "Did she seem . . . okay?"

Again, the woman waved her watering can. "Oh, that's not any of my business, is it?"

Tamar had been set on getting out of Somerset House as fast as she could, but now her feet clung to the cold tile floor as though they'd been glued in place. "I'm sorry, I didn't catch your name."

"It's Gilda. Ruben," the woman added with a frown and a small, somehow proud lift of her chin.

"Is it unusual for my mother to be leaving here in the middle of the night?"

Gilda frowned. Opened her mouth as though to speak but stopped herself short. She tried again and managed this time. "Well. It's not really my business, like I said, but I suffer from insomnia quite a bit, and I do notice a lot of comings and goings that maybe other people don't see."

"My mother," Tamar prompted.

"She has left here a few times, quite late, and not dressed the way I'd imagine she would have if she meant to. I mean if she were in her right . . . I mean, your mother is almost always very put together. Very *posh*. I'm sure you know what I mean."

Tamar thought she did. Pride in her appearance had been a Ruth hallmark since, well, forever. "You've never said anything to her about it? Or anyone else?"

"We're allowed to come and go as we please, you know. Visitors are restricted, of course, but that's for safety. The residents are allowed to do what we want." Gilda shook her head. "Not that it's—"

"Any of your business. I know. But I'm sure you can appreciate my concern. If there's something going on with my mother, I'd really like to hear about it."

Gilda sighed. "She had a fall recently. Did she tell you about that?"

"No. She's very proud, though. She might not have mentioned it so she wouldn't worry me." Tamar didn't reveal that she and her mother were not close. Had not been close in years, if ever. Ruth might have told Lovey about any health issues she'd been having, but Lovey hadn't said anything, either.

"It was in the library. I don't know if she tripped or lost her balance or what, but one minute she was on her feet and the next she was on the floor. And when she got up . . ." Gilda went to the door and peered around it, up and down the hall, before retreating back inside. She crossed her arms over her chest.

"She was what? Injured?"

"No. Well, I don't know. She had a bump on her head, I suppose. She had to, after a fall like that. But she was speaking in a different language." Gilda's thin lips almost disappeared with her frown.

Tamar tried to think if her she'd ever known her mother to be fluent in any other language. She seemed to recall Ruth taking some Spanish classes at a local college, but it had only been for a short time. She'd once told Tamar that the best way to learn a new language was by taking a lover who spoke it—going to class had ended after Ruth started dating a man named Armando who drove a red car and dropped her mother off late at night but never agreed to come inside.

"What language was it?"

Gilda shrugged. "Well, to me, it sounded like Hebrew."

Tamar wasn't sure what to say to that. She thought of the notebooks on her mother's table. The scrawled words. A chill finger tickled its way up and down her spine.

"I know she's Jewish," Gilda said. "Even if she never wants to go to services when we all go on Friday nights. On Purim, I gave her a shalach manos basket, and she acted like she had no idea what it was."

"She probably didn't. My mother was never religious. Did it sound like she was . . . praying?"

"Oh, no." Gilda shook her head. Her gaze burrowed into Tamar's own as she leaned forward, her voice lowered. A few droplets from her watering can splashed out, hitting Tamar's shoe. "Nothing that came out of her mouth sounded anything like a prayer."

"What did it sound like?"

Gilda shook her head again. "It sounded like a curse."

4

THE NOTEBOOK TAMAR had seen in her mother's room had reminded her of several she'd kept as a kid. Dream journals, given to her by her father's sister Naomi, who'd encouraged her to write down her nightmares as a way of stripping away their power. Aunt Naomi and Ruth had never gotten along, which was why Tamar had run to her when she left her mother's house. Aunt Naomi had died twelve years ago.

Tamar hadn't thought of those journals in years, but she knew where they were. Her spare room still had boxes in it she had not yet unpacked, even four years after moving in. Most of it was stuff she was sure she'd only end up getting rid of—if she hadn't missed it or needed it in all the time since she'd left New York to come back to Ohio, she surely wasn't going to need it again. She always meant to go through them, but even during the long pandemic months when she literally hadn't left the house except to take out the trash or pick up deliveries from the front porch, she'd never managed to find the energy.

Now, back from Somerset House and with an oversized mug of tea in one hand, she assessed the stack of cardboard boxes. Almost all of them had been labeled neatly in Garrett's square block printing—KITCHEN, OFFICE, LIVING ROOM.

One box did not have Garrett's handwriting on it.

The battered file box had been repaired with layers of tape, both duct and packing. It was heavier than it looked like it should be. The cut-out rectangles for handles were sharp with layers of tape and would dig into your fingers if you didn't fit them into the slots exactly the right way.

She'd run from her childhood home with nothing and had returned only once, when Ruth was at work, to gather whatever she could manage to take with her. Everything she'd taken that day, other than her clothes, was in that box. A smaller box inside it contained a few other things Lovey had given her when Ruth moved into Somerset House. Tamar had not looked at its contents. As with everything in all these boxes, if she hadn't needed it in all the years she'd been gone, she doubted she would ever need it again.

Why not throw the box away? Garrett had asked her that every time it showed up in a move, in a redecorating or repurposing of a space, or the times it simply appeared in a place it would be noticed so she would have to stick it back in the crawlspace or under a bed in a guest room, or in the back of a closet. She never told him that she'd used to go nightwalking, or that maybe she'd never stopped. He would have thought she was the one who took it out but didn't return it to where it had been, and of course, she had been. Who else would have done it?

Of course, if he'd known, he might have never questioned where she was on the nights when he woke up to find her side of the bed empty. They might still be married. Maybe she had this box to thank for freeing her from a relationship with a man who'd never seemed to know her.

It wasn't all Garrett's fault. She'd spoken occasionally of the things Ruth had done, but Tamar never, ever told Garrett about what else had happened in her childhood home. No house she'd ever lived in since then had whispers in the drains, no dark shapes ever hovered over her in the night and tried to steal her breath. No monsters under the bed or in the closets or beneath the basement stairs. He would have tried to explain it all away as childish fears, exacerbated by the monster of her mother's addictions. He'd have tried to tie up her childhood with a ribbon like a stack of letters someone kept in a box they always meant to throw away but never could.

Since moving into this house by herself, she hadn't gone walking at night. Or if she had, there'd been nobody to wake up in the bed next to the empty space where she was supposed to be. Her dreams were only dreams, not memories of waking nightmares.

Surprisingly, or not so much, the box of her childhood mementos had never randomly shown up in any other rooms of this house.

The lid needed a sharp tug to get it free, and whatever was inside the box rattled when it shook. Tamar had put it on the still-bare mattress of the guest bed, and now she took a step back from it without looking inside. She had too much to do today to mess around with this. She needed some more tea. A nap. She didn't need to go digging around in the detritus of her youth, the bits and pieces she'd never managed to fully abandon. She could put the lid back on the box.

She could finally throw the whole thing away.

In seconds, the lid was back on, slammed down with a flat hand to get it on tight. She hefted it, the familiar press of the sharp edges digging into the meat of her palms. She ignored that small sting, shifting the box until she could carry it without any pain.

Outside, she used her elbow to nudge open the flip-top lid of her oversized trash can, which protested and flopped back down, skinning her arm. She pressed the box against the side of the can, propped on her knee, and tried again. She'd missed the last trash pickup because of Memorial Day and had forgotten how full the can was, bags of trash piled all the way up to right beneath the lid. She could balance the old file box on top of that stuff, but the trash can lid wouldn't close if she did.

Instead, Tamar put the box next to the can. The garbage trucks came on Thursday, and she'd remember to take the box out to the curb along with the can. Problem solved.

"Hey! Hi!"

Tamar looked up. The neighbor from across the street waved at her. He lifted his oversized travel mug in her direction.

"Great day, huh?"

She looked up at the sun, shading her eyes. She'd spoken probably half a dozen words to this guy in the two or three years he'd lived here, most of them through the protection of a face mask. He didn't wear one now, and she could see the gleam of his ginger beard from all the way across the street.

"I'm Ross, by the way. We never officially met."

She'd met her other neighbors when she moved in, but all of them were married with kids. They were nice enough to say hi to in passing, but she didn't fit in with that crowd. One of her goals upon moving back to Kettering had been the "find real life friends" thing, but the pandemic had put a halt to that for a good long time, and honestly, Tamar kind of liked being alone. She'd been coupled for so much of her life, part of a pair, that she was relishing discovering her own hobbies. Her own time schedule. Beholden to nobody. Sure, it was a cliché out of one those books with Adirondack chairs on the front and titles with "beach" in them, but so what? She kept in touch with the people she wanted to keep in touch with and didn't really feel the lack of company. She might, one day, but for now she was okay.

Oh, shit. He looked like he was about to head across the street to what, to shake her hand? Tamar backed up toward the open garage door. Suddenly self-conscious about the fact she was wearing a thin T-shirt and no bra, she hunched her shoulders. What would be weirder, if she ran inside when he was clearly trying to be friendly, or if she too-obviously covered her boobs with her crossed arms?

"Tamar," she called back, hoping he'd stay in his own front yard.

"Tammy?"

"Tamar," she corrected. "With an 'rrrrr' on the end."

A golden retriever puppy, little more than a bundle of fluff, yipped at her from the safety of Ross's front porch. He gave it an indulgent grin. "Ah, gotcha, gotcha. Nice to meet you officially, Tamar. I moved in right before it became impossible to be neighborly, or I'd have brought you a coffee cake."

"Oh . . . that's . . ."

"I'm kidding," Ross said. "I would never have baked a coffee cake."

He laughed, so she did too. He seemed goofy, but harmless.

"You still working from home?" Ross asked.

"Yes," she said, not explaining that she'd had a work-from-home job for years. She added, because it seemed polite, "You?"

"I have to go into the office a couple days a month, that's it. I figured you were still work-at-home. My doorbell cam picks up any time your car goes in or out of the driveway. Just nice to know who's around during the day, you know? In case I need something. Oh, and don't worry about Peanut Butter here. I've got the invisible fence up. She won't leave the yard."

"She's cute."

Tamar stopped herself from asking him what the hell he could possibly need from *her*. She could be abrasive. Intimidating. Garrett had told her so. Ross was being nice. Friendly. He might even be testing the waters to see if she was single and ready to mingle, not that she was, at least not with any guy who lived across the street from her. She'd already done that, back in high school, and it had ended badly.

"Gotta get back to work. Nice chatting," she called out and ducked back into her garage, hitting the button to bring the door down before he had the chance to say anything else.

The idea that his doorbell camera monitored when she left and returned unsettled her a bit, but what could she do about it? Ask him to adjust the settings? Was he telling her as a heads-up to be nice or as some kind of creepy warning? Anyway, what did it really matter if Ross from across the street noticed when Tamar left or not, unless he was casing her house. She didn't owe him any explanations about anything she did. It wasn't like they were *married*.

"Calm down," she muttered aloud as she went into the house. "Get over your damage."

She'd left her phone on the kitchen counter when she took the box out and checked it automatically for messages. Swiping for her notifications, she saw two spam calls. A text from Lovey started off with a string of emoticons. There was a missed call from her mother too, but no voicemail, which meant she could ignore it.

What she could no longer ignore was the mess in the spare room. Getting rid of her old file box had sparked something inside her. Maybe not KonMari-level purging, but she could definitely sort through most of the other boxes and either finally put stuff away where it was meant to go or finally get rid of it.

For some of it, she made short work. Boxes of books and photo albums went downstairs to her workspace, where she put them away in the empty bookshelves. Anything labeled "Living Room" she also took downstairs and put next to the couch, although she doubted there'd be much she really wanted. When it came to the two boxes marked "Miscellaneous," though, Tamar took a small break before opening them.

Leaving her husband had not been a decision Tamar had made on the spur of the moment, even though Garrett had claimed at the time that she'd taken him completely by surprise. They both knew it wasn't true. It was his way of saving face, and she let him by taking the brunt of the blame for the failure of their marriage. He'd retained the house, the bulk of their savings, and most of their friends. What had Tamar taken, other than her freedom? She guessed she was about to find out.

The first box contained carefully wrapped glass serving bowls that had been a wedding gift. She didn't want them at the time, and she didn't want them now, which was probably why he'd sent them with her. Beneath them was a set of candlesticks, covered in wax. A challah board and cover, also wedding gifts. And there, nestled in layers of bubble wrap and tissue paper, a boxed set of six crystal wineglasses. Tamar took out the box and gently touched the delicate glass. Ruth had not been invited to the wedding, but the glasses had shown up four or five months after, exquisitely wrapped and accompanied by a simple, elegantly signed card.

As a young married couple, they hadn't been able to afford expensive glasses. These were the nicest they'd owned. They'd used them for Shabbat, filled with grape juice instead of wine because they'd met at an Al-Anon meeting and neither of them drank. Later, when they could afford to replace them with something else, the glasses had been forgotten about for most of the year and brought out only during Passover. They'd been shoved in a dishwasher even though they were clearly meant to be washed by hand. She'd never been careful with them. If anything, knowing her mother had been the one to gift them had meant Tamar was even more careless with them.

But, like her mother, these glasses had hung around.

An image of breaking glass, the sound of it and sensation of how your heart stopped in the moments between dropping it and when it hit the floor, flooded over her. She could have been remembering stomping the glass at her wedding, the lightbulb wrapped in a napkin standing in for a wineglass because it was cheaper and easier to break. Or maybe another childhood memory was trying to rise, a jelly jar knocked off the counter and spilling the contents all over the floor. Whatever it was, her hands shook the box of wineglasses hard enough to rattle them, but only for a second.

Garrett had sent these along with her as kind of a jab that she guessed he'd have told himself was kindness. She couldn't blame him. He'd married her believing they would always be together, forever and ever, and Tamar could not honestly say the same. They'd made it to twenty years, though. It should have counted for something but ultimately did not.

She'd bought herself a set of plain and standard glassware when she moved into this house, so she didn't need these. Even so, she set the box aside to take downstairs. No matter their origin or how they'd ended up in her final possession, the glasses were lovely, and she had a severe lack of pretty things right now.

Beneath the box was an envelope with her name on it.

Tamar recognized Garrett's handwriting. With a sigh, she slid open the flap and pulled out the single sheet of white computer paper, printed with text on only one side. Through the back of the paper, she could see his signature at the bottom. She didn't really want to read whatever it was he'd felt was so important that he'd had to print it out and stick it in a box but had been too cowardly to say to her face.

Her eyes scanned the printing. Then again, just to make sure she'd read it correctly. A sharp laugh burst out of her, not because she thought what her ex-husband had given her was funny, but because the only reaction could be laughter or tears, and she was choosing not to cry.

It was a get, a Jewish divorce decree, or at least it was Garrett's attempt at one. It probably wouldn't hold up in front of any rabbi, but it would also only matter if Tamar decided to get married again, and she didn't plan on ever repeating that mistake. She read over it once more. The get was his release of her, absent of any accusations or laying of blame. If she'd found this a couple of years ago, it would have hit differently. Right now, she felt only vaguely annoyed that he'd slipped it into a box of stuff he'd given her, not because she *wanted* it, but because it was what he'd believed she *ought* to have.

Taking the "Miscellaneous" box downstairs, Tamar rinsed off the wineglasses and set them to dry on a padded drying cloth. The rest of the items really belonged in a china cabinet, but she didn't have one. She found a place for the candlesticks, challah board and cover, uncertain if she'd ever use them again, but the other decorative glass bowls and items she left in the box and carried out to the trunk of her car so she could take them directly to the local thrift store for donation. She didn't need any reminders of her wedding, and it wasn't like she planned on hosting any dinner parties. The get she folded into as small a square as she could manage and shoved it into the pocket of her jeans. If she remembered to take it out, she'd file it somewhere. If it went through the wash, oh, well.

Back in the kitchen, Tamar considered calling Garrett to tell him she'd found it, but she drew up short at the sight of the kitchen counter. Of the six glasses she'd set out to dry, only one remained. It glittered in a shaft of sunshine coming through the window.

All the rest had shattered.

5

*T*HE THING THAT *comes in the darkness stands at the foot of her bed, and it watches her, and it waits for her to wake up, so she can't wake up she can't wake up it touches her toes with the claws it has instead of fingers, the grip moves up her ankles, over her calves, her knees, her shins, it reaches her hips, her belly, it will take its time and tweak under her armpits, it will tiptoe up her throat until the claws slip into her mouth and pry it open, no matter how hard she tries to keep her lips shut, it will find her tongue, it will dig into it and pull it out so she can't scream*

    so she can't scream

    scream

Tamar's shriek tore from her throat and left behind the taste of blood so thick she wanted to spit. She swallowed, hard, forcing the thick and heavy feeling to retreat. She opened her eyes, her hands in front of her to push away the thing hovering over her, but of course nothing was there.

Her hands fell back to the bed. Beneath the T-shirt she'd worn to bed, her skin was slick with sweat, but she was cold. She shivered and pulled the blankets up to her chin, not quite ready to see what time it was. She'd had a hard time falling asleep last night, although clearly she finally had since, the dreams had been nonstop. Not all had been nightmares, but that last one . . .

"Shit," she muttered and forced herself to sit up.

She swallowed again, wincing at the fuzzy feeling on her tongue. She'd been a heavy drinker for a hot minute her first semester of college, but, frightened by how much she'd liked it, she'd quit. She didn't want to become anything like her mother.

She'd joined Al-Anon. Met Garrett, whose mother also drank. They'd both stopped attending meetings for one reason or another, and eventually, the grape juice became a few sips of wine for the Shabbat kiddush blessing. Then half a glass. Half a bottle. A box. In the final couple of years of her marriage, she'd taken up drinking full force, but since moving here, she hadn't had a single alcoholic drink.

Last night after cleaning up the shards of crystal, she'd walked to the convenience store down the street and bought herself a bottle of wine. It had gone down smooth. She hoped it wasn't going to come back up the same way.

The room wasn't spinning, and it still felt as though she were laying in a puddle of sweat, so no matter what time it was, Tamar was getting up. She peeled herself out of the space her body had made in the mattress and swung her legs over the edge of the bed. She always piled her waist-length hair on top of her head in a messy bun or a braid before sleeping, but now it fell over her shoulders and stuck to her forehead, cheeks, and throat. The hair elastic must've broken. She shoved her hair off her face and tried to gather it at the base of her neck, but every motion felt like it took twice as much effort. At last, she gave up and let her head hang as she gave her body a few minutes to get used to the fact that she was forcing it to move.

She wanted to blame the wine for the nightmares, but it was never as simple as that. In the few years that she'd been a heavy user, booze and weed had kept the dreams at bay, not brought them forward. Finding religion had helped too. And, for a short time, so had being married. Even in the last days, when she was ruining all of it, her dreams had been the normal sort. The one she'd woken from just now, though, had been more than a nightmare.

It had been a memory.

With a groan, Tamar forced her feet to the floor. Made herself stand. She wasn't wobbly, but every step still felt like she was walking through chest-high water that threatened to tumble her head over heels at any second. It had been ages since she'd been in the ocean, been in any kind of large body of water, as a matter of fact, not even a swimming pool. It didn't seem fair she still so often felt as though she were doing her best not to drown.

The clock said it was still an hour before she'd normally be up. Her commute was the two-minute jaunt from her bedroom to the dining room where she'd set up her home office, and she'd never been a morning person. Probably, she thought with a twist of her mouth, because she so often slept like shit. She needed a shower to rinse off the night sweats, but she made it quick and dressed in a loose cotton gown—a schmatta, as Ruth would've said, Yiddish for "rags." You wanted to wear jeans to school instead of the skirt and blouse set Ruth had purchased? Schmatta. You wanted to pull on a hooded sweatshirt instead of a pretty cardigan? Oy, what a schmatta. Ruth wasn't *religious*, but she was *Jewish*.

Tamar frowned. The dress was comfortable, and nobody was going to see her in it. She wasn't going to let her mother take up space in her mind today.

In the kitchen, she made herself drink a glass of water, cold from the tap, while she heated water for tea. She had one bagel left and toasted it, thinking ahead to the projects she'd lined up for today. Pushing the nightmares away.

The empty bottle of wine remained on the counter with a few drops of crimson splashed around the base. The single crystal wineglass was next to it, a scant pink stain in the bottom.

She thought again of the glasses that had exploded last night while she'd been out of the room. Had they popped, one by one? Or had they gone all at once, with a tinkling crash, like a music box being knocked to the ground? At least she could explain away the reason they'd broken—she'd been stupid enough to set them upside down on the drying mat, and the delicate crystal hadn't been able to withstand the change in pressure inside the globes, or the heavier base had been too much for the thin rims to hold. Something scientific, anyway. Why one had survived was a mystery she didn't need to solve.

And, of course, as soon as she stepped into the kitchen, her foot came down on a sliver of glass she'd missed the night before. It went

deep, with a sting, and she let out a hiss that became a holler as she lifted
her foot to check the bottom of it. There was only a little blood. A
speck. She leaned against the counter to pull out the glass splinter but
couldn't find it.

"Shit," Tamar muttered.

glass shatters

broken picture frame

face crinkles now when you step down on it when you run run run limp-
ing with your foot cut and bleeding and the sound of screaming follows

She shuddered, closing her eyes against the fresh swell of memory.
She walked, gingerly, to the kitchen table and sat, pulling her leg across
her knee to look again at her sole. She could see the place where the glass
had gone in, near the old, faint scar. When she ran her finger over it, the
wound stung. No matter how she squeezed, though, she couldn't get the
hole to open far enough for her to get inside with her blunt fingernails,
nor could she see any splinters.

She put her foot down, testing her weight on it. A dull ache spread
from the now bloodless wound, but it wasn't too bad. Maybe she'd pried
the piece of glass free without realizing it.

She spent a good fifteen minutes sweeping, then mopping, the
kitchen floor until the beige tiles gleamed and the entire room smelled
in a way she could only describe as "purple," since it certainly did not
resemble lavender the way the bottle claimed. She leaned on the mop to
let out a satisfied sigh. Her house was never dirty. Tamar had long ago
determined she would never again live in filth. One of the reasons she'd
fallen in love with Garrett was because the first time he'd invited her to
his place, he'd wiped down all the counters while he cooked dinner.

By the time she'd finished, she was an hour past the time she had
meant to log in. She'd worked for this company for fifteen years and
had always made her own schedule. Her bosses didn't care when she
designed the packages for fruit snacks, jockey shorts, and headphones,
as long as she met all her deadlines, but consistency in her day helped
her be most productive and gave her the clear transition from workday
to personal time.

When Tamar took a sip of tea, she couldn't blame a change in air
pressure or delicate glass for breaking her mug. She could only blame

her own weak fingers for letting it slip free, falling and splashing hot liquid onto her bare legs. Tamar put both her hands over her mouth to hold back the scream that came out more like a hissing whistle.

The box of her childhood memorabilia, the box she had specifically put out next to the trash can, was sitting on her desk.

Tamar closed her eyes for a second, but of course when she opened them again, the box was still there. Still shut. It had some fresh stains on it along the bottom, green marks from where she'd let it sit in the grass.

The wound in her foot throbbed. Throbbed. Throbbed.

Her hands did not shake when she lifted the lid. She didn't need to see the contents in order to catalog them. A sheaf of photos had slipped mostly free of the envelope. She spotted a swirl of blond curls, the hem of a red dress. Lovey and Tamar in their matching dresses, the same photo she'd seen in her mother's apartment.

She sifted through the snapshots. Her fingers found the hard-cover of the dream journal. She almost didn't pull it out but finally did. The first pages were scrawled in a light, childish hand. Darker and heavier ink covered the middle pages, and the ones at the end were blank.

She flipped through the center section. In some places, the pen had ripped the paper. Sentence fragments, slashes of drawings, and yes, hashmarks that might have been Hebrew letters, here and there, except that she'd never learned to write that language. It looked very much like the notebook she'd seen on Ruth's coffee table. And that explained it, didn't it? Like the Raggedy Ann and the family portraits, somehow Ruth had managed to hold on to one of Tamar's old dream journals. Like the rationale for the breaking glasses, it all could be explained.

Tamar put the lid back on the box. She looked at her computer. At the clock. At the box again. She really needed to log in to work, or else she'd be here all night. Or she'd have to take a sick day or a few hours of vacation.

She was already out the front door and heading across the street before she could think to stop herself. She saw the video doorbell as soon as she got within view of Ross's front porch. She rang it, then stepped back to the edge of the concrete slab.

He looked a little surprised to see her when he opened the door. "Hi. Tam . . . ar, did I get that right?"

"Yes. Tamar. I . . . listen, I have a really weird question to ask you, and I won't blame you for thinking I'm a total freak." She drew in a breath, continuing before he had the chance to answer. She'd woken to find her mother looming over her at three forty-four. Everything had always happened at three forty-four. "Do you have the footage from your doorbell camera from last night? Probably around four in the morning."

Ross's eyebrows rose, and he opened the door wider. He pulled his phone from the pocket of his jeans and swiped his thumb down over the screen with a frown. "Yeah, hold on. I did get a motion alert around that time."

"Can you see what set it off?"

He tapped the screen a few more times, then held out the phone to her. His frown had deepened, giving him lines around his nose and crinkling more in the corners of his eyes. She'd thought Ross was a lot younger than her, but now he seemed to be more like late forties, closer to her age.

"Here," he said. "Can you see it?"

Tamar stopped herself from cupping his hand with hers to bring the phone closer to her. In the postpandemic times, touching strangers still felt gross and risky and weird. Hell, even before pandemic times. But she did lean closer, tilting her head to get the full view of the small screen and the clip he was showing her.

"Oh," she said. "I missed it."

Ross took back the phone and swiped again. He held it out to her. "There's not a whole lot to see, since it's pretty far away. I can try to zoom in—"

"Yes, please, can you?"

"Sure," Ross said as he used his thumb and first finger on the screen to do just that. He held it out to her again. "It's blurry, but I still think you can see what's going on."

She looked at him. At three forty-four, there'd been motion. He looked at her.

"I mean," Ross said hesitantly, "it's you."

CHAPTER

6

TAMAR'S SISTER HAD done something different with her hair. Something very California, very hip. The blond pixie cut was perfect on her, as was the golden glow of her tan and the breezy summer dress that bared her shoulders. Tamar ran her hand along the thick length of her dark ponytail, self-conscious for a moment at her lack of makeup, her sweatpants and oversized hoodie. Her house was chilly. At any moment, she might have to strip down to her tank top to handle a hot flash.

"Love your new haircut," she said to Lovey's face on her computer screen. "What made you go so short?"

"I went in for a trim and just decided to go for it," Lovey said with an artless shrug that conveyed every single thing about her personality in that one gesture. She ran a hand through the soft, feathery strands. "It's so much easier to take care of."

Tamar had not had a haircut, other than a self-given trim to clean up split ends, in decades. Her hair, when she took it down, reached to the small of her back. She would never cut it short. Never.

"Anyway, what did they say when you called them?" Lovey bent out of frame for a few seconds, returning with one of those fancy custom water bottles with her name on it in vinyl letters.

Tamar ran her fingers up the stem of the crystal wineglass on the desk in front of her. The call with the director of Somerset House had been useless. "Well, at first the director tried to tell me that Ruth could not possibly have gotten out without anyone knowing about it. But then she switched to the argument that she's an independent-living resident, which means she can come and go whenever she wants."

"Even if she's stumbling out of the building at midnight in nothing but her nightgown?" Lovey scowled. "What's the point of having security there if they can't keep her secure?"

"There wasn't anyone in the lobby when I took her back. I guess it's only staffed during regular hours. They have cameras and stuff, and the doors of course are locked, but that's to stop people from getting in. Not getting out."

She hesitated. What could she really tell her sister about the notebooks on their mother's coffee table? Nothing else in the room had seemed out of place. Ruth had seemed fine. Lovey hadn't heard anything from their mother about a fall, so maybe Gilda Ruben was simply making up stories.

Tamar sipped her wine. It was her second glass of the evening. Rich, earthy red, a blend. The bottom of her foot still stung from the cut, and her lower back and abdomen ached with cramps and bloating. The wine would help.

Lovey leaned closer to the screen for a second before sitting back with a frown. "You're drinking wine."

She grimaced. "I'm having killer cramps that probably will turn out to be nothing. Thanks, menopause."

"Oh, boy."

"If I skip this period, it'll be the tenth one in a row. That's almost a year. Think that means I'm almost done?" She grinned. "The doctor said I should ask my mother what her menopause experience was like, because it might give me some idea of what to expect."

They both laughed at the idea of Tamar and Ruth sharing any such conversation, their chuckles the rueful kind when there was no humor to be found.

"Anyway, it's after dinner here," Tamar said.

"It has nothing to do with the time, Tam." Lovey shook her head. "You okay?"

"No, Lovey. I'm not okay. I woke up to find her standing at the foot of my bed. Just like—" Tamar cut off her own words with another sip of wine. This one went too deep, and she coughed. Her stomach lurched, but she swallowed, hard. Then again. Her guts clenched, cramping.

Lovey's expression contorted. Tamar had told her stories over the years, only when Lovey asked, and only a few. Things had been different for Tamar than they'd been for her sister.

"Like when I lived at home," Tamar finished.

Neither spoke for a moment. Lovey drank more water. Tamar turned her glass around and around, watching the crimson fluid swirling in the oversized globe. If she filled it, she guessed it would hold almost a full bottle of wine. She wouldn't fill it, of course. Not all at once.

"What do you think about this business with the fall? Could the woman you talked to have been . . . oh, I don't know. Mistaken? Exaggerating?" Lovey asked.

"She said that Ruth fell down in the library and hit her head, and when she got up, she was speaking in Hebrew." She didn't mention how disturbed Gilda Ruben had seemed or how the older woman had described it as the opposite of a prayer.

"That does *not* sound like our mother."

They both laughed again, and in that moment the deep and fierce love Tamar had for her sister almost swept her away. They'd had their share of arguments as kids, but in adulthood, Lovey had definitely become Tamar's best friend. Living almost three thousand miles apart sucked. Not for the first time, Tamar thought about moving again to be closer to Lovey and Mark and the kids—but she'd done that once already, when she came back "home."

Mark's job meant they might need to pack up and move in another year or so, and what would Tamar do then? Follow her sister's family around the country forever? She hadn't wanted to return to Ohio, but she was here now and finally starting to feel settled in. Besides, someone needed to take care of their mother, and wasn't it her turn? She could never make it up to Lovey for running away and leaving her behind, but she could do her best to take on her share of the responsibilities for Ruth now.

"How did she seem, otherwise?" Lovey asked after a pause.

They didn't need to discuss why their mother would be bubbly and sociable with Lovey and not Tamar. Lovey had always been the favorite. It was not a role she wore proudly, not anymore, but it hadn't changed.

Tamar shrugged and sipped wine with every intention of making the glass last. "Definitely disoriented when she woke up here. She peed herself."

"Oh. Wow." Lovey grimaced, but a giggle slipped out of her that she tried to hold back behind her hand. Her mouth laughed, but her eyes did not. "Was she drunk?"

"She's been sober for years."

"So were you," Lovey said. "And now you've got a glass of wine in front of you."

Tamar frowned. "The difference is, I'm not an alcoholic. I chose not to drink for a lot of different reasons. That doesn't mean I can't handle drinking."

"You realize that's what people say when they can't handle drinking, right?"

"She didn't seem drunk," Tamar said, ignoring that question. "She just seemed out of it. I got her cleaned up. Tried to find out how she got here. She had bare feet, Lovey. Dirty and scratched like she'd walked here. But she can't have done that, could she? I mapped it. Somerset House is 17.4 miles from here. Plus, she's never been to my house, ever."

"She has your address, though," Lovey pointed out. "And she could have called a Ryde or a cab, or hell, she might have hitched a ride. She might have called some friend we don't know about."

"It wouldn't be the first time she had a friend we didn't know about, I guess."

They both fell silent at that. Through the computer screen, Tamar heard the far-off sounds of children's voices. Penelope, ten, and Archie, eight, were Lovey's youngest children. It sounded like they were having fun, despite the screeching. Lovey glanced over her shoulder and gestured vigorously at her unseen offspring before turning back to face the screen.

"She needs to be assessed for mental deterioration. She always said Bubbe Gail had it. So did *her* mother. We knew it was probably going to happen," Lovey said flatly.

"I have a meeting with the director tomorrow," Tamar said. "Anyway, I'm not sure what I'm going to get out of them but more excuses."

"They should knock some money off her rent for the month. I mean, you could raise all kinds of holy hell, couldn't you? If they can't keep their residents under control—"

"It's not a prison, Love!" A giggle slipped free, probably helped along by the wine and the lack of sleep last night.

"If she's signing herself out in the middle of the night and finding her way to your house, and breaking in—"

"She didn't break in. She used the key."

Lovey snorted. "You keep a key in the gnome?"

Growing up, the plaster gnome had lived in their front garden. Ruth had made the ugly thing in one of those pottery classes that had been popular in the seventies. Lovey had taken it when Ruth moved, and she'd given it to Tamar when she left for California. The paint had faded over the years, but Tamar had not been able to bring herself to touch it up no matter how battered it looked. She didn't have many good memories of the house on Spring Hill Drive, but the gnome had been one of them.

"Nobody would know to look inside it," she said.

"Mom would." Her sister sighed. "So. What do we do about this?"

"I told you. I have a meeting with the director tomorrow. I'll make sure they know that this isn't okay, and I'll see about getting her assessed. If she needs to move to the assisted living versus where she is now, we'll figure it out."

"I'm sorry, Tam. I should be there to help you. We're so far away now."

"Yes, because your husband has an amazing job with lots of potential," Tamar said. "What are you supposed to do? Move back to Ohio because our mother has started nightwalking?"

Lovey grimaced. She closed her eyes. Her mouth thinned. "I forgot that's what you called it."

Tamar had never forgotten it. She wanted to tell her sister about the box and Ross's camera footage. About her own nightwalking. But what could Lovey do about it other than worry? She'd always been so much younger, unaffected by the things their mother had done only to Tamar.

After she ran away, Ruth had changed, sobered up and stayed that way. It was almost as though Tamar and Lovey had two different mothers.

"It's not just the distance from here to Ohio," her sister said. "I feel like I'm not there for you."

"You *are* here with me for this, Love. As much as you can be. I know that."

Lovey watched as Tamar drained the last drops of wine from her enormous glass, the one she was never, ever going to fill all at once. "I could come out for a visit?"

"What would you do with the kids?"

"I'd bring them along. They'd love to see Auntie Tam. And Grammy, of course."

"All of them?" Tamar laughed and shook her head. "As much as I'd love to see them, and you, I don't think it's necessary right now. How did she seem the last time you talked to her?"

"Fine. Normal. She talked to the kids for a bit. Told me about a movie she'd seen. She was going on some bus trip to the outlets, and she seemed pretty excited about that. I mean, shopping was always her jam. But that was over a week ago. Could she be failing that fast? Could that fall have really hurt her?"

Tamar thought of her mother's initial lack of response. The slack expression. Dull eyes. She thought of the low, sly chuckle from the bottom of the stairs. How deceptive Ruth's fragility had seemed, especially compared to how she'd behaved once she was back in her apartment. A shudder wormed its way into the base of her spine, trying to work its way upward.

"If it did, she seemed to recover fast. I don't know. I'm hoping the director will be able to give me some insights."

"Look," Lovey said abruptly. "You have to promise me that you're not going to let her mess with you. Okay? I don't know what's going on with her, but if she's starting to get dementia or whatever we'll deal with it. But don't let her try to fuck up your life."

"I'm not going to."

Lovey sighed. "Oh, Tam. You already have."

On the desktop, Tamar's phone buzzed with an incoming call.

"Speak of the devil," she said and held up the phone screen toward her computer's camera to show her sister who was calling.

"Should I let you go?"

"No. Hang on." Tamar thumbed the screen to answer the call. "Ruth. What's up?"

A low string of muttered syllables assaulted her ear. Jolted, Tamar pulled the phone from her ear and put the call on speaker. The noises stopped.

"Ruth?" she repeated.

"What's she saying?"

"When are you coming to get me?" Her mother's voice issued from the speaker. Solid. Normal.

"I'm not coming to get you," Tamar said. "But I'll be by tomorrow to see you."

"When are you coming to get me?"

"I already said—"

"When are you coming to get me?"

"Mom," Lovey interjected. "It's Lovey. Can you hear me?"

"Goodbye," their mother said.

The call disconnected.

"That was weird," Lovey said.

Tamar looked at the phone in her hand and put it down. She wanted more wine, but that would mean leaving her desk to find the bottle, and that would alert Lovey to how much she was drinking. "*She's* weird."

Lovey left a beat of silence before she looked offscreen. There was more screeching, and this time it didn't sound like anyone was having fun. "I have to go. Call me tomorrow, okay? Let me know what the director says."

"I will."

Lovey ended the call, leaving Tamar staring at her own face reflected in the monitor. She looked again at her phone. The screen had gone dark. She took it to the kitchen while she poured herself another glass of wine, not surprised to see that the bottle was almost empty. That was okay. She had a couple more in the cross-hatch cabinet over the fridge.

The wine splashed a little over the back of her hand as she poured, and Tamar licked the drops before rinsing her hands at the sink. The tenderness in her foot flared briefly. Her lower back throbbed with cramps. The wine would make the pains go away. It could make every- thing go away for a little while, at least.

She lifted her glass. Mid-swallow, a sigh came out of her phone. It said her name, slow and sly and soft.

Tamar choked. Wine splattered. She gagged, coughing. Convulsive swallowing cleared her throat, and another burst of harsh coughing at last did the same for her lungs. Her head hung. She gripped the granite countertop and spat some pink-tinged saliva into the stainless-steel bowl, but she couldn't get her breath. Black and red flashes filled her vision as she fought to fully fill her lungs. A series of low chuckles drifted out of the phone, its screen still dark.

Tamar grabbed it up. Swiped. It took a few seconds for her Face ID to recognize her, but then her home screen showed up. The call from her mother had ended seven minutes ago. No new calls had come in after that.

She could breathe again.

First the nightwalking, then the dreams, now this. She'd been Archie's age the first time she realized that not everyone heard their names hissing out of the drains in their sinks, that if you told your teacher why you were afraid to go into the bathroom by yourself, you were "too old to believe in ghosts."

After Ruth had come in for parent-teacher conferences, stumbling, with liquor on her breath, that teacher had taken Tamar aside and apol- ogized for being too hard on her. Little Tam had been sent to the school guidance counselor, who'd asked her a lot of questions about what it was like at home, especially since her father's death the year before. Tamar had done her best to answer every question honestly, but nothing more had been done about the situation. What people thought they knew about Ruth's problems had followed Tamar through the rest of her time at school.

Well, fuck that, all of it. She poured herself a generous glass of wine and got down another bottle from the rack and opened it so it would be ready for her when *she* was ready for *it*. She went upstairs, where that fucking box waited on her bed, and she took a long, long swallow of wine, set down her glass on the dresser, and got out her vaporizer pen and the plastic prescription container of medical marijuana from the plastic bin where she kept it.

The wine had already spread its warmth through her, and the weed spread a further glow that gave her courage, if only because it made her feel as though nothing could possibly be so bad that she couldn't handle it. Tamar opened the box. She sorted through it, setting the items inside into piles. She put aside a handful of faded snapshots. Everything else went back in the box.

The lid rattled when she fit it back on. She almost ignored it but lifted the lid again to see what had caught on it. Stuck in a ragged piece of tape, a small envelope clung to the inside of the lid. She tore it free and tipped the contents into her hand. It was a delicate gold chain with a Star of David pendant on it. She didn't recognize it, but written in Lovey's familiar handwriting on the back of the envelope was an explanation.

Found this in Mom's jewelry box along with a card from your baby naming. The writing was smeared so I didn't recognize who it was from, but it was meant for you. Xoxo, Lovey

She put the necklace on. The pendent nestled in the hollow of her throat, and an odd comfort spread through her. She didn't tend toward wearing religious jewelry, but someone, long ago, had meant this for her, and it felt right to be wearing it now.

In her backyard, she threw the box and everything else it contained into the small firepit that had been one of the house's selling points although she'd never once invited anyone over to roast marshmallows at it. She doused the box with some lighter fluid she got from her shed. She lit it.

She burned it.

That night, she didn't dream.

CHAPTER

7

"TAM?" THE MALE voice sounded so hesitant that it would have been easy for her to ignore it.

She held two different doorbell cameras in her hands and had been considering the pros and cons of each for the past few minutes, her head down, not paying attention to anyone else in the hardware store. She could keep doing that. Pretend she hadn't heard her name.

"Tam," the man repeated.

Tamar looked up. She bumped into a lot of people who seemed to remember her right away, but she'd been gone so long that she often had a hard time figuring out who they were. This man, though . . . that face. The broad shoulders, the big hands that had once held her waist while they slow danced under string lights in a high school courtyard. They'd been friends since childhood and then became more. So much more. She knew him and could not pretend she didn't.

"Miguel," she said. "Hi."

"I thought that was you. I mean, it had to be you," her high school boyfriend said with a grin that looked exactly the same, even if the face in which it sat had gotten older. "I heard you moved back to town."

"Word travels fast, huh?" She put both boxes back on the shelf. She didn't really want a doorbell camera but had been trying to convince herself otherwise. This stop had been pure procrastination. She'd been on her way to Somerset House when she'd turned into the parking lot of the hardware store instead.

"I wouldn't say it's so fast. It's been what, two, three years?"

"A little more than four, actually." She nodded. "I'm surprised we didn't bump into each other before now."

Miguel shrugged. "I've only been back for the past few months myself. I was working for a private school in North Carolina for a while. Not being able to get back here easily during the pandemic proved how much my parents really needed someone around to help them out, so I took a job with Wright State and came back as soon as I could. Kind of like you did."

"I didn't come back for my mother," she said.

The flat, hard tone of her voice might have confused or even affronted someone else, but Miguel nodded. Like most of the people she'd grown up with, he knew all about Tamar's mother. He was probably one of the few people who knew more of the truth than whatever rumors had floated around.

"It's been a long time," he said after a pause.

What was that in his voice? Longing? Melancholy? Nostalgia, and a desire to reminisce? Whatever emotions were filling him up, the electronic security section of the hardware store was not the place for them to explore it.

"Do you want to get a drink with me?" Tamar asked.

Miguel grinned again. "Yeah. I do."

"Sooo, how long *has* it been?" Miguel leaned against the back of the diner booth, one long arm stretched out so he could keep hold of his beer stein.

"Oh, let's not go there. Then we'll have to talk about how we're both almost halfway to a hundred." Tamar had a tall glass of tea bristling with ice and a jaunty wedge of lemon she now squeezed. The juice stung one fingertip, burning in a small cut she hadn't noticed before. Maybe from cleaning up the broken glass? Wincing, she sucked it gently before dunking the lemon wedge into the tea.

Miguel winced. "Yeah, you're right. Let's not go there. Still, it's been a long time. You didn't come home in all those years?"

"No."

"I used to see your sister now and again, when I came back to visit my parents. She told me you were married . . . ?"

Tamar grinned. She couldn't help it. Did it matter if more than thirty years had passed, if they both sported silver in their hair and more thickness around their waists? When your first love tried to pretend that he didn't care whether or not you may or may not be available, it felt good.

"Divorced." She tilted her head to study him. "Lovey told *me* that *you* became a priest. I have to say, you don't look like one."

"That's because I'm not. I never got there. I went to seminary, but . . ." he shrugged and focused for a moment on his foamy mug. He leaned forward to turn it around in one fist, fitting his fingers into the handle, but not lifting it to his mouth.

She waited without speaking for him to continue.

"I didn't have a true calling, I guess," Miguel finished.

"I don't remember you being very religious, honestly."

He pointed at the gold Star of David pendant on her necklace. "I could say the same about you."

They both laughed, and it felt easy and fun. Like old times. He'd always been so easy to talk to, a best friend and not just a boyfriend. At least until the end.

"Sometimes," Miguel said, "things that happen to you can change your whole perspective."

"Amen." She held up her glass to his. They both drank.

Once upon a time, she and Miguel had walked past this small pub holding hands, talking about the days when they'd be old enough to sit right where they were sitting now. Back then Rooney's had been the quintessential neighborhood dive bar with a cigarette vending machine the local kids dared each other to use without the owner yelling at them. A blinking neon sign, some of the letters always burned out. Sometime over the past three-plus decades, new ownership had turned it into a hipster's idea of a dive bar. A sign advertised weekly karaoke and wing specials. They served beer that came from local breweries with clever, fancy names.

The new Rooney's was nice, but it lacked the dark and secretive atmosphere the old place had harbored. That might not be such a bad thing. At least, at one PM on a weekday, there weren't any neighborhood drunks listing on their barstools, ruining their livers and their lives. There wouldn't have been room for them here, with the families eating lunch and the romance book club in the corner talking about their latest steamy read.

"A lot's changed." Miguel had always been able to pick up on what she was thinking and feeling. "But I guess a lot has stayed the same too."

"You haven't," she told him. "You've grown up."

"As if I had a choice. You don't look much different, if I'm going to be honest." There it was again, that small, light hint of longing.

"I hope you'll always be honest with me, Miguel."

"I always tried to be."

She nodded. So they were going there. That was all right. Thirty-some years should have been plenty of time for them to get over the damage they'd done to each other and move on from it. To what, she had no idea, but hopefully to something other than sadness.

He eyed her. "Why *did* you come back, Tam? What prompted you to return to the hometown you hated so much you left it without looking back?" The longing was now tinted with a hint, just a hint, of sourness, like a shake of bitters to temper a cocktail that would otherwise be too sweet.

"I wanted to be close to my sister and her family. I'd been living so far away for too long. I thought that if I ever wanted to have a closer relationship with my nephews and nieces, I'd better make it happen. It's cheaper to live here, anyway. New York was crazy expensive." She flipped through the sugar packets in the small bin, finding the natural brown sugar and pouring it into her tea. Now it would be too sweet. She'd drink it anyway.

He'd barely touched his IPA. "Why'd you get divorced?"

"I cheated on him," Tamar said, deciding to get it all out in the open right up front. She'd asked him to be honest with her, and she owed him the same. "He found out. He wanted to work on things. I didn't."

"So you ran away."

She flinched but decided that was fair. She shrugged. "I guess so."

"So now you're close to Lovey and her family?"

"Her husband's job took them to California not too long after I moved here. It wasn't something either one of them had anticipated, but of course they had to take the opportunity." She shrugged again.

Finally, Miguel lifted the heavy glass stein to his mouth and sipped. When he set it back on the table, it clunked. He cleared his throat and shifted in his seat.

"And your mother? How are things with her?"

Tamar hesitated. It had been a long, long time since she'd talked to the man sitting across from her, and the last time she had, they'd fought. Their end had been bitter, and her mother had played a part in that. If there was anyone else in the whole world other than Lovey that Tamar could confide in about her mother, she thought it might be Miguel.

"She treats me like an acquaintance, one she barely knows," Tamar said after a moment, hating that she had to force her voice not to tremble when she described this. "She's polite, but she never asks me how I'm doing. Honestly, sometimes I think it was better when she was blatantly hating me. At least then I knew she felt . . . something. Now it's like I mean nothing to her at all."

Miguel frowned. "That sucks. I'm sorry."

"It's fine. I used to pray she'd treat me the way she does now. I guess it's true what they say, you always want what you can't have." Tamar laughed self-deprecatingly. She sat up straighter, remembering that she'd promised Ruth only last night that she'd visit today. "Actually, I was on my way to see her when we bumped into each other. She moved into Somerset House a few years before I came back to Kettering."

Miguel's brow furrowed. "She's not well?"

"You should know," Tamar said with grit in her voice, "that she is definitely not well."

"I mean—"

"She's not in the assisted-living part. At least, not so far. But she showed up at my house in the middle of the night. Used a key to get in. I woke up to find her standing over my bed. She didn't seem in her right mind, but she snapped out of it." Tamar drew in a breath, then took a drink, focusing on the tall glass so she didn't have to look at his face.

He hadn't believed her back then when she'd told him similar stories. There was no reason to think he'd believe her now. But when she looked up, all she saw on Miguel's expression was concern.

"Did she say why she was there in the middle of the night?"

"At first, she didn't seem like she was capable of saying anything. When I got her back to her place, all she'd say was that she wanted to see me. She wouldn't own up to being confused. She wouldn't even tell me how she got there." Tamar forced a chuckle that came out sounding weak. "But it was just like . . . never mind."

"What?"

"You'll think I'm crazy. Or lying." She tried to keep her tone neutral but failed. The crack in her voice gave away just how much his past accusations still hurt.

Miguel shook his head. "I promise you, Tam, I won't."

Still, she couldn't quite bring herself to tell him of her fears. He knew all about her mother's alcohol and drug addictions, her promiscuity, her verbal and physical abuse. Tamar's voice shook. "You didn't believe me then. I needed you to believe me, Miguel. And you didn't."

He reached across the table and took both of her hands. His had always been so much bigger, and they engulfed hers now. His fingers were warm and strong, the way his arms would be if she allowed him to hold her.

"Tam, listen to me. Back then, I was just a scared, stupid kid who didn't know his head from his ass. I know I let you down. I know I should have been there for you, and I wasn't. You tried talking to me about what was happening, and I should have known you were telling me the truth. You'd never lied to me in your life, even when it might have been better if you did."

"I can't blame you. Haunted houses are for movies and books. Not real life."

They stared at each other across the table.

"You *should* blame me. I promised you I'd be there for you, I promised to protect you, and I failed you," Miguel said.

"Everyone did," she said sharply. "I ran up and down that street, banging on doors, begging someone to let me in. She was coming after me with a knife. I'm not sure if you knew that. But she was drunk out of her skull and probably high on something she found on the floor of a seedy hotel room."

"That night . . ." He gulped in air and squeezed her hands again. "Do you know how many times over the years I thought about what happened and how I wish I could've changed it all? I thought so often of trying to reach out to you and tell you I was sorry. But then I heard you got married, and life got messy for me too, and I just never got up the courage to do it. And the further away from it we got, the easier it was to tell myself I'd only imagined it all."

"You don't have to be sorry. I did the same thing. Looking back, I told myself over and over again I'd made it all up. Dreamed it, maybe. Like living with my mother wasn't bad enough, I needed to invent ghosts and monsters too?" Tamar made a face. "Like you said, you were a stupid kid. So was I. You couldn't have done anything else for me, even if you'd wanted to."

Miguel shook his head. "No, you don't understand. I'm not just sorry I let you down. I'm sorry I never told you that I did believe you."

She laughed self-consciously. "Miguel . . ."

"I didn't answer the door for you because I wasn't in my house," he told her. "I was in yours. The things you told me that were going on in that house. I saw it for myself. Why do you think I almost became a priest?"

CHAPTER

8

S HE AND MIGUEL talked for so long the night crowd started arriving
to fill in the booths and barstools. Their waitress had gone off shift,
replaced by another. They'd eaten too much bar food, ordered more
drinks.

They didn't dive into any details about what had changed Miguel's
mind about believing all the things she'd told him back then, and that
was fine with her. There was so much else to get caught up on, no need
to dwell on those horrors. Most of the time, only her dreams let her
relive the full truth of what had happened the last night she ever lived
in the house on Spring Hill Drive. It was a trauma response, according
to one of her Al-Anon mentors. Not being able to remember all the
details.

On the sidewalk outside, Miguel reached for her hand as naturally
as he always had for the short walk to the parking lot. He didn't let it go
until they reached their cars, parked next to each other toward the back
of the lot. He leaned against his.

"Have you ever been back to the house?" he asked with a tip of his
chin toward the street that led to both of their childhood homes.

"No." She leaned against her car, across from him.

"Maybe you should go by."

She laughed. "Sure. That doesn't sound like a sequel to every bad
horror movie ever made."

"You hate horror movies," he said.

"I don't anymore. They're my favorite. Maybe because compared to living in that house, they all seem so ridiculous."

"What about your husband? Did you ever tell him?"

"Oh, never. No way." She laughed, but sadly. "He knew my mother and I were estranged. He knew about her addiction issues. But he never met her, and I never told him about the house being haunted."

"Nothing about the night you left?"

"No," she said. "I've never told anyone about what happened that night. Not even Lovey." Tamar drew in a shaking breath. "I just left her there, Miguel. I left her behind and abandoned her."

"Your mom always treated her better than she did you."

"But how did I know for sure that if I left, she wouldn't turn on Lovey? I didn't. I just . . . got out."

"You had to," Miguel said. "And your mom sobered up. Your sis was fine."

"Yeah. They were both fine." It was hard to keep the bitterness out of her voice, but she tried hard.

"I'm sorry. I know it doesn't change anything now, but . . . I've been so sorry for years." He'd kept his words light, but there was a darkness beneath them. One she understood. His pause indicated that he had more to say, but he wasn't saying it. Finally, he cleared his throat. "At first, I thought maybe you were dead."

"Oh, Miguel."

His voice shook a tiny bit. "You'd tried it that once, when we were fifteen. I thought you'd finally done it. She was telling everyone you ran off. She had the police looking for you."

"And you didn't believe her?"

"She lied about a lot of things, didn't she?"

"Yes. She sent them to my aunt's house to get me, but I'd turned eighteen. There wasn't anything they could do." She thought about reaching for him but wasn't sure that would be cool. "Did you really think—"

"I guess I wanted to believe that would be the only reason you could have for not telling me where you were. Never reaching out to me."

Her throat closed, but she forced out her reply. "I'm sorry."

"I know it was because of everything I said to you before that. I knew it then too. I was so stupid, Tamar. You were already talking about leaving to go to college, and I was afraid that once you got there, you'd find someone you liked better. That you'd break up with me."

"So instead, you broke up with me," she said.

"I was an idiot."

"You broke my heart," she told him, blunt and honest, but not harsh.

He nodded. "I know. I'm sorry. If it makes you feel any better, you broke mine right back."

"What kind of asshole would I be," she said, "if that made me feel better?"

"The kind who forgives me?"

She held out her hand for him to shake. "I'll forgive you, if you forgive me."

"Done." He shook but didn't let go of her hand.

For a moment, she thought he was going to pull her close. Kiss her. Put his arms around her. They'd kissed under this streetlamp before. Why not do it again?

Because thirty years, she thought as Miguel dropped her hand, thirty years was a long time ago.

"Where'd you meet him?"

He was talking about Garrett.

"Al-Anon. Seemed like we had a lot in common. I didn't find out until much later that wasn't really true, and basing a life off the perception of shared trauma was not really the best reason to be with a person." She hesitated. "What about you? I haven't asked. Did you ever get married?"

Miguel laughed. "Nope. Studying to be a priest turns out to be a real hard hit to the dating life."

"What about when you realized you weren't going to be a priest?"

"Well, when I realized I wasn't going to be a priest," he said with a sly tip of a grin, "I was having so much fun making up for lost time that I didn't want to get married."

They both laughed at that.

"My mom wishes I'd settle down. Give her some more grandkids. But I told her my brother already handled that. I was going to be a professional funcle, not a dad. How about you?" His laughter faded. "Did you . . . ?"

"I never had any kids. No."

"Did you want any?"

The question could have been offensive, but from Miguel it felt thoughtful and full of care.

"My husband did, but he never pushed for it, and I never wanted any, so I never offered. After we were married for ten years, it was pretty obvious we weren't going to become parents. He talked to me about adoption, but again, he never made any real attempts at convincing me one way or another, or even figuring out how to start the process." She shrugged. "I knew that about him. I could have talked to him about making that effort, but it worked in my favor that he didn't bother. That was true about a lot of things, I guess. Until it wasn't anymore."

They both fell silent for a few moments.

"We would've had an adult child by now," he said at last. "We might've been grandparents."

"We might've," she agreed, ready to tell him she hadn't spent her life looking back with regrets.

Before she could, her phone hummed harshly from her purse. She pulled it out and showed him the screen quickly. "My mother."

"Do you have to answer it?"

"I don't want to," she told him with a sigh. "But I suppose I should."

Silence greeted her after she said hello. She could hear breathing.

"Ruth?"

"When are you coming to get me?"

"I'm not coming to get you. I told you that before." She pitched her voice lower, half-turning away from Miguel although he'd done the polite thing and pulled out his own phone to give her a semblance of privacy. "I'm sorry I didn't make it there today. I'll try to get there tomorrow, but I have a lot of work to do. So I might not. Are you all right? Do you need anything?"

"I need you to come and get me."

"I just told you—"

"An ungrateful child," her mother said, "is sharper than a servant's tooth."

The call ended. Tamar pulled the phone away from her face to look at it. There was the mother she remembered. Harsh of word, martyred, mean. "It's *serpent's* tooth, for fuck sakes."

"Hmm?" Miguel looked up.

"That," she said, "was my dear mother. She wanted to know when I was coming to get her. Keep in mind, I never told her I was coming to get her. She needs to be assessed for mental deterioration. I know I have to take her, I just . . ."

"It's hard," he said.

She nodded. "I never in a million years thought I'd be in this position. Never thought I'd move back here. *Never* thought I'd be the one who ended up being responsible for her."

"Maybe there's a reason why you came back, Tam."

"You mean like a Higher Power reason? Like God?"

Miguel smiled. "Yes."

"I don't think I believe in God," she told him.

"I definitely do. I believe we are given what we need to help us get to where we're supposed to be. Even if we don't want it, even if we don't understand it at the time." He slipped his phone into the pocket of his jeans. "I mean, look at us, standing here together after all this time."

Tamar had no good answer for any of that. Her phone hummed again. Another call from her mother. She didn't answer it this time, and the call went to voicemail.

"It was really great running into you," she told him sincerely.

"Maybe we can do this again?"

"Sure," she said, unable to hide her grin at the idea.

They reached for each other at the same time, both awkward. Both hesitant. Stepping into his arms, Tamar closed her eyes. The embrace was strange and familiar at the same time. Nostalgic. Also hopeful. She squeezed him for a moment before taking a step back.

They exchanged numbers, marveling at how they hadn't even had cell phones the first time they'd ever done that. Miguel texted her ten minutes later as she pulled into her driveway, and although she *knew* she ought to know better, she knew she shouldn't let her heart beat faster, she shouldn't think of this as anything but an old connection that wasn't going anywhere . . . the sight of his name and number on her phone made her feel as though there'd been no thirty-plus-year absence of him in her life.

Let me know you got home safe, his message said. In high school, when they'd lived across the street from one another, she would have blinked the porch light for him to know she was safely inside.

She texted him back, still standing next to her car with the garage door still wide open. *I'm home.*

Safe?

The next text that came through was a simple gif of a blinking porch light.

Safe, she replied.

"Hey, neighbor." Ross's voice came up too close behind her, and Tamar jumped, a hand over her heart.

She dropped her phone, wincing at the crunch as it hit the asphalt. She already knew before she picked it up that it would be cracked and broken. Unfortunately, it also wouldn't turn on.

"Oh, shoot, I'm sorry. Wow." Ross held up both hands. "I didn't mean to scare you."

Tamar folded her fingers over the broken phone, her voice terse. "Can I help you?"

"Yeah, I got this by mistake." He held up a small box, tilting it so she could see the address on it. Hers.

She softened and took the package. "Thanks."

"I was going to say that we should exchange numbers or email addresses, you know, in case of something like this. I get a lot of packages for your house, even when I tell the delivery guys they have it wrong. Because I'm 123," Ross said. "You're 132."

"I'd be happy to exchange numbers with you, Ross, but . . ." she held up her broken phone.

His mouth twisted. "Oh, man. I'm really, really sorry. Maybe if you try to turn it off and then back on?"

"Yeah, I'll check it." She had the sinking suspicion the phone was totally dead, no matter how hard she tried to revive it. She'd just paid it off.

Ross pulled out a receipt from his pocket. "If you have a pen, I can write it down?"

Pulling a pen from her purse, Tamar scribbled her phone number and email address. Ross did the same with his, then tore the receipt in half and handed her the part with his information on it. She tucked it into her bag, shifting the box beneath her other arm. She waited for him to leave, but he stared expectantly.

"Nothing weird on the cameras," he said finally, when she gave him a pointed look.

Heat rose in her throat and flushed her cheeks. "That's good."

"Just thought you'd want to know. If you were worried about it."

"I wasn't, really, but thank you." Again, she softened. He was weird, but he was also nice. She turned her body to point the package at him. "Thanks for bringing this over."

"You're welcome. Just being a good neighbor, you know? When I'm expecting a package, I get really disappointed if it doesn't arrive when I'm expecting it."

"It's a new book I've been looking forward to," she explained. "So thank you for bringing it over."

She gave him a nice smile that he returned. She backed up a couple of steps, no longer waiting for him to take the hint that it was time to end the conversation. She looked over her shoulder at him as she hit the button to close the garage, but although she watched until the door completely shut, the last view she had was of his shoes, steady and unmoving in the same place.

9

TAMAR DID NOT make it back to Somerset House as soon as she'd promised. In fact, it took her a week to force herself to finally return, and even then, she almost missed the turn to the parking lot because her brain simply didn't want her to go. She waited in her car too long before getting out, telling herself she just wanted to hear the rest of the song on the radio.

Finally, she had no more excuses.

Unlike many of the other doors in this corridor of Somerset House, Ruth's was closed. Nor did it have a message board on it, although there was a bare spot, slightly more faded, that made it seem as though there once had been. Tamar rapped her knuckles lightly on the door, but nobody answered. She touched the keypad but didn't tap in the numbers her mother had used a few mornings ago. They were easy to remember. Lovey's birthday.

Tamar's childhood bedroom door had been taken off the hinges by her mother, more than once, for some infraction of rules so complicated that it had been impossible to avoid breaking them. Privacy had been a privilege, accorded or withheld by her mother's whims—and maybe by how much she was drinking that day.

Still, that didn't make it right for Tamar to bust into Ruth's apartment, not even if she thought her mother might be in some kind of distress. Hurt, perhaps. Fallen and unable to get up.

The hand she'd raised to knock lowered slowly to her side, and Tamar took a step back. It could be a few hours before anyone on the staff thought to check on her mother. Hell, based on the way she'd waltzed out of here last week in the middle of the night without a single person noticing other than nosy Gilda Ruben, it could be days. If something bad *had* happened to her, Ruth could die alone on the floor before help arrived.

While she stood there pondering this possibility, the door opened. Her mother was there. She looked fine. She frowned when she saw Tamar.

"Tammy? What are you doing here?"

"I told you I'd be by to check on you," Tamar said. "See if you wanted to go out to lunch or something."

"Oh, honey, I wish you'd called first. I have some plans. I hadn't heard from you in over a week." Her mother's mouth curved down into a frown that seemed genuinely upset.

"My phone was broken. It took me a few days to get a new one. But you're right, I should have called first." She studied her mother but tried not to make it obvious. She waited for Ruth to ask her inside, but she did not. Tamar shifted her weight from one foot to the other, looking around her mother's shoulder to see if she had a guest that she didn't want Tamar to see. The apartment looked empty.

Ruth looked over her own shoulder in the direction Tamar was looking, then back at her. "What?"

"I thought maybe you had company. Or something."

"I'm alone," her mother said. "I'm always so alone."

There was a hint of the old martyrdom in her mother's voice. The slightest trace of a whine, a "poor pity me" that set Tamar's teeth on edge. Tamar eyed her. "I thought you said you have so many friends here."

"I do." Ruth gave her a curious look. "Why? What does that mean?"

Had she already forgotten what she'd said not a full minute before? Tamar studied her harder, looking for any signs that her mother was fucking with her. She couldn't tell.

"I wish you'd called first," her mother repeated. "I have plans today."

"That's fine. Did Ms. Carr say anything to you about having some evaluations done?"

Ruth tilted her head, her brow furrowing. Her mouth thinned. After a second or so, she shook her head. "No. I don't think so. Why?"

"Because of what happened last week," Tamar said more gently than she'd thought herself capable of being.

Her mother's eyes went wide. "What happened last week? What do you mean?"

"When you came to visit me? In the middle of the night?"

It was clear by her mother's agitated expression that she either didn't know what Tamar was talking about, or she didn't want to discuss it. Her hands, fingers malformed with arthritis, opened and closed before she settled them on her hips. Her chin went up. Jaw set. Gaze flashed.

"Just what are you getting at, Tammy?" Fear trilled in her voice.

"I'm going to go have a chat with Ms. Carr. Okay?"

Her mother's frown deepened. "Fine. I've got a bus trip today. We're going to the art museum."

"All right. Well . . ." Tamar hesitated, always on uneven footing with her mother. Never sure if a hug felt right, only knowing that not hugging felt wrong.

She didn't have to worry about it for more than a few seconds, because Ruth stepped back into her apartment and closed the door in her face. Tamar stood there for another moment, shaking her head and letting a low chuckle seep out of her. She put her palm on the door, her head hanging, her eyes closed, as she contemplated what she was doing here.

Her childhood and teen years had been awful. Her mother had been terrible. Tamar had escaped that, made her way in life, taken care of herself. More than that. She'd made herself a *success*. So why did she stand here, hand on a closed door, wondering how she was supposed to help the woman who'd shut it in her face?

You're cold. Do you know that? You don't care about anyone but yourself.

That had been Garrett's accusation, and it had dug in deep like a splinter working its way directly to her heart. Festering and poisoning her, mostly because Tamar knew it wasn't true. If anything, she had always felt too much. Cared too much. She'd given too many people the benefit of the doubt, trusting until they gave her a reason to stop. Her ex-husband would never admit to his part in the end of their marriage or all the things he'd done over the years to wear away her trust in him. He would only and ever always blame her for what he could "prove" she'd done. Tamar had always thought he was angrier about that than anything else—that after years of vagueness, she'd given him something concrete. A definite end. It had been better, in the end, that he hated her enough to kick her out than to keep on trying and trying to get him to listen to her when she knew he never would.

Tamar's fingers curled against the cold wood. She pressed her forehead to it too, but only briefly in case anyone was watching. She stepped back from the door, lifting her chin. It was too easy to drown in the past, especially when you were ignoring the lifesaver being tossed your way.

A recent online thread on social media had proclaimed that Gen X was the "whatever" generation, and Tamar felt that strongly now as she took another step back from her mother's closed door. *Whatever.* She had work to do at home. She didn't have time to stand here in the hallway letting herself get lost in emotional upheaval.

On the way to the director's office, Tamar passed by Gilda Ruben's room. It was cracked open, and she expected to see the woman peering out from inside. Instead, she glimpsed a different woman mopping the floor. The room itself had been stripped of any personal décor.

She stopped and pushed the door open a bit more. "Excuse me?"

The janitor looked up, leaning heavily on the mop. "Yes?"

"Do you know what happened to the woman who lived here?"

"You a friend?"

"No. I mean, we were acquaintances."

The other woman shrugged and began mopping again. "I'm not allowed to discuss the residents. You'll have to talk to Ms. Carr about it."

The dismissal was clearly not personal. Unsettled, Tamar kept moving down the hall. Her inquiry about making an appointment with the director had been answered with Ms. Carr's "open door policy" encouraging the family of residents to simply drop in. Tamar didn't like that. It sounded like a good way to be shunted off.

Lovey had always been the one to deal with the Somerset House director, the billing, all of that. All Tamar knew about Ms. Carr was that she seemed a lot like a high school superintendent—you might see her in the halls sometimes, and she might even know your name, but you generally didn't have much to do with her unless you were causing some kind of trouble.

The director's door was slightly open when she got there. Tamar rapped lightly, which made the door swing open. Ms. Carr sat at her desk, her chair spun around to face the large window overlooking the building's backyard. When Tamar cleared her throat, the woman turned her chair slowly to face her.

"Can I help you?"

"I'm Tamar Glass. I came to chat with you about my mother."

Ms. Carr blinked rapidly, then sat up straight. Her welcoming smile revealed brilliant white teeth, perfectly straight. She waved a hand at the chair in front of her desk. "And your mother is . . . ?"

"Ruth Kahan."

The waving hand stopped. Ms. Carr frowned. Tamar was already taking a seat, but the director's expression was no longer welcoming.

"Ohhh, yes," she said. "Your mother and I had a conversation this morning."

"You did? About what?"

"I'm sorry, did you make an appointment, Ms. Glass?"

"Your email to me said you encouraged drop-ins." Tamar's hands clenched. So did her jaw. She forced both to release.

Ms. Carr shuffled some papers on her desk. "It's just that I'm very busy right now—"

"You didn't look very busy," Tamar pointed out crisply. She knew what getting the runaround sounded like.

"Well," Ms. Carr said, "I suppose nobody can ever really know what's going on with someone else, can they?"

They stared at each other across the desk. Tamar looked at the papers the director had been shuffling. They'd spread out from a manila folder, and although she couldn't see the name on it, the papers looked as though they had a legal letterhead on the top of them. Seeing her look, Ms. Carr quickly put the papers back into a pile and stuffed them back into the folder, which she turned face down so Tamar couldn't possibly see what was written on the tab.

"Considering that my mother managed to leave Somerset House in her nightgown in the middle of the night and nobody stopped her, considering she made her way all the way across town to my house and I had to bring her back here, and considering that not a single person on your staff here, including you, followed up with me about it, I'd say Somerset House certainly *doesn't* know what's going on."

Ms. Carr's brow furrowed. She placed both of her hands on top of the folder. "We take a lot of pride here at Somerset House in providing an exemplary residential experience. But there are limits to what anyone could expect."

"Look, I didn't come in here to fight with you about whether or not it was okay that my mother went night—went wandering." Tamar cut off the private word she had always used, and when Ms. Carr looked as though she meant to interrupt, she cut her off too. "Because it's not okay, and I'm sure you know that. I came here to see about getting her some kind of assessment."

"I'm afraid we won't be able to accommodate you with that, Ms. Glass."

For a moment, Tamar couldn't answer. "I'm sorry—what?"

"You'll need to arrange your mother's mental assessment privately. We aren't able—"

"Hold on. What do you mean, you're not able? My sister did a lot of research before we settled on Somerset House, largely in part because of your reputation in transitioning independent-living residents to assisted or full care, if needed. She was very clear—"

"You weren't part of that research, though, were you, Ms. Glass? Your sister did that all by herself. You, in fact, only recently returned to the area. Isn't that right?" Ms. Carr's nails dragged faint scratches along the back of the manila folder.

The sound was not quite as brutal as fingernails on a chalkboard, or teeth biting a fork, but a shudder still tiptoed up and down Tamar's spine. She sat up even straighter. "My sister was in complete communication with me. I might not have been here physically, but I was part of the process."

"Were you, though?" Ms. Carr's entire expression distorted into one of fake concern.

Taken aback, Tamar narrowed her eyes. She'd never been one for confrontation. Not unless she was pushed into it.

"Were you?" Ms. Carr prompted.

"I can find the residence agreement, if you want," she replied. "I didn't bring my copy along, but I'm sure you have one on file."

Ms. Carr blinked again, that same double-fast and somehow bird-like flutter of her eyelids. "Not necessary, Ms. Glass. I'm canceling your mother's contract with us. I have the paperwork in progress. We here at Somerset House think it would be best if you found your mother other accommodations."

From outside, a lawnmower hummed. A faint and distant sound of voices, shouting, came through Ms. Carr's closed windows. She twitched, her eyes shooting toward the glass before locking back on Tamar's. Every line of her body screamed with tension, barely controlled.

"What do you mean, you think it's best if I find my mother 'other accommodations'?" Tamar had done her best to keep this entire conversation calm. Steady. Anything but accusatory or sheeplike or Karen-esque. She'd failed.

The director leaned back in her chair. The high-backed leather had seen better days. What looked like a series of cat scratches marred the surface just over her left shoulder. The arms were both ragged at the ends. Maybe the result of endless hours of fingers tapping against them, the way they were doing now.

"I'm very, very sorry," Ms. Carr said. Her voice shook.

And here was the thing—Tamar believed her. She wanted to make the director into a villain, ready to cast an old lady out into the snow and cold, but looking across the wide desk in need of a polish, all Tamar could manage to find was a swelling measure of sympathy.

"I understand your concerns," Tamar began, but Ms. Carr lifted a hand.

"I'm not sure you do. Conversations like this are never easy. If you want to know the truth, I hate them on every level." Ms. Carr rubbed at the space between her eyes with one fingertip. She wore a dirty bandage on that finger, the adhesive black and gummy on her skin. When she looked up at Tamar, her expression had warped. There was nothing professional in that face any longer. Pain shone in the woman's eyes, and something else Tamar could not quite identify.

"Somerset House runs on a bare-bones budget, Ms. Glass, as I'm sure you can guess. We rely on endowments and donations and state funding, along with the residents' rent, of course. Which most often doesn't cover the entire expense of their support."

Silence.

Tamar understood Ms. Carr was waiting for her to speak, but she had nothing to say.

"Residents like your mother, the self-supporting ones . . ." she trailed off and, to Tamar's alarm, put both her elbows on the desk. Leaned forward. Placed her face in her hands. Her voice muffled, she continued, "But your mother. Your mother."

"What about my mother?" Tamar's voice buckled into a squeak. Her fists clenched in her lap again, but she managed to keep her jaw from going too tight.

So many times, too many times, someone had spoken to Tamar about her mother. The police. The hospital. The neighbors. The manager at the supermarket. The debt collectors.

"I can pay more. What do you need? I have money. I can make a donation. What do you need?" Tamar repeated, more urgently this time. "Look at me."

Ms. Carr lifted her head and seemed to get ahold of herself. Faint circles shadowed beneath her eyes. Her lips were dry and split, with the remnants of the lipstick she'd put on this morning lining each fissure. Fine lines had worn themselves into the brackets around her mouth and were starting to carve themselves around her nose.

"I'm sorry. That won't be possible."

Tamar sat up even straighter, mindful of the crackle in her spine. "You said Somerset House needs money."

The director shook her head. She'd appeared to be in her mid-thirties when Tamar came into the office, but some trick of the light now showed her as being much older. Her hair had turned from blond to silver. No. To white. Her fingers curved into claws on the desktop.

"I'm sorry," the director repeated, her voice a monotone. "But your mother . . ."

Tamar stood. Hands shaking. Voice shaking. "What has my mother done? Tell me!"

Ms. Carr blinked rapidly and sat up straight in her chair. She smoothed her hair back from her face. Pressed her lips together. She put her hands flat on the desk in front of her. When she finally looked up to meet Tamar's eyes, her own gaze had gone a little dazed. Like she was coming out of a dream.

Maybe it was Tamar who'd been dreaming.

"She's been . . . unkind. To other residents. And the staff. She's been disruptive."

Tamar sat and linked her fingers together in her lap, tight, tight, tight, to keep her hands from flying upward and around as she spoke. "So, she's been mean. Isn't your staff trained to handle that? She's clearly got dementia or she's starting to, anyway. Somerset House is supposed to specialize in care for people like her."

"Nobody could care for someone like her." Ms. Carr's voice was so low, so rasping and soft, that for a moment, Tamar was not convinced she'd heard her correctly.

"What does that mean?"

"She's been unkind," the director repeated. "Abusive, both physically and verbally."

For a second, Tamar allowed her eyes to close. But only for a second. "I'm sorry, but again, it's a symptom of her illness—"

"Is it, though? *Is* it?"

"I don't know what you mean."

Ms. Carr leaned back in her shabby chair again without speaking.

Tamar rubbed the inside of her arm, over the place where the scars had faded. She stopped when she saw the director's eyes drifting to the spot and pressed her palm to cover it.

"When the community guinea pig died," the director said bluntly, "we assumed it was an accident."

Where's Fluffy? What happened to Fluffy?
He went to live on a farm.

"But when Mr. Patel's cat was found dead," Ms. Carr continued in the same soft monotone, "that was definitely not an accident."

"Are you saying my mother killed a man's cat?"

"She laughed about it," Ms. Carr cut in. "*Laughed*, Ms. Glass. Poor Mr. Patel's angina flared up. We thought he was having a heart attack. And then there was her . . . altercation . . . with Gilda Ruben."

Ice crystallized in Tamar's entire body. "What altercation?"

"I'm not at liberty to disclose any resident's private information."

"But you just—"

"I could be fired," Ms. Carr said.

"Is Gilda okay?"

Silence.

"She passed away," Ms. Carr said.

Tamar sat up straighter in her chair. "From what?"

"I'm not at liberty to discuss—"

Tamar scowled and waved away the question. "What did you and my mother talk about this morning?"

The director's nails dug into the soft, pale-yellow paper of the file folder. One broke as Tamar watched. She flinched. Ms. Carr did not.

"I won't," Ms. Carr said through gritted teeth, "discuss it."

The woman was unhinged.

"I thought," Tamar whispered, "Somerset House was supposed to help people like my mother."

"She's going to have to leave. I'm sorry. We can't take care of some-one like *her* here." It seemed as though the moment the words left the director's lips, something lightened in her. Her back straightened. Color returned to her cheeks. Her eyes sparkled. "Yes, yes, that's the only solu-tion. Your mother has to go."

"But where am I supposed to take her?" Tamar cried.

Ms. Carr shrugged. "Home with you?"

"I can't do that."

"Isn't that the problem today? Nobody wants to take care of their families anymore. Old people used to die at home, surrounded by their children and grandchildren. Now they get carted off to places that pre-tend to be better for them, but how could anything possibly be better than dying at home with your family?"

"My mother isn't dying," Tamar said sharply. "And that seems like an odd point of view for someone in your position to hold."

Ms. Carr's eyelids fluttered. Her gaze sharpened. "I can put in a word with some other facilities, if you want. But they're all so full, there are waiting lists. And of course, I'd have to be honest with them about the reasons we are terminating your mother's residency here. I'll have to tell them everything."

Tamar stood. "Do I need to get a lawyer?"

"We have one," Ms. Carr said.

She had the money for a lawyer, but did she really want to bring this fight? Tamar swallowed the lump in her throat. "When do you need her to move out?"

"I'm working on the paperwork right now. But she'll need to be gone by the end of next week."

There was nothing else to say. Tamar didn't offer her hand, or even a farewell as she turned on her heel. She pretended not to hear what Ms. Carr said as she left the director's office.

"We talked about secrets," the woman whispered to herself. "How did she know my secrets?"

10

"YOU CAN'T TAKE her home with you." Lovey's image on the screen blurred and pixelated for a few seconds, her voice lagging behind the motion of her mouth. "You can't take her to *live* with you, Tam."

Tamar set the phone on the counter as she filled the electric kettle. "What choice do I have? They have a lawyer. According to the residential contract, she can be evicted for being disruptive or destructive."

"I just don't understand," Lovey said. "She's been so good for so long. Once she stopped the booze and drugs, she was . . ."

Her sister trailed off, looking embarrassed. The subject of their mother's addiction was a sore one. Lovey had said long ago that she didn't blame Tamar for running away and leaving her behind, but Tamar had always wondered if that were really true. She didn't blame Lovely because Ruth had decided to change her life after it was too late to affect Tamar, but there *was* resentment. They didn't really talk about it. It was easier that way.

"I have an appointment for her to be evaluated by her doctor to see what might be going on, and she's on three different waitlists for places. But until one accepts her, she'll have to stay here." Tamar drew in a breath. "It'll be fine."

"Oh, Tam." Lovey shook her head.

Tamar leaned on the counter to stare into her sister's face, so small in the phone screen. In the background, Archie was dancing with what looked like a stuffed bear while fifteen-year-old Judah seemed to be taunting his twin sister Helena with one of those plastic guns that shot foam bullets. All of the kids were blond, mini-replicas of her sister.

"It'll just be for a few weeks. Maybe a month, just until another place opens up," Tamar said.

"What about what the director said? About telling other places about what she allegedly did?"

Tamar shook her head. "I told them if they accused her of killing someone's cat, I'd sue them for libel. They have no proof that she did anything to anyone. Laughing at someone's misfortune is shitty, but it's not an admission of guilt."

Lovey rubbed her forehead and leaned closer to the screen. "Seriously, though, what the fuck?"

"I don't know," Tamar said.

"Do you think—?"

"I don't know," Tamar repeated. She didn't *want* to know.

"But . . . she can't live with you, Tam." Lovey said this as though it was the first time. She didn't have to explain why.

"What choice do I have, Lovey? What fucking choice? They're kicking her out. Where else is she supposed to go? With you? How do you want to get her to California? Walk?" Tamar clamped her teeth tight to stop herself from shouting again.

The kettle screamed.

Tamara added boiling water to the infuser section of her teapot. She watched the loose leaves unfurl in the hot water. Steam curled out. She put the lid on the pot, and she let the tea steep.

"You don't have to try so hard to be the better person, Tam."

At this, Tamar looked into her phone's camera, hard. "Who says I have to try hard?"

"That's not what I meant," Lovey said. "I meant that I understand if you don't want to take her in."

"Right now, we don't have any other options. Anyway, she's our *mother.*"

In Lovey's background, a child began to wail. Lovey twisted in her seat to look over her shoulder before turning back with an exasperated expression. She sighed.

"You have to go," Tamar guessed.

"Tam. Listen. We'll work this out. Okay? I do have to go now, but we'll figure something out."

The image flickered again, stretching Lovey's face. Her voice broke into electronic babble. Tamar used this as an excuse to thumb the call to an end, then tapped a text quickly to her sister telling her the call had failed, not to try back.

Give the kids a kiss from Auntie Tam.

The message turned from delivered to read while she watched, but Lovey didn't reply.

The decision had been made, no matter what her younger sister said about it. And where did Lovey get off, anyway? She lived on the entire other side of the country with her perfect house and perfect husband, her perfect tribe of children. Her perfect *life*.

The vehemence in this train of thought unsettled Tamar's stomach. She loved her sister. Everyone loved her. That's why she was called Lovey, instead of her given name, Lavinia. Everyone had always adored the sweet-tempered little blond girl with the curls and big blue eyes, the one who never made a fuss, who excelled at school, who made friends easily and kept them.

Instead of tea, Tamar poured herself a glass of wine. She'd stopped at the liquor store on the way back from Somerset House and picked out a full case of bottles, different varieties. This one was a little too sweet, but in the end, did she really care what it tasted like? She wasn't drinking it for the flavor but for the warmth it would flood through her and the hum in her brain it would block out. She was drinking it because getting a little tipsy made the rest of everything so much easier to deal with.

She was drinking it because she was her mother's daughter.

For years, while her friends were getting blackout drunk and high on whatever they could ingest, Tamar hadn't touched a single drop or smoked a single puff. She'd never made a big deal out of it, never really shared her reasons why, even with people she was really close to. She'd remained adamantly sober without preaching to anyone else about it. She'd married a man with a similar outlook about intoxicants, and for a long time, everything had been fine. Until it wasn't.

When she finally started drinking, she hadn't bothered to hide it from Garrett. She was an adult, she'd said. She wasn't going to let alcohol, or the fear of it, run her life. It had been a lie. She'd chosen to drink as a way of pushing him out of her life, because he otherwise refused to go. And even then, becoming a drunk hadn't been enough. It had taken a blatant affair to get him to let her leave. By then, though, she'd discovered how much she really liked being not-sober. One of the first things she'd done once moving to Ohio was to get her medical card for "chronic pain." The pain was real. The cause for it? Old injuries. A fall down the basement stairs when you were fifteen, it turned out, could really fuck you up for the rest of your life.

Glass in one hand, laptop in the other, Tamar went upstairs to her bedroom. She got her vaporizer pen out of the nightstand and filled it with a small amount of flower.

"Thanks, Mom," she said to the empty room as she drew in her first hit.

As soon as the warmth began spreading through her, easing the tension in her neck, shoulders, and back, she let out a long, grateful sigh. Why had she waited so long to discover just how good, how fucking *good* it felt to lose control of your mind? No wonder Ruth had always been wasted.

Settled on the bed, wine close at hand, she opened her laptop and quickly rearranged some meetings. All of her projects were on target, but she made sure to build in some extra time in case the next couple of weeks went sideways from dealing with her mother. She messaged her bosses and let them know, briefly, what was going on and that she'd most likely be working outside regular hours for the next few weeks. Then she pulled up a browser window.

All she had to type in was "Gilda Ruben," and the woman's name came up immediately. Her obituary was short and to the point. She was survived by a married son with three children. No siblings. She'd been active in her synagogue Sisterhood and liked reading and crocheting. There was no mention of her cause of death, only that it had been unexpected.

There were other ways to find things out. Tamar wasn't often active on social media, but she did belong to the local neighborhood and town groups. A quick check of those brought up a small mention of "Did anyone hear about the accident at Somerset House?" The comments on the post were sparse. One chimed in that the details were scarce, but "apparently, it was ruled an accident, not a suicide."

Tamar shut the laptop lid and put it on the bed next to her while she swung her legs over the side. She took the glass from her nightstand. Drained it. The wine went down smooth as silk, but instead of going to the kitchen to pour more, she took another couple of hits off her pen.

Old people died all the time. That was life. Gilda Ruben had been a busybody who'd apparently had "an altercation" with Tamar's mother. That did not mean that Ruth had actually been responsible for the other woman's death. As far as Tamar knew, her mother had never *killed* anyone.

But she certainly had tried to, hadn't she?

Tamar's frequently aching back was a reminder of that. She hadn't fallen down the stairs by accident. Ruth had pushed her. Tamar would never forget the feeling of cold cement beneath her cheek as she lay sprawled at the bottom of the basement stairs, or the sight of her mother's silhouette at the top of them.

"You're so fucking eager to see what it's like to die," Ruth had said in a voice flat and devoid of emotion. "Why not let someone else help you."

She hadn't died, obviously. Her mother had never spoken to her about it again. Two years after that, Tamar had run away from the house on Spring Hill Drive, and her mother, forever.

Until now.

11

"THIS IS . . . nice." Ruth looked around the guest room from her spot in the doorway but didn't go through it.

Behind her, Tamar shifted the suitcases in each of her hands to get a better grip. They were heavy, and her mother was simply standing in the doorway without moving. "Can you move, please, these are—"

"Oh, sure, of course. I'm sorry, honey." At last, Ruth moved into the bedroom and toward the window on the far wall.

Tamar followed and set the suitcases down next to the closet, then worked her fingers free of some of the stiffness. Ruth had brought only her personal belongings with her, choosing to put the furniture she'd been using at Somerset House into storage until she was accepted to a new residential facility. Her expression looked as though she might be regretting it now, but honestly, where would any of it have fit? Tamar didn't have and didn't want a house crammed full of junk like the one she'd grown up in. She never wanted to live that way again.

"Well, isn't this just . . . lovely." Ruth turned around in a slow circle, taking in everything about the bedroom Tamar had set up for her.

Tamar looked around the room. This bedroom was at the top of the stairs, at the opposite end of the hall from the primary. The previous owners had renovated the house to include a Jack-and-Jill bathroom shared with the third, empty bedroom. She'd left it as it had been when she bought it, with soft gray walls and carpet. She'd added matching white and gray curtains, a white iron bed frame, a distressed pale gray dresser. Everything was neutral, bland, without much personality. She'd never had overnight guests.

"It's so very . . . nice." Her mother's voice wavered, and she bit her lower lip.

Tamar held back the flinch and bit the caustic remark in half to keep herself from saying it aloud. "You know this is only temporary until we get everything figured out with a new place."

"Like staying in a hotel." Ruth perked up.

"I hope it's better than that," Tamar said stiffly.

Her mother didn't seem to notice she'd made an insult. She pulled open the closet door and rattled the hangers inside. She opened the top dresser drawer, then the others, all the way down to the bottom. She peeked into the bathroom before turning back to Tamar. "I'm sure it will be fine. As you said, it's only for a few days, and then I can be out of your way."

"Do you need anything else right now? There are extra blankets in the closet, and there should be shampoo and toothpaste and stuff in the bathroom—"

"I brought my own," her mother said. "It's in my suitcase."

Tamar nodded. Ruth opened the top dresser drawer again and looked inside. She shut it again. She sat on the bed, facing the window, her back to her daughter. Her shoulders slumped a little, and she let out a sigh. Tamar stepped back toward the doorway.

"I'm going to let you get settled while I check in at work. Don't forget, we have your doctor's appointment at three today. We'll need to leave at two-thirty. Okay?"

"Do you really think I need to see a doctor?"

Tamar paused, one hand on the doorframe. "Yes. I do. Don't you?"

"I'm fine," her mother answered without turning around.

"You're not fine," Tamar replied bluntly. "You left your apartment in the middle of the night in your pajamas and broke into my house—"

"Is it so wrong to want to see my daughter?" her mother cried.

"You were disoriented. You were . . ." Tamar stopped to clear her throat so her voice didn't shake. "You need to get checked out. It's a requirement for the places we're applying for. If you want to be approved, you need a doctor to sign the paperwork."

Ruth said nothing.

"I've really got to check in on some work." Tamar looked at her phone. "You have a couple of hours before we need to leave. Help yourself to whatever you'd like in the kitchen. Get settled. I'll be in my office."

Downstairs, she got herself in order. Despite the multiple extra bedrooms and the study off the kitchen, Tamar had set up her home office in the formal dining room. The light was better, with windows looking over the backyard and the garden she'd been slowly planting. It was closer to the kitchen, in case she needed to top off her tea or grab a snack. Unlike the study that was meant to be used as a home office, there was no way to close off the dining room with a locked door, but she lived alone, so who would bother her during the day? Under normal circumstances, nobody. But today . . .

"Do you want some lunch?"

Tamar looked up from the computer monitor. "I didn't hear you come down."

"I'm making something to eat. It's lunchtime," her mother said. "Are you hungry?"

"I don't usually eat until a bit later. Thanks." Tamar turned back to the computer but remained aware that her mother hadn't moved from the open doorway between the office and the kitchen. She looked up. "But like I said, help yourself."

"It's no trouble. I'm making it for myself anyway."

"No. Thank you," Tamar said. "I don't want anything."

Her mother disappeared into the kitchen. There came a sound of opening and closing cupboards. The clatter of dishes.

"What are you working on?"

Tamar looked up again, pressing her lips together against an irritated huff. "A project."

Before she could stop her, Ruth had crossed the room to peer over Tamar's shoulder. "What is it?"

"It's a package for a new brand of cheese crackers. And I promised I'd have the draft sent by one, so if you could just—"

"You always were so artistic," her mother said. "Always drawing or coloring something. I have to say, for someone with such an eye for color in your work, Tammy, you really don't use it much in your house."

"I like simplicity, and I don't have to justify myself to you."

Her mother did that blinking thing she seemed to have taken up as a habit, and it irritated Tamar even more. "Of course, you don't."

"Look," she said with a sigh. "I really need to get this finished before the doctor's appointment. I need you to not interrupt me when I'm working. If I didn't make that clear, I am now. Okay? If I'm in this room, I'm not to be interrupted."

A glimmer of anger flickered across her mother's expression but faded quickly as she nodded and backed away, hands up. "Of course. I'm sorry. I'll leave you alone. You know, I don't need you to take me to the doctor. I can call for a Ryde."

That would have made Tamar's life much easier, but she didn't trust her mother to tell her the truth about what the doctor said. "I arranged my schedule to take you. It's no problem."

"I don't need you to go with me."

"You do," Tamar said.

It was the same voice her mother had used on her as a child, and the words hit like thrown stones. Ruth flinched and took a step back. She straightened and opened her mouth, but nothing came out but a small sob she quickly hid behind her hand.

In the next second, she burst into tears. Huge, racking sobs. She stumbled away as though blinded by her tears, knocking into the stack of books on the sideboard and sending a few hardcovers askew. One fell, pages fluttering, landing face down on the hardwood floor. Ruth bent to pick it up but fumbled it, dropping it again. Another sob lurched out of her. She turned and swiped at her face.

"I'm sorry, Tammy."

There'd been many times her mother had started a sentence with those words, only to continue on with "but" and a long explanation about why she really didn't need to be sorry, because she wasn't the one who'd done anything wrong. This time, though, she went silent. Expectant.

Tamar shrugged. "I'm not sure what you want me to say."

"That you forgive me. I know I was not the best mother in the world." Ruth's hands shook as she reached in Tamar's direction, almost as though she were seeking a hug.

Well, she wasn't going to get one. Tamar might have taken on the responsibility for her mother's care, but that did not extend to blatant lies to save Ruth's feelings. "Not the best? You weren't even a *good* mother."

Ruth flinched. Hung her head. She turned her face toward the window and stared out of it for a long time as her throat worked and her shoulders shook with repressed sobs. She was so small now. The woman who'd loomed larger than life back then had become almost the size of a child herself—no, Tamar corrected herself. Not become. She'd always been that size but had seemed bigger when Tamar was smaller.

"I can't change anything that happened back then," Ruth said finally.

"Nobody can."

Ruth's chin went up. Her lips trembled. She drew in a sniffling breath and blew it out, and then, to Tamar's surprise, nodded firmly. "You are exactly right. I'm not asking or expecting you to forget anything that happened back when I was sick. I'm just hoping you can forgive me now. So we can move on."

"When you were *sick*." Tamar let out her own breath, slowly.

"Yes. When I was sick," her mother repeated. "When I was hurtful to you. When I wasn't myself."

"And you're yourself now?" The question came out sounding more like a challenge than she'd intended.

It took a few seconds for her mother to nod, but she did. "I hope I am. I suppose the fancy-pants doctor you're taking me to will tell us both all about it. All I can do is apologize. Make my amends to you—"

"Amends. Uh-huh." Tamar shook her head. "You can't make amends to me now. You can't change what you did, and you can be all the sorry you want, but it doesn't change the past. I realize that saying you're sorry is part of your journey, but I'm not required to go on it with you."

They stared at each other until Tamar broke the gaze and went back to work. Her mother stayed in one place for a few more moments, but she finally turned toward the kitchen doorway. She paused.

"I understand why you're so angry with me, Tammy. I hope you can find it within yourself to one day forgive me," Ruth said. "Because if you can't, then it will become like the devil himself inside you, and that will be worse than anything you think I ever did."

12

Ruth was quiet on the way home. Dr. McAllister had gone through some simple cognitive tests and a personality assessment, as well as ordering a full panel of bloodwork and a urine test to check for UTIs. Tamar hadn't sat in on the appointment, but she'd chatted with the doctor after. Ruth had passed the mental tests, but they'd have to wait for the other results to see if there might be something physical to explain what was going on.

"I'm sorry," Ruth said as Tamar pulled into the garage and turned off the car. She sat staring straight ahead out the front window. "I know all of this is a real inconvenience. I just want you to know that I do appreciate it."

Tamar held back the sigh. "Let's just go inside, okay? I still have some work to get caught up on. You can watch some TV or something, can't you?"

They both got out of the car, Ruth a bit slower than Tamar. She hiked her purse over her shoulder and smoothed the front of her dress. She hung back until Tamar looked at her.

"I can make us both a nice dinner," Ruth said. "How does that sound? You can get your work done while I do that."

"You don't have to."

Ruth waited until they got into the kitchen before she tried again. "I'd like to. It's the least I can do, after all. I know, how about I make us grilled cheese? You always loved the grilled cheeses."

Tamar allowed herself the indulgence of remembering her mother's grilled cheese sandwiches—layered with two or three different kinds of cheese, mayonnaise instead of butter on the outside of the bread to create a perfect gooey, crispy treat. She used to add crispy bacon, thin sliced red onion. The sandwiches were fancy, but always served with canned tomato soup, sometimes with cheesy fish-shaped crackers tossed on top, others with a side of saltines. The nights Ruth made grilled cheese could always be counted on as sober nights. If it was in the summer or on school holidays, she'd put Lovey to bed and let Tamar stay up late to play cards with her. Snap, Old Maid, Spite and Malice.

There had been good times, sometimes.

"We could play some cards later?" Ruth said hopefully, as though she'd read Tamar's thoughts.

"Sure. That sounds fine. Let me finish up the project I need to turn in. It'll take me about an hour."

"Perfect." Ruth smiled. She paused, tilting her head to look at Tamar. "That's a pretty necklace."

Tamar backed up a step, out of reach from her mother's inquisitive fingers trying to touch the pendant at her throat. "You don't recognize it?"

"Should I?"

"Someone gave it to me for my baby naming, apparently," Tamar said and watched her mother carefully for any signs she remembered who it might have been.

Ruth's eyelids fluttered rapidly. She reached again for the necklace, and this time, Tamar didn't move out of reach. Her mother's fingertips lifted and dropped the pendant. She shook her head with a small and apologetic chuckle. "That was a very long time ago, I'm sorry to say. I'd guess it came from one of your father's relatives. Where did you find it?"

"It was in a box of things Lovey had put aside for me before you moved to Somerset House."

Ruth still showed no signs of recognition. "I didn't know you'd become so religious. But I suppose there's a lot I don't know about you."

"I really need to get to work."

Her mother nodded firmly. "Yes. Of course, go, go, go. You do that, I'll fix dinner. Do you have everything I should need?"

"I don't know. Probably?"

"I'll make do," Ruth said with a smile. "Don't you even worry about it. It'll feel good to cook a meal again. I enjoyed the dining options at Somerset House, of course, but there's nothing quite like a nice, home-cooked dinner. Even if it's only sandwiches."

And it was nice to finish up her work and go into the kitchen to find the table set with steaming bowls of soup and a platter of sandwiches oozing cheesy, delicious goo over the sides. Ruth turned from the sink where she'd been scrubbing the frying pan. She gestured at the table.

"Sit, sit. You didn't have any bacon or mayonnaise, so they won't be quite the same. But still good, I hope."

Tamar sat. "I'm a vegetarian, I don't allow pork or shellfish in my house, and mayo is the condiment of the devil."

Ruth paused, her hands full of soapsuds and blinked rapidly, looking confused. "You're a vegetarian? Since when?"

"Since a long time," Tamar said.

Her mother frowned. "Well. I didn't know. I should have known? Did I forget?"

"I don't think you knew," Tamar told her. "So, no. You didn't forget."

"You used to love mayonnaise."

"People change."

Ruth's lips trembled, and she rinsed off the pan and put it in the dish rack, then dried her hands on the towel hanging on the oven door. "I hope you like the sandwiches anyway."

"They look great. Sit. Please." Tamar waited until her mother took the opposite chair before putting a sandwich on her plate.

They both ate in silence for a few minutes.

"As soon as I can get out of your hair, I will," Ruth said finally. "But in the meantime, I'd like things to be better between us. I mean that. No forcing it, no demands. Okay? Let me just try."

Tamar nodded stiffly. "All right."

After dinner, Tamar cleaned up the kitchen while Ruth spoke with Lovey on the phone about what the doctor had said. She took the call in her room, so Tamar couldn't listen in, but when she came back to the kitchen she was in a good mood.

"Your sister says hello," Ruth told her. "She asked you to give her a call later."

"Sure. Okay. Did you want to play cards?" Tamar kept her voice steady and neutral. She wasn't even sure if she wanted to play cards with her mother, but if Ruth said no, it was going to feel like a rejection.

"Oh, I think we could do that," her mother said with a smile, but raised a finger to shake at her. "I warn you, though, I've gotten a lot better at it! I'm not going to let you win the way I did when you were small."

"I wouldn't dream of it."

Ruth beamed, but her eyes glistened with unshed tears. She drew in a shaky breath. She opened her arms as though in the offer of a hug, but Tamar didn't move to embrace her, and Ruth put them back at her side. They stared at each other awkwardly for a few seconds, until Tamar moved.

"I'll get the cards," she said. "So we can play."

CHAPTER

13

Ruth beat Tamar soundly at three games of gin rummy before begging off to go to bed.

"I need my beauty sleep," she said. "Now more than ever."

She paused in the kitchen doorway to look back. "You remind me of my mother. Did I ever tell you that?"

Tamar looked up from the cards she'd been sorting to put back in the boxes. "Bubbe Gail?"

Ruth's mother had died shortly after Lovey was born. Tamar had only the vaguest memories of her as round and soft, with long dark hair. The memory of a smell, something powdery like lilac or talcum, came back to her.

"She was so beautiful when I was young, I thought I'd never be able to live up to her. I didn't look much like her, not the way Lovey favors me . . ." Ruth trailed off for a moment, her gaze going distant. Her hand twitched on the doorframe before she focused again on Tamar. "But you look so much like her that sometimes, I could almost forget you're my daughter and not my mother. Good night, honey."

"Night."

"Oh, the necklace," Ruth said, pivoting on her heel. "I remember now. It was from her. Good night, honey."

"Good night," Tamar said again.

In her own bedroom, Tamar settled in with the new book, a light-hearted romance she hadn't yet had the chance to crack open. She was having a hard time getting into it, even though the tropes were all ones she usually devoured. The conversation with Ruth kept playing over and over again. She touched the pendant. It felt warm in her hand, almost hot against the base of her throat. Or it could be her skin that was flushed and sweating, in the midst of a hot flash.

Stretching, she opened the drawer on her nightstand to pull out the small sheaf of photos she'd salvaged from the box. She flipped through them, finding the one she wanted. In it, infant Tamar was cradled by her mother, who stood next to her own mother. *Three generations*, said the words scrawled on the back of the photo in faded ink. The picture itself had faded into oranges and yellows.

She held it closer, searching her grandmother's face for any resemblances she could pick out. They had the same dark eyes and thick brows, untamed on Bubbe Gail's face and honestly getting there again on Tamar's, who'd done away with excessive plucking a few years ago. The same dark hair, as mentioned by blond Ruth. Tamar looked even closer, discerning a tiny glitter against the front of baby Tam's lacy gown that might've been the necklace, but she couldn't be sure. She returned all the pictures to the drawer and sat back against her pillows with her book again.

Tonight was the only time Tamar could recall Ruth ever speaking of her own mother without animosity in her voice. She'd never given any reasons for why she'd reviled Bubbe Gail, but it had always been clear that she had. Kind of the way anyone who'd met Tamar after she was eighteen understood she was estranged from her mother without necessarily ever hearing any reasons why.

"Family trauma," she murmured aloud. One of the several times she'd attempted counseling, a therapist had told her about it, how emotional damage done to a child can return when that child becomes a parent, thus passing along what could be considered a family curse.

Whatever.

She had a book to read, and she wanted to get a good night's sleep so she could get up early in the morning to catch up on work. When her phone lit up with an incoming text, Tamar assumed it was from Lovey and took her time reaching for the phone. Her sister would want to go over what the doctor's visit had found out, but since it was basically nothing, Tamar wasn't in a rush.

On a good night, Tamar was able to knock out half a book, but on a good night, nobody was texting her. Even with it on silent, the repeatedly lighting screen still distracted her until finally, she put down her book and picked up the phone. It wasn't her sister.

It was Miguel. She hadn't heard from him since the day they'd met at the hardware store. Her phone had been broken, and then she'd been so busy with everything else, she never got the chance to message him and see if he'd tried to get in touch.

Hey. I was thinking about you. Are you awake?

With the phone clutched in her hands, Tamar tried to ignore the sudden rush of her heart pounding. She typed slowly. *Yes. What's up?*

Maybe she'd waited too long to reply, and he'd already gone to sleep. It was after midnight. Well past time she should be in dreamland. But she held on to the phone a minute longer, watching to see if a return message arrived.

When the text went from "delivered" to "read," Tamar couldn't hold back the giddy chuckle that slipped out of her. She held her breath, waiting for his reply. The three bouncing dots at the bottom of the screen teased her, then stopped. Nothing. Then they started again. Stopped. A flurry of giggles sifted from her. She fell back onto the pillows, eyes closed, but flipped the switch on the phone's side to activate sound.

A ping.

A message.

What are you doing?

She snapped a picture of her book cover and sent it without additional explanation.

Nice. Looks steamy. Could give a guy a complex, having to live up to the standards of a book like that.

Nobody should think the standard of mutual concern for each other's happiness, willingness to work on your issues and a guaranteed happy ever after is too high, Tamar typed, and, aware that the subtleties of tone didn't always transfer over text, added, *but yes, it's also nice and steamy.*

Point taken. He added an embarrassed emoji. *Forgive me?*

She sent the winking face emoji.

Do you realize what we would've done if we'd had text messaging back then? We'd have been up all night. Every night.

Instead of using flashlights to send codes back and forth through our bedroom windows. It would've been a lot easier, she typed.

They sent a few more texts back and forth. Small talk. She was just about to tell him she was signing off when his message came through first.

I had a great time catching up. I'm hoping you'd like to do it again.

She didn't type a reply right away. Moving back to your hometown and reconnecting with the boy who'd broken your heart was such a cliché, wasn't it? All that history between them. First, the years of friendship, then the heartache. Tamar had never yearned to get back together with Miguel; once she'd left her mother's house and Kettering, she'd turned her back on everything, including him. She'd never thought of him longingly, never held him up as an example, good or bad, of what a relationship should be like. She'd spent a lot of time forgetting him, as a matter of fact, because thinking about him hurt too much.

But seeing him had lit a small fire inside her, and it warmed her now, with her phone clutched in both hands like some kind of precious object she had to be careful not to drop. The pounding of her heart couldn't be ignored, no matter how hard she tried.

That would be great.

The next reply was not words, but a photo of Miguel's grinning face and a thumbs-up. He looked goofy in the photo, and charming, and nostalgia swept over her in a rush. She took her own picture in reply, making a goofy face too.

I always liked that about you.

She laughed, brow furrowing. *What? My pig nose?*

The way you always were able to have fun. You were always willing to look or act silly. No matter what happened, you never took it too seriously.

Her smile faded. *I think we both know that wasn't true all the time.*

Three dots, bouncing. Nothing. Nothing. Nothing. And finally, *Can I just call you?*

Yes.

She turned off the sound on the phone again, mindful of her mother sleeping down the hall and remembering how those flashlight messages had alerted her to hover over the phone, ready to lift the receiver off the cradle before it fully rang, so she could answer it before her mother could hear it. Late night conversations on summer nights, her room so hot her hair stuck to her forehead, tasting sweat every time she licked her lips. Soft laughter, and then later, frantic, frenzied tears.

When her phone screen lit with the call, she almost didn't answer it. Her fingers swiped, though, and she put the rectangle of glass and plastic to her ear. "Hi."

"Hi." Miguel cleared his throat. "It's late. You probably want to get to sleep."

"I was hoping to read most of this book." She looked at the book, open and face down on the bed. "You should try it some time."

He laughed. "Oh, ho, ho, you assumed I'm still not a reader. I'll have you know, I read things all the time now."

"Oh, you do?" She settled into her pillows, phone pressed to her ear, and smiled.

"Sure. I read the back of the cereal box, billboards, emails . . ." he laughed.

"The Bible?"

"No," he said. "I don't read that anymore."

She'd been trying to make a light joke, but it had clearly failed. "I'm sorry. I didn't mean to make fun."

"It's fine. I can talk to you about the Bible all day long, if you want. I no longer need it for myself," he said, and after a pause, added in a lower voice, "I went through a real crisis of faith, don't get me wrong, but it was a long time ago. Not such a big deal anymore."

"Do you want to talk about it?"

"We used to talk about everything, didn't we?"

"Yes," she said, her own voice going low too. "Until we didn't."

She thought he might have disconnected by the silence that tickled its way into her ears. Then she heard him breathing. She closed her eyes and waited for tears to come; it had been decades since she'd wept about their breakup.

"I've missed you, Tam."

He'd want her to say the same to him, but she couldn't, could she? How could you miss someone you pretended you'd never even met? She'd done her best to ignore the empty, aching space he'd once filled, and she'd gotten so good at it that she hadn't missed him at all.

"I just can't believe you're back here. And I'm back here. It feels like . . . fate," Miguel said.

Tamar's laugh sounded a little watery. "I don't believe in fate."

"Feels like a second chance, then. Does that work better for you?"

"Miguel . . ."

"You don't have to make me any promises. Okay? But I'd like to take you out. As friends. You know, the way it used to be, before everything got so messed up. I'd like to talk to you about all the things we should have said to each other back then and get caught up on everything that happened since. No pressure for it to become anything else. I promise."

She sighed. He'd always been so persuasive. "I've got my mother here with me now, and I'm not sure for how long. It's kind of put me behind on a bunch of work, plus, having her here . . ."

"Wow. Yeah. What's up with that?"

The story took a few minutes to get through, and she didn't share all the details, but there was relief in knowing that she didn't have to explain the backstory for him to understand why having her mother here was disruptive.

"I'm proud of you, Tam. Forgiveness is hard."

"Oh, I haven't forgiven anything. But I try really hard in my life not to be a horrible person, that's all." She rubbed at her eyes, grainy now with the need for sleep. A yawn pried open her lips.

"You're not a horrible person," he said. "You're not even a bad person."

She was going to take a chance on him, and this, and whatever might happen. "When do you want to go out?"

The rattle of Tamar's bedroom doorknob stole her attention from his answer. She tensed, sitting up straight in bed, her head cocked.

Listening. Shadows blanketed the far side of the room, so she couldn't actually see the knob turning, but she heard it.

"Shh," she said, too abruptly.

"Tam?"

"I'm sorry. I heard something." She strained, listening, eyes also boring through the darkness between her bed and the door.

The knob rattled again.

Her throat squeezed tight as her heart pounded and her mouth dried, and she clutched the phone to her ear with fingers so stiff they almost dropped it. In the next moment, Tamar forcibly shoved away that reaction. That was stupid. She was in her own bedroom. She was an adult. The only thing on the other side of her door was her mother, who probably heard her voice or saw the light from under the door and needed something from her.

"I think my mother's at the door," she whispered into the phone.

"Do you need to go?"

"Yes. I'd better see what she needs."

Miguel let out a low chuckle. "Was she listening in? The way she used to?"

"Possibly. Probably." She laughed too and made her fingers relax. "Let's talk later, okay? About going out."

"Tomorrow," he said firmly. "I'll call you."

They said their goodbyes, and she put her phone on the nightstand so she could slip out of bed and go to the door. She pressed an ear against it, listening, but could hear nothing. The urge to get on her hands and knees, to look through the crack at the bottom of the door, was so strong that she started to bend before catching herself.

She was an adult, in her own home, and she was allowed to stay up as late as she wanted, talking to whomever she pleased.

When she pulled open the door to reveal nothing but the dark hallway beyond, Tamar let her breath seep out of her pressed-together lips, a held-in scream that lost its oomph. She scanned the shadows, but they all remained silent and still. Her heartbeat slowed. She swallowed, but the sour, metallic taste on her tongue wouldn't wash away.

Her habit of late-night tea had begun in the final days of her marriage, when sleeping next to Garrett had become intolerable, but she'd not yet been willing to admit it. She'd made up excuses, instead, for staying up late reading, or working, or catching up on television shows she knew he'd never watch. She'd pretended she wasn't tired, and drinking coffee would've made that an obvious lie. She'd made tea, instead.

Quietly, she went down the hallway toward the stairs, passing the closed third bedroom door.

Ruth's door was wide open, and Tamar's feet slowed as she approached it and the pale square of light on the hallway carpet from the streetlamp's glow coming through the windows. Superstitiously, she didn't want to step into it, as though it would make a sound, as though it would break like glass and wake her mother. She couldn't go around it—the light stretched all the way to the wall. She couldn't jump over it either.

Her heart pounded again. She was being stupid and silly. Either she was going downstairs to make some tea, or she should go back to bed. She put a foot into the square of light, then another, still trying to be as quiet as she could, so she didn't disturb her mother.

As it turned out, she needn't have worried about waking anyone. As Tamar passed the open door, she paused to peek inside. Her mother sat on the bed, facing the windows. Her hair, tumbling down all over her shoulders and down her back, shone silver, but the rest of her was darkness. She shifted a little when Tamar looked in, her face turning slowly, slowly, not quite into a profile but the mere hint of a brow. Nose. Mouth, lips moving with words that Tamar couldn't hear. A hitch of breath that might've been a sob. No. Definitely was.

If sympathy for any sorrow her mother felt was trying to nudge its way into Tamar's heart, it had been thoroughly blocked years ago. No amount of card games was going to fix that. Without another word, she passed the bedroom and went downstairs. Thinking of Miguel, she headed for the kitchen. She switched on the light.

She stumbled back, trying to scream but only able to hiss with terror, her mouth opening and closing as she grabbed at the wall to keep herself from falling.

Her mother sat at the kitchen table.

"Why, Tammy," she said with a tilt of her head and a small, confused smile. "You look like you've seen a ghost."

CHAPTER

14

"Tammy?" Her mother struggled out of the chair.

Tamar put up a hand to hold her off. "I'm fine. You just startled me. I thought—"

it is my mother it is not my mother it is my mother it is not my mother it is a dream it is not a dream it is a dream it is not

Her mother waited with an expectant expression, but Tamar didn't finish. The surreal sense of the past coming back washed over her, so she focused on concrete details making up the present. The cool tiles under her bare feet. The lack of pain from the place on her foot that had been cut with glass. The goosebumps on her bare arms. She wished she'd thought to grab a sweatshirt, but in the next moment, an internal heat rolled all through her. She fanned her face while Ruth gave her a curious glance.

"Hot flash," Tamar said.

"So that's why you're up."

Tamar shrugged.

"The older you get, the less sleep you need. Nobody ever told me that. I remember my grandma walking at night. I'd listen to the creak of the floorboards as she paced in her bedroom, but it wasn't until I got old myself that I understood why. The closer you get to sleeping forever, the more important it seems to stay awake as much as you can." Ruth's eyes narrowed as she looked Tamar up and down.

"I'm making myself some tea. Do you want some?" Tamar asked.

"A glass of wine would be better." A minute ago, she'd sounded a little melancholy. Nostalgic. Now she sounded a little sly. "But of course, I don't do that anymore."

Tamar looked automatically to the counter where she'd left the last bottle of wine she'd opened. The decorative octopus stopper was still on it. No glasses were next to it, or on the table, or in the sink. She looked back at her mother's face.

Ruth frowned. An emotion flickered in her gaze and was gone as fast as she could blink. "You don't trust me, do you?"

"To be honest? Not really." Tamar filled the electric kettle with her back to her mother and concentrated on slowing her pounding heart. Her hands shook a little, spilling water. She fit the kettle into its base and turned it on, then found two mugs in the cupboard and set them on the counter. By the time she pulled down her tea chest, she'd managed to push away her anxiety and make herself like stone. It was a little trick she'd picked up in childhood, cowering from her mother's screams and threats. If she made herself a statue, she couldn't feel anything. Nothing could hurt her.

Not even Ruth.

"I haven't touched the booze for years, Tammy. Sorry. *Tamar.* You know, every time I say it like that, I think about your father. Maybe that's why I prefer to call you Tammy. I don't like anything that reminds me of him."

The kettle's clear glass shone with the blue light indicating it was heating. Tamar studied the bubbles forming in the water. "If you hated him so much, why did you marry him?"

"Nobody gets married because they hate someone," her mother said. "That comes later. I'd think you'd know all about that, wouldn't you?"

The water was almost boiling. Tamar tore open the foil packets containing the tea bags and put one in each mug. She glanced over her shoulder.

"If you hated him so much," she repeated evenly, "why didn't you divorce him?"

"I didn't have to. He took himself out of the equation. But I don't suppose you ever stopped to think that maybe that's the reason why I hated him so much?"

Tamar turned off the kettle before it could whistle. "Anything you ever said about him was negative and hateful. What was I supposed to think?"

"He left me," her mother rasped, "with a child and a newborn infant. He left me without a single word of warning. He left me, like the life we'd built together was no better than a pile of shit. He. Left. Me."

"He left *us*!" Tamar cried. "All three of us! But you always made it about you!"

Her mother flinched. Her shoulders hunched. "You couldn't possibly begin to understand what it was like. Your husband goes missing. What do you assume? That he's having an affair. That he has made a mockery of everything you built together, your family, your marriage. All of it, betrayed. What would you have done, if you'd thought your husband was cheating on you?"

"If he'd gone missing, that would not have been my first assumption." Tamar turned back to making the tea, filling each mug with hot water and taking one to the table. She set it in front of Ruth but went back to the counter, where she leaned with her own mug. She had to hold it away from her face to keep the steam from bathing it. She was hot enough as it was.

"The times you went missing," Ruth said quietly, "what did your husband assume about you?"

Tamar didn't ask her how she knew about anything that had happened between her and Garrett. Lovey might have said something. Perhaps Ruth had made her own assumptions. At any rate, Tamar didn't care about being judged. Not by the woman sitting at her kitchen table, anyway.

"What happened in my marriage has nothing to do with what happened with Dad."

"Doesn't it?" Ruth's eyes narrowed again. She hadn't touched the mug in front of her. "If you can blame me for everything bad that happened in your life, then you also have to accept that what your father did absolutely affected you and who you are."

For a moment, neither woman spoke. Ruth at last put her hands around the mug, lifting it with shaking hands that sloshed hot liquid over the sides before she put it down. She turned her hands palm up, then down, looking at them, then placed them on the table. She looked at Tamar.

"There was so much blood," she whispered. "I never knew a person could have so much blood inside them."

Tamar's knees threatened to buckle, so she slid into the chair across from her mother. "You never told us what happened. I asked Aunt Naomi once, but she never gave me any details."

Ruth's lip curled, perhaps at the mention of her former sister-in-law's name. She closed her eyes. She shuddered, once, before making a visible effort at keeping herself still. Her fingers scratched at the Formica tabletop, and Tamar winced at how bent and swollen the knuckles had become. This was her future, she thought suddenly. Violently. Her own hands ached, not in sympathy, but in anticipation.

"He said he was going out for a pack of cigarettes, but when he didn't come home after an hour, I knew something was up. Of course, we had no cell phones then, so I couldn't track him. Couldn't even call him. I tried the bar first." Ruth opened her eyes and met Tamar's gaze. "He'd been drinking a lot. He usually did it at home. I was always grateful for that."

Tamar swallowed hard, but the lump in her throat still threatened to choke her. Memories overlapped each other. Ruth, staggering drunk, crying out from the bathroom as she got sick. Breaking glasses. Spilling bottles. Passing out on the couch and not waking up when they got home from school.

"Why would you be grateful for that?"

"Because it was cheaper," her mother said flatly. "Because if he was drunk at home, I didn't have to worry that he was driving around. We had one car. He was the breadwinner. It was the seventies, and I was a stay-home mother with a high school education. I couldn't afford for him to crash the car or lose his job. If he did it at home, at least I knew where he was. But he'd started going to Rooney's. He said . . ."

"What?" Tamar prompted.

Her mother shook her head. "I don't want to say. I don't think you want to know."

"Tell me."

"He said that he couldn't stand being in the house. That it smelled of sour milk and baby shit. That you . . ." her mother cleared her throat but met Tamar's gaze without flinching. "He said that if he had to listen to you whining for one more second, he was going to lose his mind. So he started going to Rooney's after work instead of coming home. He'd stay there until he could be sure you were in bed."

Tamar didn't know what to say to that. Her heart hurt, but she couldn't be sure why. She didn't remember her father as anything other than a shadow figure who'd smelled of cigarettes and Old Spice cologne. She remembered his laughter and the rumble of his voice reading her a book. She did not remember him hating her, but her mother certainly always had.

"That's why you said it was my fault," Tamar managed to say.

"Did I?" Ruth sounded shocked.

Tamar nodded. "Yes. You'd say it was my fault, what he'd done. To be fair, you were usually drunk when you said it."

Silence.

Her mother sighed, hanging her head. "I'm sorry. There isn't anything I can do to make it up to you. I know that. All I can tell you is that I'm sorry."

Ruth's apology sounded sincere, but that didn't necessarily mean she was. She'd say she was sorry for anything, if she thought it would get her what she wanted. She'd apologize for things she didn't even believe she'd done.

Tamar shrugged. "There *is* something you can do. You can tell me what happened that night."

"Why do you want to know that?" her mother asked. "It's a horrible story."

"I need to know."

Ruth eyed her with a familiar, calculating gaze. "I called the bar first, but they said he'd been there and gone already. I asked them if he was alone when he left. They wouldn't tell me, one way or another. I took that to mean that he'd gone with someone. I wasn't surprised. It made sense. We hadn't been together that way in months. Lovey's birth had left some damage. And I was tired, so damned tired. She was a perfect baby, no fussing, slept wonderfully, but you—"

"You can say it," Tamar told her stiffly. "I was a nightmare child. I know. You used to remind me, all the time."

"Is that why you never had any of your own? Because you were worried you'd have a child like yourself?" Ruth's second attempt at drinking some tea went better this time. Her hands still shook, but she managed a sip without spilling.

"No. I never had any of my own because I was afraid if I had any children, they'd have a mother like you," Tamar said coolly, surprised that her voice didn't shake. She'd imagined saying something similar without ever believing she really would.

The mug thumped onto the table. Tea splashed. Her mother drew in a long, heavy sigh.

"I asked Mrs. Estrada from across the street to watch the two of you. You remember her."

Miguel's mother.

"Of course."

"I called a friend to pick me up, and we drove around town until I found your father's car. It didn't take long. I'd figured I'd find him at the seedy motel just off the highway, and I was right."

"What friend?" One thing she well remembered from her childhood was that her mother's "friends" were almost all male.

Ruth bristled. "His name was Roger. He and your dad and I had all gone to school together. He knew your dad had been having some trouble."

A vague memory of a dark-haired man with a bushy beard poked at her mind, but her mother was still talking.

"We found your father's car exactly where I'd expected it. At that motel. Roger tried to stop me from going in, but I had to know. He wanted to come in with me, in case your father *was* with someone else, and in case he turned violent. But I made him stay in the car while I went in. The door was unlocked. Can you imagine that? Doing what he did, without even locking the door?"

"What exactly did he do?" Tamar managed to ask, despite her dry mouth and throat. She couldn't even bring herself to sip any tea, worried her stomach would reject it immediately.

"He drank a bottle of Scotch, took a bottle of my sleeping pills, and used a hunting knife to slit his own throat. There was blood everywhere. So much of it, I thought for a moment that someone had spilled paint. That's what it had to be, right? Spilled a gallon of paint, because there was no way any one person could bleed so much. But he did," Ruth said flatly. "And he died there, alone."

For a moment, silence swelled between them. A clock ticked, or maybe it was the click of Tamar's jaw as she pressed her lips together against a low cry of horror, not sure why her mother's words hit so hard. She'd always known her dad killed himself. She'd never had any false hopes it hadn't been awful.

"We all die alone" was all she could think to say.

Her mother leaned forward, across the tea-stained table. Her gnarled fingers crept around the mug like spiders that had been hiding and now crept out, ready to bite. She gave Tamar an awful grin that showed leaning teeth gone gray. "If we're lucky."

15

Lovey had called and texted, checking in, but this was the first time in the week since their mother had come to stay with her that Tamar had been able to spend more than a few minutes chatting with her sister. Rearranging her work schedule had been harder than she'd thought—not the rearranging part of it but getting time to work on the projects. There'd been several more doctor's appointments, and a tour of one facility that had been so depressing neither she nor her mother had been able to discuss even one good thing about it. On top of that, Ruth had been melancholy and needy for attention, interrupting Tamar no matter how many times she'd warned her to stay out.

"Hang on," Tamar said now in a low voice to her sister on the phone. "Let me just make sure she doesn't need anything."

She found her mother standing in the living room, arms crossed over her chest as she stared out the windows overlooking the street. Ruth didn't turn as Tamar came in. Tamar stood next to her for a moment, also looking. Ross was tending to the small front patch of his garden.

"He tried to talk to me this morning when I went outside to check the weather," Ruth said.

Tamar nodded. "Yeah, he's very friendly."

Her mother barely looked at her. "He's got his nose in everyone's business, that's what he has. Look at that dog. He's going to let it shit in your yard, just you watch, Tamar."

Tamar had never seen Peanut Butter stray outside of the white flags set up around the perimeter of Ross's yard. Without getting into it, Tamar left her mother there and took the phone upstairs. She locked her bedroom door behind her and took the extra precautions of going into her bathroom and locking that door behind her too. Her mother had taken up the habit of following her no matter what room she went into.

"Sorry," she said into the phone. "She's complaining about the guy across the street. I came upstairs to make sure she didn't hear me talking about her."

"What did the doctor say?"

Tamar flicked her bathroom window curtain to look down to the street below. Ross was still in his own yard, but instead of working in the garden, he'd stood up and was facing her house, shading his eyes. "She's definitely showing signs of deterioration, but he couldn't say how long it would be before she needs full-time care. Her physical health is pretty good, other than some normal age-related things. Her hands shake, but he said it's not from anything degenerative."

"Did you tell him what happened?"

"Yes," Tamar said.

"And?"

"He said he couldn't explain exactly how she managed to get to my house, but it could've been a dissociative fugue. Memory loss," she added. "Like a precursor to something more."

"Well, shit. How are you doing with her there?"

Tamar was explicitly grateful in that moment that this was an audio-only call. She hadn't showered for two days. Her hair was a tangled mess. She had bags under her eyes. "It's been a challenge."

Outside, Ross was waving at something she couldn't see. Tamar watched him, her fingers touching the window. She couldn't hear what he was saying, but he looked animated. He stood at the edge of his yard, waving his hands, pointing at the garden. Then at her house. Peanut Butter ran around his legs, barking.

From downstairs came the faint sound of a raised voice.

"I think she's yelling at the guy across the street." Tamar pinched the bridge of her nose. "She was complaining about him earlier."

"What's he doing?"

"Nothing. I mean, he's kind of over-friendly, but he's all right." She leaned to see if she could glimpse her mother, but the porch overhang hid any sight of her.

As she watched, Ross bent to pat the puppy's fuzzy head. It sat, wagging its fluffy tail. Ross went back to his garden. Tamar turned her attention back to the phone call, distracted immediately by the soft slither of her necklace slipping off her throat and falling to the floor.

"Well, schnitzel," she said, which was something Garrett's mother had taught him to say instead of shit.

"What now?"

"My necklace broke." She coiled the chain and pendant together and put them in the glass ashtray on top of her dresser, making a mental note to get the chain repaired.

"Any updates from any of the places she applied to?" Lovey's voice crackled. Hissed with the fuzz of a broken connection. Faded.

Tamar held the phone away from her ear, not sure if the call had failed. "Hello?"

They traded "hellos" for half a minute before Lovey's voice got clear again.

"No," Tamar told her. "Nobody's gotten back to us. The place I took her to seemed like it would be happy to have her, but . . . Lovey, even I couldn't do that to her. It was pretty bad."

Her sister's voice crackled again. ". . . for taking . . . this . . ."

"What?"

"I said, 'thank you for taking care of all this.' I know it can't be easy, Tam. Especially with the past relationship and everything. I just want you to know, I'm here for you. If I could get out there, but the kids have school, and—"

"You took care of it all without my help the first time."

"It's different this time," Lovey said. "And she and I have a very different sort of relationship."

Screams from outside tore her attention from the phone call. Tamar went to the window again. Ross stood by his front door. The puppy was a foot or so on the wrong side of the invisible fencing. The dog jumped the curb and ran into the road. Tamar couldn't hear what was getting its attention, but it seemed to be focused on something on the other side of the street.

Her side.

Ross shouted again, waving his hands, already heading for the dog. It danced in the middle of the road, taking a few steps toward Tamar's house, turning in a circle and backing toward its own lawn, then forward again. It got close enough to the invisible fence to yip and yelp as the electric collar zinged it, preventing it from getting back to its yard. Ross called out again. The puppy headed back into the street.

"What the . . . ?"

"What's going on?" Lovey asked.

"Hang on," Tamar said. "There's something wrong with my neighbor's puppy."

A horn blared. Ross shouted again. Running now, he pelted toward the street. The dog didn't move, cowering against the asphalt. Just as Ross reached it, scooping the puppy into his arms, a white SUV plowed into them both.

Ross and the dog both went flying. Blood spattered up and over the vehicle's white hood and sprayed the windshield. The SUV squealed to a stop. The dog's howl cut off abruptly.

Oh, no. Oh, fuck, she thought, staring in gape-mouthed horror. The sight of Ross's crumpled body, just out of sight except for one foot, made her stomach twist and knot.

"I'll call you back." Tamar disconnected and shoved her phone into her pocket before taking the stairs two at a time. Only her hand on the railing stopped her from plummeting down when her foot slipped. She hit the hardwood floor at the bottom and skidded in her socks, almost falling again as she ran for the open front door.

Ruth stood on the front porch, a watering can in one hand. Puddles dried rapidly on the concrete porch below the plant stands Tamar had filled with colorful annuals a week or so ago. The flowers had all gone dead and brown, littering the porch with their petals.

Words came out of Tamar's mouth, but they were nonsensical and mostly just noise. She pushed past Ruth, whose body was as stiff and solid as stone. Water from the sprinkler can spattered Tamar's lower legs as she jumped down the two concrete steps to the sidewalk. Her phone slipped free of her pocket at the impact, and she grabbed for it, playing a juggling game as it slipped from her hands. She caught it moments before it hit the pavement.

In the street, a woman was screaming.

She'd been driving the SUV. Now she stood in front of it, several feet away from Ross's bent and broken body. The puppy lay a few feet beyond that, silent and still. The SUV's back passenger door opened, and a little boy tumbled out, calling for his mother. She screamed at him to get back inside, but it was too late. He'd already come around to the front of the big vehicle and saw what had happened. He began to scream and cry.

Tamar found herself with an armful of a stranger's child. The little boy clung to her, wailing, and she scooped him up on instinct, turning to shield his eyes from the sight of all the blood. She tried to hush him, but she couldn't be sure if anything was coming out of her mouth but her own sobs.

The driver bent over Ross with her phone in her hand. Calling 911, by the sound of it. She didn't touch the still-unmoving Ross, but she barked information into the phone while the puddle of blood from underneath him grew bigger and bigger, spreading out the same way as the water from Ruth's sprinkler can—and Ross, it seemed, would soon be just as dead as those flowers.

One leg bent beneath him at an angle that could only happen if it were broken. White bone jutted through a hole in his jeans just below the kneecap. His head was turned to one side, facing away from her, and his arm had been flung out toward where the puppy lay. A fluffy tuft of soft beige fur fluttered from his fingers.

"It's going to be okay," she said into the little boy's ear. The words were a lie, but what else was she supposed to say?

The puppy stirred. It rolled onto its back, small legs running against the air. It finally got to its feet and staggered, disoriented, and shook itself. It ran slowly to Tamar's yard and flopped into the grass.

The sound of sirens filled the air.

Tamar put the kid back in the car, making sure to buckle the seat-belt. Thinking of her nieces and nephews, she engaged the child lock on the door and closed it again. The ambulance and fire truck were pulling into place as she closed the SUV's door. A police car, lights flashing but no siren, joined them. The woman who'd been driving looked almost catatonic as she knelt on the pavement next to Ross's body. A paramedic knelt next to her, holding her hand. In her other, she held her phone.

"Did you see what happened?" The police officer asked Tamar.

She blinked and tore her gaze away from Ross. She looked at the officer. "His dog ran into the street, and he ran after it. That's all I saw."

Over the officer's shoulder, Tamar could see her front porch. Her mother had put down the sprinkler can. She'd picked up the dog.

"Is there anything else you can tell me about what happened, ma'am?"

"I'm sorry," she said. "I can't tell you anything."

CHAPTER

16

H ER ALARM HAD been going off for a few minutes by the time
Tamar finally managed to wake up. She'd been dreaming it was
a fire alarm, and for a moment, she still smelled smoke. She swam
against the wave of blankets trying to hold her under, but at last managed to grab her phone from the nightstand and tap the bleating alarm
to silence. She yawned. Stretched.

Shit.

Her mother.

Tamar struggled up onto one elbow, but her room was empty. She
fell back onto the pillows with a small groan and double-checked the
clock. It was the first time in months that she'd actually needed her
alarm to wake up. After the horrific scene with Ross yesterday, Tamar
had medicated heavily before going to bed. Wine and weed, a soporific
combination that must've knocked her out so thoroughly that, until the
ringing started, she hadn't even dreamed.

At least she hadn't had any nightmares about Ross's broken and battered body catapulting into the air after being slammed by a white SUV,
or about her mother's wicked grin as she clutched the dog she may or
may not have lured across the street. Their conversation last night about
Ross's accident had been brief and full of tut-tuts and what-a-shames
from her mother. The dog had been handed off to one of Ross's friends

when he was taken to the hospital. Tamar had not asked her mother
what part she'd played in any of it.

She didn't want to think about it.

With a small groan, Tamar stretched. Her neck and spine crackle-
popped. She rolled onto her side for a second, then flung the covers off.
The room was stifling and muggy, which explained why her blankets
had felt so unwelcoming but not why her muscles were all so stiff and
sore. She groaned and sat up.

At the foot of the bed, dirt and grass were smeared all over her pale
blue sheets. Tamar's yawn became a squeaking groan. She scrambled
away from the mess, pushing with her feet, leaving more stains. They
were coming from her feet, also covered in mud and weeds.

Tamar went very, very still.

She looked to her bedroom door again, still closed, then at her feet.
Mud encrusted them, dug deep even under her toenails. With trembling fingers, she touched her left sole. Then the right.

She got out of bed and tore the sheets from it, bundling them into
a pile she tossed on the floor. She went to the bathroom and ran the
shower hot enough to scald, but she didn't care that it was too hot as she
got in and scrubbed at her skin. Mud swirled around the drain and bits
of grass clogged it until she bent to scoop it away and toss it into the can
by the toilet. She scrubbed over and over, wincing at the sting of hot
water and soap in a few small, fine cuts on her feet. She saw no real
wounds, but a dark bruise was starting on her left big toe. Another on
her instep. A few scattered black and blues were decorating her shins, a
constellation of injuries she couldn't remember getting.

Where had she gone?

What had she *done*?

Tamar's nightwalking had never taken her far beyond the house,
and much of the time, not even out of it. In the house on Spring Hill
Drive, Ruth had also been prone to leaving her bed in the midst of
dreams, claiming she didn't remember what she'd done the night before.
But even in the worst times at Spring Hill Drive, nothing like this had
ever happened.

Tamar huddled under the water. It was starting to cool. She pulled
her fingers through her hair, wincing when they hit the first tangle.

There were so many that her hair felt like a doll's tresses that had been washed and dried—plastic, stiff, coarse, matted. She shampooed and conditioned quickly but stayed beneath the spray until it went too cold to bear. Teeth chattering, she got out.

She tripped on the bathmat and her wet feet slipped on the tiles, but she caught herself on the towel rack. It came out of the wall. Shoddy installation. A protruding screw scraped over the back of her hand, bringing blood.

Breathing hard, Tamar found her balance. Naked, she stood and watched the bright crimson bead up on her skin and slid over it. A single drop hit the floor and left a mark on the white tile that disappeared when she dragged a toe across it.

At the sink, she studied her reflection for anything else that seemed wrong. Her ribs felt tender. Her back, sore. There were no visible bruises there, but her skin in some places felt soft, like overripe fruit that would split if you pressed it too hard.

Bile rushed up her throat and into her open palm before she could stop it. Shuddering with sickness, Tamar spat into the drain. She rinsed off her hand and opened her mouth to rinse it too. She waited to see if she was going to really puke, but although her stomach corkscrewed inside her, nothing else came up.

She brushed her teeth hard enough to make her gums bleed and spat pink froth into the sink. She wrapped herself in a towel and went to her bedroom to sit on the edge of the bare mattress while she dragged a comb through her hair. It took her a good ten minutes to get out all the knots. By the time she'd finished, her arms felt like jelly, but her stomach was growling.

Her bedroom door was still locked, exactly as it had been last night when she'd finally collapsed into sleep. The metal doorknob, warm under her palm. The wood, also warm. She was sweating. She'd have to check the thermostat settings. Hot flashes were one thing, but this was bordering on ridiculous.

Remembering the smell of smoke, feeling ridiculous but unable to stop herself from checking for a fire, Tamar got onto her hands and knees and pressed her cheek to the floor. The crack beneath the door was about an inch or so, but she could glimpse the hallway floor. No smoke or shadows. No signs of anyone standing there, waiting for her to open the door.

On her feet, she put her hand to the doorknob again, this time unlocking and turning it to open the door with an almost violent jerk. She got ready to scream. Her breath leaked out of her in a hissing sigh. Nothing was there, and of course there wasn't. She wasn't in the house on Spring Hill. She was in her own.

She sagged in the doorway for a second, the pounding of her heart easing a bit. At the far end of the hall, her mother's door was closed. She'd have to pass by it to get to the stairs. Tamar drew herself up straight. Her feet hurt a little, even with the soft comfort of her slippers to protect them. When she passed her mother's bedroom, she didn't pause to listen at the door.

In the kitchen, every single cupboard and drawer were open.

All of the knives in the silverware drawer were facing in the opposite direction. Every mug had been turned to show only the blank backs of one-sided designs. The dinner plates had been stacked on top of the salad plates. Nothing was missing, but all of it was a mess.

"Fuck." The word slipped out of her in a harsh whisper, guttural. Not surprised. How many times had Ruth shaken Tamar awake, blaming her for the nightly mess-making? Even when Tamar had been too small to reach the cupboards by herself, her mother's perfectly manicured finger had been pointed at her.

In the middle of the table sat an oversized glass ashtray. In her childhood, it had held the same pride of place at the kitchen table, almost always full of cigarette butts rimmed with crimson lipstick, one always still burning. No lipstick adorned the single cigarette resting in the ashtray now, but it had burnt into a long tube of ash. She couldn't see a pack anywhere or any other loose cigarettes. Tamar took a step back, her heart thumping with a sudden harsh ferocity she had to ease by pressing her palm to her chest. She blinked rapidly, but of course the ashtray remained, the length of ash was still there, and the scent of smoke still lingered. That's what had woken her.

Her mother had not been a smoker for years. Lovey had been very clear that she wouldn't allow their mother to visit the children if she still smoked, so Ruth had quit. At any rate, Somerset House did not allow smoking indoors, and Tamar could not recall seeing any cigarettes when she'd been helping her mother unpack.

Her mother seemed to have taken up other old bad habits, so why not smoking too?

"Oh, I see the 'ghost' is back." Ruth spoke from the doorway leading to the hallway. She used air quotes around the word and laughed.

Tamar had been sweating, but now her entire body ran with chills, like a fever. "What?"

"The ghost of horrible inconveniences," her mother said after a second. "The one that used to haunt our house. A little ghost named Tammy? Who liked to make mischief?"

"Why would I have rearranged everything in the cupboards in the middle of the night?" Tamar challenged.

"Well," Ruth said with a huff in her voice, her fingers toying with the neckline of her blouse. "*I* certainly didn't do it."

"Did you hear anything last night?" Tamar asked after a moment.

Ruth's hesitation was blatant. A flurry of emotions crossed her face. Her sly smile twisted into lips pressed tight and a brow furrowed in confusion. She shook her head but didn't speak.

Tamar held up the ashtray. "I don't want you to smoke in the house."

Her mother's eyelids fluttered. Her chin tipped up. Her lipstick had curdled in the corners of her mouth.

"I wasn't smoking," she said.

"Right, I know," Tamar snapped, irritated, "the cigarette was."

Her mother's head tilted. The old joke, *her* old joke, seemed to go right past her. She frowned.

"I wasn't smoking," she repeated. "Smoking's a filthy habit, Tammy. I gave it up long ago."

She sounded like she was telling the truth, or at least believed she was.

Tamar gave her a suspicious look. "Was someone else here?"

"Nobody came here who wasn't already here," Ruth said.

"Where did you get the ashtray? Is it the one from my room?" When her mother shrugged, Tamar put her hands on her hips. "I don't want you going into my room. I don't go through your private things, and I don't want you going through mine."

"The ashtray was mine," her mother said. "You stole it from me."

This was true, but nevertheless, Tamar frowned. The idea of Ruth creeping into her room while she slept, hovering over her without waking her, sent a swirl of disgust all through her. "It was in my room."

"It was mine," her mother whispered in a low, hoarse voice. Her eyes gleamed, her fingers curled, and her nails made a gut-twisting noise against her palms. "You took it from *me*. It. Was. Mine."

She had taken the ashtray because her mother loved it. She had wanted to smash it into pieces on their kitchen floor, but no matter how many times she threw it down, it would not break. So she took it with her instead. She'd used that ashtray to hold her spare change, earrings without mates, loose paperclips and buttons, for more than thirty years. It had moved with her every place she ever lived since leaving the house on Spring Hill Drive. She'd stolen it from her mother, true, but that ashtray was *hers*.

"Please stay out of my room." She'd made that same request back then too, and it had always been ignored. But things were different now.

She rinsed the ashtray quickly and took it upstairs. The only evidence anyone else had been in there was the scatter of coins along the top of her dresser, left behind where the ashtray had been. She scooped them into her hand and put it back. The coins clattered gently against the glass. Something glinted in the tufts of the rug when she took a step back—her broken necklace. She picked it up and replaced it in the ashtray. Nothing else seemed to be missing.

Nothing but her memories about what had happened to her last night.

At the top of the stairs, she listened and heard the faint sounds coming from the TV, but nothing else from Ruth. She went to the guest room. The door was open, but Tamar stayed in the doorway. She didn't want to be a hypocrite. She scanned the pale carpet for any signs of mud or grass or anything else that might indicate Ruth had also gone wandering, but all she could see were some faint marks left by the vacuum.

So it had only been her. Downstairs, Tamar checked the front door. Like her bedroom door had been, it was locked. So were the French doors off the kitchen that led to the deck and the fenced backyard. The garage door too. No way to tell which door she'd left through or where she'd gone.

All the wine and weed last night should have kept her asleep all night, and yet she'd still gone nightwalking. She'd rearranged her cupboards without remembering it. The little ghost that had haunted their old house, her mother had said. It had done more than cause inconveniences. It had wrought terror.

And, until just now, Tamar had thought she'd left it behind when she ran away.

CHAPTER

17

THE HOUSE ON Spring Hill Drive looked almost the same. The shutters and front door had been painted a cheery, welcoming red instead of the faded avocado green Tamar remembered. Instead of overgrown grass with dry, dead patches, the front yard was trimmed neatly, and a garden bloomed with black-eyed susans and coneflowers below the living room windows. The bushes that had once been wild and untamed were shaped into boxes. It looked like the sort of house a nice family lived in.

Sitting in her car with the air conditioning on full blast was better than being at home, where she felt constantly coated in a sheen of sweat because the fucking A/C never seemed to kick on. She could sit here all day and work on her laptop. Sit here all day and then drive home to deal with her mother.

She didn't have to knock on that door.

Tamar gripped the steering wheel so hard her fingers hurt. She had not been back to this house since the day she'd returned to stuff her backpack with whatever she could take. It had been quiet, dim inside, the air thick with dust that danced in the bars of light shafting through the mostly closed curtains. There'd been no sign of what had happened there the night before she ran away other than the missing picture on the wall. Every scrap of glass had been cleaned up. The sewer stink had been replaced with the smell of fabric softener and smoke.

Drive away, she thought. You don't have to do this. You don't have confront the past.

But she had to know. Everything she had told herself over the years was no more than a child's overactive imagination, had it been real? The nightmare memories she had, were they the truth? She had to find out. She *did* have to.

Tamar got out of her car. She looked up and down the street, wondering if any of the old neighbors still lived here. If she knocked now, politely, would any answer? Would anyone remember her? Once she'd run up and down this very street, banging on the front doors and begging to be let in; the only person who'd answered lived four houses away and had died ten years ago. She'd seen the obituary. She'd sent flowers but had not attended the funeral.

She knocked, hard enough to hurt her knuckles, but thought for sure that nobody would open the door. Like Ross, the people who lived here had one of those fancy doorbell cameras, and she stood in front of it self-consciously, wondering if they were looking at a screen, deciding if they were going to shout through the speaker for her to get the hell off their front porch. She raised her hand again to knock, but the door swung open.

To her surprise, because who allowed their kids to open the door anymore, a little girl with a tumble of strawberry blond curls stood there. She gave Tamar a suspicious glance and put a hand on her hip.

"Are you selling something? Because my dad says if you are, you can—"

"Kayla." A tall man with sandy hair and glasses opened the door a little wider and put a hand on the child's shoulder. He gave Tamar an embarrassed smile. "We're still working on not repeating things we hear at home. Can I help you?"

"I . . ." Tamar looked at the little girl, not sure what she thought she might see. Dark circles under her eyes? Tangled hair, dirty fingernails, a look of wariness. That would've been Tamar at that age. She cleared her throat. "I used to live here. I haven't been back in a really long time, but I was driving past and—"

"Oh, wow. You're Ruth's other daughter."

Taken aback, Tamar hesitated. Then nodded. "Yes."

"She had photos of you and your sister all over the place." He opened the door a little wider and looked over his shoulder reflexively before turning back to her with a smile. "Honestly, it was one of the things that made us fall in love with the house. Seeing how she'd had the framed photos arranged. We're trying to do the same thing. We just don't have as many pictures yet."

"If you live here for almost fifty years, you might catch up," Tamar said. She tried to imagine her mother choosing photos. Picking out frames. Hanging them, points of pride. All she could recall was the sound of crunching glass. Her foot, mostly healed, stung with the memory.

"Would you like to come in?"

Now that he'd invited her, Tamar didn't want to go inside. She took a step back, almost off the concrete front porch. They'd added wrought-iron railings, and she grabbed one to stop herself from tipping back off the edge.

"Kayla, this lady used to live here when she was a little girl. Just like you."

"You can see my room," Kayla said. "Maybe it used to be your room. But it's my room now, you can't have it back."

"Kayla," her father admonished.

Tamar shook her head. "You don't have to worry about that. I would never try to move back into your room." She looked up at the man in the doorway. "If you don't mind me coming in. I mean, I'm a total stranger—"

"I recognized you at once," he said. "I just wasn't sure from where."

She followed him through the front door and into the entryway that she remembered as dark and unwelcoming. Now, cheerful late afternoon sunlight came in through the transom windows above the door and the glass panels on the side. It striped the hardwood floor. A chubby calico cat sunned herself in one block of light. A decorative wooden shelf showed off a collection of thriving houseplants in another.

"Have you done a lot of renovations?" she asked, taking it all in.

"Mare? We have a guest," the man called out toward the back of the house. To Tamar, he said, "To be honest, it wasn't in great shape when we bought it. So, we've done a lot of repairs. But no real renovations. The house had such great bones."

Oh, it had bones, all right. The kind you're supposed to keep in the closets. Tamar didn't say so, of course. She eased in a few steps and looked to the living room on the left.

"Hello?" A pretty red-headed woman appeared through the kitchen doorway and onto the small landing at the bottom of the stairs. She wiped her hands dry on a dishtowel and gave the man a curious look.

"This is—I'm sorry, I didn't catch your name."

"Tamar Glass. I'm Ruth Kahan's daughter."

"Mommy, she used to live here! Maybe in my old room!" Kayla gave Tamar's hand an excited tug. "C'mon, you want to go see it? I have a princess bed!"

"Hold on, Kayla. Let Mommy and Daddy talk to Ms. Glass for a few minutes first. Why don't you go upstairs and play?" The girl's mother gestured toward the stairs, her eyes on Tamar. When Kayla went up the stairs, her gaze followed before returning to Tamar's. "Hi. I'm Mare Landry. This is my husband, Bill. And you met Kayla."

"Yes." They shook hands.

Mare's grip was firm, unhesitant, and slightly damp. Or maybe it was Tamar's hand, sweating. Either way, they both wiped their hands on their thighs surreptitiously after touching.

"I was driving past. I'm sorry to barge in. I haven't been here in so long, I just stopped on impulse."

She hated herself for how easily the false words came out. How quickly just coming through the front door could make her a liar again. Neither Mare nor Bill seemed to notice, or if they did, they didn't question her reasons for not telling the truth.

"I recognize you from your photos," Mare said. "Your mother had them all over the place."

"Bill told me." Tamar smiled.

To the left and right, walls of about three feet long created a tiny hallway, with open doorways into the living room on the left and dining room on the right. Straight ahead were two steps that led to the landing. The stairs to the second floor rose to the right and another couple of steps went down into the kitchen, straight ahead, like a small bridge.

Tamar looked around, trying to picture this plethora of photos they'd both described. In her childhood, this wall on the left had been hung with religious art in dark wood frames, inherited from her father's parents when they died. A dancing pair of Orthodox men in fur hats and black coats in one, a pair of women with kerchiefs covering their hair, lighting Shabbat candles, in another. Tamar had been in college before she'd understood what was going on in those pictures, and the realization had hit her like a slamming door. Faith had been in her house all along, but her mother had never shared it.

"When I was a kid," Tamar said, pointing to the small wall space on the right that divided the dining room from the entryway, "we had a ship hanging there. Someone had hammered small nails into a board and used different colored strings to make a picture of a ship. And, wow, I'm also remembering a macrame owl."

She didn't mention the religious art.

"Can I get you something to drink? Cup of coffee? Water?" Mare asked.

Tamar hesitated. "I really don't want to take up your time. I shouldn't have—"

"I'm glad you did," Mare interrupted. She shared a glance with her husband. "Actually, Tamar, we have some questions about the house that maybe you can answer."

The floor shifted under her feet, but only hers. Tamar kept herself upright because falling down in front of Mare and Bill would be more embarrassing than anything she could think of. Mare must have sensed the internal stagger, though. She reached a hand to touch Tamar's upper arm, not taking it, but she seemed ready to.

"How about some coffee?" Mare asked, and must've seen Tamar's hesitation, because she added, "Hot tea?"

Tamar nodded. "That would be great. Thanks."

"I've got some stuff I need to do out in the garage," Bill said. "Mare?"

"We'll be fine," she said. "Let's go into the kitchen."

Tamar paused in the doorway.

Nothing looked the same. The dark wooden cabinets now gleamed a soft cream. The yellow and green patterned linoleum was gone, replaced by golden brown laminate that complimented the house's original hardwood. Color splashes of orange, red, teal, and lime green were all over the place. Sun shone in through the sliding glass doors, turning the entire space into something bright and cheerful.

"Different, huh?" Mare asked as she gestured for Tamar to sit at the small table tucked into a corner. She put a kettle on the stove burner and took down two oversized mugs from a cupboard. She put them on the table, along with a small basket brimming with teabags, in front of Tamar. "Pick your poison."

Tamar chose a packet of Earl Grey. "You've done an amazing job here. This room is . . . it's so different. Bill said you hadn't done much renovation. But I barely even recognize anything."

"Just redecorating," Mare agreed. The look she gave her kitchen showed her pride. The look she gave Tamar was a little more concerned. She leaned against the counter as she waited for the kettle to whistle. "Your mom had lived here alone for a long time, and she hadn't been keeping up with it. It's honestly the only reason we could probably afford to buy in this neighborhood. I feel bad, sometimes, about what we paid."

"You paid the asking price," Tamar told her. "You don't have to feel bad about it."

Mare nodded, but only after a second. "How long has it been since you were in this house, Tamar?"

"I left here right before I turned eighteen. So, a long time."

Mare blew out a breath. "Wow."

Tamar waited, then, for the questions. Why had she left home so young? Why had she never returned? But Mare only took the now-whistling kettle off the burner and poured them both mugs full of hot water. She took the lid off a cookie jar and put what looked like home-made chocolate chip cookies onto a small plate that she also set in front of Tamar. She sat at the table and dunked her own teabag in her mug.

Tamar wrapped her hands around the mug, not daring to sip yet. Steam wafted off the tea. She looked again around the kitchen, marveling at how cozy it felt. How warm and welcoming.

"You lived here for your entire childhood?" Mare asked.

Tamar nodded. "Yes. My parents bought this house when they got married. I came along a few years later. Then my sister some time after that."

"How's your mother doing?" Mare blew on her tea, but it must've still felt too hot, because she put down the mug and picked up a cookie instead. She offered the plate to Tamar, who took one.

"She's . . . honestly, she's not doing very well." Tamar bit into the cookie. She wanted to weep at the sweetness of it.

"I'm sorry to hear that. We knew she was going into Somerset House when we bought the place from her. Is she still . . . ?"

"Ah, well, she's with me now. At my house. Until we can find someplace better for her." Tamar braved a drink of tea, burning her tongue. She winced, but it was good. She took another cautious sip.

"It's hard when our parents start to fail. I lost my mom a few years ago."

"Were you close?" She had no idea why she asked that question. Mothers and daughters were always supposed to be close. To suggest anything else was an insult.

Mare didn't seem to be offended.

"Yes," she said. "It was hard on me when she died."

Tamar nodded.

"It's probably hard to have her living with you too." Mare's tone drifted slightly upward, not making her words a full question, but leaving it as a possibility.

"Yes. It is," Tamar answered simply and with relief at saying so out loud.

It was Mare's turn to nod.

"You said you had some questions? About the house?" Tamar tried to keep her tone light and neutral, but her voice shook a little.

"Yes. I'm not sure if you can even answer them," Mare said.

"Have there been problems?"

Mare gave her a curious look. "With the house? Nothing unusual, especially not for an older house. It was built in what, 1943?"

"Nothing unusual," Tamar repeated. "That's . . . good."

Mare's brow furrowed. "What kind of problems would you think we might have?"

"Electrical? Do the lights flicker?"

"No," Mare said after a beat.

Tamar sat back in her seat. "Plumbing issues? A sewer smell, even though nothing seems backed up?"

"No," Mare repeated, this time adding a shake of her head. "Nothing like that. We had the house inspected before we bought it, of course. There were a few things here and there that we knew would need to be fixed, but nothing like what you're describing. We haven't even had any new leaks, and the inspector said we should probably expect some—"

"Leaks?"

They couldn't see the dining room from this spot, but Mare's gaze went in that direction. "The dining room ceiling had a huge spot in it from where a leak from the upstairs bathroom had been badly patched. Maybe it happened after you moved out?"

"No," Tamar said around the tightness in her throat. "That happened when I still lived here. The bathtub overflowed."

"There was a bathtub upstairs?" Mare sounded surprised. "Oh, wow. There's only a shower there now. We thought maybe that's where the leak had come from, when they redid the bathroom. I never imagined a tub in there. It doesn't seem like there could even be enough room."

Tamar closed her eyes for a moment too long to be a blink. Self-consciously, she tugged her sleeve down over her wrist. The scar had faded long ago. When she looked at Mare, the other woman smiled. It looked genuine.

"Maybe you want to take a little tour around? See what's changed?"

Or what had stayed the same.

"I couldn't ask you to do that," Tamar said.

Mare waved a hand. "Don't be silly. I'd be happy to. First of all, I love bragging about what all we've done to this place, considering it was such a—since we put so much work into it."

"You can say it was a dump." Tamar laughed a little sheepishly.

"It wasn't a dump," Mare corrected, but gently and with humor. "It was a house that needed some love."

"Probably desperately," Tamar said in a low voice.

The women stared at each other across the table. Mare nodded after a moment, her smile somehow solemn. Tamar took a sip of now-cool-enough tea.

"If you really don't mind," Tamar said, "I'd love to see the house."

Mare's expression brightened. "Oh, good. Because then you can tell me all about the secret room."

"Which one?" Tamar asked.

Mare's brows rose before knitting. "You mean there's another one?"

"Oh, yes," Tamar said. "More than one."

18

Mare and Bill had discovered the canning cellar already. They'd kept the long narrow shelves, now sporting neatly organized bins of tools instead of rows of canned goods and spiderwebs. They'd replaced what had been a bare overhead bulb with a new fixture. They did not, as it turned out, know about the small door set into the paneling at the far end of the long, narrow space. When Tamar pushed it open, it revealed a windowless concrete room, another bare bulb fixture swinging overhead.

She braced herself when the door opened, but there was nothing in the room except the drain set into the floor.

"It's a cold cellar," Mare said with marvel in her voice. "My grandma had one just like it. It must run behind the craft room."

She meant the small room at the far end of the finished basement. They'd looked at it already—what had once been a dimly lit rumpus room overcrowded with brown flowered couches and a television set on top of the old console TV that no longer worked had become another well-lit and cheerful space with a distinct purpose. Cabinets lined the walls. A good-sized table was set up with a sewing machine and various art projects.

The cold cellar hadn't changed at all.

curl up tight like a pillbug curl in a ball the door is closed and it won't look here for you

it won't find you oh it will find you it
found you

"We found this." Mare pulled a cardboard shoebox off a shelf in the storage room. "We didn't know what they were, but it didn't feel right to throw them away."

Tamar lifted the lid, which remained attached to the box. Inside was a cluster of metal and ceramic cylinders. Some were broken. All were empty. A pile of torn and dirty scrolls littered the bottom of the box.

"They're mezuzot," she said. "Um, a mezuzah is a scroll written with a Hebrew prayer. You're supposed to put them on all the doorposts of every room where people live. They protect the house. The cases protect the scrolls."

Mare's eyebrows rose. "That sounds like a lovely idea. Too bad she took them all down."

Tamar closed the lid of the box and held it out to Mare. "Yeah. Too bad."

"I guess that explains all the small holes we found in just about every doorframe." Mare waved the box away. "Would you like them? Some of them look very intricate. Like they might have been expensive."

She doubted that. Her mother wouldn't have spent a lot of money on anything religious—that she'd ever had mezuzahs on the doorframes at all was a surprise to Tamar. She couldn't remember ever seeing them. She hadn't even known until she became an adult what one was or why Jews put them up.

"Family heirlooms, maybe?" Mare prompted gently when Tamar didn't answer right away.

She gave herself a mental shake. "I don't think so. But yes, I'll take them. They have the name of God on them. If the scrolls have been damaged, they should be taken care of in some special way. I'm not sure how, but I can find out."

From the floor drain in the back room, formerly hidden and now found, a whisper burbled forth.

it finds you always it finds you
Tamarrrrr

Tamar froze. An icy chill centered itself at the base of her throat, stabbing. Sweat trickled down her spine. She clamped her arms over her belly to stop the shiver.

Mare didn't seem to notice either Tamar's discomfort or the sibilance hissing from the drain. She stepped fully into the small concrete room, taking a small, slow spin. Tamar almost grabbed her but stopped herself. She had *not* heard her name here in this room where once she had cowered, eyes closed, and waited to die. She was only remembering that once she had.

Mare looked at her. "Do you want to go back upstairs?"

"Yes. Sure." Tamar dared to glance over her shoulder at the cold room as Mare closed the door. It blended back into the paneling, once more keeping its secrets.

The stairs creaked exactly the same as they always had, the wood groaning and protesting each step. The railing of smooth, polished wood was different. No more splintery two-by-four with rough-hewn ends that bit your palm if you dared drag along it. Nothing grabbed her ankles either.

The four bedrooms upstairs were the same, other than fresh paint. The shared hall bath had a new tile floor and a stall shower that did indeed take up only half the space once occupied by the tub. The toilet was in the same place but now sat in a corner made by the wall that filled in the place where the tub had once been.

The secret room in the bedroom closet was still where it had always been.

"Kayla just loves this," Mare explained as she pushed open the small, square door inside the closet of the room they were using for guests.

Inside, the sloping eaves made a crawlspace that had been fully carpeted—floor, walls, ceiling. A scrap of burnt orange shag ran along one section. Shorter green pile wrapped around the corner. Faded blue covered the ceiling.

"She spends hours in here playing," Mare said.

They'd strung fairy lights along the ceiling and piled colored cushions on the floor. Books were scattered on the pile. Dolls and stuffed toys watched from small bins that lined the low section where the eaves met the floor. When Tamar bent to look into the small space, she drew in a quick breath. It still smelled the same, like hot wood and dust.

Tamar touched the place on the doorframe where she and Lovey had written their names and the dates. They'd drawn smiley faces. Tic-tac-toes.

"We didn't paint over it or anything," Mare said at the sound. "It didn't seem right."

"Tam and Love's Clubhouse," she murmured aloud and looked over her shoulder at Mare. "That's from a long, long time ago. Do you mind if I . . . ?"

"Not at all. Go on in." Mare gestured with a smile.

Tamar had to kneel to crawl into the space. When this place had been hers, she'd often spent hours in here too, but not playing. She'd gone inside the carpeted room and pulled the door shut behind her, hiding at the far, far end, closing her eyes and ears to the sounds of what was going on in the rest of the house. To know Kayla had made this space something special and wonderful seemed impossible, but clearly, the little girl loved this space.

Tamar crawled a bit further, but instead of reaching a dead end to the long, low corridor, she found a small room big enough for her to stand up in. Kayla had set it up with a small table and a tea set. Dress-up clothes and other costume pieces spilled out of a lidless bin. Mare was right behind her. The space was tight for two adults, so Mare hung back a little bit.

"I've never . . . this wasn't here when I lived here. It looks like it was broken through the wall into the space where the tub and linen closet used to be."

"We didn't notice this until after we moved in. We didn't crawl back here when we looked at the house originally."

Tamar turned, slowly. In the glow of the fairy lights strung all over, she saw something on the bare plywood wall. "What is that?"

"It's what I wanted to ask you about," Mare said.

Tamar leaned closer. The room had not been finished with more carpet scraps. Not even drywall on this side. Something had been scrawled onto the plywood in thick, dark strokes of what looked like permanent market. Tamar leaned closer to read it.

"It was supposed to be mine," she whispered the written words out loud.

"We assume your mom wrote it," Mare said from behind her. "Honestly, we did paint over this, but you can see how it just keeps bleeding through the paint. Kayla says it doesn't bother her, but it's kind of . . ."

"Creepy. Yeah."

Tamar shuddered at the idea of her mother crawling along the dark space. Pulling herself upright. Scrawling her message.

Waiting for one day, some day, when Tamar would come back home and read it? Except she never had. Whatever renovations her mother had made were done after she left.

"Any idea what it means?" Mare asked.

Tamar shook her head and turned away from it. She didn't want to freak Mare out, especially since her little girl was so happy in this space. The walls were closing in. Tamar tried to draw a breath, but the whispers from the drain were sifting up, up, through the exposed pipes that. They ran through the wall in front of her. Helpless to stop herself, she put a hand on one of them. The metal chilled her. She pulled away.

"Can we get out of here? It's a little claustrophobic."

"Of course." Mare backed up, bending and then getting on her hands and knees to crawl out of the space.

Tamar followed as fast as she could. She was almost out when something grabbed her hand. She yanked it. Pain seared through her palm. A stinging heat flooded her. Tamar cried out and yanked her hand free. The blood looked dark in the soft white glow from the string lights.

"Are you okay?" Mare asked from outside the closet.

Tamar backed out as fast as she could, getting to her feet with a stumble that knocked her shoulder against the doorframe. She cradled her hand, burning now, against the front of her. Blood smeared onto her dark blouse.

"Oh! Oh, my gosh," Mare cried. "What happened?"

"I must've caught it on a nail or something." Tamar pressed her fingers against the long slit in her palm, but the blood welled up anyway.

"Let's get that cleaned up." Mare guided her to the bathroom.

Tamar washed the wound in the sink while Mare dug out a small bin of adhesive bandages and antibiotic creams from beneath one of the cabinets. She held out the tube to Tamar, who used a bit of the clear goo on the cut. More blood smeared. Mare handed her a wad of toilet tissue, and Tamar used that to stanch the bleeding.

It wouldn't stop, she thought. She was going to bleed forever. She watched red bloom up through the white paper.

"I'm going to see what got you. If there's a nail sticking out, I don't want Kayla catching herself on it. I'll be right back," Mare said.

Tamar nodded and pressed the tissue hard against the cut. As if on cue, Kayla came out of her room at the end of the hall. She peeked in at Tamar with wide eyes.

"Did you get a boo-boo?"

Tamar nodded and looked out the doorway. "Is that your room down there?

"Yep, that's my room."

"Mine was the one right there at the other end of the hall. The one with the playroom in the closet," Tamar said. She deliberately didn't look at the tissue in her hand.

"That's the guest room for when Nana and PopPop come," Kayla explained seriously. "But when they aren't here, I can go in my playroom whenever I want. Did you go in there when you lived here?"

"All the time," Tamar said. Mare had not come back yet. "Tell me, do you ever hear anything in that room?"

"Like what?"

"Like whispers? Or someone saying your name?"

"No," Kayla said with a frown. "Should I?"

"No. Absolutely not," Tamar told her.

"Did you, when you were little?" Kayla put her little hands on her hips and gave Tamar a long, hard stare that said she wasn't settling for any bullshit.

Fortunately, Mare returned before Tamar had to answer. "I couldn't find anything. Kayla, love, don't go in the playroom until Daddy can check it out, okay? Miss Tamar hurt her hand on a nail that might be sticking out."

"Okay," Kayla said, still giving Tamar a steady stare.

"How's it doing?" Mare asked.

Tamar took the paper away and rinsed her hand again beneath some cool water. The bleeding had slowed. She took some fresh tissue and pressed it to the cut. This time when she took it away, she was able to coat it with antibacterial ointment and use a couple bandages.

"It's the worst place for a cut," Mare pointed out. "You'd be better off with a gauze pad and some medical tape. I don't have any, though. Sorry."

"Oh, no. No, it's fine. I'm sorry I caused such trouble," Tamar began, but Mare waved her to silence.

"Thank you for finding it instead of Kayla." Mare pulled the little girl against her side for a few seconds. "Go on back to your room and play, Kay-kay. But stay out of the playroom for now."

Back downstairs in the kitchen, Tamar declined another cup of tea. "I really should get going. I've taken up way too much of your time. I'm sorry I couldn't tell you what the words on the wall meant."

"Thanks for showing me the cold cellar addition. I've been wanting to get into canning," Mare said lightly, although her gaze seemed shadowed. "Tamar, if you don't mind my asking. What kinds of problems were you thinking we might have here?"

Tamar shook her head, unwilling to say aloud everything she'd been thinking. Mare's sympathetic look didn't do much to encourage her to share—she'd seen looks like that too many times to trust them. But when Mare sat down at the kitchen table again and gestured for Tamar to return to the seat she'd occupied before, Tamar took it.

"You don't remember me at all. But I remember you. My oldest sister Janelle was in your class at Pierce High." Mare paused. "Janelle Kenney?"

Tamar vaguely recalled the name. "My high school years are . . . blurry."

Mare laughed lightly, but not like she thought Tamar's statement was funny. "Yeah. That happens."

Tamar sagged in her chair. "So, you knew my mother before you bought the house from her?"

"I knew about this house and your family. Not much about your mom, specifically. I heard rumors about why you left when you did. They went around for a while."

"I bet they did."

"But if there's something about this house I should know—"

Tamar bit the tip of her tongue lightly, then shrugged. She met Mare's gaze. "If something was going on in this house, Mare, I think you already would know."

"We fixed the electrical issues, and the plumbing hasn't ever been a problem."

Tamar thought of flickering lights. The stink of sewage and other things. She swallowed bitterness. "Have you ever come down here to the kitchen in the morning and found all the drawers open, all the cupboard doors open?"

"No," Mare replied, but after a hesitation.

"Have you ever heard someone saying your name even when you're alone in the house?"

"No," Mare repeated, a little quicker this time. She cocked her head to look over Tamar's face.

"Have you ever had nightmares?"

Mare frowned. "Everyone has nightmares, don't they?"

Tamar put her hand over the scar on her wrist. "Not the same kinds."

They sat in silence for a moment or so after that. A bird flew past the sliding glass doors, casting a shadow over the tile floor and turning Mare's head in that direction for a second before she looked back at Tamar.

"Are you telling me this house is haunted?"

"Yes," Tamar said, and the relief spilled out of her into that single word that hung in the air between them, solid and unbreakable. Untakebackable. She waited for Mare to laugh, or to get angry and tell her to get the hell out.

Mare frowned but did not raise her voice when she answered. Her brow furrowed, but with concern, not anger. She reached across the table and briefly touched the back of Tamar's hand.

"I saw the listing for this house online and something told me I had to see it. I just knew. Our realtor had a heck of a time getting your mother to agree to a showing. She canceled on us twice, once as we pulled into the driveway. But we did finally get in to see it, and the second I walked through that front door, I knew, I just knew, this was the house for us." Mare paused and leaned back in her chair. Her eyes held Tamar's. "It was not in good shape. They'd dropped the price on it several times already. We came in even a little lower but offered to take it as-is. She took our offer. Our realtor said it was like she'd been waiting for just the right family. When we moved in here, it felt to me as though this house drew in a huge, long breath of relief, and it's been full of care and love ever since."

Tamar pressed her fingertips beneath her eyes to hold back the tears that threatened to spill down her cheeks. Mare got up from the table and returned with a box of tissues. Tamar took one to blot her face.

"I'm glad," she said when she could be certain her voice would remain steady. "I'm really glad to hear that."

"We love this house," Mare said. "I know it sounds silly, but I think if a house can love, it loves us. I've never felt anything but safe here."

After that, there didn't seem to be much to say. Tamar cleared her throat and tried to find some words, but silence again fell between them. Mare didn't seem inclined to break it, so they sat and stared at each other.

What would Mare say, if Tamar told her everything? The whole truth about what had gone on in this house, these rooms, in the very spot where they now sat? If she told her what her mother had once screamed at her, and why, it would change Mare's feelings about this house. It would ruin it for this family.

So instead, Tamar pushed away from the table. She found a smile that felt fake but must've looked sincere, because Mare returned it. She held out her hand, and Mare took it to shake.

"It was nice meeting you, Mare. I'm sorry I barged in on you like this. You and your family have done an incredible job with the house. It looks loved, for sure."

At the front door, Tamar thought about turning back once more, but she didn't, even though she could feel Mare's gaze on her all the way to her car. She would never come back here. There was no need to visit, no need to encroach on this family's happiness. If a house could love, she thought as she got in her car, and her throat got tight and her hands gripped the steering wheel tight enough to turn the knuckles white. If a house could love, it had not loved her. That was one truth, and here was another: Her old house had never been haunted.

It had always been her mother.

CHAPTER

19

TAMAR DIDN'T EXPECT an answer from Lovey right away, not with the three-hour time difference. Still, when her sister didn't reply well past the hour she would usually have been awake, Tamar tried again. The text went through, but Lovey did not reply.

Her workday was fucked. There was no way she could concentrate on anything, not with the aches in her back and feet. After visiting her childhood home yesterday, she'd spent a sleepless night, but at least she hadn't gone nightwalking, and when she got downstairs this morning, the kitchen had been the same way she'd left it when she went to bed.

"Tam," said Ruth from the doorway to the dining room. "I know you said not to bother you when you're at your desk, but I'd like some coffee."

"I don't drink coffee. Make a pot of tea if you want something." Tamar turned back to her computer. The files she'd been working on had shut down while she wasn't looking. She clicked the program to bring them again, but her computer screen flickered and then went completely black.

"Language," her mother scolded when Tamar let out a curse.

Sweat ran down between her breasts, but she refused to fan herself or pull at the neckline of her T-shirt. She restarted her computer, hoping that would fix the glitch. The familiar startup chime sounded wobbly, like it came from far away.

The computer booted to a black screen with a circle struck through by a line.

Tamar closed her eyes. Her computer was only a few years old and had been the best she could afford. It was fast and had, until this moment, never given her any problems, no matter how many programs she had open.

"I don't like tea. Maybe you can drive me to the store so I can get a coffeemaker, if you don't have one," Ruth said, still standing in the doorway.

"I have to work today. I can take you later." Tamar wiggled her mouse, but the screen didn't change. She pressed the button at the back of the monitor to force the computer to shut down.

Ruth burst into loud, braying sobs. She bent over as though she'd been punched in the gut. She pounded one fist into the other. Her body wracked with her wails.

Tamar cringed, spinning in her office chair. Her hands moved automatically to clap over her ears, but she held them forcibly at her sides. She was not a child.

Her mother rocked back and forth, still crying. She lifted her tear-streaked face. Tamar had seen those kinds of tears before. They'd vanish the second Ruth got what she wanted.

"Stop it," Tamar ordered. "Cut it out!"

"I want coffee!"

Tamar eyed her without saying anything. Ruth slumped into a chair at the kitchen table, putting her head in her hands. She'd chosen the only chair Tamar could see from her desk.

"I just want coffee in the mornings. Is that too much to ask? You have no idea what it's like to be made to feel so unwelcome." Another squall of sobs worked their way out of Ruth's throat while Tamar kept her silence. "You have no idea what it's like to be so unwanted!"

"Order a coffeemaker online," Tamar said. "It'll be here in a couple of days."

Her mother looked up and dashed tears from her face with furious hands. "That doesn't help me right now."

"Order one now. Then take a walk down to the convenience store on the corner and buy a cup of coffee. It's just a few blocks from here. A walk would be good for you." It would get her mother out of the house for a bit, and that would be good for both of them.

"You expect me to walk that far?"

"You walked from Somerset House to here," Tamar said. "I think you can make it to the end of the block."

Ruth straightened. She frowned. "It's so easy for you to say that."

"It would be so easy," Tamar said, "for you to do it."

"Fine." Her mother got up, a little unsteadily, and put a hand on the back of the chair. "Order me a coffeemaker, and I'll get dressed and walk myself to the store."

It had not been meant as a negotiation, but if that was what worked, Tamar was fine with it. "Okay."

"Fine," her mother said.

"Yes."

Without another word, Ruth left the kitchen. Tamar rubbed her forehead against the threat of a headache. She hadn't had one in ages, not like this, but the familiarity of the pain throbbing behind her eyes was another reminder of when she'd lived with her mother. At her desk, she restarted her computer once again, wishing as hard as she could for it to boot up without a problem. This time, it did, but she was wary and made sure to run her backup program immediately. While her external hard drive whirred, she ordered a coffeemaker. She opened the project she'd been working on, packaging for a set of boxer shorts made from bamboo fibers. She was having a hard time getting all of the information on it that the company wanted to display without the package looking too crowded.

Her sister still had not returned her message.

Tamar focused on her work but was too antsy to accomplish much. She went to the bottom of the stairs to see if her mother was ready to leave. Ruth was looking down at her, her toes slightly over the edge of the top stair. She wasn't holding on to the railing.

"Are you okay?" Tamar asked.

Ruth wobbled.

A sound like the flap of wings, a rush of breath, a crash of waves, pushed Tamar back a few stumbling steps. She gulped in some air but still felt as though she were drowning. At the top of the stairs, her mother hovered, floating.

Then came the slap of a hand on the polished wooden railing as Ruth grabbed it. Held it. She wasn't falling down the steps, and she wasn't flying down them either. Tamar blinked, blinked, and swallowed hard at the slice of breath caught in her throat. The headache swelled, no longer a throb but an incessant and endless pulsing behind both eyes, deep in the upper reaches of her sinuses, even into her jaws. Her teeth ached. Heat wrapped around her, suffocating and thick. Her eyes closed and opened, closed and opened. Closed. Opened. Blink, blink, blink.

When she opened them, her mother was stepping off the bottom stair.

"What's wrong with you?" Ruth asked suspiciously. She put her hands on her hips, her black purse slung over one arm. She'd put on a red blouse and navy skirt. Makeup. Her hair was piled into an ornate bun. "Tammy? I asked you what's wrong?"

"Nothing. Just . . . nothing. Do you have your phone with you? Cash?"

Ruth laughed with good humor and patted her arm. "Of course I do. I even wore practical shoes."

She pointed her toe to show off the thick-soled walking shoes. Tamar's laugh didn't have the humor her mother's had. Ruth hitched the purse higher on her arm. Her smile was warm, her eyes a-twinkle. "Well. I'm off."

"Maybe you should wait a little bit. It's hot today, and it's only going to get hotter," Tamar said.

"I drink my coffee in the morning. If I have it after noon," her mother said, "then I can't sleep. You're the one who told me I should go. You're the one who said it would be good for me. It's not so hot yet. It's barely ten in the morning."

"Sure. Fine. You're right." But watching her, Tamar couldn't help noticing how frail her mother seemed. "I could drive you."

"Not necessary," Ruth said crisply. "I'll take a nice little walk and get some air, and you can get your work done. I'll be fine. I've been walking since before you were born."

Tamar had to laugh at that, with more humor, this time. This was Lovey's mother, she thought, watching Ruth smile. The one who made jokes. Who was considerate of others. The mother who loved and was loved in return.

"Call me if you need something," Tamar said.

At the front door, her mother turned back to look at her. "It used to be me sending you off into the world and worrying that you'd be all right."

Before Tamar could answer, Ruth had gone out the door, closing it behind her. Tamar stood in the hallway, silent, before moving quickly to look through the narrow windows on the side of the door. Ruth was already moving down the sidewalk, her gait slow but steady. She moved with purpose. She waved at the next-door neighbor mowing her lawn, then at the guy from the delivery truck handing off a package to someone across the street. Tamar watched until she got to the corner.

The text she was anticipating from Lovey had not arrived, but one from Miguel had. Guilt poked at her. She'd meant to call him back but, in the turmoil of yesterday's accident with Ross, had forgotten. She tapped his contact information now, a call and not a text.

"Hey," she said without preamble when he answered. "I'm sorry, I'm caught up with a lot of stuff going on here. I don't know if I'm going to be able to make it tonight."

"Bummer. But that's actually okay, because I'm almost at your house right now," he said, surprising her. "I picked up some bagels and thought you and your mom might like some. I was going to drop them off on my way to the gym. Is that cool?"

Tamar looked at her work-from-home outfit. PJ pants, a soft T-shirt, slippers. "Uh, give me ten minutes?"

"I'll be there in seven," he said.

It took her five to braid her hair and pin it up. She swiped on some mascara. Lip gloss. A bit of powder. She even changed into a T-shirt dress that flattered her figure, because why not? She was already at the door when he pulled into the driveway.

He grinned when he saw her and held up a brown paper sack bulging with bagels redolent with garlic. Her stomach rumbled. With everything that had been going on this morning, she hadn't eaten yet.

"How come you're not at work?" she asked.

"Day off. July fifth," he said, watching her face. "You didn't remember the holiday?"

She forced a laugh. She hadn't even heard any fireworks last night. "These days, I'm lucky if I remember anything. Can you come in for a bit?"

"I was hoping you'd ask." He followed her inside, looking around the cool, dim interior of her front hall. "Where's your mom?"

"She went for a walk. Come into the kitchen."

She toasted them each an everything bagel and, digging further into the bag he'd brought, found sliced lox wrapped in white deli paper, a small carton of whipped cream cheese, and another of sliced tomatoes, onion and even capers. She looked up, jaw dropping, to see him grinning with clear delight at watching her discovery.

"This is what the guy at Barry Bagels said you needed for a proper bagel breakfast. Did I get it right?"

She laughed, shaking her head. "Yeah. You sure did."

"You'll have to arrange it for me. I've only ever had plain bagels with butter." He sat at the table. "I know, it's a sacrilege of some kind, right?"

Quickly, she slathered the toasted bagels with the cream cheese, lox, and toppings and slid his on a plate toward him before taking the chair across from his. Miguel took a big bite. His eyes went wide. He chewed rapidly and swallowed.

"It's fish, it's like a big slice of raw fish!"

"Umm, yes," Tamar said. "That's what lox is."

They both laughed and laughed some more. Laughed so hard they both had to wipe away tears. She laughed so hard her belly hurt, which allowed her to forget the twinges in her back and cut-up feet. Even the wound in her hand felt better.

They were still laughing when her phone rang. Tamar thought it would be Lovey, but instead her mother's number and name showed on the screen. It wasn't her mother's voice on the other end.

"Hi. Is this . . . Tammy? Your mother is Ruth Kahan?"

"Yes," Tamar said warily. "Who's this?"

"My name's Heather. I'm here at Orchard Park. The elementary school." The woman paused. "Your mother is here. She seems a little confused."

"Oh, no. I'm sorry. Is she all right?" Tamar got up from the table.

"She's not hurt or anything. She just seems a little . . . like I said. Confused. Um, I think you need to come and get her. Do you know the playground?"

"Yeah. I'll be there in five minutes. Can you keep her there? Is she going to wander off or anything?"

"No, I don't think so. But you should come right away," the woman said.

"Can I get your—" The call disconnected. "Number. Shit."

Tamar turned to Miguel. "I have to go pick up my mother. Apparently, she never made it to the convenience store. Or maybe she did, but she's at the playground now. The woman who called me said she seems confused."

"Do you want me to come with you?" He was already gathering their plates for the trash.

"You don't have to do that," she said, grateful he'd asked. "You said you were on the way to the gym."

"After eating all that? Nah. I'll go later. C'mon. I'll ride along. Besides, it'll be nice to see your mother again. Right?" He winked.

The playground was beyond the convenience store and down a bit. By the time Tamar parked her car, she could already see Ruth's bright red blouse from across the playground. She sat on a bench, her purse on her lap. A woman with a baby in a stroller was next to her.

"Hey," Tamar said, approaching. "What's going on?"

Ruth looked up. Her fingers tightened on the purse handles. "I got a little lost. Nothing to be worried about."

Tamar looked at the woman with the baby. "Heather?"

She nodded and gave Ruth a sideways look. She lowered her voice. "Can I talk to you for a minute? Over here?"

"Ruth, stay here. I'll be right back."

"I'm not a dog," Ruth snapped. "You don't have to tell me to stay."

Heather moved them a few feet away and turned her back to Ruth, still pitching her voice low. "She was making the parents uncomfortable. Offering some of the kids candy from her purse. I'm sure she didn't mean anything by it, but I'm sure you understand."

"She didn't pull up in a white van," Tamar said, irritated. Embarrassed. "She's an elderly woman who's got a little bit of confusion going on. She hasn't seen my sister's kids in a while, maybe she thought—"

"It wasn't candy," Heather interrupted. "She was trying to give them drugs."

Tamar gaped. "What?"

"Drugs," Heather said again, the word drawn out and finishing with sibilance.

"What kind?"

"Marijuana gummies."

"Where the hell would she get—?"

"How should I know?" Heather asked, affronted. "They had a prescription label on them. Just get her out of here. And if she's that bad off that she can't remember how to get back home, you should get her some kind of care. Really, shame on you for letting an old, confused lady wander around."

Tamar looked at her mother, who was sitting with a smile, happily watching the children play. Her stomach knotted. "Thanks for calling me. Ruth. C'mon. It's time to go home."

Miguel was waiting outside the car for them when they got back to it. "Hello, Mrs. Kahan."

Ruth stared at him. "Do I know you?"

"I'm Miguel Estrada. My parents used to live across the street from you on Spring Hill Drive."

"You used to date my daughter," Ruth said.

Tamar and Miguel shared a look.

"Yep," he said easily. "That's me."

"I'll hold your purse while you get in the car." Tamar opened the back door while Ruth climbed in. She shut the door and opened the purse to pull out a rectangular bottle. She muttered a curse, and when Miguel gave her a confused look, she held it up. "These are mine. She took my weed gums and tried to feed them to kids on the playground."

"Shit."

"Yeah," she said. "Damn it, Miguel. What am I supposed to do with any of this? With her?"

Ruth rapped on the window, waving her hand and making exaggerated mouth motions. Tamar ignored her. Miguel frowned.

"I'd say let's start by getting her home," he said. "And then I guess you can go on from there."

She reached for his arm as he made to get into the front passenger seat. "You don't have to deal with this. When we get back, you should just go."

"If that's what you want me to do, I will. But I'm also okay to stay and figure this out with you. Whatever you need." He looked determined and also hopeful.

After a second, she nodded. Relying on someone generally meant being let down. "Okay. Sure."

In the five-minute drive back to the house, Ruth said nothing even when Miguel tried engaging her in conversation. She got out of the car, with help, and went into the house also in silence. She was halfway up the stairs when Tamar called out to her.

She held up the prescription bottle. "You took these from my bathroom."

Ruth turned on the stairs, one hand on the railing. "I have no idea what you're talking about. Those candies were in my purse. I didn't put them there."

"You could have made those kids really sick." Tamar glanced at Miguel who'd kindly gone into the kitchen to give them some privacy. "You need to come down here and talk to me about this And how you got lost."

"It was hot. I was tired. I asked the woman if she'd mind giving you a call to come get me. That's all. End of story. Fini!"

Tamar shook her head. "Did you forget where I lived?"

"Fuck you, Tamar." Her mother said in a gritty, raw voice so low and full of malice that it sent Tamar back a step. In the next minute, Ruth moved down a stair. Her eyes went wide, her mouth curving down. "Oh, Tammy. I'm so sorry. That just came out of my mouth, I have no idea why I would say that. I'm sorry."

"You should probably just go upstairs to your room." Her fists clenched at her sides.

Ruth nodded. She seemed about to say more but turned and went up the stairs slowly, almost pulling herself along by the railing. At the top, she looked down once more before she went into her room and shut the door.

Tamar pulled out her phone and tapped an angry message to her sister. *CALL ME.*

There'd been no reply, and none came now, but she used her phone to check her email for any updates from work as she went to find Miguel. There was an email from Lovey. It had come an hour ago, and when she refreshed again, another came in.

I've been calling you and texting you, but you're not answering me. What's going on?

It took only a few seconds to pull up Lovey's contact information, and as soon as she did, Tamar saw at once why her sister had not been replying. She fixed the problem and sent one more text.

Our mother blocked your number on my phone.

CHAPTER

20

RUTH HAD STAYED in her room for most of the day, only coming out when Miguel left. She and Tamar had eaten a mostly silent dinner of takeout Chinese, and after the meal, Tamar had gone back to work so she could catch up on everything she'd been letting slide. Her mother had gone into the den to watch TV.

Tamar had drained the rest of her bottle of wine and opened another.

She took a long, slow sip. The wine slid down, down, into her stomach, where it rolled around before settling. She took another sip, this time deliberately holding the wine on her tongue before swallowing. She had the prescription bottle in front of her. The white label on it keeping it sealed had been cut open, but she couldn't be sure if she'd done it or Ruth had.

Tamar usually preferred to vape the flower for a quicker high that didn't linger. The gummies often left her feeling spacey for too long. In fact, if the woman at the playground hadn't given her this bottle, Tamar would probably have forgotten she'd ever had it in the first place.

If she leaned to the right, she could look down the hallway toward the study. The flickering light of the television cast shadows from the doorway, but the volume was too low for her to hear it. Tamar took a longer, deeper drink. When the warmth hit her, she shuddered, but she didn't stop drinking until the glass was half empty.

"Oh, c'mon now, Tam, don't be such a pessimist," she whispered to herself as she held the glass up against the sheen of shifting white and gray coming from the study. It reminded her a lot of how the lights had so often flickered in the house on Spring Hill Drive. How her computer had glitched and flickered just that morning. She braced herself for a rotten stink but smelled only wine. "This glass could be considered half full."

The day had started off bad and kept on going. She'd come downstairs to find the kitchen a wreck again. Her computer had totally shit the bed, and her laptop screen was far too small for her to use her graphics programs without it being a pain in the ass. She'd ordered a new desktop, but it wouldn't be delivered for three weeks. The toilet in the powder room had overflowed, and now the kitchen smelled like an outhouse.

The only good thing was that Ruth had not spoken a word to her all day.

Tamar had called her sister to tell her about what had happened. Lovey had, at first, been apologetic. Sympathetic. Concerned about their mother's mental health, her sister had asked to speak to Ruth. They'd spent fifteen minutes on the phone, with Ruth's bedroom door shut, so Tamar couldn't hear what they were talking about.

Whatever it had been, Lovey's entire attitude had changed. When she got back on the phone with her, Lovey was unconvinced that Ruth was the one who'd blocked her number. Did Tamar leave her phone lying around, unattended? No. Had she given their mother any opportunity to grab it? Also, no. As for the drugs she'd been trying to pass out on the playground, that, too, was Tamar's fault for not keeping her drugs in a more secure place. Lovey, run ragged by her brood of children, hadn't had time to discuss all of this.

"Figure it out," she'd said. "If you can't handle her being there, you'll have to hire someone to come in during the day."

Easier for her sister to say from her golden castle in California, and Tamar had told her so.

She and Lovey rarely fought, but this time they'd both ended up shouting. Tamar had looked up at one point to see Ruth lurking in the doorway. She'd hollered at her to get out. Lovey had shouted at Tamar not to be so mean to their mother.

It had been a shitshow.

She opened the lid of the gummy bottle and tipped out a couple of the square, soft candies into her palm. A quarter of one was enough to get her loopy. She'd never taken a whole one.

The cupboards had all been open. The knives, sharp tips pointing in the wrong direction. The mugs and plates moved around. She had not imagined this.

Her mother at the top of the stairs, the sound of wings and rushing wind. The shadow floating. Ruth at the bottom of the stairs between one blink and the next. She had not imagined that.

Children on a playground, tempted by a woman who looked like a grandma offering them candy that could make them sick, hell, Tamar thought, could possibly kill them. This was also not something she'd created in her own mind. It was real. It had happened.

It was starting all over again.

She finished off the other glass of wine.

She contemplated a ruby square of corn syrup and cannabis. She used her fingernails to cut it in half. Then again. She ate a quarter of it.

Then she ate the rest.

She would drink and drug herself into oblivion and pass out in her bed, door locked, and she'd be way too blitzed to go nightwalking. And if her mother got into some trouble in the night? Fell down the stairs on her way to fuck with all the kitchen cabinets and drawers, or wandered out into the street and got run down like a puppy someone was encouraging to jump the fence. If something bad happened to her mother while Tamar was deliberately unconscious . . .

Would that really be So. Fucking. Bad?

The thing standing at the foot of her bed has no eyes. Only black holes glittering with tiny crimson pinpricks of light. The rest of its face is all mouth, another black hole glinting with the points of many serrated teeth, in rows like a shark or a lamprey or a leech.

Tamar knows this because of the pictures she looked up in the encyclopedia at the library. None of those things are exactly what this thing is, with its long arms that reach its hands nearly to the floor and its long, long legs that bend in odd directions, like a dog's hind legs. This thing is different.

This thing is—

"Mom?"

It makes a noise, a long, low growl but not that of an angry dog, of something else, a grinding, gritting noise. It's how teeth would sound if rubbed against sandpaper. It's what the night sky sounds like when it is filled with bugs that want to sting you. It's an ocean full of oil that drowns everything it touches.

It is her mother laughing at her for tripping over nothing on the floor. Crying that nobody loves her, will ever love Tamar the way her mother does. Screaming because the cupboard doors are all hanging open again, and she slams them over and over again; it is her mother ripping the plates from the shelves and throwing them on the floor in a rage.

Tamar's bedroom door is off its hinges. Mom pays for this house. That door. If she wants it gone, it is gone. There is no such thing as privacy in this house, not for little bitches who disobey.

The mother-thing hovers over her bed, long arms dangling. Feet with toenails as thick and yellow as hooves scratch along the comforter as she moves up, up and over, to hang in the air over Tamar's open, silent-screaming face.

Spit dribbles from the thing's cavernous hole of a mouth.

It slides between Tamar's lips. It stings. It tastes like puke and smoke and sucking on a penny. It is electric and sharp, the sting of touching the fence that says don't touch. It is poison.

And it will kill her, if she doesn't get away.

"Let me in," *the mother-thing says in that gritty gravel voice, that horror movie voice, that voice that is older than the stars it hates so much because they are bright and shining and it is dark and because they remind it of where it once was and where it can never be again.*

Let. Me. In.

But she refuses.

And she runs.

"Tammy? Let me in!" Ruth's voice, muffled by the door, got louder. She knocked.

Tamar couldn't sit up, not right away. Everything low inside her lurched and roiled, and she struggled up from the tangle of her sheets thinking something was holding on to her feet. It was only her blanket, too heavy for the summer, but which had been taken from her closet at some point and layered over the end of the bed.

The nightmare lingered, but that's all it was. A dream. A memory about the night she'd left home.

Surprisingly, she did not feel sick to her stomach. Her head didn't hurt. Not yet, but she felt an inquisitive throb beginning that might become something worse if she didn't drink some water or take a few ibuprofen. She was coated in sweat, her T-shirt as damp as if she'd splashed water on it.

"Let me in!"

"I'm sleeping," Tamar barked out.

Ruth stopped banging on the door. "It's late."

"Shit." Tamar rolled to look at her phone. Nearly eleven AM.

Multiple missed calls and texts filled her phone's notification screen, but she couldn't look at them right now. She had to pee so bad her stomach was cramping. She kicked off the blankets and swung her feet over the edge of the bed.

Now the nausea hit her but not from anything she'd consumed last night.

Black dirt on her feet. Green grass stains. A clover leaf clung beneath her big toenail. Angry red scratches raked over one foot, ending on the sole. When she stretched them out, her legs bore the same signs of abuse. Scratches, bruises, and filth.

She muttered a low cry when she got out of bed and her feet hit the floor. They ached and stung like she'd walked for miles in stilettos. Her calves hurt even worse, as did the small of her back. Her neck and shoulders hummed with pain. She staggered to the door and unlocked it. Yanked it open.

Her mother stood on the other side of it. "It's time for school. You're going to miss the bus."

"You're joking, right?"

Ruth waved a hand and meandered down the hall toward the stairs. She called over her shoulder, "I'm not driving you if you miss it. You'll have to ride your bike. Or walk. You know how to walk, don't you, Tamar?"

She paused at the head of the stairs and looked back at her daughter, still stationed in her bedroom doorway.

"You seemed to have done a lot of walking last night."

And then she threw herself down the stairs.

CHAPTER

21

FOUR DAYS AGO, Ruth had rolled down the stairs like an acrobat, boneless. A visit to the ER in an ambulance had turned up no injuries beyond the bruise on her forehead. No broken bones and allegedly, no recollection of how she'd fallen in the first place.

This was not new. Her mother had often come home from her nights out sporting bruises or sprains. Once, a cracked tooth and a black eye that she hadn't been able to explain away as clumsiness. Her deliberate flight down the stairs had been the first time Tamar had witnessed her purposefully doing something to hurt herself.

She never wanted to see that again and had turned the downstairs study into her mother's room. There would be no excuse for Ruth to climb the stairs now. She'd also installed an exterior lock on her own bedroom door to keep her mother out of it when Tamar wasn't able to lock it from the inside.

The doorknob still jiggled every night, and the whispers sifted underneath the door, and Tamar still woke from horrible dreams that were actually memories.

Her phone call to the agency had resulted in a flood of applications for the position. Shawn was her seventh interview in the past two days. At least six-four, with dark skin, a head of tightly twisted black curls cropped close to his head, and the build of a dancer, Shawn was the youngest person who'd applied for the position, but he was also the most impressive. His handshake, firm. Eye contact, unwavering. He gave off a steady, calm vibe, and Tamar appreciated that. Some of the other applicants had been too intense, too cheerful, or too edgy.

"I'm sorry, I missed that. Is it hot in here?" Bleary eyed, she struggled to hold back the yawn threatening to crack her jaw.

She'd had the HVAC guys out three times already, but although there was supposedly nothing wrong with the air conditioner, her house was always way too hot. The last time, the tech had clearly insinuated it was all in her head. She'd been tossing and turning for nights on end, waking drenched with sweat. It was terrible during the day too, but the nights were the worst.

The young man sitting across from her didn't seem to mind or notice. He grinned. "No problem. I said that I had references. They're on the paper there. And yes, it's a bit warm. Not too bad, though. I like the heat."

"I hate it." She looked at his paper. He'd already told her he figured she had a lot of caregivers to interview and that he wanted to stand out. So far, he had. "You said you've been traveling for the past few months?"

He nodded. "Yes, ma'am. My last client passed about eight months ago, and I decided to take some time before getting back to work. I love travel, and I hadn't been able to go anywhere for a while, you know?"

They spoke briefly about where he'd gone and what places he'd liked best. They both had a fondness for New Orleans, despite the heat. It took twenty minutes for Tamar to decide to hire him, but they chatted for another twenty before she ended the conversation by offering him the job.

"I'll give your references a call, of course," she said, "but unless they tell me you're a monster, I think you're going to be a great fit. All you have to do is meet my mother and see if you both agree."

"I'm free right now," he offered, standing. "Honestly, I'm ready to get started as soon as you have me sign the papers. I loved taking six months off, but my bank account didn't."

"I converted the study into her room, so she wouldn't have to use the stairs," Tamar explained, keeping her voice light. "It has a small bathroom off it that she has for her private use. There's a powder room off the kitchen for you during the day."

In her room, Ruth's gaze was fixed on the television. Animated animals cavorted on the screen along with live-action people. Her laughter stopped abruptly when she saw them both in the doorway. One of her mother's favorite movies, one she'd shown Tamar and Lovey over and over, was *Mary Poppins*. To this day, Tamar couldn't hear "A Spoonful of Sugar" without gagging at the remembered flavor of the thick, oily castor oil her mother had fed them for any illness or injury, no matter how slight. It had embarrassed her at Disney World, but she hadn't told Garrett why she'd gotten sick.

Apparently, Ruth had brought her own DVD of the film, because Tamar certainly had never owned a copy. Now she used the remote to pause it. "Who's this?"

"I'm Shawn, ma'am. I'm here to see if you might be amenable to me coming to keep you company during the days." He moved toward her, hand out.

Ruth took it without standing and allowed him to shake it. She looked at Tamar. "Will he take me shopping?"

"Shopping. Hair appointments. Ice cream," he said with a grin. "Whatever you like."

Her mother's eyes narrowed as she looked him over. "Do you play cards?"

"If I don't know the game, I'm sure you can teach me."

She smiled. "Well, then, Shawn. I suppose you and I will get along just fine."

"Where's your coffee pot?" Her mother's querulous voice came through the doorway to Tamar's office. Ruth leaned against the doorjamb, her shoulders hunched, like the wall was the only thing keeping her standing.

"It should be on the counter. It came yesterday, but I haven't taken it out of the package yet." Tamar said without turning around.

She bent to peer closer at her laptop screen, hating how much smaller it was than her broken desktop. She scaled an image a little bigger, then changed her mind and reverted it to the original size, her mind far away. With Shawn starting tomorrow morning, she'd be able to dive back into work and get caught up.

"I *need* my morning coffee."

Tamar turned with a frown. "It's almost dinner time."

Her mother said nothing.

"I got the coffeemaker, but I didn't get to the store yet to buy any coffee. I can make us a pot of herbal tea. How about that?"

"I guess that would be okay," Ruth said. "Do you have any cookies?"

"I'll see what I can find. Come on."

In the kitchen, her mother sat at the table while Tamar filled the electric kettle. Tamar opened the fridge to hunt for a lemon to squeeze into the tea but couldn't find it. Most everything had been shifted around inside, her mother's doing, so with a sigh, Tamar moved things around until she could find what she was looking for. A single, lone lemon, not in the best shape, was hiding in the vegetable drawer, and she pulled it out with a small noise of triumph. She really needed to get to the grocery store, another chore she'd be able to accomplish more easily once Shawn started working.

When she turned back around, all the cupboards and drawers were open.

Her scream lodged in her throat, dying into a whisper.

"What—" she said. It was the only word she managed to get out before her lips slammed shut.

She didn't want to ask too many questions, afraid of what the answer might be.

Ruth hadn't moved from her place at the table. She sat with her mouth slightly open. Eyes a little glazed. Distant. For a moment, Tamar glimpsed a flash of awareness in her mother's gaze, but it was gone almost at once.

"Ruth," she said. "What did you do?"

She'd been turned way for no longer than a minute. Ruth could not have done it. Tamar closed her eyes, tight and tighter. The lemon in her hand was all at once too heavy. It threatened to drag her to the floor, to her knees, or flat on her face.

She waited for the gust of foul breath on her face, but all she could smell was a hint of vanilla. Some lavender. She opened her eyes.

All the cupboards were closed. All the drawers shut. Her mother still sat in the same place at the table. She had her hands crossed in front of her. She looked expectant.

"Do you have the coffee ready, Tammy? And some cookies. Oh, I'd like some cookies."

Her mother had called it the ghost of horrible inconveniences, but it was so much more insidious than that.

"Ruth . . ." her voice trailed to silence as she swallowed hard against the lump in her throat. "I told you, I only have tea."

"But cookies?" her mother said, this time with a small sideways smile that tipped only one corner of her mouth.

"Sure. Yes. I'll see what I have."

The lemon thumped a little on the counter as Tamar set it down with shaking hands. She hesitated before pulling open the pantry door, but inside, the floor-to-ceiling wire shelves were mostly bare. Her decades of being a housewife were in the past. She always shopped for a single person living alone and had often reveled in ordering takeout on a whim. Her search turned up a package of Fig Newtons, barely out of date. She gave herself a minute, then another, to catch her breath before turning around.

The kettle was boiling.

"Tea," her mother said. "Tammy, the tea!"

"Just a minute."

"Get my fucking tea, Tamar," The mother-thing said, all grit and growling.

That was not her mother's voice. It came from her mother's throat, past her tongue and teeth and lips, it came out of her on the breath from her lungs, but it belonged to something else. Tamar didn't turn around.

Tamar felt heat on the back of her neck, followed by the chill draw of a fingertip over her bared skin.

She shuddered and held her breath. Every muscle went stiff and taut and straining. She closed her eyes and clutched the package of cookies in both hands. The plastic crinkled and rustled. A floorboard creaked.

She whirled.

Her mother sat at the table in exactly the same position she'd been in the entire time. "If you don't have coffee," her mother said, "I guess I'll just have tea."

The kettle screamed, but Tamar did not.

22

S OFT, COOL SAND beneath her feet.

Tamar opened her eyes and stumbled forward. She landed on her hands and knees, her shins banging onto a ledge of concrete. Her fingers dug into fragrant bits of shredded bark.

Mulch.

She shuddered, pushing herself upward and onto her feet. She stood in a sand pit. She was in the playground a mile or so from her house, the one where her mother had tried to give the kids the stolen marijuana gums. It was night. A soft, cool misty breeze caressed her face, promising the rain that began in the next moment. She tipped her face upward, closing her eyes and letting the cold splatters tickle her mouth until she opened it and drank.

This dream. So real. The taste of the rain, metallic but fresh. The smell of the sand, the mulch, the pang in her shins from where she'd banged them. The creak of chains, a swing in motion.

Her eyes flew open. She wasn't dreaming. This was all real. She was in a playground in the middle of the night. In her pajamas. Her feet bare.

A few yards away, a figure hunched on one of the swings, slightly in motion.

"Ruth?"

It turned its face toward her. The eyes, blank dark spaces lit with the tiniest pinprick of red light. The mouth, a gaping hole, teeth glittering like stars. A guttural noise issued from the emptiness, diving straight into Tamar's eardrums. Piercing right into her brain.

Tamar took off at a run, aware of the pain in her feet on the rough surfaces of the playground. Only after she'd run a few feet did she stop and turn with her fists clenched and panting breaths tearing at her lungs. If this was not a dream, she couldn't leave her mother behind. And if it was, she'd have to face the monster sooner or later.

She reached her mother in a few dozen strides. She put out a hand to stop the swing. It was her mother, only her mother, nothing more. Ruth still had on the blue-flowered nightgown she'd worn to bed. Her feet were bare like Tamar's, but hers were unscratched. They were also clean, especially in comparison to Tamar's own filthy toes. Ruth's misshapen fingers gripped the chains of the swing. She smiled.

"How did you . . . how did we get here?" Tamar looked around. The swing set was close enough to the parking lot that she could see all the empty spaces. Her car wasn't there. That was good, wasn't it? She hadn't driven them there in a blacked-out state.

So how did they get here?

She looked down again at her bare feet. There was her answer. They'd walked. At least, *she* had walked. Tamar straightened, wincing at the strained muscles in her neck, her shoulders, her back. Remnants of a dream returned to her, a dream that, like so many she'd been having since her mother came to stay, was not a dream at all.

"I carried you," she whispered. "On my back."

Her mother said nothing. Shafts of moonlight, split from the tree branches overhead, glittered in her eyes as she looked toward Tamar. Her smile warped.

"I carried *you*," her mother said. "Oh, you used to hate walking, didn't you? You insisted on wearing those tippy tap shoes, the sparkly gold ones with the buckle. They were too small for you, but you wouldn't give them up. They pinched your toes. Rubbed your heels into bloody sores. But you loved the way they tipped and tapped, didn't you? And we had to walk so far that day, didn't we? So I carried you. You were so heavy, too old to be carried, almost seven, but what choice did I have? I carried you."

"I don't remember that."

Tears pricked behind Tamar's eyelids. Her eyes themselves felt gritty. Scratchy. She tried to draw in a breath and then another, but it caught in her throat and stuck there. She choked on it. Coughing, she tried again to breathe in and felt only the squeeze of a fist on her throat.

"I carried you away from trouble," her mother said again, in a sing-song this time. Her voice had pitched lower. Gravelly. "So now, you carry me."

The laughter gurgled out of her like gas bubbles coming up from the bottom of a swamp. Fetid. Noxious. Each popped from her lips with a small noise, and Tamar could smell every single one. Some dank stench rose from the depth of her mother's guts and rose up, up, and out, a cloud of odor that choked her further.

She staggered back and stepped on something sharp that sliced into the sole of her foot. The same foot that had been cut by the broken wineglasses and, years ago, by a shattered picture frame. With a cry, she lifted it to counter the pain, but unbalanced, she was heading for a fall. Her arms pinwheeled, reaching out but finding only air.

At the very last second before she toppled over, her mother's hand flashed out. Fingers gripped Tamar's wrist. Squeezing. Grinding. That hurt too, more than the cut on her foot. Ruth yanked her forward. Where had she gained the strength?

In the next second, it all changed. Her mother's fingers slipped away from Tamar's wrist. The old woman fell forward, face-planting onto the chunky mulch spread beneath the swings. She flailed, crying out, writhing with her nightgown tangled around her ankles. Her hair fell free of its bun and around her shoulders.

"Ruth!" Tamar fell to her knees in front of her. She pushed at her mother's shoulder, bony and frail, to turn her. Tamar slipped a hand beneath her mother's neck to cradle it as she helped her to sit. "Are you okay?"

Predictably, Ruth didn't answer. She let out a long, soughing sigh that lifted her shoulders. Her feet pushed against the mulch, digging beneath it.

"Stop. Let me check you out. Stop," Tamar repeated, harshly this time.

"Where am I? Why are we here?" Her mother gripped the front of her T-shirt. She clung to Tamar, shaking. Weeping. Afraid.

What could Tamar do then but hold her?

A bright swath of light swung over them, then beyond, and back again. The beam from a cop car's searchlight. The car had pulled into the empty parking lot.

"C'mon. Let's get you up. On your feet."

Behind her the crunch of feet on the mulch came closer. Another light pinned itself on them, this time from a flashlight. With her hands holding her mother upright, she couldn't turn all the way around, but she could see a tall figure from the corner of her eye.

"You all right? Miss?" The light swung again.

"It's my mother," Tamar said. "She's . . . not well. She went wandering. I'm trying to get her home, officer, can you help?"

In seconds, the man knelt beside her. "Is she hurt?"

"No. She fell off the swing. I don't think she's hurt. Just disoriented. And tired." Tamar shifted her mother's weight, what little where was of it. She met the officer's eyes. "She'll be fine, once I get her home."

"Ma'am?" He shone the light on her mother's face. "Are you all right?"

"She'll be fine," Tamar repeated. She put a hand up to block the light. "Can you please not shine that in her face?"

"Ma'am, are you all right?" The officer asked again. "Can you tell me your name?"

"I've had many names," her mother said.

"Her name is Ruth," Tamar told him.

He shone the light on her face, blinding her for a moment before she held up a hand. The brightness still streamed through her fingers and found its way into her eyes until she turned her head.

"Do you have any identification on you?"

Tamar moved, shifting as best she could into a squat, so she could lift her mother into a sitting position. The officer took a step back to give them room but didn't do anything else to help. Tamar winced again at the pain in her wounded foot.

"Is that your blood?" The cop shone the light to a splash of crimson on her dirty foot.

"I cut myself. Look, are you going to help us or not?"

"Do have any identification on you?"

"Right. Let me just grab my passport. Oh, that's right," Tamar said, "I'm in my *pajamas*. I ran out after my mother when I realized she'd gone missing. So sorry, I didn't think to grab my purse."

She couldn't tell him she'd woken up here with no recollection of how she'd managed to get here herself, much less with her mother. She couldn't tell him of the mornings she'd woken with aches and bruises she couldn't explain, her feet dirty and scratched. She could not tell him of how her mother had escaped from Somerset House and walked all the way to her house, all by herself, with no idea how to get there.

"This is my daughter. Her name is Tammy Glass. She lives at 132 South Sheffield Drive." Ruth paused for a second and rattled off Tamar's cell phone number. "You can call her if you want to."

"I don't have . . ." Tamar looked at him. "My phone is at home."

"Ma'am, I'm going to take you to my car, all right?" The cop offered his arm to Ruth.

Ruth took it, leaning on him heavily. "Well, aren't you just a fine young man? And so handsome too. Are you single? Tamar isn't married."

He gave Tamar a somewhat amused glance at the befuddled granny routine. "I'm married."

"Oh, your wife is a lucky lady. Oops, I shouldn't assume. Maybe it's your husband?" Ruth covered her mouth against a flirtatious giggle that took Tamar back in time. Her mother had flirted with everyone. The guy at the post office, the grocery store clerk, all of her teachers from elementary to high school.

"As a matter of fact, I do have a husband," the cop said. "His name is Bruce. Come with me?"

He was escorting her like he was taking her to the prom, and Ruth was eating it up. Tamar watched them walk away from her. Ruth moved slowly, unsteadily, supported by the officer.

Tamar's foot hurt. Her blood had soaked into the mulch. She limped when she walked, but if she didn't catch up to them, it looked as though they were going to leave her behind.

"Doesn't he worry about you?" Ruth was saying as the cop led her to his patrol car and opened the front passenger door for her.

That did not seem right. Tamar had had far fewer run-ins with the police over the years than her mother ever had, but surely, they didn't go around putting people in the front seats of their cars, even if they didn't think the person was breaking the law? By the time she caught up to them, however, Ruth was firmly ensconced in the passenger seat.

"Hey," Tamar said. "Hello?"

The officer turned. She could read his badge now. It said Phan. He opened the back door for her and waited for her to get in. She did, hesitantly. The back of the patrol car smelled like feet and fast food. Her stomach curdled.

The drive home took about five minutes, but she sat in the back seat for another three while Officer Phan helped her mother out of the car and into the house. By the time he got back to the car, Tamar was convinced he'd forgotten all about her. In fact, when he got into the driver's seat, she was sure of it.

"Hey," she said. Then, softer, with a rap on the screen between the front and back. "Officer Phan. Can you let me out?"

He turned to look at her through the screen. His expression was blank. He frowned. Got out, opened her door, and let her out. He stared at her for a long uncomfortable minute while she balanced on her unhurt foot and waited for him to do or say . . . something. He stared at her for so long that the tension and anxiety from her nightwalking began to morph into fear that he was going to arrest her. Or hell, the way his hand went to his weapon for a second, shoot her.

"Officer Phan," Tamar managed to say, her voice hoarse. "Are you okay?"

"You have a good night. Take care of that mother of yours," he said. "She's a real lady."

Then he got in his car and pulled out of her driveway as Tamar stood and watched him, incapable of doing anything else.

Across the street, a light was on in Ross's living room. With the sheer curtains drawn, everything inside was blurry, but a figure looked as though it were peering out. When had Ross come home from the hospital? Was he okay? Tamar was ashamed to admit she had no real idea; if anything, she'd been avoiding even thinking about what had happened to her neighbor and whatever part Ruth might have played in his accident.

But he had that camera system set up, she thought. He would have footage of them leaving the house. If she could see it, she could . . .

"What?" she muttered aloud. "See yourself being hag-ridden by your own mother?"

At least she'd know, Tamar thought. Her foot might have stopped bleeding, but when she put it down into the soft and too-long grass, the pain made her hiss. She'd know what really happened.

But didn't she really know already?

Inside her own house, the study light came on. That room had slatted blinds, and she had a decent view of Ruth pacing back and forth in front of the window. She looked like she was talking, her hands waving. Mouth moving. She turned, her face contorted, as she shook her hands in a fury. She flailed and moved out of sight. Then back into it. As Tamar watched, her mother punched herself in the face.

Then again.

Again.

"Shit." Tamar ran as best she could, limping, to the front door.

It was locked.

She pounded the keypad, which beeped cheerily but did not let her in. She tried again, slower, fingers trembling. This time it worked, and she yanked the front door open and ran inside. Her foot left splotches of blood with every step. By the time she got to the closed door of the study, she anticipated finding her mother on the floor, perhaps covered in blood. She flung open the door.

Ruth sat on the edge of the bed that had taken the place of the couch. She wore a placid and serene expression despite the purpling bruises on her face. She hummed under her breath, something wordless, the tune familiar but unnamable. A lullaby. She smiled but didn't look up as Tamar entered the room.

"Ruth?"

But her mother only hummed and smiled, and then she lay down, curled on her side, her head on the pillow facing away. The humming stopped. Her shoulders lifted, then dropped. Tamar went around to the side of the bed to face her, certain this time she would see the blank gaze of death.

Ruth was sound asleep.

CHAPTER

23

"**B**UT IT'S YOUR milestone birthday!" Lovey's protest rang out through the screen.

Tamar gave her sister a stolid look. Lovey had been trying to plan a trip for her and Mark and the kids to fly out to Ohio for her fiftieth. There was no way Tamar was going to let her sister bring her family around Ruth.

No fucking way.

She had always protected her sister as best she could from the things that happened in their house. The drinking, the drugs, and the strange men Tamar found in the kitchen in the mornings when she got up for school. None of them had stuck around long enough to pretend to be stepfathers. None of them had ever seemed like possible allies.

"It's not a good time for me right now. I have a lot of work, and getting Ruth into some kind of facility is taking longer than I thought it would," Tamar said. "It's just not going to work, Lovey."

"But . . ." her sister's shoulders slumped. She looked tired and sad. She shook her head and leaned in closer to the screen. "I want to do something nice and fun for you. Maybe even give you a little break from Mom?"

Yes, yes, yes, a thousand times, please. Take her away from me. I don't care where she goes, just make her go away.

But not to Lovey. Not around the children. Ruth could not be trusted with them. It was bad enough for Tamar to see Ruth's disintegration. How much worse would it be for the people who loved her?

Ruth had never done the things to Lovey that she'd done to Tamar. But what if she started?

Tamar's need to see her sister was a bone-deep ache, a relentless internal throbbing, the persistent dull pain of a tooth about to crack. She'd moved away from the friends she'd cultivated in New York. The pandemic had kept her from traveling and later from making new friends. And Lovey, with her family, had been so far, so far, for all this time, and it had been so long since Tamar had been able to hug her.

She had always protected Lovey, and she always would.

Tamar kept her expression neutral. "With Shawn here, it's been great. No trouble at all. Really."

"But that's only during the day, isn't it? You said she's been getting more frail. You had to move her downstairs. What about at night?"

"She's fine," Tamar said. "I have one of those fancy baby monitors, so I can hear if she gets up."

She hadn't bothered to put a lock on the outside of Ruth's door. A lock, it seemed, wouldn't be enough. If Ruth wanted in . . . or out . . . well, she'd get what she wanted.

Lovey frowned. "No more nightwalking?"

"Nope."

"But you said she's not talking anymore."

Tamar shook her head. Since the night at the playground, her mother had barely spoken at all, and if she did walk at night, she didn't take Tamar with her. "No, not so much. She's gone basically nonverbal. But she seems happy and content."

"No response from any place you applied?" Lovey sounded frustrated.

Tamar shook her head again. "I've got it on my list of things to do, to follow up with them all."

"Can I help? Make some calls, anything?"

"Look," Tamar said, "I'm working on it. And I love and appreciate that you want to visit me for my birthday, but honestly, I just can't right now. I just can't."

Her sister sighed. "You're drinking again?"

"Again. You make it sound like I hit rock bottom and had some dark moment. I didn't drink for years because I didn't want to," Tamar said. Her wineglass was empty. She'd done a few hits off her vape pen before this call.

"And now you want to?"

"I'm turning fifty," Tamar said wryly. "If you can't acquire a few bad habits in your lifetime, what's the point of getting older?"

Lovey laughed but didn't seem amused. "I worry about you. That's all. I know you always had a real issue with her drinking. And I don't blame you," she added hastily. "I'm sure it was awful."

"It was. I'm glad you never had to know it the way I did," Tamar said.

"I just wish . . . I don't know. Are you okay? Tell me you're okay, and I'll stop worrying." Lovey's expression turned anxious.

"I'm okay. I promise." Tamar cocked an ear for the sound of voices from downstairs. She could hear a male voice singing along with "Chim Chim Cher-ee." "Shawn really has been great. A real blessing. Listen, Lovey, I have to run. Shabbat starts in a couple of hours, and I have some work I have to finish before I knock off for the night."

Lovey looked surprised. "Oh. You're doing that again?"

"Again with the 'again,'" Tamar said lightly.

"I didn't know. That's all."

There was so, so much that Lovey didn't know.

"The Reform shul had its food festival," Tamar explained. "I ordered a few meals to support them, and since they were promoted as a family Shabbat ready-made meal, I'd figured I'd make a night of it."

Her first month of college, Tamar had been startled into accepting an invitation to attend a Hillel Friday night Shabbat dinner and service. Startled because she'd wondered how the girl who'd invited her had known that Tamar was Jewish. Startled that anyone voluntarily attended religious services. She'd become a regular after that first night.

Shabbat had always brought her peace, something she could definitely use.

"And Mom's okay with it?"

"Ruth," Tamar said, "seems to be okay with mostly everything these days."

Lovey frowned. "I guess that's better than if she was combative?"

"It is."

"Before you go," her sister said, "at least check your email. If you won't let us come out to celebrate in person, at least look at the gift I got you."

"Okay. Hang on." Tamar settled the laptop as she picked up her phone and swiped to check her inbox. She laughed, incredulous, and looked at her sister's expectant face. "Whaaaat?"

"Do you hate it?"

"No, of course I don't hate it. I've been looking at getting one." Tamar peered at the email letting her know that Lovey had gifted her a complete test kit and results package for DNATESTER. "Wow."

"I got one for me too. And for Mark." Lovey beamed. "I thought it would be so interesting, you know? We don't know anything about our family history, really."

Because their father had sliced his own throat in a seedy motel room when Lovey had been an infant. Because their mother had despised her own mother and never allowed her to be part of her life. Because, Tamar thought, maybe there were some things that were simply meant never to be known.

"Well, this is exciting," she said.

"You really like it?"

Lovey looked so hopeful how could Tamar break that bubble? She'd spent the entire first eleven years of her baby sister's life protecting her from everything she possibly could and the next thirty-plus years trying to make up for abandoning her. Lovey had forgiven her, but that was only because she had no idea what horrors Tamar had willingly left behind even knowing her sister might be the next target. Tamar had never forgiven herself for that; she probably never would, just as she would never tell Lovey about everything that really happened back then.

"I love it. Thank you. It's perfect," Tamar said.

For once, she was the one who had to get off the call because she had something pressing. It was a relief to end it, so she could let the fake smile fade off her face. She had some time to finish up some work before she had to pick up the food and come home, light the candles and pour the wine. She'd invited Shawn to stay but wasn't surprised or offended when he said he had other plans. He'd leave work tonight at five, and he wouldn't be back until nine in the morning on Monday. That left an entire weekend for Tamar and Ruth to be alone.

She needed to prepare herself.

CHAPTER

24

ANXIETY ASSAULTED HER with the strength of a fist to her chin as Tamar waited on Ross's front porch for him to answer the door-bell. She held a paper and foil wrapped package in each hand. If he was at home, he'd be able to look at his doorbell camera and see who it was. He could choose not to answer the door.

She knew he was there, though. She'd seen the lights on in his house for the past few nights, and she'd watched his friend's car come and go. This last time, the friend had returned Ross's puppy. That had to mean he was at least up and about again. Right?

She was almost ready to turn away when the door opened.

Ross looked better than she'd expected. His leg was in a cast and a brace of some kind, and he had a crutch under one arm. His face still bore mottled bruising, much of which had turned to a sickly yellow and green. He had stitches in his lower lip that looked almost ready to come out.

"Hi," he said.

"Hi, Ross. I brought you these." She held up the packages of food. "I ordered four from my synagogue to support their food festival, but I only need two. It's matzah ball soup, some roast chicken and potatoes, a couple of homemade challah rolls and salad. Oh, and I think there's pie or cake for dessert."

At first, he said nothing. The puppy appeared and sat, panting, at his feet. He bent, carefully, slowly, to stroke a hand over its head.

He straightened. Carefully. Slowly. "That's really nice of you. Thanks."

"I can bring it in for you. It just needs to be warmed up a little bit. Or you can put it in the fridge for later? Or freeze it," she added, saying too much, talking too fast.

Ross blinked. After a silent moment, he stepped aside to let her pass him. She stepped into his cool, dim interior and followed the square of brightness back to the kitchen at the back of the house.

"You can put one in the fridge," he said. "And if you don't mind warming up the other one, I'd appreciate it."

"Sure. No problem."

"Would you like to stay?" he asked from behind her as she bent to put one package in the refrigerator.

Tamar turned. "Oh, that's really nice, but I have to get back home. My mother . . ."

"Right," Ross said. "Your mother."

"She has a caregiver, but he leaves at five o'clock." It was almost four-thirty now.

Ross licked his stitches and winced. "How is your mother?"

"She's . . ." Tamar cleared her throat. She stepped toward him. "Ross. I'm sorry about what happened. Did she . . . was she . . . ?"

"I don't really remember anything," he said with a curious cock of his head. "They told me that it's common after an injury like mine to blank out as much as a few days leading up to the accident. I guess that's a blessing, isn't it? If you believe in that sort of thing. Do you?"

"Believe in blessings? I guess so." Tamar removed the foil from one food container before putting it in the microwave and turning it on.

Ross sat heavily in a kitchen chair with his injured leg stuck out in front of him. The puppy went to its water bowl and slurped sloppily. It came back to Ross and lay down, nose in its paws.

"If you believe in blessings, I guess you have to also believe in curses, huh?"

She turned to face him. "Yes. I suppose you do."

"You came over to see my footage again, didn't you?" He sounded resigned.

"Do you have some I should see?" She wasn't going to play any kind of games with him. He didn't look to be capable of it, and she wasn't in the mood.

"I think so. But every time I try to remember what it is," Ross said, "I find myself forgetting what I was trying to look for in the first place."

The microwave beeped, but Tamar didn't take the food out of it. She stood in place as though her feet had been nailed to the floor. The cut she'd gotten on the playground throbbed, rotten like an infected tooth, although she'd cleaned it every single day and it looked as though it was healing just fine.

"Here." Ross pulled his phone out of his pocket and slid it across the table in her direction. "It's the DingDong app. Just pull it up and check the history."

She did, hesitant and feeling weird. Using someone else's phone, even with permission, felt as intimate as a kiss. She opened the app and scrolled through the days to find the one she needed. She took a deep breath and tapped the screen. It took a few seconds to load, but when it did, she choked on her own saliva, which ran, hot and bitter, down the back of her throat. She wanted to spit but could not.

The short video clip showed exactly what she'd half remembered. Ruth, mounted on her back as though they were playing a game of horsey. Tamar, barefoot, wearing pajamas, stumbled out the front door and shut it behind her. Locked it. She stepped off the front porch. Walked across the lawn. Ruth riding her, both hands fixed around Tamar's throat and her feet propped in Tamar's cupped hands like stirrups. She kicked them into her daughter's ribs the way a person on horseback would dig spurs into the beast's sides. The clip ended as they headed down the sidewalk toward the corner.

Tamar deleted it.

She handed the phone back to Ross. She finished warming his food and put it on the table for him. She gave his dog a thorough petting, not because she liked dogs one way or another, but because she couldn't apologize for what she now was certain Ruth had done.

Going to see the old house had convinced Tamar that her childhood home had not been the problem. Seeing the video had cemented what she'd tried for years to wash away like sand beneath waves. Something was very, very wrong with Ruth. It went beyond the drinking, the drugs, the promiscuity.

Something was inside her mother. It had always wanted to hurt Tamar. It still did.

"Thanks for the dinner," Ross said in a much brighter voice than he'd had when she came in. His expression looked more present too. "I appreciate it. You're a good neighbor."

"It's the least I could do," she said, and meant it. "The very, very least."

He looked at the clock. "Should you get going? You said you needed to get home to your mother."

"Oh, I do," Tamar said. "I absolutely do."

Tonight, they would light candles and sing the blessings Ruth had never bothered to teach her. They'd celebrate a sabbath Ruth had never seemed to acknowledge. And after that, Tamar thought as she stepped out onto Ross's front porch and closed his door behind her . . . after that?

She thought she might kill her mother.

25

Tamar waited until Shawn left for the weekend before setting the table as the food warmed in the oven. She put out candles in her crystal candlesticks and laid the embroidered challah cover over the rolls from the food festival packages. She added two wineglasses and uncorked a bottle of red. She even added a two-handled pitcher for hand washing.

Then she called her mother to Shabbos dinner.

When she didn't come, Tamar went looking for her. Ruth stared without expression at the television. She had to be guided to the table, but she sat without protest and put her napkin on her lap without prompting. She smiled, but her gaze didn't quite focus on anything until she saw the two glasses of wine.

She'd drunk most of hers before Tamar could stop her. Great gulps of it, red wine splashing from her mouth and staining the front of her yellow blouse. When she put the glass down and grinned, her teeth were pinkish.

"You're supposed to wait for the blessing," Tamar said.

Ruth frowned, her gaze cloudy. Her mouth slightly slack. "Huh?"

Ah. Speech instead of the silence Ruth had kept up for the past few weeks. Tamar gestured at the table settings. "It's Shabbos. There are blessings you say first."

"If you must." Her voice was clear this time. Ruth sat back and held up her glass for more.

"You shouldn't have any more. You shouldn't have any wine at all."

Her mother shrugged. "And yet you gave me the glass."

Tamar didn't immediately pour a second round. Gone was the smiling, charming woman who'd called her honey, the woman her mother had become and remained in the years after Tamar left her behind. This Ruth sounded more like the one Tamar remembered.

"Aren't you supposed to just say no?" Tamar asked.

"Who are you, Nancy Reagan?" Ruth's laugh caw-cawed out of her. She waved the empty wineglass. "I'm a grownup lady. Fill 'er up."

Tamar did, generously. She'd known it would only be a matter of time before the real Ruth returned. She'd been waiting.

"I'm starving. Where's dinner?"

"We're going to say the blessings first," Tamar said again.

She'd said them for years and should have known them by heart but used the little prayerbook to make sure she wasn't messing them up. First, the candles. Then the wine. She lifted the glass and let the sing-song words fall off her tongue. She wanted to let herself get lost in the ritual and beauty of the ancient prayers, but she made herself carefully watch her mother instead.

What was she looking for? She didn't quite know. Hissing, recoiling, like a vampire confronted by a crucifix? Ruth didn't so much as sneer when Tamar said the prayers. She even hummed along, a surprise since Tamar would have bet good money her mother didn't know the tunes. Ruth sipped daintily at her second glass of wine. She symbolically washed her hands with the pitcher and even accepted the torn chunk of challah roll dipped in the sprinkle of salt. If any of the spiritual trappings brought her harm, she wasn't showing it. In fact, the only sign at all of anything changing was that ratcheting laughter and the sly smiles.

"This was nice," Ruth said when dinner was finished and Tamar had taken away the plates to put in the dishwasher. Her words were the tiniest bit slurred. "I'd forgotten how nice it could be."

"Did you ever observe Shabbat?" Tamar asked.

"My mother did. So, we did, when I was a child."

"Why didn't you, when you were raising us?" She wanted more wine but held off pouring it.

Ruth looked thoughtful. "Didn't I?"

"No. Never."

Her mother sighed. "I suppose I didn't feel like it. It's hard raising little ones, especially by yourself. Friday nights were my time to relax. Making a big dinner, slaving over the stove . . . aren't you supposed to rest on the sabbath? All of that was so much work. Typical, isn't it? Men make the rules, but women do the work."

Friday nights had been Ruth's night out. She'd hired a babysitter more religiously than she'd ever lit candles or blessed wine and bread. She'd stopped doing even that when Tamar was ten, leaving her behind to watch over Lovey while Ruth went out to Rooney's or wherever she went. Sometimes, she came home in the wee hours of the morning. Sometimes she came home by Saturday afternoon. Most of the time, Tamar hoped her mother wouldn't ever come home again.

"I like Shabbat. I find a great comfort in it," Tamar said. "Too many people get frenzied about the weekend, filling it up with things to do. I like the idea of forcing yourself to take some quiet time."

They stared at each other. Ruth lifted her glass and drained it of the remnants of the wine. She held it out for more.

"You shouldn't have any more," Tamar told her.

Ruth held out the glass.

Tamar filled it, then her own. That was the last of this bottle. They lifted their glasses to each other in a silent toast. It was the first time she'd ever shared a drink with her mother.

"Let's sit outside. It's a nice night," Ruth said after a bit. "Bring another bottle, Tamar. You started this. You might as well see it to the end."

To the end, Tamar thought as she opened another bottle and poured them fresh glasses. They both went out onto the flagstone patio in her backyard, where she switched on the softly twinkling fairy lights she'd strung along the fence. What *was* the end of this?

Ruth settled into the wicker rocker and took the glass from Tamar. "You have this nice backyard, all those pretty string lights, and you never use them. You never have anyone over. You're so lonely."

This was neither true nor false. "I spent twenty years being lonely when I was with someone. I'm alone. Not lonely."

"You should find yourself a new man," Ruth said authoritatively.

Considering that all of her recent texts to Miguel had gone unread and unanswered, Tamar didn't think that was likely to happen. "I don't need a man to be happy."

"You don't even have any friends."

Tamar shifted in her chair to look her mother in the face. "Is that what you think? That I'm some lonely, friendless, frigid loser?"

Soft laughter. "Aren't you?"

"I have friends. They don't live around here, but I do have them. I used to travel to visit them, before we went on lockdown."

"Why don't you go visit them now?" Ruth asked.

"Because," Tamar said, "now I'm dealing with you."

Ruth pursed her lips and drank some more wine. "I'm not stopping you from living your life. If you want to travel, you should go. I always wanted to travel, but instead I had kids. I should've—"

She stopped herself. Shrugged. Sipped daintily with the greed of an alcoholic trying to pretend she didn't want to gulp.

"You had the right idea," Ruth said finally into the silence between them. "Not having children."

"You're particularly chatty tonight. What's up with that?"

Ruth shifted in her chair to look at her. "What do you mean?"

"Is it the wine? It loosens your tongue? You've been basically silent since Shawn started coming. Don't you like him?"

"I like him just fine," Ruth told her. She drank some wine. "I'm not sure what you mean."

Tamar didn't pursue it. If Ruth wasn't going to acknowledge that she'd hardly said more than a sentence or two since the night Officer Phan had brought them home, there was no use arguing about it. In the grass, fireflies shimmered. The soft night air, cool compared to the heat of the July days, carried the sound of voices on the breeze. The houses on either side of hers were alive with light and the sound of children playing in the backyards, but the privacy fence blocked the sight of them.

"Why did you hate your mother so much?" Tamar asked quietly.

Ruth let her head fall back to look up at the sky. There was too much light pollution to really see the stars. "I didn't hate my mother."

"You acted like you did," Tamar said, unwilling to let her mother rewrite this bit of history.

Ruth looked at her. "My mother wanted a son. When she had me instead, she made it very clear that she wished she'd never borne a daughter. I guess something like that stays with a person. But I don't know why you think I hated her. I loved her."

Tamar waited for her mother to ask why she hated her, but Ruth didn't. Instead, they both sat and sipped wine and stared up at the sky in which they could not see the stars. After a while, Ruth's head dropped. The last drops of her wine spilled as her glass tilted, and Tamar rescued it before it fell out of her loose fingers. A small snore wuffled out of Ruth's lips.

"Why do you hate me?" Tamar whispered.

Her mother's eyes glinted, half-open. She smacked her lips and shifted in the chair. "I don't hate you. I love you. I've always loved you, and I always will."

Ruth had always lied. She always would. But in that moment, Tamar allowed herself to believe that maybe what her mother had said was true.

Leaving Ruth snoring in the chair, Tamar took the empty glasses and bottle into the kitchen to clean up. The low rise of her mother's voice drifted to her through the screen of the open French door. She turned off the kitchen lights and stood at the door, watching Ruth's slumped shape. She hadn't moved. She murmured, though, a string of words Tamar couldn't quite catch.

Drunk, Tamar thought guiltily. She'd not only permitted but encouraged her elderly, alcoholic mother to get drunk. She would never tell this to Lovey, or to anyone, that she'd gotten her mother drunk so maybe Ruth would slip and fall in the shower. Hit her head. Maybe she'd choke to death in her sleep. Maybe she'd slip while using a too-sharp knife and bleed out while Tamar slept.

Ruth spoke again, a louder mutter this time. "I needed you."

"It's time to go to bed," Tamar said.

Once Ruth was settled in her room, Tamar went upstairs and took a shower. She slipped between clean sheets that were too heavy for the heat. She tossed them off and checked the thermostat, which claimed the temperature was sixty-three degrees. She was never going to be able to sleep, not with her hair sticking to her cheeks and throat, not with her pajamas slowly dampening with sweat.

Things had always been worse in the summer.

She'd imagined her mother dead, and she'd imagined killing her, but in the end, of course she hadn't been able to go through with it. It was the lack of sleep driving her to this madness. Of course she couldn't *kill* her mother. The best she could do was hope for her to die all on her own.

Tamar opened her eyes wide to look at the ceiling. Light streamed in from her windows. She had slept, after all. She almost didn't dare move, testing her body for fresh pains that flared as she moved her feet against the mattress. She could feel dirt clinging to her skin. She could smell it on her, and she bit back a cry as she forced herself to sit up.

Ruth lay curled on her side, facing away from her. Her feet and clothes were clean. She stirred when Tamar got out of bed and opened her eyes. They stared at each other for a long, long time before Ruth spoke.

"Where am I?" she said.

CHAPTER

26

*T*AM'S BODY ACHES. *Her lower back, her belly, the places inside of her. The back of her hand is bruised from where they put the needle in. The medicine was supposed to keep her calm, even make her sleepy, but she was wide awake the whole time. She shouldn't have been able to feel anything, but she felt it all.*

The bleeding isn't bad, though. No worse than a regular heavy period. She's supposed to take it easy for a few days, which she plans to do. Lovey is at sleepaway camp for the next two weeks, so Tam will have the house to herself while her mother is working . . . or out . . . or in bed, hungover.

She hasn't spoken to Miguel since last week. The breakup shouldn't have been a surprise. They were planning to go to college in different places. She'd never believed they were meant to do something dumb like get married young. She hadn't expected him to be so adamant against the abortion.

"Don't I have a say in it?" he'd demanded.

"Unless you're the one who has to be pregnant and give birth," she'd said, "no. You don't."

It wasn't the first time they'd fought—their friendship had begun in elementary school and only turned romantic when they became juniors, so they'd had plenty of stupid arguments throughout the years. This fight had been different. Miguel had cried. Tam had not.

Now she tosses and turns in her bed, too hot because even though the house has central air, her mother insists on closing the upstairs vents and setting the thermostat high to keep the electric bills low. Her mother loves the extreme heat. It gives her an excuse to walk around half naked. When Tam has a house of her own someday, she vows that she will never be too hot or too cold. Ever. For now, she suffers with sweating and kicks off the covers even though it makes her feel too exposed. Vulnerable.

*She looks toward the doorway. Her mother took the door off the hinges months ago, claiming that if Tam was going to fuck a boy in **her** house, she'd lost the right to privacy. Tam and Miguel had never done it in her bedroom, anyway, only in the basement rec room or in the back seat of his car. Once in his room when his parents were away for a couple of days. They'd only done it a handful of times overall, but it really had only taken that one time.*

Tam rolls onto her side. The hallway outside her bedroom is dark, but the shadows move. It's summer. Things are always worse in the summer. The stink of rot filters even through the closed air vents. Doors slam open and closed on their own. The TV runs through channels all by itself. The doorbell rings, insistent and jangling, at midnight, and two in the morning, and three forty-four, and at five, but nobody's there, so a full night's sleep is almost impossible. Sometimes she thinks she would agree to anything, no matter how terrible, if only she could sleep.

Her eyes close. She draws in a breath. The smell is there. Something thick, cloying. The water in the bottom of a vase of dead flowers. The clot of hair you pull from a shower drain. She presses her face to the pillow to block it out, but she can't.

The floorboards creak.

Terror seizes her. No matter how many times this happens, she can't ever stop being afraid of it. A hot gust of breath washes over her bare legs. With a whimper, without looking, Tam digs her feet below the sheet and blindly searches for it so she can cover herself. If it touches her, she's going to scream.

It touches her.

She shrieks and punches at nothing. Her fists pass through nothing but shadow. She flails, her feet tangling. She's trapped in the bed. Her closet door slams open and shut, over and over. Her dresser drawers do the same.

It laughs.

The throaty chuckle pushes another wash of stink over her. Tam screams again. She wrenches her feet free and rolls, falling out of her bed. A slow, hot gush of blood oozes out of her, leaking around the edges of the thick pad and down her thighs. She stumbles to her feet.

"Leave me alone!" Tam shouts. "Why can't you just leave me alone!"

In the doorway, something looms. Its head touches the top of the door-frame. Its thin arms reach nearly to the floor. Its legs bend, but not at the knee.

The hall light comes on. The doorway is empty for a second or so until her mother centers herself in it. Her makeup is smeared. Lipstick worn off. Mascara and eyeliner drawing tear stains on her cheeks. She wears a cotton nightgown, the buttons undone nearly to her crotch. Her blond updo is squashed, lopsided.

"What the hell is going on in here? Tammy? What . . . Oh, for . . . what did you do?"

Tam looks down at herself. Blood trickles down her legs. She shakes.

Her mother's fingers curl into claws. "What. Did. You. Do?"

Tam cannot, will not answer her. She tries to push past to get to the bathroom but makes it only a few feet down the hallway before her mother reaches out to grab her arm and spin her around. The slap is hard and unexpected. Her mother has been awful enough to shove her down the stairs, but she's never, ever hit her.

Ruth slaps her again.

It is the first time Tam thinks of her mother by her given name, but how can she call this woman mother after what she is doing? Ruth's fist crunches Tam's nose. Her cheek. Her lip. Her eye. There is more blood. Tam tastes it, bitter and metallic and somehow reminding her of that stink that always heralds the arrival of the thing that haunts this house.

Tam staggers back hard enough to hit the wall. Framed photos fall, glass crashing, and she steps on one. Pain slices her foot. She cries out.

Ruth hits her in the gut.

Tam doubles over. When she gets up, breathless, sick with pain, she launches herself at the woman in front of her. Her own fists fly. It's Ruth's turn to stagger back, back, back. Her elbows knock more photos off the wall. She puts up her hands to shield her face. Tam hits her wherever she can.

The growl is low, a rabid dog sound. When she lowers her hands, Ruth shows off a grin full of blood-smeared teeth. Her eyes are dark holes, a void, twin crimson pinpricks. Her mouth yawns, gaping, black and open and endless, ready to swallow up everything in its path.

Tam closes her eyes. This is her mother. This is not her mother. This is a nightmare.

This is not a dream.

"You killed it," Ruth says.

*"It's **my** choice!"*

*"No, no, no," Ruth says. "It was supposed to be **mine**."*

Tam forces her eyes to open. Ruth pants. Her hands reach, grabbing but missing.

Tam runs.

She runs out into the street in nothing but her pajamas, blood smearing her body, her feet bare. She runs across the street to hammer on Miguel's door, but no lights come on inside. What time is it? She runs to the house next door, looking over her shoulder at her own front door, which hangs open and reveals nothing but blackness beyond it.

Nobody will open their door for her. She screams, pounding. A light comes on in one house. The curtains flick to the side. A face peers out. But nobody opens the door.

Where can she go, if nobody will help her? Where can she go without money, clothes, no shoes, her body still recovering from a fifteen-minute procedure that, she is convinced, saved her life. What can she do but run and scream and pound on doors that will not open?

27

G ROWING UP IN Kettering, Tamar had always thought their family
was one of the only Jewish families in town. That was how Ruth
had made it seem, anyway. When Tamar moved back, she'd been
shocked to discover multiple synagogues within a few minutes of her
house.

She and Garrett had always belonged to a Conservative congregation. Temple Beth Shalom was Reform, but the website had used the
most welcoming language, and their calendar had featured several
events geared toward singles or adults-only. She paid her dues every year
and dutifully bought her tickets for the High Holidays, and she promised herself that one day soon she'd become active again, but time had
passed, and she never had.

The synagogue was a nondescript gray and brown building on the
corner of two busy streets in an otherwise residential area. The parking
lot was empty when Tamar pulled in, but the website had said their
office was open from nine until three on Thursdays, and it was just after
two now. She turned off the car and pulled the box from the passenger
seat to put on her lap for a moment while she lifted the lid. Inside, the
jumbled mezuzot and the torn and dirty scrolls didn't look any different
than they had in the basement of her childhood home. She shook the
box a little, dislodging a few of the cases to reveal a few more scrolls. She
took one out and unfurled it. Water and dirt stained the cream-colored

parchment, smearing the Hebrew words she wouldn't have been able read anyway.

She'd texted to tell Miguel to tell him she'd visited her old house, since he'd been the one to suggest it. Mostly, she wanted to tell him that the house on Spring Hill Drive had never been the problem. She wanted to tell him about the things going on in the house she lived in now. Because she had to tell someone, didn't she?

Garrett had always shouted at horror movie characters who'd stayed in the place where scary things were going on. He'd never understood how terrible, even terrifying things can become normal. How you can get so used to being scared all the time that you can become almost numbed to it. But Miguel might understand why she didn't simply run screaming from her house now and never come back, because he knew what she'd gone through in the past.

Her fingers tapped out another message but deleted it. There was reaching out, and then there was chasing. He'd answer her when he had a chance. Or, he wouldn't.

She might have sat there for five more minutes. Maybe ten. But a police car entered the parking lot, making a slow revolution around the outer edge. It slowed as it neared her car. Someone might have called them from inside. Tamar did look suspicious, just sitting there, and synagogue staff would be smart to call for help before they actually needed it.

She got out of the car, box in hand, and gave a nod to the police officer in the car. The cop returned it and rolled up his window as he drove away. Slowly. Watching. She could see his eyes on her in his side mirror.

Tamar didn't look back at him as she went up to the synagogue's front doors, where she pushed the intercom doorbell. She gave her name and the reason why she was there. She held up the box in the direction of the camera and was buzzed inside.

The office window was the sliding kind, like in a medical office. It faced the lobby, where signs on the walls still reminded people to socially distance, to mask up, to get their vaccines, although no such measures were currently in place. A big corkboard featured newer notices—the Jewish food festival, the religious school activities, a schedule of services. A reminder, bigger than the others, that the High Holidays were approaching, and tickets were available through the shul's office.

"Can I help you?" The woman behind the glass had to ask the question twice before Tamar heard her.

She held up the box again. Her hands were sweating. The internet had told her most synagogues would have a place to put damaged religious items.

"I emailed briefly with the rabbi about bringing these in? She said there was a genizah here?" Tamar stumbled a bit on the word, not sure if she was pronouncing it right.

"Oh. Sure. Hang on a second." The secretary bent back to her desk, lifting her phone and murmuring into it. She watched Tamar through the glass. She put down the phone and gestured as the second set of doors buzzed her an entrance. "Rabbi Feldman's office is down that hall to the left. She said to go on back."

The rabbi's office looked out onto lush green grass that sloped down to a stream where Tamar knew the congregation gathered for the annual Tashlich observance, throwing crumbs into the water in a symbolic tossing away of the year's sins. It was the same as every other clergy leader's office that Tamar had ever been to—cluttered with books and papers and smelling faintly, always faintly, of something she could never figure out. Like a library or a used bookstore. A good smell.

"Hello?" She knocked on the rabbi's open door.

"Come on in."

Tamar, box held in front of her, entered. Rabbi Feldman was bent over her desk, rifling through a bunch of folders and papers, but she looked up when Tamar came in. She smiled. Gestured.

"Come in," she repeated. "What can I do for you?"

"I have these." Tamar held out the box.

For a moment, the rabbi frowned in confusion before her eyes widened. "Right, right. You have the box of old mezuzot."

"Yes." Tamar put the box on the desk. The moment it left her hands, she wanted it back. She curled her fingers against her palms instead, not reaching.

"You said you found them in the basement of your new house?"

"No . . . the people who bought my mother's house found it in the basement. And they gave it to me."

"Oh, yes, of course. Your childhood home?" The rabbi looked at Tamar from the corner of her eye before opening the box. "Oh, these are lovely."

"Yes. My childhood home. But I don't remember ever having a mezuzah anywhere. My mother wasn't religious."

The rabbi gestured at the chair across from her desk, and although Tamar had not expected to stay longer than a few minutes, she sat. Rabbi Feldman took her own chair. She pushed her folders and papers out of the way and closed her laptop, pushing it also aside. She settled the box on the desk between them, the lid open. She took another peek inside before sitting back.

"Some of these look like antiques. Do you mind if I take them out?"

"No, not at all." She ought to leave, Tamar thought, but could not make herself go.

She watched the rabbi set out all the scroll cases, lining them up neatly side by side. Some were small and metal, others longer and taller, crafted of ceramic. One was bigger than the others, of glass that had been molded into ripples and waves.

"I know that one," Tamar said after a second. She closed her eyes in an extra-long blink, remembering. She looked at the rabbi. "It was on the front door, but only when I was really young. Before my sister was born."

"So, these were all probably in your house then too." The rabbi sat back. "But your mother took them down and put them in this box."

"Yes. I guess so."

"Any idea why she'd do that?" The rabbi sounded curious, not judgmental.

"Because she wasn't religious," Tamar repeated.

The rabbi made a small, assessing noise and peeked again into the box. "The scrolls are definitely no longer kosher. I can take care of properly disposing of them for you. Some of the cases are broken, but many of them are still okay. Are you sure you don't want them?"

"I . . ." A hot flush crept up her throat and into her cheeks. She took up the large glass one and turned it over and over in her hand. "This one. But I don't need the rest of them."

"Would you mind if I used them for young families moving into their first place? Many times people don't have the money to buy both a scroll and a case. I'm setting up a program here for people who want to become more observant get help with things like this."

"That sounds really nice. Sure." Tamar hesitated. The rabbi had a nice smile. "We never celebrated anything when I was growing up. Once, I asked my mother why we didn't have a Christmas tree. She said because we were Jewish. So I asked her why we didn't have a menorah, and she said because she was an atheist."

"Are *you* an atheist?" The rabbi asked, again without judgment.

"No. I don't know." Tamar laughed and shook her head. "I'm still trying to figure it out, I guess. I am more observant than my mother was. Well. I was for a while. Not so much lately."

"Yeah? What happened?"

"I got divorced," Tamar said. "The life I had when I was married didn't seem to fit me as well once I started living by myself."

There was a beat of silence, but it wasn't awkward. The rabbi opened her desk drawer and pulled out a small plastic bag with a zip top. Inside, a small cream scroll. Rabbi Feldman slid it across the desk toward her.

"Here. You'll need a kosher scroll for it."

Tamar hesitated. "Oh, I didn't bring any cash—"

"My gift to you," the rabbi said. "Anyway, the value of these cases is far more than this single scroll. You're doing a mitzvah."

Tamar took the small bag and the glass mezuzah case. "Thank you."

She didn't intend to use either one of them, but she didn't know how to insist she didn't want them.

"You're a member here?"

"I pay my dues."

The rabbi laughed. "That makes you a member, then. I haven't seen you at services. But I'm new myself. I started in early 2020, which meant I spent a lot of time *not* meeting my congregants. Were you active before? When you were married?"

"Not here. I grew up here and moved back here after the divorce. I joined because I thought I'd want to come to some of the social events, meet other Jews."

"So I have to ask, Tamar, is there something we can offer you here that would make you more inclined to participate? We have a welcome committee that's supposed to reach out to new members, send invitations for Shabbat dinners, that sort of thing."

"They did."

The rabbi nodded. "Ah."

"I ordered from the food festival," Tamar said after a pause. "They sent the tickets, but I didn't have anyone to sell them to. I work from home. So I just bought all four meals. I hadn't done a Shabbos dinner in a long time, but having the meals prompted me to do it."

"That sounds lovely," Rabbi Feldman said.

Tamar leaned forward a little, uncertain why she was talking so much, sharing so much, but feeling somehow desperate to share with someone. "My mother is living with me right now. It's been a difficult adjustment. I thought maybe having a nice ritual to share would help. No. That's not quite true."

She shook her head, trying to steady her voice. She drew in a breath, horrified that she might burst into tears. The rabbi reached for a box of tissues and, without a word, pushed them gently across the desk toward her.

"I do not have a good relationship with my mother, Rabbi."

"Many of us don't."

Tamar took a tissue, although so far she'd managed to fend off the tears. Once the initial confession was out, it felt easier to keep going. "She had a drinking and drug problem when I was growing up. She was hard to live with. I ran away from home right before I turned eighteen and didn't have much to do with her until I moved back here."

"You returned home because she needed you?"

"Oh, no. My sister and her husband were here, and their kids. I wanted to be close to family, and after splitting up with my ex, it seemed like a good time to make a big change. But my sister moved away and my mother . . ."

"She came to stay with you. Can I ask why?"

"She was kicked out of Somerset House. Nobody else will take her. We put in applications, we've had her assessed, but nobody's answering my calls." Tamar scrubbed at her lips with the back of her hand.

Rabbi Feldman sat back in her chair. "Are you familiar with the term sandwich generation? The ones taking care of elderly parents while also raising kids of their own?"

"I never had kids."

"I'm sorry. I shouldn't have been so careless to assume," the rabbi said.

Tamar shook her head. "It's not a sore subject or anything like that. But that would describe my sister, for sure. Anyway, they moved to California for her husband's job, so she couldn't take my mother. It was supposed to be temporary."

"But it's looking more permanent. Do you have someone to help?"

Tamar nodded. "I hired someone. He's been great with her."

"Do you have someone to help *you*, Tamar?" The rabbi asked gently.

Tamar shook her head.

"Well, I hope you'll consider me someone who'd like to help you, then. And," Rabbi Feldman added with a laugh, "you are not required to come to services, although I'd love to see you here."

"I should get going. The caregiver leaves at five. But, Rabbi . . . thank you," Tamar said sincerely. She stood.

The rabbi stood too and offered her hand. She didn't shake but squeezed Tamar's gently before letting it go. "I'm a listening ear anytime you need one. I mean that."

"Thanks, I'll keep that in mind," Tamar said with no intentions of ever taking the rabbi up on her offer.

Nobody believes children when they say they've seen something lurking in the closet or under the bed. Children are told it's all in their heads, or they've been having a bad dream. Nobody believes children who say they've seen a monster.

Nobody believed adults either.

CHAPTER

28

SHAWN OPENED THE door between the garage and the kitchen before she'd even turned off the engine. Tamar's heart sunk at the sight of his expression. This could not be good news.

"I'm not late, am I?" She fumbled with her phone as she got out of the car, swiping to check the time. "It's only four forty-five—"

"I need you to come inside here so we can talk," Shawn interrupted.

This was not the polite, soft-spoken young man she'd interviewed and hired, and it wasn't the upbeat, professional young man who'd arrived at work with a smile for the past two weeks. Shawn looked angry.

He also looked . . . scared.

He moved back from the doorway as she approached and led the way to the kitchen. He didn't stop at the door to the study, through which Tamar could hear the television. She paused to peek around the half-open door. Ruth sat motionless in her recliner, feet up, legs covered with the ugly burnt orange and avocado green afghan that had been spread across the back of the couch during Tamar's childhood. She stared at the TV, lips parted, eyes wide and blank.

By the time Tamar caught up to Shawn in the kitchen, he'd put on his sweatshirt and slung his bag across his chest.

"What happened today?" She wasn't sure if she ought to sit or stand. She hung her purse on the hook near the door, and her keys, but she kept her phone clutched tight in her now-sweating palm. Bitterness collected in her mouth, forcing her to swallow again and again. The house felt hotter than the air outside.

"I've been at this job for five years," Shawn said. "I don't want you to think that I'm not used to handling difficult patients. Okay?"

"You had excellent references. I believe you." Tamar grabbed a bottle of seltzer from the fridge and poured some into a glass. The fizz tickled her lips when she lifted it to her lips, but at the first sip her gut convulsed, and she put the glass back on the counter.

"I know that these people can't really help the things they say or do. I know that." His voice shook. Broke.

Tamar, confused, looked at him. "What exactly did she do?"

"You told me she'd had some trouble with her previous situation. You said she hadn't gotten along with some of the other residents, and that you weren't happy with how the facility handled it. You told me," Shawn said, "that your mother had wandered off more than once, and you couldn't trust the staff there to make sure she was safe."

"All of that is true," Tamar said, although he hadn't come out and accused her of lying. "Shawn, I'm sorry, but you're going to have to explain to me what's going on."

He shook his head and pulled the hooded sweatshirt closer around him. He crossed his arms. He would not look at her.

"Look," he said. "I've had people in my care be inappropriate with me before. They lose their control and their sense of what's right or wrong. Their minds aren't right, but their bodies can still work, you know what I mean?"

"Are you saying my mother came on to you?" Tamar put her hands on her hips, pressing her fingers into the sides of her belly. An old habit. Her fingertips didn't touch. Too much softness there. Nausea rose in her throat, but she forced it back.

"You don't sound surprised," Shawn said.

She sighed, choosing her words carefully. "My mother was . . . promiscuous. When she was younger."

Hey, little girl, is your mama around? No? Well, then, how 'bout you? Are you your mother's daughter?

Mom shows up to the pizza party at school to help hand out slices of soggy pizza and juice mixed from a powder, the reward to the class for surpassing their reading goal. She wears a low-cut blouse that shows the lacy edges of her bra. Her jeans are tight. She wears white high heels with them, the toes and heels worn with black smudges. She smells of Emeraude perfume, and her lipstick is always a little too bright.

Shawn's expression remained distraught. His lips trembled when he spoke. "I'm sure you can understand how careful I have to be, Ms. Glass. A young Black man, taking care of an elderly white woman? Life isn't *Driving Miss Daisy*. If your mother accused me of being inappropriate with her, I could lose my license. Hell, I could go to jail."

Tamar straightened her shoulders. "My mother has become basically nonverbal."

"No." He shook his head and pointed a finger at her. "She's mostly nonverbal with *you*."

She took a moment to let this sink in, thinking of last Friday night. "She talks to you?"

"Oh, yeah. She talks." He zipped the hoodie with several jerking motions and shoved his hands deep into the pockets. Pulling in on himself.

She recognized the posture of someone trying to make themselves smaller. "You never said anything to me about it."

"She started off fine, you know? Telling me good morning, how nice it was to see me again. I thought, hey, she's got some clarity. That can happen. I'll roll with it." Shawn shrugged. "She'd been declining since I started here, which wasn't a shock or anything. I didn't want to get you excited about something that might've been a one-time thing. People do that, you know? They hear their loved one talking in full sentences, and they get their hopes up that it means they're getting better. But then I figured out that she didn't want you to know she was in there."

"In where?" Tamar looked automatically down the hall toward the study.

"In here." Shawn tapped his finger to his temple. "Your mom, she doesn't want you to know she's *in there*."

Tamar took a long slug of the fizzy water to wash away any words that tried to come out. The cool liquid slid down her throat and hit her stomach like a handful of rocks. She turned away from him until she could take a breath.

"Why," she asked, "why would she do that?"

"That's between the two of you. It's not any of my business, and I'm not trying to make it my business either. I'm giving you my notice, right now. I'm done here."

"What exactly did she say to you?"

He closed his eyes for a moment before fixing his gaze on hers. "I've had people in my care call me names. Be racist right to my face. I've had them be as vile and nasty as you can ever imagine. And you know, sometimes that's just the illness talking for them, but at the same time, you know it's their real feelings, and no matter what you do or how you act, you're never going to be good enough for them. They don't want your help, and they won't take it, even if they need it. I've left jobs because of that. And, like I said, I've had clients get frisky with me, and usually I can just put them off, you know? Make sure they understand I'm not here for that. But I have to be careful, Ms. Glass, because people are really quick to believe the worst of other people."

To Tamar's discomfort, Shawn's eyes gleamed with tears. His voice shook. He looked away from her, tension in every line of his body.

"I came in to ask her if she wanted her lunch. I've been encouraging her to eat at the table, not in front of the TV on a tray—it's better for her, you know?"

Tamar nodded, not stung by his subtle implication that her habit of setting her mother up in the den in front of the TV and leaving her there all day was not a good choice. She knew that. It was the best she'd been able to do.

"She'd taken off her dress and was . . . spread out on the bed . . . waiting for me. I backed up and asked her if she needed help getting dressed, or help maybe with the bathroom. You know. Maybe she'd had an accident or spilled something on her clothes. But she only laughed. It was . . ." He shuddered. Went silent.

Tamar didn't need a description. She could remember the rough, ratcheting caw, caw, caw of her mother's laughter. Not the way she giggled at jokes or laughed out loud at funny movies. He was talking about that sly laughter. The cruel kind, when she knew she was upsetting you and simply didn't care.

"She asked me if I'd have sex with her, only she didn't say it like that."

"No. I can imagine how she'd have phrased it." Tamar's voice broke apart. "I'm sorry, Shawn. She's not well."

"When I told her that wasn't going to happen and she needed to be more respectful to me and to herself, she told me she could make me do it, if she wanted. She could *force* me to." His voice shook to a stop. He rubbed at his mouth with his palm. "I need some water."

Without waiting for her to reply, he opened the cupboard and pulled out a glass he filled from the tap. He drained it. Put the glass down. When he looked at her again, his jaw had set. His eyes didn't show any tears this time. He looked furious.

"We got into it a little bit, me telling her she needed to get dressed and not act like that. I said I was happy to help her, but she needed to stop being inappropriate. But I was scared already."

"That she was going to say you'd assaulted her if you didn't do what she wanted?"

"Yes. I already knew she was capable of lying. She does it to you every day."

Tamar had to sit at the table. She rested her head in her hands. "I'll give you the full month's pay. I don't expect you to give me two weeks' notice. And I'll provide you with a good reference. Okay?"

"There's something about her you didn't tell me, isn't there? Something about why she had to leave Somerset House. I know the people there. They'll put up with just about anything, so long as they get that money. If they kicked her out, whatever she did had to be really bad. She tried this with someone there, didn't she?"

"No. It wasn't . . . I told you, she didn't get along with some of the other residents, and they weren't able to keep her safe."

"Uh-huh. Okay."

Like mother, like daughter

"What did you just say?" Tamar lifted her head.

Shawn shrugged. "I know you're not telling me the whole truth, but that's fine. I'll be glad for the reference and the money. You should hire a woman next time. She might take to that better."

She knew she had to stand but couldn't bring herself to try. When she looked at his face, she frowned. "Is there something else?"

His mouth opened, but nothing came out. He tried again, gaze cutting down the hall toward the study before settling back on hers. His voice went thin and wispy.

"It's just that . . ." He shook his head. Shoved his hands deep, deep into the hoodie pockets. Shoulders hunched. Making himself less of a target to avoid attention.

It broke her heart to see what damage her mother had wrought. "What, Shawn?"

"She told me that I'd like it. No, that I'd *love* it. I'd love it so much that I'd want her to get inside me." His expression distorted.

Tamar assumed his horror was her mother's offer of something other than vanilla sex, but Shawn kept going.

"She said I'd beg her to get inside me. And . . ." He shook his head again, this time putting a hand over his mouth, as though trying to hold back his words, but they came out anyway. He spoke between his fingers, his jaw clenched so every word sounded strained, like speaking hurt his mouth and throat. "But right then, Ms. Glass, you have to understand, when she was talking to me like that, it wasn't what she was telling me that was so awful. Words are only words, especially from a person whose mind isn't clear, you know?"

"I know," she whispered.

"The most awful thing," he said through chattering teeth not even the grip of his fist on his jaw could stop, "the most awful thing was that it was true. Something in her voice made me want to do it all. Why would I feel that way, Ms. Glass? What did she . . . what did your mother do to me?"

29

"YOU THINK YOU'RE *pretty, don't you?" The slur in Mom's words tells Tam everything she needs to know about where this conversation is going.*

She turns from the mirror, curling iron in her hand. She's been trying to figure out how to get her bangs higher, the way the other girls at school wear them. Her eyes and the inside of her nose sting with the scent of cheap hairspray. Her hair is still flat.

"You," Mom says, "think you're So. Fucking. Pretty."

Tam carefully, so as not to draw attention to it, unplugs the curling iron.

"You get that from me." Mom's tone has changed. She pushes Tam away from the mirror to admire herself. Her lips skin back from her teeth, a couple of them smeared with crimson. She turns her face side to side. She lifts her chin.

She opens her mouth, wide, wide, wide, staring down the hole of her throat. When Tam tries to inch away, her mother's hand snaps out, gripping the sleeve of Tam's blouse. It has puffed sleeves. She bought it with birthday money she got from Aunt Naomi. Mom holds her in place as a low, guttural chuckle issues out of her gaping mouth.

"Look at us," she says. "Look how pretty we are."

The mirror cracks.

Her mother springs back, letting go of Tam's arm. Spiderweb cracks spread rapidly, distorting their reflection. None of the glass falls out, and in seconds, all that's left is a broken mirror.

Mom looks at her, eyes narrowed, brow furrowed, lips tight and sealed up. Tam's heart pounds. She doesn't want to look into the mirror, afraid of what will be in the reflection behind her. A dark, looming figure with claws for hands? A hazy human shape, nothing but empty holes for eyes?

"What did you do?" Mom whispers as she backs away from Tam. Her hands shake. Tam can smell the gin on her breath.

Tam doesn't answer.

Later, the stink of gin and bile wakes her a few seconds before the pain in her scalp as she gropes her head and finds it shorn to her chin. When her mother snaps on the overhead light, she holds up the hank of Tam's ponytail.

"Not so pretty now, huh?" the mother-thing says.

She will take Tam to her own hairdresser that afternoon, claiming Tam had tried to cut her own hair and botched it. Tam ends up with an angled bob, bangs cut straight but too short across her forehead.

Four years later, she will run screaming into the night, begging the neighbors to help her, but finding none who will open the door. She will leave the house on Spring Hill Drive and never come back.

She will never cut her hair more than a few inches at a time ever again.

Tamar sat straight up in bed, heart hammering, throat dry. She'd had a hard time falling asleep last night, at least until she'd vaped. Now she was slow, logy. She fumbled for the lamp on her nightstand. The tickling, feathery sensation that she'd felt all over her arms and cheeks was hair.

Her own hair.

Tamar's hands flew to her head as she cried out. She expected to feel the heavy weight of the messy bun she always slept in, but her fingers skated over prickly shorn strands, so close to her scalp in some places she could feel her skin. In others, longer hair remained, but all of it was cut short. She got out of bed and staggered to the full-length mirror on the back of her door. She clutched at her head, trying to deny what she saw.

Her hair was gone.

Rage shook her entire body as she stared at her reflection. She had to turn away from the sight of it—her sad, bare scalp, the longer, wispy strands that were somehow worse for having been left intact. She slammed open her bedroom door so hard the knob crunched a hole into the wall.

She took the stairs two at a time, skidding down the final few. The kitchen lights were on but flickering. The sink gurgled as she passed the kitchen doorway. A stink wafted to her. She ignored it. Smoke and fucking mirrors, tricks without treats. She would not allow herself to be distracted.

At the end of the hall, the door to the study that had been converted to Ruth's bedroom was locked.

Tamar threw her entire body against it, rattling it in the doorframe as she yanked the knob.

Again, again, she slammed her body into the door. Beneath her palm, the knob twisted. The distinct noise of the simple lock disengaging clicked into her ears, but it was too late, she was already falling through the now-open door that no longer resisted her.

Tamar landed on her hip, the hand that had been gripping the knob still hanging on to it but her arm scraping along the edge of the door. She let go and fell hard onto her side.

Tamar was so convinced she was going to see her mother standing over her that she automatically put up her hands in defense—but there was no need. Her mother was there, all right, but she sat on the edge of the bed, facing Tamar but unmoving.

Ruth's head hung, limp gray hair covering her face. Her breathing was harsh and heavy, rattling. She didn't look up when Tamar got to her feet and stood over her.

"Ruth." Tamar's voice cracked, then shattered. "Why? Was it because I confronted you about what you said to Shawn?"

Her mother didn't answer. Didn't move. Tamar bent, but cautiously, to lift her chin so she could see her mother's face.

Deep furrows marred the papery cheeks. It looked like she'd raked her fingernails down her own face. Blood dotted the cuts here and there, and small specks of it splashed onto the front of her white nightgown. Her lips were slack, eyes wide and staring but not seeing anything.

"Ruth." Tamar snapped in front of her mother's face but got no response.

Her fury was fading, replaced not with calm but another low level of frustration and anger. There could be no doubt about who'd snuck into her room and cut her hair, but how would she be able to hold her mother accountable for it? Tamar took her mother by the shoulders and shook, gently at first, then harder. Ruth's head rolled on her neck. Her jaw snapped.

Breathing hard, hating herself for resorting to violence, Tamar took a few steps back. She forced herself to swallow. She forced herself to take a breath, then another, while she counted. Ruth didn't move. Didn't make eye contact.

Tamar looked around the room and spotted what she'd been searching for—a heavy pair of rusted shears that had come from a box of sewing supplies on the bottom shelf in her office. So her mother had found the shears, come upstairs, bypassed the lock on Tamar's bedroom door, snuck into the room and cut off her hair, then came back here, all without waking up Tamar. Then what? She'd fallen into a catatonic state?

"I'm not buying it. You hear me?" Tamar tried to keep her voice steady, but it shook as she wheezed.

Her mother said nothing.

Discomfited, Tamar bent to look at her again. Her mother's gaze was like a star—glittering but distant. She did not see Tamar at all.

And no matter where she looked, Tamar could not find a single strand of her hair anywhere.

CHAPTER

30

IN THE MORNING, Ruth was herself again, whatever that meant. Cheerful, talkative in a way she hadn't been for weeks. She claimed not to remember cutting Tamar's hair.

"Remember, honey, you used to do that to yourself. A lot. I had to hide the scissors from you. Well, I had to hide all the sharp things, didn't I?" Ruth simpered and had the audacity to cast a significant look at the scar on Tamar's wrist.

The lights didn't flicker, not this time anyway, but Tamar was being gaslighted, all the same.

If the stylist at the walk-in shop wondered what the hell had happened to Tamar's head, she didn't ask. She simply trimmed away the long and wisping strands and buzzed the rest of it while Tamar sat, silent and red-eyed, trying not to wail.

When it was all over, the stylist brushed the hair off the plastic cape and put her hands on Tamar's shoulders. "Not everyone can pull off this look, hon, but you can. You've got a beautifully shaped skull."

Tamar choked back a sob.

Frowning, the stylist leaned closer to whisper, "If you're not safe at home, honey, I can get someone to help you."

"It was my mother," Tamar said. Somehow, this felt more shameful than if she'd admitted to spousal abuse. "She's got dementia. She didn't mean to."

Now Tamar sported a buzz cut that was just barely longer on the top. She felt so much lighter without all that hair that she found it hard to believe she could keep her feet on the ground. When she caught sight of her reflection, she saw a stranger. People stared. She lifted her chin and put a roll into her hips, pretending she didn't care.

She did.

When she opened the door from the garage, the faintest smell of burning wafted to her nose. "Hello?"

No answer.

Alarmed, Tamar went to the kitchen, where she found a pan left on the stove with what looked like the remains of a grilled cheese sandwich on a plate left on the counter. The bread was black. Another sandwich, untouched, was on the counter, scattering scorched crumbs across it. Two bowls of soup were in the microwave. Her mother had tried to make them both the only meal she'd ever been proud to share with her daughter.

This was why she hadn't already taken Ruth out somewhere and dumped her like an unwanted kitten. Why she hadn't held her under the bath water until the bubbles stopped coming out of her nose. Because of those memories, the infrequently good ones. Because of the way her mother had turned out to be something better than she'd been when Tamar was younger. Because Ruth was her fucking mother, and Tamar, no matter what had happened over the years, no matter how much she had hated and sometimes still hated her, she wanted her mother to love *her*.

"Hello?" Tamar called out as she headed for Ruth's bedroom. "Are you in here?"

She peeked around the doorframe. Ruth sat in the recliner, feet up, eyes unmoving from the action on the TV screen. The menu for the *Mary Poppins* DVD showed a loop of chimney sweeps popping in and out of chimneys. The sound had been muted, making their grins maniacal instead of cheery.

"Ruth?"

Slowly, slowly, her mother's head swung in Tamar's direction. Her fingernails made a dull scratching against the arms of the chair as she curled her fingers deep into the fabric. It was worse than the scrape of something on a chalkboard, worse than the bite of teeth on a fork. Tamar shuddered, heart sinking. The burned pan and sandwich had been a clue to what she might find, but this was full proof that no matter how coherent her mother had been this morning, she shouldn't have left Ruth alone.

Her mother turned her attention back to the TV. She lifted the remote from her lap and pointed it at the screen, pressing the play button. The menu screen faded as the DVD hummed and whirred in the player with a grinding sound. The screen went dark. She looked at Tamar.

"Leave me be, Tammy, I'm trying to watch my shows."

Another flash of memory. Her mother's shows had been the afternoon soaps. *Mary Poppins* had become a more recent obsession, but the sentiment was the same, as was the same dismissive tone. Tamar bristled.

She was an adult.

This was her house.

Her mother was a guest here, not in charge.

Tamar stepped in front of her mother's chair to turn off the television. The room had only a single window. The blinds were closed against the beat of late afternoon sunlight. "I don't want you using the stove when I'm not here."

Her mother peered up at her from lashes thickly coated with mascara. The rest of her face was not made up. Her mouth worked, pursing, making deep wrinkles in her face. "I was hungry."

"I left you a sandwich in the fridge," Tamar said, and added, "Did you forget?"

"I didn't *forget*. I *wanted* a grilled cheese. You always used to love my grilled cheese sandwiches. They were your favorite. You didn't have mayonnaise, though. Or margarine. I had to use butter. That's why it burned."

"Mayonnaise is a culinary abomination," Tamar whispered.

Her mother's eyebrows rose, and her lips pursed. "The sandwich you left me was an abomination."

"You can't use the stove if I'm not here. Especially if you're going to burn things."

Her mother's gaze grew shifty. Sly. Her eyes darted from side to side before settling back on Tamar's. Her expression smoothed, becoming neutral.

"Okay" was all she said.

It was a win that ought to have felt better, but Tamar didn't push it. "I'm going to make cauliflower tikka masala for dinner. With rice. It should be done in about an hour."

"Oh, that's right. You're a *vegetarian*." Her mother's nose wrinkled. "Fine."

She lifted the remote and held it out to the side, turning the TV back on. She waved a hand at Tamar to shoo her out of the way. Chimney sweeps started their singing and dancing again.

"Um diddle diddle," her mother said, "Um diddle fucking aye."

Tamar's back straightened at the curse word, but her mother was busy pressing the menu buttons to start the movie. In the kitchen, Tamar quickly disposed of the burnt sandwich and put the pan in the sink to soak. She prepped the cauliflower and turned on some music. Dancing alone in her kitchen was one of her favorite ways to cook. Garrett had always complained about her choice of music. She turned it up louder now.

They were going to have to talk about what had happened with Shawn, although Tamar already suspected Ruth was going to play as dumb about that as she had about the nighttime haircut. Tonight, Tamar wouldn't drink too much. She wouldn't vape any weed. The damage had already been done, but she'd be a fool to think there couldn't be more. She had to be alert.

While the veggies roasted and the rice steamed, she thumbed through her call records, checking to see if she'd somehow missed a voicemail from any of the facilities they'd applied to. Nothing. It was after hours now, but she dialed what had become several familiar numbers and left more messages for directors. She put an extra edge of desperation in her voice, hoping that would help but realizing it probably would not. How many calls like that did they field every day? Dozens, most likely. Dozens of families urgently trying to find a place to put their loved ones. Or their hated ones.

Shawn had told her he wasn't going to lie if someone asked him specifics about what Ruth had done. He called it the "missing stair."

That people who knew about problem patients but didn't share that information only contributed to other caregivers getting tangled up in a mess like the one Ruth had put him in.

There were other agencies. Or she could go with a private hire. Or maybe one of the homes would finally call her back, and she could unload this burden she was beginning to fear she would have to carry until her mother died.

Her mother wandered into the kitchen about fifteen minutes before Tamar was done cooking. She wrinkled her nose before setting the table without being asked. She did it slowly, methodically, but not completely. She put out sharp knives but no forks. Coffee mugs instead of glasses. She took her seat and waited while Tamar fixed the mistakes, but she didn't comment on anything.

Tamar dished them both plates of hot tikka masala, adding a few warmed pieces of naan she'd pulled from the freezer. She watched her mother drag her fork through the reddish-brown gravy, then stir the white rice and peas. Ruth took a bite of naan, chewing slowly. She grimaced, upper lip curling. Her throat worked as she swallowed.

"You don't like it," Tamar said.

Her mother shrugged and teased a few grains of rice free from the small serving. She pushed them onto her fork with a fingertip. She made another face as she tasted it, but Tamar wasn't paying attention to the theatrics.

She gestured at the thin red welt across the back of her mother's hand. "How did that happen?"

"I don't know." Her mother tucked her hand out of sight beneath the table.

"Did you burn yourself making the sandwich?"

"No," her mother said. "*I* did not."

They stared at each other across the small table. After a moment, her mother dug the fork into the food on her plate and shoved a huge bite into her mouth. She chewed, deliberately staring into Tamar's eyes. She took another forkful and gobbled that too, chewing and swallowing, gravy and rice smearing over her chin.

Revolted, Tamar shoved a napkin toward her. She ate a bite of her own food. This was one of her favorite meals, perfected over the years, but tonight it tasted bland and flavorless. She wiped her lips, hoping her mother would get the hint, but Ruth simply continued shoveling the food into her mouth. At least she chewed with her mouth closed.

"Why did you take the mezuzahs down at the old house?" Tamar hadn't meant to ask the question, but it came out anyway.

Her mother stopped chewing. With her mouth full, she said, "What?"

"I got a call from the people who bought your old house," Tamar lied smoothly. "They were doing some cleaning out in the basement, and they found a whole box of mezuzahs. They asked me if I wanted them."

Her mother's lips parted, revealing the inside of her mouth, stuffed with partially chewed cauliflower and rice. "What?"

Food sprayed. Tamar winced. She pushed another napkin toward her mother, who ignored it.

"They were in pretty bad shape, so I took them to the synagogue to ask the rabbi what I should do with them."

"You don't have any in this house," her mother said around the mess of food in her mouth. She swallowed hard.

Tamar watched the lump in her mother's throat swell, sliding down the column of her throat. "I never put any up, no. But I kept this one."

From her pocket, she pulled out the large glass mezuzah case she'd saved. "The rabbi gave me a scroll for it. I thought I'd put it up at the front door. I thought it would be nice. But I want to know why you took them all down?"

"You're lying. Where did you get that?"

Tamar was never going to admit the truth about how she'd ended up at the house on Spring Hill Drive. "I told you—"

Her mother started gagging.

Tamar recoiled automatically. "What the hell—"

Her mother puked all over her plate. The kitchen table. Down her chin, over the front of her blouse. It ran from her mouth in slow-motion waves, much of it barely chewed. She retched again, more vomit pouring from her mouth to puddle on the table. It began spreading in a relentless wave toward Tamar, who got up from her chair so fast it fell over behind her.

"Dis . . . gusting . . ." her mother gasped between gags and more vomit. "This food . . ."

Tamar clapped a hand over her own mouth to hold herself back from sympathy puking. She bent over the sink, certain she was going to lose her own dinner, but she managed to hold it back. She ran the water, cold, to splash her face and to help block out the sound of more thick, wet retching gags, more splattering.

When she turned around, her mother sat with both hands flat on the table. Puke dripped from her chin. It had splashed upward, into her eyelashes. It covered everything on the table in front of her. Puddles of it oozed to the table's edge, streaming onto the floor.

It was full of long, dark hair.

You think you're pretty, don't you?

Tamar's heart seized. Her throat closed. She choked on her own spit.

"See what you made me do?" Her mother gritted out. "You see what you made me do?"

It was an ancient accusation, but it still dug deep, deep, deeper. Tamar flinched. She splashed her face with more cold water and turned off the faucet. She could not take in enough of a breath to center herself, not with the sour stink of stomach acid hanging in the air. She allowed herself a heartbeat or two to close her eyes, though, before she turned.

"You are never going to do that again. Do you understand me?" She spoke calmly, despite wanting to scream.

Her mother's expression rippled. No. Her fucking face shifted and twisted, a gamut of expressions running over it. She grinned, vomit and strands of Tamar's hair stuck between her teeth, but it passed so fast Tamar could not be sure it was not a grimace. Her mother hung her head, shielding her face, but her shoulders went up and down. Laughter? Tears?

"I'm just an old lady," her mother whined. "An old, sick woman. What are you doing to me, Tamar? Why aren't you helping me?"

She wasn't falling for it, Tamar told herself even as she pulled a wad of paper towels from the holder. She braced herself, turning. Her mother looked pathetic. Hunched. Definitely weeping.

"C'mon," Tamar said at last. "Let's get you cleaned up."

As Tamar stripped off Ruth's soiled clothes, her mother stood as docile and complacent as she'd been the night Tamar had woken to find her standing at the foot of the bed. Tamar dropped the blouse and skirt directly into the washer as her mother stood, shivering, in the center of the kitchen. In the small bathroom off the study, Tamar got the old woman under a warm shower and started rinsing her off. When she took the clip from her mother's hair, the thin gray strands fell to cover her face. Resentment and fury surged through her. Ruth still had all of *her* hair.

"I can take care of it myself," her mother snapped. "I'm not a fucking infant."

Hesitant to leave her mother alone in the shower but knowing the longer she waited to clean up the mess in the kitchen, the worse it would be, Tamar stepped back.

If her mother slipped and fell, hit her head . . . well, she could end up dying, couldn't she? Or becoming so incapacitated that she'd need to be hospitalized? Tamar's teeth clattered together with such a sudden force that she nearly clipped off the tip of her tongue.

Her mother's head turned. Water streamed over her face, cutting channels in the gooey vomit still clinging to her chin. She stared.

She smiled.

Tamar backed away, leaving her there.

Ruth had eaten her hair. *Eaten* it. Tamar had managed to fend off the sympathy pukes until that moment, but thinking about the full reality of what her mother had done now made her run for the powder room where she fell to her knees in front of the toilet and vomited over and over, her eyes closed so she didn't have to see what she was throwing up. She was terrified she would find the bowl filled with hair. She flushed without looking. Vomited again. Flushed.

She got up and washed out her mouth at the sink. Splashed her face with cold water. She gripped the sink, leaning over it, shaking. Minutes passed. Maybe hours, days, weeks, years, an eternity, she could no longer judge time. When she at last opened her eyes, she expected her reflection to show her a madwoman, but she looked the same as she always had except for the shorn head. She turned her face from side to side, trying to admire the shape of her skull. Trying to find a way to feel beautiful.

It took her an hour to clean the kitchen, leaving it with the stink of bleach so fierce it made her eyes water. She'd stripped out of her own clothes and washed everything in scalding water. Naked, she stood in her laundry room with her hands on the washer, her eyes closed, as she gathered the strength to go back and check on Ruth. She put on a trench coat from the closet, unwilling to be vulnerable in front of her mother.

Ruth had put herself to bed. Her body looked small under the covers, which rose and fell with each soft breath. As she had the other times, she was turned away from the doorway, so Tamar couldn't see her face. She'd left the light on, and when Tamar switched it off from the doorway, Ruth shifted.

"Can you leave it on, please, Tammy? I'm afraid of the dark."

Tamar turned the light back on without a word and left the room. Afraid of the dark? What a joke.

Ruth *was* the dark.

31

"Just pick something, please." Tamar did her best to keep the irritation out of her tone, but she must not have done a very good job because the woman passing by her with her own cart gave her a sharp glance. She also gave one to Ruth, who'd been standing in the cereal aisle for at least seven minutes without yet being able to decide what she wanted.

The same woman was in the next aisle too, when Ruth wavered between English muffins and whole wheat bread, and in the next when she lingered over creamy or chunky peanut butter. Without Shawn to help during the day, everything had fallen to Tamar. They'd been in the store for almost an hour and had only managed to select three items from the list Tamar had gone over with her mother before they left. She'd expected the trip to take about an hour, tops, so she could get home and get back to work. At the rate they were going, she'd be lucky if they got home before it was time to make dinner.

Ruth held up the list she'd shown Tamar earlier. "I need chicken noodle soup. And beef vegetable. I need some things with *meat* in them."

Tamar sighed. They'd already been up and down the canned soup aisle. It was on the other side of the store. "Let me run and get it for you. Okay? Just stay here."

"I need some pork and beans too!" Ruth called after her as Tamar started toward the soup aisle.

Tamar went back to the cart. "You know I'm not going to get you any pork and beans. I can get you some vegetarian baked beans if you want."

"I need some meat. I'm not a vegetarian! I'm going to fade away from lack of protein!"

"I don't allow pork in my house, Ruth." Tamar kept her voice low, firm but not angry. "Do you want the vegetarian beans or not?"

"They're no good without that little piece of pork fat in the can," Ruth said. "So, no."

"Stay here."

It took three minutes for her to jog to the soup aisle, grab a few cans she was sure her mother wasn't going to eat and only wanted her to get so she could be bumptious about it. The woman from earlier was standing near Ruth when Tamar returned to the cart. From a distance, Ruth looked to be animatedly talking, using both of her hands to gesture. Both women turned when Tamar approached.

"Hi," Tamar said warily. "Can I help you?"

"Oh, I'm not sure, hon," the woman said with a broad, genuine smile. "But I think I might be able to help you."

The woman seated across from her at the kitchen table reminded Tamar of Mary Poppins, minus the parrot-headed umbrella and bottomless carpet bag. Not in appearance—Sally Henderson wore comfortable scrubs and shoes designed for someone on their feet all day. A small gold cross nestled in the V-neck of her scrub top. Her hands were big, the nails blunt but shiny with red polish. She had the cheery smile of the movie nanny, and pink cheeks, and a nose sprinkled with freckles that suggested that the gray hair she wore pushed back from her face with a wide headband had once been red. She had the same brisk demeanor as the infamous nanny.

She'd given Tamar her number in the grocery store, explaining that she was a retired nurse who had a lot of experience working with "people who need a helping hand." It had been clear that Ruth was immediately taken with her.

And Tamar was desperate.

"Nobody will call me back," she told Sally now. Ruth was in her room and had not come out to see who'd rung the doorbell.

Sally nodded. "So many of the places have waiting lists. Short staffed, you understand? A lot of workers passed during the virus years, and a lot didn't want to go back to such risky work. I myself decided against returning to my former job. So I understand."

"We had a daily caregiver who I thought was fantastic, but . . . he didn't work out."

"Your mother didn't like him?"

"Oh," Tamar said after a second, "I think she liked him too much. Look, Ms. Henderson—"

"Sally. Please." Her smile was as warm as the blanket you tuck around yourself as you read your favorite book.

"Sally. My mother is . . . she can be . . . difficult." Tamar cleared her throat, trying to think of what to say. How to describe Ruth's behavior.

"Is she combative? Forgetful? She seemed alert and mobile in the store, but I know how easily older people can change how they act. Like that." Sally snapped her fingers.

Tamar held back a sigh and kept herself from rubbing the headache brewing between her eyes. She pushed away thoughts of filthy feet and sullied sheets. Honesty might be the best policy, but it wasn't the only one.

"She's definitely still mobile. She's had some periods of not speaking a lot, but she seems past that, for now. Look, Ms. Henderson . . ." Tamar drew in a breath. "My mother and I haven't had the best relationship over the years. I don't always react to her with kindness or patience because of that. We can be contentious with each other. To be honest, I don't know how she'll be with you."

"I suppose we can find out, can't we?" Sally nodded once.

Hope was a balloon trying hard to yank its string free from Tamar's grip so it could fly away. She held on tight. "What exactly made you give me your number, if you don't mind my asking?"

"I saw the two of you struggling in the grocery store. I've worked with people like your mother for the past fifteen years. Before that, I was in pediatrics," Sally said. "But I found it was easier on my heart to help people who'd had a chance to live their lives, rather than the babies who'd never get the opportunity."

"I like that you're so open about that. I hate the double talk that so many people try to use when they talk about my mother. She's dying, that's the way it is," Tamar said. "We all die."

If her blunt words shocked Sally, the nurse kept that to herself. In fact, she nodded, her expression solemn. She reached to pat the back of Tamar's hand, the one resting on the table, gently.

"Yes, we do, and it's my privilege to help make those last days as comfortable and fulfilled as I can. I mean that," Sally added, maybe thinking that Tamar wouldn't believe her. "I really believe it's my calling. And forgive me for saying so, Ms. Glass, but you look like you could really use a break."

Tamar blinked, owl-eyed. "I haven't been sleeping very well."

"She walks in the night?"

Tamar thought of waking in the morning. Her mother, curled on her side in Tamar's bed although she'd gone to sleep in her own, her feet clean as a baby's. She didn't need to see Ross's camera footage or get taken home in a squad car to know that *someone* was still walking at night, and it wasn't her mother.

"Are you looking for an overnight position?" Tamar asked abruptly, adding before Sally could reply, "Or maybe live-in?"

She had no idea what that would mean in terms of salary, responsibilities, none of that. In that moment, she didn't care what it would cost. She was desperate for sleep.

"I share a house with my sister and her kids," Sally told her with a smile. "I am absolutely open to a live-in position."

It felt a little like taking the heavy blanket off the bed for the first time in the spring—there might be a day or two of chill still lingering, but change was in the air.

"I'll have to check your references," Tamar said.

"Of course."

"And we'll have to talk to my mother about it first."

Sally inclined her head in agreement. "Absolutely. I wouldn't dream of accepting a position without making sure she's on board. I could talk with her right now, if you'd like."

"I converted the downstairs study into her room, so she didn't have to climb the stairs." Tamar was already up from the table. "I work from home, so I'm here all day, but I need to be able to do my work. So . . . well, she's been watching a lot of television. I'd like her to have more activity than that."

"Of course, of course," Sally followed her from the kitchen into the hall toward the converted study.

"I have another room upstairs. It has an attached bath. You'll have free run of the house, kitchen, laundry, whatever you need." Tamar paused just outside the doorway, listening for a moment to the sound of chimney sweeps dancing along the rooftops of London. She looked at Sally. "She's watching *Mary Poppins* again."

Sally leaned to look past Tamar. "May I?"

Tamar stepped aside to make room for Sally to pass her. The nurse went into the room. For a moment, Tamar didn't follow. She held her breath. Sally wasn't speaking.

Not for the first time, Tamar imagined finding her mother's body. Maybe she'd simply slipped away. Her body, slouched in the recliner, her last moments fading to the sounds of animated animals singing and dancing. Maybe, Tamar thought with a fierce, bright, and useless hope, maybe her mother had already died.

"Hello there, Ruth. I'm Sally. I met you in the grocery store yesterday. Do you remember me? Is it all right if I come in and sit with you for a bit?"

Tamar stepped into the room. Her mother had turned toward Sally with a frown. She lifted the remote and clicked off the movie.

"Who are you?"

"I'm Sally. I'm a nurse. I'm going to sit here on the end of the bed, if that's all right?"

"I'm not sick. I don't need a nurse. I'm only going to be staying here for a little while longer, then I'm going home."

Sally didn't seem phased. "Your daughter Tamar asked me to come in and say hello. See if you and I might get along. What do you think?"

Ruth narrowed her eyes and gave a shifty glance from Tamar and back to Sally. "She's paying you to take care of me?"

"Sally's just meeting you to see if you're compatible," Tamar said. "We talked about this. You're staying here with me, not going back to Somerset House."

"I had my own room there," her mother said.

Tamar looked at Sally, who'd taken a seat on the end of the bed. "You have your own room here."

"They had a garden there. Tammy won't let me have a garden here. She says I'll track in bugs and dirt."

"I *have* a—" Tamar sighed and pressed her fingertips between her eyes. "If you want to plant something in the garden, we can talk about it."

"Ruth, if I was to come live here with you and your daughter, I'd be able to help you with whatever you needed. So Tamar can work. She needs to be able to do her work, doesn't she?" Sally had a perfectly soothing voice and manner. Her previous experience in pediatrics was showing.

Tamar tensed, expecting her mother to snap at the nurse, but Ruth smiled.

"You like *Mary Poppins*?"

"I love most of the Disney films. I used to watch them with my little girl all the time." Sally patted Ruth's arm. "My favorite is *The Apple Dumpling Gang*."

"I haven't seen that one in a long time," Ruth said. "We could watch that one, I guess."

"I'm going to have Sally come out with me to the kitchen and talk some more. Do you need anything?"

But they'd already lost her. She'd clicked on the TV again and was focused on the screen. She didn't respond.

"I told you, sometimes she doesn't have much to say," Tamar told Sally when they'd returned to the kitchen table. "It's worse when it starts to get dark."

"Sundowning," Sally said with authority. "It can be harder for them in the evening, for some reason. They get confused. Is there anything else I should know about your mother before we talk about the next steps?"

Tamar shook her head. The lie rose easily to her lips. "I don't think so."

"Well, then. I'll let you get back to work and wait to hear from you." Sally got up.

"Wait. I mean," Tamar said, too hastily. Too desperately. "Could you start today? Stay here tonight?"

If Sally was here, she would be alert to anything Ruth might need in the night. Tamar could lock her door and sleep all the way until morning. If Sally was between Ruth and Tamar, maybe her mother would take the nurse instead.

Sally's brow furrowed. "You don't want to check my references or anything?"

"I like you. Ruth seems to like you. I know it's sudden, but I really need someone here. Definitely to be there for her overnight, and we can work out what to do during the day, I know you can't work twenty-four hours a day—"

"Well, hon," Sally interrupted gently, "neither can you. We can talk about the hours you'll need me most and work it all out."

Tamar's breath tried to force its way out of her with a sob, but she managed to keep her composure. "Thank you, Sally. You're a godsend."

Sally laughed and touched the cross necklace at her throat. "I don't know about that. But I would like to help you and your mother. I'll need to go back to my sister's house and tell her what's going on. I'll pack a few things. I can be back tonight."

"Should we talk about money? I—"

"Do you ever just have a really good feeling about someone, Ms. Glass? Just a gut instinct?"

"Please, call me Tamar. I don't think I'm a gut instinct kind of person, to be honest."

Sally grinned. "Well, I am. I have a good feeling about coming here to help you. So, I'm going to trust that you and I can work out all of this to our mutual benefit, so we can both help your mother. All right?"

"Yes. Thank you. Yes." Tamar reached to shake the older woman's hand. "I just need to get some sleep."

"I understand, Tamar. I'm going to chat with your mother for a few minutes and tell her what's going on, and then I'll go and finish making my arrangements. If that's all right with you?"

"Yes. Thank you. That will be perfect. Thank so much." Her relief flooded out of her.

Sally walked to the hallway, turning back for a second to look over her shoulder. "I wanted to tell you, that short hairstyle really suits you. Brings out your eyes and your cheekbones. I'd never be brave enough to go that short, but on you, it really works."

"Thank you." Tamar accepted the compliment as graciously as she could. "My mother did it for me."

CHAPTER

32

"YOU LOOK GOOD. Better. Like you've been getting some rest."
Rabbi Feldman pushed the oversized mug of tea across the
metal tabletop toward Tamar. Her gaze took in the newly visible shape
of Tamar's skull, but she made no comment about it.

Tamar wrapped her hands around the mug. Despite the August
heat, she welcomed the warmth. "I used something to help me sleep."

"Ah." Rabbi Feldman settled deeper into her seat and picked a scone
from the serving dish between them. She contemplated it, turning it
one way. Then the other. She touched the tip of her tongue to the cream
piled thickly on top, then bit into it with a small, happy sigh.

Tamar waited for questions, but the rabbi simply nibbled at her
scone. She set it down. Took up her fragile teacup. Sipped. At last, she
looked up and met Tamar's gaze.

"I'm guessing it wasn't something you got over the counter?"

"Technically, I did. I have a prescription."

Tamar took a drink of tea, tensing at the anticipation that it would
roil in her stomach the way everything she'd tried to eat lately did. She
wished that when she'd called to ask for a meeting that she had insisted
they meet at the rabbi's office, not in this tea shop. She had a suspicion
she might break down in tears before this conversation was finished,
and she didn't want to do that in public.

"When I was in college, I smoked weed almost every day," Rabbi Feldman said casually. She took another bite of her scone and shrugged. "I rarely, if ever, drank, but I was a *total* stoner."

Tamar did not know what to say to this, so she took a scone from the dish between them and put it on the small plate in front of her. The rabbi had said all this in her normal, conversational tone. A few people looked toward them but didn't stare.

"Have you struggled with addiction, Tamar?"

"I don't know how to answer that." She broke her scone into four pieces as equal as she could make them. "I took a lot of diet pills in high school."

Rabbi Feldman looked at the mess of crumbs on Tamar's plate. "Do you want to tell me about it?"

"They helped me stay awake," Tamar said.

"And you were afraid to sleep?"

"My mother," Tamar began, but lost her voice. Her throat closed up tight, the way it used to when she tried to eat, so the food couldn't get down it.

The rabbi gave Tamar a sympathetic smile. "And now she's living with you and she's ill. You feel responsible. But resentful?"

"I *am* responsible," Tamar said. "She has no place else to go. She's supposedly on a few different wait lists, but nobody will return my calls. My sister lives too far away, and she has her own family to worry about."

"You have yourself to worry about, Tamar." The rabbi reached across the table to touch Tamar's wrist, lightly. Quickly, before withdrawing.

Tamar stared at the torn-apart scone and deliberately lifted a bite of it to her lips. It was sweet but dry. She ate the entire piece, then picked up one with jam and cream on it. She ate that too, expecting more rebellion from her stomach and again feeling none.

"This is really good," she said.

The rabbi laughed. "You sound surprised."

"I haven't had much of an appetite lately." She took another bite but slower this time. Pacing herself. Every time she tried to eat, she felt the tickle-tickle of long hairs stuck in her food, catching in her teeth, wrapping around her tongue. No matter what she tried to eat, it tasted like her mouth was full of hair.

"The issues you had with your mother when you were younger. Are they still there? Does she say unkind things to you about what you eat or your body?"

Tamar frowned. "I never said—"

"I just guessed. Was I wrong?"

"No," Tamar admitted after a second. "She was incredibly cruel, especially when she'd been drinking. But she got better. She stopped drinking and doing drugs."

"People with cognitive decline can become mean," the rabbi said. "How is she now?"

Tamar bit her tongue, trying to force the words. Rabbi Feldman waited, patient and nonjudgmental. Tamar found her voice. "There's something wrong with her. And it's been wrong for a very long time."

"Is she drinking again? Drugs?"

"No. It's not that. It's something else." Tamar clenched her fists to stop her hands from shaking. "Rabbi, do Jews believe in ghosts?"

Rabbi Feldman stayed quiet for what seemed like a very long time before she said, "That's an interesting question."

"Does it have an interesting answer?"

"The Torah forbids all attempts at communication with the dead," Rabbi Feldman said. "Which leads to the interpretation, then, that there are dead to communicate with. Which leads to the interpretation that when we die, our spirits do go on to some place, some afterlife, from which we might be able to reach out to those left behind."

"But we're not supposed to try?"

"According to passages in Leviticus and Deuteronomy, no. Maimonides defined evil spirits as mental illness," the rabbi said. "But the Talmud includes a few stories about demonic entities, the shedim or mazikin. Spiritual demons that inhabit this world and can provoke interactions between the dead and the living. And of course, there are also stories about dybbukim, the souls of the dead that have somehow managed to enter a living person, causing mental illness."

Tamar frowned. "So there are ghosts and demons? Or not?"

"Have you ever heard the saying 'two Jews, three opinions'?"

"Yes. Of course. It means that we dissect and discuss and debate. It's why the study of Torah is considered something you can do for your entire life without ever knowing everything about it."

Rabbi Feldman smiled. "Yes. But it also means that if there are two Jews and three opinions, that would mean that one of them is able to hold two opinions at the same time, perhaps even two opposing ones. We study to be able to understand the nuances and complexities of Jewish law, and the more we know, the more we understand how several different interpretations can have legitimacy. It behooves us to keep an open mind, so to speak."

"So, what does your open mind tell you?" Tamar asked.

The rabbi smiled again. "I side with Maimonides on this one, Tamar. While there have been stories about demonic possession, I think, especially in our modern context, that rather than something possessing a person to cause mental illness, the illness itself is the possession. Not something supernatural. We are talking about your mother, aren't we?"

"Yes." Tamar sat back in her chair with a frown.

"Struggles with addiction are definitely a mental illness," she said. "But any demons that possess an addict, while they can be spiritual, are not, in my opinion, literal."

Rabbi Feldman's words were meant as a comfort, but they didn't hit quite that way. There should have been relief, but Tamar only felt the same unease. Rabbi Feldman must've sensed it, because she leaned forward a bit and touched the table next to Tamar's plate, a small tap of her fingertips only, before she sat back.

"That doesn't mean I think the struggle of dealing with addiction can't feel like wrestling with a very real, very physical demon, Tamar."

Tamar laughed. "You think I'm also an addict?"

Rabbi Feldman's lips pursed, but she said nothing.

"I will readily admit to you that I abuse weed and wine, Rabbi," Tamar said. "But I'm not an addict, and my mother doesn't drink anymore. She hasn't for years. Any pills she takes are medications, and honestly, her health has been so good that she really doesn't even take anything regularly."

"Just because someone isn't using doesn't mean they can't or won't fall back into patterns of additive behavior. Your mother doesn't have be drinking to be cruel. You're allowed to have mixed feelings about caring for her."

"One Jew, a hundred opinions," Tamar said.

Rabbi Feldman laughed. "Something like that, yes. Have you thought about counseling?"

"I called you."

"Well," the rabbi said. "That's a good place to start."

Tamar drew in a breath. "But let's say there *is* something evil inside someone? A demon or a malevolent spirit. Or, okay. Let's say it is only their own mind, but they *believe* it's a demon. What do you do for them?"

"There'd have to be an exorcism, I suppose."

"Do you know how to do one?" Tamar asked.

Rabbi Feldman contemplated her. "Not really, no. I can't say that I've ever been called to perform one."

"But if you were? Would you? Could you? Hypothetically speaking," Tamar added quickly, sensing a negative answer from the rabbi.

"I suppose I could find out how it's done. But if I was asked to do one, I'm sure I'd encourage counseling or psychiatric help first. You know," the rabbi said, "nobody would blame you for putting your mother into a facility."

"I tried. I wanted to. Nobody was getting back to me." Now, she thought, how could she risk putting Ruth into any place where she could hurt other people? "Anyway, no matter what she did in the past, she's my mother. Right?"

"Love can be the worst poison you ever ingest," Rabbi Feldman said.

Tamar's laugh spilled out of her. She shook her head. "Do you know the poem 'In the Desert'? Stephen Crane?"

"I don't think so."

She'd memorized this one for a college course and had never forgotten it. She recited it in a low voice now, aware of the crowd around them.

In the desert
I saw a creature, naked, bestial,
Who, squatting upon the ground,
Held his heart in his hands,
And ate of it.
I said, "Is it good, friend?"
"It is bitter—bitter," he answered;

"But I like it
"Because it is bitter,
"And because it is my heart."

Tamar finished with a self-conscious laugh. "That's how I feel about my mother. I don't love her, and my heart is bitter because of it, but I want her to love me. I'm *starving* for her to love me. So I keep eating my own bitter heart."

"If that's all you eat, you'll always be hungry," the rabbi said gently.

"Yeah," Tamar said. "But it's all I have."

33

*D*ID YOU CHECK *your results yet?*

The text had been sent an hour or so ago, but Tamar had been deep in the design she'd been creating and hadn't noticed the chime of her phone. She thumbed the screen to send her reply.

Not yet. Why?

Instead of vibrating with another text, her phone buzzed with an incoming video call. Frowning, Tamar answered. Lovey's face loomed before she pulled the phone away. She looked frazzled.

"Hang on," she said.

Her phone whirled, giving Tamar vertigo, as Lovey somehow wrangled her two youngest kids before holding up the phone again in the right direction. She moved, looking over her shoulder.

"Are you in the pantry?" Tamar peered close to see the shelves of canned goods and snacks.

"I had to come in here and shut the door, or else they'd be bugging me. And I don't want them to overhear this." Lovey let out a breath that blew her bangs off her forehead. "Tam, you need to log in and check your results. No. Wait. Don't, I'll just tell you. Shit. What did you do to your hair?"

Tamar stiffened, her chin going up. She forced a smile. "You don't like it? I thought yours looked so . . . fresh and summery . . . I decided to go for it."

She thought Lovey might probe deeper, but her sister only stared.

Finally, Lovey cleared her throat. "You look gorgeous. Of course. I'm just shocked you'd go so drastic."

Tamar forced herself not to give in to the tears that always seemed to be waiting to burst out of her when she thought about her hair. "I needed a change."

"It looks great. I bet it's so much cooler too." Lovey touched the fringes of her own hair, her gaze cloudy.

"What were you calling about?" Tamar propped her phone against the side of her laptop as she clicked to bring up a new browser window. She typed in the website address for the DNATESTER site and waited for it to load the login screen.

"I don't want you to freak out," Lovey said.

"*You* are freaking me out."

Lovey took another big breath. "Hang on, Tam, don't log in just yet."

But it was too late. Tamar had clicked to get access to her account. The screen populated with a simple menu attached to her profile, which she had not bothered to complete. She saw a few messages waiting in the inbox and clicked on it.

"Your results are in!" cried the oldest message, sent a couple of days ago.

She let the cursor hover over it but didn't click. She looked at her phone screen and her sister's face. Lovey looked as though she'd been crying.

"I thought it would be a fun thing, Tam."

Tamar nodded. "Yeah, it seemed like it could be. What's wrong?"

Lovey drew in another breath and let it out. Her gaze sharpened. "Where's Mom?"

"Sally took her to get her nails done."

Lovey's brow furrowed. "Good. I don't want her to overhear this."

"Lovey," Tamar said, frustrated, "please just tell me what's going on."

"You . . . are my half-sister," Lovey said.

Tamar huffed out a breath. This news seemed to have come as a real shock to Lovey, but Tamar assessed it quickly and did not find herself surprised. It wasn't anything she'd ever thought about before—Dad had died when Lovey was only a baby and Tamar barely into second grade. She had very little recollection about what life had been like when he was alive, but Lovey couldn't have any memories of him at all.

"Well," she said after a pause, "you do remember how she was when we were younger, don't you?"

Lovey frowned. "I know the stories you've told me. But . . ."

"You figured it was because she'd been a young widow, right? A lonely young widow, a single mother, looking for love?" It was the narrative Ruth had always put forth, for sure.

"I guess I never thought about it, really," Lovey admitted. "She said Daddy was our father, and I believed her."

"People always had a hard time believing we were sisters." Tamar ran a hand over the dark bristles of her hair and gestured at the screen while Lovey did the same with her pale blond locks.

"But I never thought it could be because we didn't have the same dad."

"Me neither. But I also can't be totally shocked." She looked at the computer and the messages waiting for her. "I'm checking my results now."

"Tam, wait. There's something else." Lovey pressed her eyelids closed with her fingertips. She briefly pinched the bridge of her nose before looking again at Tamar. "I also have two half-brothers. They're younger than me by a few years. Daddy died when I was two months old."

"Okay, so our mother slept with some other guy while she was still married and got pregnant with you, and that guy had other kids later," Tamar said.

"Don't you get it, Tam? Dad must've found out. What if that's why he . . ." Lovey trailed off.

Both of them were silent, thinking about this.

"We can't ever know, Lovey."

Lovey drew in a hitching breath and swiped at her eyes. "Just . . . I always . . . she always said he was just a coward who took the easy way out. I always thought that meant he didn't want to be a dad again, that maybe having me put too much strain on him—"

"Oh, no, Lovey! No." Tamar wished she could reach through the screen and hug her sister. "Hang on."

She went to the far wall of her office and pulled down the framed photo that had gone with her to every place she'd ever lived. It showed their father, or the man they'd believed was their father, in a hospital room. He held newborn Lovey in one arm, his other around Tamar. He looked at them both with an expression of such love it had sometimes taken Tamar's breath away.

She held up the photo in front of the screen so Lovey could see it. "Look at this. That's not the face of a man who didn't want to be a father. He loved you. He loved both of us. I don't remember a lot, but I remember that."

"Maybe the truth came out and he couldn't handle it."

"Even if that's what happened, it still doesn't mean it was *your* fault, Lovey."

It was hers, wasn't it? Ruth had always said so. Even hearing her mother's version of what happened the night he died had not convinced Tamar it was true.

Her sister took another shaky breath. "I know. But it's still weird to find this out. That we only share the same mother, not the same dad."

"We never really had a dad," Tamar reminded her. "So it's not that different, is it? It doesn't change anything about *us*. It doesn't change who we are to each other."

Lovey gave her a watery smile. "No. It doesn't."

"I'm going to check mine now." Tamar clicked before her sister could interrupt.

The message came up with a link to her results. Grumbling inwardly at how many hoops she had to jump through, Tamar clicked it and waited for that screen to load. When it did, she sat back, mouth open. Speechless.

"What?" Lovey demanded.

Tamar looked closer at the screen. She read the results, then again. She blinked. Sat back. She looked at the phone and at her sister's face.

"My biological father is still alive."

Lovey's kids had needed her, so their conversation had been truncated, but Tamar didn't mind that so much. Getting off the call with her sister meant that she could stare in disbelief at the words on her laptop screen without having to temper her reaction. She could take her time in processing it without having to be strong for her sister.

With numbed fingers, she typed out a message through the site's internal system, introducing herself to the man linked to her and asking it he'd be willing to meet to answer some questions. He would probably assume it was about her heritage, possibly even about seeing if the two of them could form some kind of relationship, but Tamar did not actually care about any of that. She'd lived her whole life without a father figure and wasn't aching for one now.

Within a minute, she had a reply. Her biological father's name, he shared, was Roger Adams. He'd be happy to meet her, any time she wanted.

Roger.

This could not be a coincidence. It had to be the same man who was with Ruth the night Jake Kahan had committed suicide in that motel room, and she was going to find out the truth from him.

34

A WEEK PASSED, THEN another, and then a third before Tamar started to feel as though she could trust that Sally was there to stay. The nurse and Ruth had struck up a surprising compatibility, both a surprise and a relief. Ruth was still in an obvious mental decline that often got worse in the evening—sundowning, Sally had told Tamar it was called. Ruth paced, argued, sometimes tried to leave the house, but Sally was there to be a compassionate and effective friend and caregiver. Honestly, with Sally there, Tamar had stopped trying to get any of the facilities to return her messages.

Sally seemed to keep Ruth grounded in herself, which meant that the dark thing inside her could not get out.

Sally, Tamar thought, was saving both their lives.

The two older women had started binge-watching old television series, sometimes staying up until almost midnight, which was fine with Tamar because that meant she was able to get to bed at a decent time without worry. She helped Ruth with breakfast in the morning while Sally used her personal time then and again around dinner time, although she also often ate with them. It wasn't a standard schedule or arrangement, but it was working for them all.

Today Tamar got to her desk early, glad for a softly quiet house. If she stayed on track, she'd be finished with the day's work by the time she had to leave.

She and Roger Adams had a date for lunch.

Buckling down, she got an hour's worth of work done before she noticed the taste of sweat every time she subconsciously licked her lips. Her armpits were damp. So was her crotch, so wet that in the powder room, Tamar expected to see the signs of her errant period, but nope, she was simply sweating so much she'd soaked her panties and leggings. Her reflection showed beads of moisture pearling at her hairline, sliding down her face, collecting on her upper lip. She ran the water in the sink, hoping to splash herself with coolness, but the water from the faucet was as tepid as a heated pool.

Things had always been worse in the summer.

She went to the fridge to grab some iced tea. The pitcher was empty. She sighed, irritated, and made some more, only to discover when she pulled out the ice cube trays that they had not been refilled. Tamar bent over the sink, shoulders hunched, biting her tongue to hold back the curses she wanted to shout.

"Good morning!"

Tamar jumped. Sally was so quiet that she hadn't heard her come to the kitchen doorway. She put a hand on her heart. "You scared me."

"Sorry. Is she up yet? I slept in a bit later today than usual." Sally didn't move from the doorway and cast a glance down the hall toward Ruth's closed door.

"I haven't heard her. Is it hot in here, or am I just flashing?" Tamar waved a hand in front of her face.

Sally laughed. "It does feel warm."

"I'll check the thermostat. I have a lunch meeting today. Is there anything you need me to pick up while I'm out?" Tamar filled the trays and put them in the freezer. She put the pitcher of warm tea in the fridge, sans ice.

"Oh, yes. She's been asking for a few things. I'll give you a list?"

"Sure. Can you text it to me?"

"Sure thing, dingaling," Sally said, and laughed.

Tamar paused. "My father used to say that. It's one of the few things I remember about him."

"Did he?" Sally looked surprised.

"I think he did. Anyway," Tamar said, shaking herself free of memories. "Just let me know what you need, and I'll grab it."

The thermostat was set to sixty-three, but no cool air was coming out of the vents. According to the HVAC guys who'd come out several times already, nothing was wrong with the system. Sweat trickled down her spine like the tracing touch of a bony fingertip, and Tamar shuddered so hard she clipped the tip of her tongue with her teeth.

The doorbell rang.

"Ross," she said. "Hi."

"How are you doing?"

She swiped a hand over the damp brush of her skull. "Aside from the fact my house is hotter than Satan's taint, things are just dandy."

He blinked and handed her a package with her name on it. "This got dropped off at my house."

"Thanks. I got a message it had been delivered," she said, adding in a joking tone, "See, I really need one of those fancy doorbell cameras like you have. It would have proven they didn't leave it here."

"I don't have that anymore." He looked past her shoulder, into her house. Ross turned abruptly and headed back for his own house, leaving her staring after him, not knowing what to say. Tamar gathered her wits. She went after him, calling his name, then again.

"What happened to your camera?"

"I took it down. It's not cool to spy on your neighbors," he shot over his shoulder without stopping.

Tamar didn't keep following him. She watched as he went into his house, though, shutting the door behind him. After a second, his living room curtains twitched as he peeked out. He must've seen her still watching, because he closed them tightly.

Uneasily, she took the package to her office. She'd left her phone on the desk, and it hummed with a text. She didn't recognize the number.

Tamar, it's Miguel. I got a new phone, new number. If this is overstepping, I'm sorry, but I wanted to reach out one more time. Please get back to me if you want to.

It might be hard to read tone in a text message, but it wasn't impossible. Miguel's message sounded terse and stilted. Hurt. Frowning, Tamar swiped her screen to reply.

Call me.

He did, within the minute.

"I thought you were ghosting me," she said without preamble. "I sent you a few different messages and never got an answer, so I stopped."

"I messaged and called you about twenty times," Miguel said. "You never answered me."

"Shit. Hold on." Tamar took the phone from her ear and put it on speaker, then pulled up her contacts list. Her frown twisted her mouth so hard her lips hurt. She sat, her knees suddenly weak. "Your number was blocked."

"Why would you—you know what, it's fine. You don't have to explain. Whatever it was, I'm sorry."

"No," she said. "I didn't do it. This happened with my sister's number once before too. I thought it was just a glitch or a mistake or something. I'm sorry, Miguel. I definitely did not block you."

A beat of silence.

"Was it *her*?"

Meaning Ruth. "I don't know how she'd have managed to get to my phone. But yes. I think it was."

The jiggle of a doorknob handle. The soft brush of feet on carpet. The dent of a mattress from a new weight upon it. Nighttime visits could not always be prevented with a lock on the door.

Tamar had been sweating hot all morning, but now a frigid cold flooded her. She clenched her jaw to stop her teeth from chattering. The sweat beneath her breasts felt like it had turned to beads of ice. Even her nipples rose to tight, hard points that pressed the soft fabric of her T-shirt bra.

"Let me check something else real quick." She thumbed her screen again. She hadn't added any of the facility numbers to her address book, but when she looked up the string of numbers in her "blocked" list, they were all there, along with the one for Somerset House.

"Everything okay?"

"No . . . I mean. It'll be okay now, I think." She took the call off of speaker and lifted the phone to her ear again, this time with a quick glance toward the doorway. She hadn't heard anything from her mother's room, but that didn't mean she wasn't awake. "I'm so sorry, Miguel. I really didn't block you."

"I believe you. I just thought you weren't interested." His laugh sounded uncertain.

Hers was lower, softer. "Oh. I'm interested"

"I'm really, really glad to find out otherwise."

"I'm really glad you didn't give up on me."

"Tamar. I don't intend to give up on you ever again."

She wanted to believe him.

"Hi, excuse me? Oh, sorry. You're on the phone." Sally had knocked on the doorway.

Tamar held up a finger and said into the phone, "I have to take care of some things. I have a lunch meeting today with—well, it's a lot to tell you about. I should be done by about two. Can we—hang on again. Sally, would you be all right to stay with my mother for dinner today?"

"Of course."

"Miguel? Can we meet for dinner?" Quickly, Tamar sorted out the day, arranged it all with Sally and went upstairs to take a quick, cold shower. She dressed carefully. She was having not one, but two meetings with men who'd impacted her life.

She would never have Ruth's skill with cosmetics or her fashion flair—Tamar leaned toward skinny jeans and band T-shirts, flowing gypsy skirts and tank tops, not much like the tailored and matchy-matchy style Ruth preferred. And her hair . . . Oh. Her hair.

Tamar wept again for her shorn head, her sobs tearing at her throat as she stifled them so Sally wouldn't overhear. She tried not to mourn for something as shallow as her appearance. Women lost their hair for worse reasons than a mother's whim. And yet, that didn't matter. Her hair had been her identity, long and thick and full. Her one beauty, she'd always said, quoting her childhood favorite *Little Women*, and Ruth had destroyed it.

The only plus was that her long hair would've made her even more miserable in the house's sweltering temperatures. The cold water had, like the kitchen sink, been tepid at best. Minutes after stepping out of the shower, she was still damp even though she'd wrapped a towel around herself.

She frowned at herself in the mirror as she patted her face dry and smoothed it with lotion. It had been weeks since anything weird had happened here. She hadn't woken with dirty feet and an aching back. She hadn't even dreamed up old memories.

She should cancel her meeting with Roger Adams.

She didn't need to know about anything he had to say. Not really. Whatever was in the past should stay in the past.

Tamar shed the towel and went naked into her bedroom, where she'd left her phone. She wasn't going to let it out of her sight again, not after what she'd found out about the blocked numbers. The sight of herself in the full-length mirror distracted her, and she turned toward her reflection.

Fifty hadn't been terrible to her. She touched her short hair. She lifted her breasts, feeling the weight of them. She put her hands on her belly, not flat, but not covered in stretch marks or scars. Her pulse throbbed faintly beneath her palms. The cramping and other PMS symptoms had finally stopped, and no period had arrived for over a year. She thought she might finally be finished.

"Welcome to the crone years," she whispered with a sudden gleeful, giddy smile. "You made it."

Where had that come from? That uprush of almost frantic relief, somehow tied to the realization that her body had at last ceased its preparations to grow a child she would never bear? Tamar pressed her belly harder, imagining her uterus as a fist-sized lump, shriveling. Never fully used, now useless.

Electric tingles rippled through her, and it took a minute to figure out what it was.

Joy.

Tamar sank onto the bed, still staring at her reflection. She'd never missed having children, no matter many well-meaning friends—or strangers—sympathized that she'd never known the glory of mother-hood. She rarely shared with anyone that she'd chosen to terminate a pregnancy. People judged, stones in hand, even when their houses were made of glass. Society didn't seem to understand deliberate childless-ness, and it surely didn't celebrate it.

Until now, though, there'd always been the knowledge in the back of her mind that she could end up pregnant, whether she wanted to or not. Now there would be no more chance. Oh, yeah, she knew about change-of-life babies. Ruth had been one. She'd always made so much of how, unlike her own mother, who'd borne her only child in her late forties, *she* had been a young mama. But that wasn't going to happen to Tamar. She wasn't sure why she felt this so strongly, but . . . she was safe.

Safe.

35

"How is Ruth, anyways? As beautiful as ever? She was always such a looker. I guess you take after me—with the dark hair, I mean."

Roger Adams turned out to be a dapper gentleman who still wore the bushy beard Tamar recalled, only now it grew in shades of gray and white instead of deep black. He gestured with the good grace enough to look embarrassed that he'd said something so callous. He cleared his throat and shifted in his seat in the diner booth.

"Sorry," he said. "That came out wrong."

She stopped herself from running a self-conscious hand over her still mostly bald head.

"It's fine. It was always so obvious I didn't favor her the way my sister did." Tamar sipped some iced tea from her sweating glass. The restaurant didn't offer straws. Her palms were wet with condensation. She'd grown so used to the heat at home that the air conditioning in here was almost too much.

They'd chatted briefly when she arrived. He'd told her that his wife had passed away a few years ago, and that his kids had bought the DNATESTER kit for him so he could learn more about his heritage. He had three daughters, all married with kids of their own. Had he been surprised to find out he had a daughter he'd never known?

Not really.

"Look," he said now. "Jake and I were buddies, you know? All of us went to school together. Knew each other forever. Your dad and I—shoot. I guess I shouldn't call him that? Your dad, I mean." He frowned and jammed a french fry into a puddle of ketchup.

"It's fine." Her own food sat untouched in front of her.

"Well. anyway, Jake and I worked together at the graphite factory. We all went out together a lot back then. So when your mom asked me to meet her at Rooney's, I didn't think anything of it. And then . . ." Roger shoved a fry into his mouth and chewed furiously.

Tamar waited patiently for him to finish, but he kept eating. "You two had an affair?"

"It wasn't that." Roger looked affronted and shocked. Ketchup smeared his lips. He wiped them with a napkin and leaned closer, lowering his voice. "She said she needed a baby, but Jake couldn't do it. He'd had mumps or something as a kid. His swimmers didn't swim."

She pinched her mouth shut against a bark of laughter. "What?"

"She was desperate to have a baby, and your dad couldn't give her one." Roger took out a bandanna from his shirt pocket and mopped his face with it.

Tamar had to sit with this information for a minute. Her mother, desperate to have a child? That didn't feel right.

"Did he ever find out about what you'd both done?" Tamar drank more iced tea so she didn't have to look at his red face.

Roger didn't answer.

She sat back against the diner booth. "Is that why he killed himself?"

"I don't know. I swear to Jesus, I don't know. All I can tell you is that we were together a couple of times before she got pregnant, and after that, she didn't want anything to do with me. I was dating my wife at the time, and we were going to get married, so I was fine to keep it all a secret. And . . . Tammy, hon, your dad was so happy to become a father. What was I going to do, tell him you weren't his? You *were* his, as far as he was concerned. But then he ended up doing . . . that . . . in the same motel." Roger shoved the bandanna away and drank half his glass of cola, then stifled a burp. His face didn't get any less red, but he seemed calmer.

"Same as what?"

The old man sighed. "That's where you were conceived."

She took a minute or so to digest this. "The night he died, were you with my mother? When she went to the motel room?"

Roger's head hung. "She called me, frantic. How could I say no? He was my friend."

And Ruth always got what she wanted.

"She told me he slit his own throat."

He looked up, eyes wide. "That's what they said happened, but I don't see how anyone could've done that to themselves. I mean his head was . . . his got-damned head was . . ."

Tamar's hands linked tight in her lap as her body tensed. "It was what?"

"Well, it was almost nearly off his fucking neck," Roger spat out in a hoarse whisper.

He looked at her, his eyes rimmed with red. The lines around his eyes and mouth deepened, and for a terrible moment, Tamar was reminded of her meeting with Ms. Carr, how the woman had aged in front of her eyes. Roger had been elderly when she got to the restaurant. Now he looked ancient. She began to fear he might actually have a heart attack right there at the table.

Roger took in a long, shaking breath and went on. "There was blood everywhere, and you were just sitting there—I'm sorry. I haven't thought about this in years."

Hot and cold, hot and cold, her entire body ran with shuddering chills that swelled into an inferno of heat only to revert to ice again. Tamar's jaw clenched so hard she couldn't speak. She could hear Roger asking her if she was all right, but his voice was very far away. Everything had gone so very far away.

She wrestled herself back from the edge of unconsciousness and found her voice. "What the fuck?"

"You were there," Roger said. "You don't remember?"

"Here." Roger shoved the glass of ice water she hadn't yet touched across the table toward her. It slid on a track of moisture, almost going over the edge and into her lap.

Tamar couldn't drink it, not without choking, but she took a piece of ice from the glass and pressed it to the base of her throat where so recently she'd worn the Star of David. She tucked a piece in her mouth. Then took another and rubbed it on her wrists.

"I'm not going to faint," she said aloud, trying to make that the truth.

"You didn't remember that, did you? Hey, can we get some more water here?" Roger waved at the server, who brought a pitcher to refill their glasses.

Tamar waited until the server left before she answered him. "No. My mother told me she'd left me at home with the neighbor from across the street."

"You were there. Sitting on the bed. There was blood everywhere in that room, but you didn't have a speck of it on you." Roger shook his head. "Ruth had gone in first, because she'd said she wanted to see who he was in there with. If it was some woman. She was always so jealous."

I carried you away from trouble

Tamar fought a shudder. "Considering she'd fucked another man to get a baby, that seems pretty hypocritical."

Roger winced. "I know that later on she got herself in a bad kind of place, Tammy. She did . . . things. But she wasn't always like that. Losing your dad, knowing what he'd tried to do to you, changed her."

"What do you mean what he tried to do to me? Did she say he tried to kill me? Because he found out he wasn't my real father?"

"I don't know what he wanted to do in there," Roger admitted. "But he ended up not harming a hair on your head. Only himself."

Tamar slowly sipped water, feeling her equilibrium returning. "I never knew any of this. I didn't even know *she* was there that night until a few months ago."

"I'm sure she kept it from you to save you from knowing it. That would've been an awful thing to tell a child, wouldn't it? Maybe she saw that you didn't remember it, and she was trying to help you," Roger offered.

She doubted that. She took the folder with the check the server had left and slipped her credit card into it. She waved away Roger's offer to pay for lunch, and she declined the box the server offered for the food she hadn't been able to finish.

In the parking lot, Roger said, "I'm sorry about all of this, Tammy. I really am. I should have reached out to you long before now. I guess I thought . . . I wondered if maybe one day you'd get in touch with me, like maybe you'd find out. Maybe Ruth would have told you."

"I appreciate that you met with me, Roger. I'll stay in touch."

She had no intentions of doing that, but it seemed rude to say so. They parted with a handshake, not a hug. When she got in her car, she blasted the air as cold as it would go and sat in the parking lot for a long time before she felt like she was no longer too shaky to drive.

They'd spent too long at lunch, and now it was almost dinner time. Tamar had a real desire to cancel her plans with Miguel, but when she looked at her phone and saw the sweet text from him letting her know how much he was looking forward to it, she couldn't bring herself to disappoint him. Not again.

She also wasn't quite ready to go home and face her mother.

Instead, she drove out of town to the Lucky Inn, the seedy motel where her father had died. It was still in business, its condition not much better than she imagined it had been when Jake Kahan had taken his own life in one of the rooms. She didn't know which one, so she parked in front of the long building and studied them all. Some of the doors stood open, housekeeping carts outside. Most were shut. A few cars took up spaces in the lot. A sign offered free WiFi and cable television.

None of it looked familiar. She remembered nothing about that night. Yet Roger had said her father had taken her there, then killed himself. Why? For what purpose? Did he mean for her to be a witness? Had he intended to take her life too? He was dead and would never be able to answer her, and Ruth . . . well, Tamar had always known her mother was a liar.

A quick call home reassured her that Sally was still willing to be on duty even after dinner. Even late into the night. She'd make sure Ruth was all right, she reassured Tamar.

As if Ruth could ever be anything close to all right.

CHAPTER

36

S HE MET MIGUEL once again at Rooney's, but she waited outside for
him to arrive. She wasn't hungry, and the place was crowded with
people playing trivia. It would be too loud for talking, and she desperately needed to talk.

"If you're not too hungry, maybe we could just walk?" she suggested.

Miguel had looked happy to see her, but now his expression was
tight with concern. He nodded, his gaze skimming over her shorn hair.
He didn't ask questions. She was sure he already knew who'd done the
cutting.

"Absolutely. Whatever you want."

So, they walked. By the time they reached the end of the parking
lot, they were on a residential sidewalk lined with trees. He took her
hand. They turned the corner and were on their old street. If they kept
walking, they'd pass right by their old houses. They kept walking.

"I'm not sure I believe in God," Tamar said finally.

He didn't seem to find this out-of-the-blue statement strange. His
fingers squeezed hers. "I do. Not the one in the Bible, not the one I was
supposed to convince other people was real. But I do believe in God."

She stopped and turned to face him without dropping his hand.
The street was quiet, the house in front of them dark. Laughter lilted
from some backyard. Bugs whirred. Summer sounds. Things had always
been worse in the summer.

"Why?" she asked.

"Because if I didn't, I wouldn't be able to believe in an afterlife. And without being able to believe there's something for us after we die, I'm not sure how I could get through life at all."

"If you believe in God, then, do you believe in the devil?"

He shrugged. They started walking again, slowly, traversing the places in the concrete where it had buckled from the tree roots. Some of the yards had fences—she could remember running along them with a stick, rat-a-tat-tat. Picking flowers from the vacant lot that now had a house on it. So much had changed in this neighborhood, so much of it for the better.

"I think there's evil in the world," Miguel said. "Yes. If Satan is the Adversary, I suppose, then, yes. I do. But the devil as in horns and a pitchfork? I don't think so."

"What about demons?"

"Yes. I believe in demons." he said. "So do you."

They stopped walking again. Ahead of them, midway down this street, was his old house. Hers, across the street. Both had lights on. She faced him. He took her other hand.

"We never talked about what you saw that night," she said. "I need to know."

He cleared his throat. "I came over to check on you. The door was unlocked and I was used to letting myself in. I felt terrible that I hadn't gone with you to the clinic, even though you told me you didn't want me there. I heard you both upstairs, screaming. Glass breaking. I saw you run down the stairs, but I was too scared to shout after you."

Tamar frowned. "Because you thought you'd get in trouble?"

"Because I saw it," he said. "All those years you told me about the things that happened in your house, but I never really believed you. I mean, I knew your mother drank too much and all that. But the other stuff . . ."

"You mean that my house was haunted. I always knew you didn't believe it," she said with a small laugh. "Who would? After I ran away from there, I convinced myself I'd imagined it all. Maybe even as a trauma response, you know, to block out what she'd actually done."

"You didn't imagine anything. You ran out the front door. All of the doors in the rest of the house were slamming open and shut.

Cupboards too. The entire house smelled like something had died. And then . . ." he paused with a shudder. He looked at her. Light from the nearest house glittered in his eyes.

"Then?"

Miguel's entire body shook. He closed his eyes for a second, then looked into hers. "I saw it."

"My mother?"

"No. It. The thing, whatever was causing it all. Tall. Thin, but bent. Claws. Red eyes. It looked at me, and I ran. That's the last thing I remember until I woke up in my own bed the next morning. I had scratches all down my back, though. Like something had raked me with long claws as I ran away."

They were both silent.

Tamar's voice rasped when she finally spoke. "The last thing she said to me before I ran out was 'You killed it,' and when I said it was my choice, she said, 'It was supposed to be mine.' I used to think that meant the choice was supposed to be hers. Like, she was my mother, she had the right to decide for me. But now I think . . ." she shuddered, remembering what Roger had told her about Ruth wanting a child. "I think she meant the *baby* was supposed to be hers. Like she wanted to do something to it. Or with it."

Miguel frowned. "Whatever that thing was, Tam, it wasn't your mom."

"That's the problem, Miguel. It *was* my mother. It still is."

"I told myself it wasn't real," he said finally. "But it put the fear of Hell in me. I was sure it was my punishment for getting you pregnant, for not stopping you from having the abortion."

"It wasn't—"

"My choice," he cut in. "I know. So maybe seeing that thing was my punishment for not being there to support you."

"Oh, Miguel. None of it was a punishment for you at all." She drew in a shaking breath.

This man had broken her heart, and she had broken his. All these years, each had carried the burden of that mutual cruelty. It was time to let it all go.

She kissed him, pushing up onto her toes to reach his mouth with hers. The brush of lip on lip was soft, not demanding, nothing like the passionate tangle of tongues and swapping of spit they'd shared in high school. This kiss was sweet and warm, but also full of promise, and when she pulled away from him, he unlinked one of their hands so he could touch his mouth.

"All these years, I thought you hated me because of what happened," he said.

She shook her head. "I was angry at you for a long time. But I never hated you."

"What are you going to do?"

Tamar didn't know if she meant about them or about Ruth, but it didn't really matter because her answer to both was the same. "I don't know."

"If it's a demon, there has to be a way to get it out of her."

She laughed aloud, trying to keep it down so they wouldn't alert any of the people at home. "This is crazy. You know that?"

"I know what I saw," Miguel said.

Her laughter eased. "Will you help me?"

"Yes," he told her. "Always."

They walked back to Rooney's but didn't go inside. Instead, they both drove to the diner on the outskirts of town, the one that had been there forever. The one open twenty-four hours with a menu twelve pages deep. The one right across from the motel where Jacob Kahan had cut his own throat so deeply that he'd nearly self-decapitated.

The hostess seated them in a comfy booth big enough for eight, with a view across the street of the Lucky Inn. Tamar flipped through the selections on the small tabletop jukebox, reading the names of the songs aloud to Miguel as they both laughed and groaned at the memories. They ordered coffee and big breakfast platters, and they made small talk until the food came.

She passed her portion of bacon and sausage over to him with raised eyebrows. "You want?"

"You keep kosher?"

Tamar laughed and shrugged. "Kind of."

"Growing up, I knew you were Jewish, but I have to admit I had no idea what that really meant, other than Santa didn't come to your house.

Obviously, when I went to seminary, I got a little more educated." He dragged her plate of meat across the booth next to his. "I will gladly take this plate of pig off your hands."

She was surprised at the strength of her appetite. She spread a thick layer of strawberry jam on her toast and piled the slice with soft, cheesy scrambled eggs and crispy home fries. She looked up to see Miguel watching her with amused eyes.

"You still do that," he said.

"I still do." She lifted the sloppy egg sandwich toward him in a salute to youth and days gone by.

The first bite was bliss, and she closed her eyes to let herself sink into it. They ate in companionable silence for a few minutes before she pushed the still-brimming plate away with a sated sigh. Diner breakfast was her favorite thing, but there was always so much of it.

Tamar waited until the server had filled their white ceramic coffee mugs again and left them before she said, "So. What should I do?"

"We need to confront it," Miguel said confidently. "Cast it out."

"First of all, how are we supposed to do that? Second," she said, counting on her fingers, "what happens to it once it's cast out?"

"Your mother won't be possessed anymore. It'll go back to Hell or wherever it came from." He said this with a little less confidence.

Tamar sipped coffee and looked across the street to the motel. "She had so many years where she was okay. After I left, she turned her life around, really got her shit together. It took me too long to forgive her for the things she'd done. Now I'm wondering if I missed my chance to have the relationship with my mother that I always wanted. Maybe it's too late."

"Maybe the demon went dormant for some reason, while you were gone." He poked at his omelet but then pushed his plate away too. "It would be a good thing to find out."

"Maybe," Tamar said quietly, "without me around, my mother could just focus on the kid she loved more. So she didn't need to drink and do drugs to forget how terrible it was to have me there."

Miguel scowled and took her hands across the table. "That's bullshit. People get sober for a lot of reasons, Tam. But you'll never convince me that was hers."

She let him squeeze her fingers and let herself take comfort from that small embrace. "Lovey got me one of those DNA test things. We found out we were only half-sisters. I met my biological father earlier today."

"Wow. How was that?" Miguel frowned and stroked the backs of her hands with his thumbs.

"He told me Ruth asked him flat out to get her pregnant because her husband couldn't. He said she was desperate for a baby. But if that was true, why did she always hate me so much, and love my sister so much, instead?"

Tears scalded her eyes and throat, and she sniffed them back. Miguel shook his head. His fingers stroked hers.

"I don't know," he said. "I'm sorry that I don't have a better answer for you."

"He said I was there the night the man I always thought was my father killed himself. I don't have any memories of that at all. Not of being there, not if he tried to hurt me, nothing. *She* told me she left me and Lovey with your mom." Tamar looked at him. "But the weird thing is, as soon as he said that to me, I knew it was the truth. I don't know why it happened, but that story felt right."

"The only way to really know is to ask her."

She shook her head and took her hands from his. "She'll lie about it."

"If you confront her with the truth, she might not. Getting sober makes a big difference for a lot of people," Miguel said.

"What does being possessed do for them?" She meant to say it lightly, joking, but the words came out garbled and higher pitched than normal. Her throat had tried to close tight around them.

He waved toward the server for the check and gave Tamar a steady stare. "I say we go find out."

CHAPTER

37

THE HOUSE WAS mostly dark and quiet when they pulled into the driveway. The now-familiar flickering blue light from the television in Ruth's room was no guarantee that she was still awake, but the dim golden glow coming from the window of Sally's room meant that the nurse, at least, had gone upstairs. Tamar parked in the garage and got out to wait for Miguel.

"It's kind of late," he whispered, although they were still in the garage, and there was no way for anyone to overhear them. "What if she's sleeping?"

"I hope she is. Then we'll have to talk to her in the morning," Tamar said and waited a beat to see if he understood the unspoken invitation.

In the garage's shadows, Miguel's eyes gleamed. "Oh, really?"

She smiled but said nothing.

Their earlier kiss had been warm with nostalgia. This one was hotter, alive with promise. They weren't kids anymore. Whatever they did together now would not be done with youthful optimism but with the reality of adulthood. Kissing Miguel felt less like a second chance and more like an entire new one.

When they stepped away from each other, her heart was beating so fast she had to put a hand over it. "Whoa."

"Yeah," he said. "Agreed."

It was too tempting to ignore her mother and whatever was happening with her. She could be selfish and greedy and needy. She could explore all the things they'd done so furtively and frantically as teenagers in the much slower and luxurious manner befitting grown-ass adults.

She took him upstairs.

They passed the slightly open door of Sally's room without pause, but Tamar heard the familiar snort-whistle of the nurse's snoring. She took Miguel into her bedroom, shut and locked the door.

If in the past they'd both been fumble-fingered, overeager, desperate with the need to do it all before they could get caught, now they were both . . . not hesitant or cautious, at least Tamar didn't feel that way. They weren't reluctant, but they definitely took their time.

Coming with him was like coming home.

The house was still too warm, but naked, it was bearable. Sweating, they both collapsed onto the pillows with the sheets tossed off to the foot of the bed. His hand found hers. Their shoulders touched. When she rolled to face him, she kissed his bicep and pressed her face to the smell of his body, the scent of effort and exertion and ecstasy, and she breathed it in with a giddy sigh that made him laugh.

He kissed the top of her head. They might have fallen into a discussion about what they were doing, or where this might go, but instead they both lay in contented silence. She listened to the sound of his breathing syncing with hers.

From the baby monitor on her nightstand came a low, slow hiss. A crackle of static. The sound of what might have been a voice saying her name. Tamar hadn't turned the monitor on in weeks, since Sally was supposed to be on night duty.

Tamar sat up, aware of Miguel's hand on the small of her back as she leaned toward the monitor. She meant to turn it off, but another sibilant whisper issued forth. Not her name this time, but a wordless chuckle that sounded a like air escaping a balloon. *Sss sss sss sss.*

She swung her legs over the edge of the bed, already searching for the clothes she'd tossed aside. "I should check on her."

"I thought you had the nurse for that?"

She looked over her shoulder at him. "You came here so we could confront her. So, let's go do that."

"You also said we could wait until the morning. It's the middle of the night," Miguel said.

"That's when it comes out."

He nodded after a second and also started to get dressed. She moved in front of him as he buckled his jeans. She waited for him to look at her.

"You don't have to do this with me, Miguel. This isn't your responsibility."

"I'm here," he said. "I want to help you."

Quietly, they left her bedroom and tiptoed down the hall. Sally's door was now closed, no sounds from within. Together, they went downstairs. Outside Ruth's room, Tamar paused to listen but heard only silence.

She pushed the door open a little and eased her way into the room. For the first time in months, she didn't crave weed or wine, and not because she wanted a clear head. The idea of letting everything turn into a blur was simply not appealing to her in that moment.

Miguel believed her.

As a kid, Tamar had learned quickly nobody listened if she talked about the monster that hovered over her at night or the things that happened in her house. As an adult, she'd forced herself to blame everything on Ruth's addictions, giving all of it an explanation firmly based in reality, not a hint of supernatural to it at all. There was relief in being able to share the truth with Miguel, but some anxiety too.

If Ruth was in fact possessed by a demon, how were they going to get rid of it?

As usual, the TV light flickered. Ruth lay curled on her side in bed, facing away from the door. It all looked normal. As Tamar turned, gesturing at Miguel to move back, into the hallway, the floor creaked. Tamar froze. Slowly, slowly, she half turned.

Ruth was sitting up in the bed. With the TV light behind her, her face was in shadows. Tamar could make out a faint gleam of her teeth as she grinned. Another glint of light in the places where her eyes should be. The shine of her teeth disappeared as her mouth yawned, wide and wider, and a low, horrible hiss issued forth.

Miguel was still in the hall and probably couldn't see past Tamar. He must've heard the noise, though. He must've seen Tamar's face. He took her by the upper arms and moved her out of the way so he could step into the room.

The lamp next to Ruth's bed clicked on. She was sitting up, but blinking, her face creased from the pillow. She frowned.

"Who are you? Get out of here, or I'll—"

"Ruth," Tamar said. "It's me. This is Miguel Estrada. From across the street on Spring Hill Drive. You remember the Estradas, right?"

"What's he doing here?" Ruth clutched at the collar of her nightgown. Then her expression changed, eyes narrowing, mouth pressing closed for a flicker of a moment before she smiled and nodded. She relaxed. "Miguel. Of course I remember you. My goodness, how you've grown up. Come over here and let me see you properly. How is your mother?"

Just like that, she was the portrait of a slightly befuddled but beloved granny. Sweet enough to draw flies. Well, Tamar thought, shit drew flies too.

Miguel went into the room and took Ruth's offered hands, pressing them between his own. He sat on the bed next to her, facing away from Tamar. Ruth focused her attentions on him, peppering him with questions about his family and what he'd been up to. Miguel answered her questions conversationally, calmly, never taking his gaze off her face. He didn't let go of her hands either.

Tamar watched, first from the doorway, then from the recliner set up in front of the television, which she turned off. Miguel's conversation with her mother lasted a few minutes, no more than ten, before Ruth looked at her daughter.

"I suppose I don't need to ask what he's doing here so late," she said. "I hope you kids are being careful."

Tamar burst into a string of giggles at the absurdity of this statement, along with the embarrassing realization that neither one of them had even mentioned condoms, much less used one. She hadn't been that careless in decades. Never, in fact, not even back then, when the positive pregnancy test had been as much of a surprise as one would now. She could see Miguel thinking about it too by the way his expression twisted.

"It was good to see you, Mrs. Kahan. It's late, I really should get going." He patted her hands and stood, giving Tamar a look.

Ruth reached for the remote to turn the TV back on, then settled onto her pillows. "Well, I'm up now, I suppose I'll just watch something. Good night. Tammy, please try to be a little quieter at night. I was sound asleep."

"I'm sorry about that, Mrs. Kahan. I thought if you were up, I'd like to say hello. Since we haven't seen each other in so long. But I'm heading home now. Good night." Miguel did a strange thing then. He pressed his hand to the top of Ruth's head, the way you might say good night to a child.

It didn't seem to bother her. She beamed up at him with a big, broad smile. Tamar didn't think she'd ever seen her mother look at Miguel that way. She'd always been either sullen and snarky toward him, or oddly and grossly flirtatious. Ruth was already focusing on the television as they left the room.

Tamar walked him to the front door, half hoping he'd ask if he could spend the night but relieved when he didn't. On the front porch, he kissed her. His hands fit neatly on her hips. His touch felt right, like it was meant to be there.

"That was kind of weird," she said.

He shrugged and gave a self-conscious laugh. "You mean what she said about us being careful?"

"All of it. But yes. That."

"You don't have to worry. I had a vasectomy years ago."

They both burst into stifled laughter.

"We didn't ask her anything," Tamar said.

"It didn't seem to be the right time. I can come over again, though. During the day. We can ask her to tell us more about the night your father died, see what she says. She might have a different story for you, or it might be the same. But at least you'd know you tried. But . . . Tam . . ." he hesitated. His gaze went to Ruth's window, lit by flickering gray-blue light. He looked back at her. "Whatever happened back then, I don't think it's part of her anymore."

Her back stiffened. Shoulders went tight. Her jaw clenched so hard she had to force herself to relax it.

"What do you mean?"

Miguel shook his head, then lifted his hand to show the small crucifix attached to an equally petite and delicate set of rosary beads. The entire set fit into the palm of his hand, invisible until he showed it to her. "While we were talking, I was pressing this against her hands. And before I left, I touched it to her forehead."

Tamar blinked. "And? So what?"

"It's a rosary I had blessed by the Pope," Miguel told her, like she ought to know what that meant.

She frowned. "Okay, but what does that have to do with anything?"

"She didn't try to get away from it. It didn't seem to burn her or anything. It's a holy object," Miguel told her patiently, as though he didn't grasp why she didn't understand.

He wasn't trying to be patronizing, Tamar knew, but that was how it felt. She wanted to laugh but not with humor. She stepped away from him, back toward her front door.

"It's a holy object for you," she said.

"It was blessed by the Pope," Miguel repeated. "A demon would recoil from it."

He held it up again, as though showing her would guide her toward comprehension. The problem, though, was not in her comprehension. Tamar shook her head.

"It's a holy object for *you*," she said again, emphasizing.

"For demons too." He sounded frustrated. He closed his fingers around the rosary and drew it close to his body. "The first test before attempting any kind of exorcism is touching the afflicted with a holy object. She didn't even flinch when I did."

She took in a small, sharp breath. "Miguel, my mother is Jewish. We don't care about your Pope. Or your Christ. That test means nothing."

The tension between them earlier in the night had been the good kind; this most definitely was not. He pushed the rosary into the pocket of his jeans and then put his hands on his hips. He rocked a bit on his toes, then went so far as to step off the porch and onto the walk, still facing her.

"I'm sorry," she said, although she really wasn't. "But Christianity is not an accurate default, even if Christians automatically assume so."

"No. I'm sorry," Miguel said after a long moment in which she was sure he was going to turn on his heel and leave without a reply. "You're right. I shouldn't have assumed."

"It was worth a try. I understand why you thought it might tell us something about her. Or it," Tamar said. "But you can see, can't you? Why what you did is in no way proof of anything?"

"I was trying to help."

"I know you were," she said.

"I guess I should get going. It's really late." He looked at the sky, as though that would tell him the time. "I'll call you. Okay?"

"Sure. Yes. Please," she said. "I'd like to see you again."

He wasn't going to call her, she thought as she watched him get into his truck and drive away. He might not have become a priest, he might not be religious, but she'd made him feel stupid. She couldn't even be sure he'd waved at her. She watched until his brake lights winked at the end of the street as he turned the corner before she went inside.

She stopped in Ruth's room before going upstairs. She expected her mother to be sleeping again, but Ruth was wide awake. She stared at the television with a glazed expression, her lips loose and parted. She'd drooled a little.

Disturbed, Tamar turned off the set again and went to the side of the bed. "It's late. You should get some sleep. C'mon. Lay down."

"Do you think," Ruth whispered as she allowed Tamar to press her to the mattress. "Do you think he put a baby in you?"

Tamar fluffed her mother's pillow. The temperature outside was summer cool, but this room was sweltering. Ruth didn't seem to mind. She wriggled, reaching for the blankets, and Tamar helped her pull them up.

"No, Mother. I do not think he put a baby in me."

"Too bad," Ruth said.

"Why? Because you think I need a baby at this point in my life?" Tamar asked sharply.

"No, Tamar. But *I* do."

CHAPTER

38

A ROSARY WOULDN'T PROVE the presence of a demon possessing her
mother, but something else might. Tamar had not asked Ruth if
she wanted to attend Rosh Hashanah services with her. She'd simply
told Sally she could have the day off, and she'd told Ruth to get dressed
and get in the car.

"We're here." Tamar looked through the windshield at the front of
the synagogue. The parking lot was full. People headed for the front
doors, guarded by a cop hired for the day to provide security. She looked
at her mother. "Are you ready?"

Ruth wore a clean blouse and skirt and a full face of makeup. Without Sally to help her, the heavier hand showed in the amount of blush
and eyeliner. She didn't answer at first, but then leaned forward to peer
through the glass. "This isn't the nail salon."

"It's the synagogue. We're here for High Holiday services," Tamar's
voice was calm, but she studied Ruth for any hint at all that she knew
what was going on.

"I thought we were going to the nail salon." Ruth frowned and
rubbed her hands on her thighs, back and forth, back and forth.

"Sally takes you to get your nails done. Today, we're going to
services."

Ruth turned in her seat. Her voice rasped. "I didn't know you got
so religious."

Tamar didn't bother with a reply. She got out of the car and went around to the passenger side, only to discover that her mother had locked the door. It didn't matter. Tamar held up the car's remote and booped it as she looked through the glass at Ruth, who was steadfastly staring straight ahead. Tamar opened the door and held out her hand.

Ruth took it and allowed herself to be helped out of the car. Her fingers pinched on Tamar's elbow, but she followed willingly enough. She hesitated once as they approached the synagogue's front doors. She smiled at the police officer stationed there.

"Hello, handsome." Ruth's voice was distinctly flirtatious, pitched lower and still raspy. She fluttered her eyelids.

The cop must've been used to elderly women making eyes at him, because he tipped his head toward her. "Ma'am. You have an enjoyable holiday, okay?"

"My daughter Tamar is making me go," Ruth said.

Tamar and the cop exchanged looks. He gave her a nod. She managed a smile.

Ruth hung back again as the greeter opened the door for them and stepped aside so they could pass through the double doors and into the entryway. Only Tamar's gentle grip on her shoulder kept her moving forward. Ruth's shoulders were tense and tight, but she didn't make any audible protest.

She looked around the entryway with wide eyes. "Where is this?"

"Welcome to Temple Beth Shalom. I'm Veronica."

Tamar knew Veronica Alster by name. She was head of the Sisterhood, active on the Hebrew School committee, a board member. Her name was signed to the food festival call-to-action letter that arrived every spring, along with the four tickets every congregation member was expected to sell or purchase themselves. She had finally stopped calling to invite Tamar to the Sisterhood meetings.

Veronica held out a hand to Tamar's mother. Ruth didn't take it. Veronica withdrew it with a small, commiserating smile toward Tamar. She gave them each a program.

"I'm Tamar. This is my mother, Ruth."

"Oh, Tamar. Glass, yes?" Veronica beamed. "Welcome, welcome. It's so nice to see you both here."

She guided Ruth into the sanctuary. Tamar had chosen seats in the first row of chairs set up behind the permanent pews, one seat on the outside aisle. If they needed to leave abruptly, they'd be able to duck out the sanctuary's back doors without calling too much attention to themselves.

Tamar gave her mother a side-eyed glance. She couldn't even have guessed how long it had been since her mother had been inside a synagogue, much less a High Holidays service.

Still, as the rabbi and cantor took their places on the bimah and the congregation settled into their seats, Tamar could not deny the sense of peace washing over her. Her mother shifted in her seat and muttered. Tamar tensed, turning to her. Ruth stared straight ahead without expression. After a second, still without looking at her, she took Tamar's hand. Held it loosely with her own gnarled fingers.

Tamar caught Veronica looking at them, the other woman's eyes dropping to those linked fingers. She smiled at them both and mouthed something that looked like "how sweet." Self-conscious, Tamar did not drop her mother's hand.

Rabbi Feldman wore a colorful tallis in shades of blues and greens over a crisp white clerical robe. Her mesh kippah was pinned to her fall of dark hair with what looked like butterfly pins. She had a bright, warm smile as she looked out at the congregation from her place at the lectern.

The rabbi welcomed them all to the service, and it began. As the cantor's voice led them all through the opening melodies, Tamar allowed herself to relax a little. She squeezed Ruth's hand briefly, expecting her mother to let go, but she didn't. Her grip tightened a little instead.

Tamar bent forward to pluck a mahzor from the back of the pew in front of them. She tugged gently to free her other hand from Ruth's grip. Her mother clutched harder.

"Let go," Tamar said quietly.

Ruth bore down. Her nails began to dig into Tamar's skin. Tamar tugged again, looking around to be sure nobody was watching this. The hot flush of embarrassment crept up from her belly and into her throat and higher, into her face, turning it red. With one hand holding the heavy prayer book, the other imprisoned by her mother, she felt trapped.

Powerless.

The cantor's voice swelled, joined by the rabbi and the congregation, but Tamar couldn't join them. Her throat was dry and tight.

"Ruth, stop."

Her mother moaned. The sound vibrated, not quite out of hearing range but still low. Her hand tightened. Harder, harder.

Tamar winced at the sting as her mother's fingernails broke the skin on the back of her hand. She tried again to pull free, but it was like tugging against a statue—no, a vice that was slowly, inexorably, closing. Her finger joints popped as her mother squeezed.

Tamar's breath fought for freedom out of her throat even as she fought to remain calm, showing nothing, desperate not to let on to anyone around them that a battle was going on. Bright sparks fluttered around the edges of her vision as the pain in her hand worsened.

Was her hand bleeding? She imagined wet heat sliding down her fingertips to drip onto the dark blue and gray carpet. She tried to look at their linked fingers but could see only the back of Ruth's wrinkled and age-spotted hand.

Her mother moaned again. Louder, this time. It turned heads. Brows furrowed, faces looked concerned. Tamar kept her back straight, staring ahead, painfully conscious of the attention her mother was bringing to them. Ruth moaned again, and Tamar turned to her.

"Shh," she murmured, too aware of the weight of eyes upon her.

The woman in front of them turned fully around to look at them. "Is she all right?"

"I think she's fine, but let's go, okay?" Tamar put her other hand over Ruth's. "Let's get up. Okay?"

"Do you need help?"

Tamar shook her head. "No, it's fine. She hasn't been well. Come on."

She tried to stand, but her mother's grip got even tighter. Ruth grunted. Something flashed across her expression, and then she settled.

Tamar tensed, not daring to relax. Her hand ached, but at least she couldn't see any blood. The cantor finished the prayer, and in the few beats of silence before the next began, the sound of Ruth's breathing seemed very, very loud.

At least, until she started to scream.

The shriek rang out like an alarm bell. The cantor had begun singing and kept on, dutifully ignoring the commotion, but everyone else looked at them.

Tamar stood, pulling her mother upright along with her. Somehow, she managed to get Ruth to follow her, out of the row of seats and toward the door out of the sanctuary. Ruth screamed again, louder this time. Tamar managed to get her out into the entryway, where her cries echoed even louder.

"Do you need some help? Is she okay?" The man at the door asked. He had a basket of kippot in his hands.

Ruth let go of Tamar's hand and flailed at him. She hit the basket, sending fabric skullcaps flying to scatter on the floor. When the man bent to pick them up, she kicked toward his face.

Tamar pulled her away in time for Ruth's foot to miss him. Her mother staggered. Tamar caught her. The man straightened, his eyes and mouth both wide.

"I'm sorry," Tamar muttered as she dragged her still-shrieking mother toward the front doors.

The police officer stationed at the doors opened one. His hand was on his gun as he came into the entryway. The man handing out the kippot took a few steps back, his hands going up.

"I'm sorry," Tamar repeated, louder over and over. She wrestled her mother toward the front doors. "She's not well."

Ruth screamed again. It echoed through the entryway, ringing in Tamar's head. The man staggered back, dropping the couple of kippot he'd managed to pick up. The cop put his hands over his ears. Tamar pushed Ruth through the doorway.

Above them, the stained-glass window cracked with a loud noise.

Tamar shoved her mother onto the sidewalk beneath the vestibule overhang and the car drop-off. Ruth stopped screaming as quickly and sharply as a radio being switched off. She sagged in Tamar's grip, nearly falling.

"Ma'am, do you need me to call an ambulance?" the police officer asked.

Tamar shook her head. "No, she's okay now. I'm so sorry."

She repeated it a few more times, not daring to look behind them as she helped Ruth across the parking lot to her car. By the time she got her mother into the passenger seat, the police officer had gone back to his post. He watched them, his sharp gaze spearing her even from across the parking lot. Nobody else had come out of the synagogue, but a few late arrivals gave Tamar some curious looks as they headed for the front doors.

She buckled Ruth's seatbelt, leaning close. "We're going home now. I hope you're happy. You embarrassed the shit out of me."

Ruth frowned. "Why would you take me to that place?"

"It's a synagogue. It's Rosh Hashanah. I thought you might like it," Tamar said.

Of course it was a lie. She knew her mother wouldn't like even a regular religious service, much less the much longer High Holiday one. She'd taken Ruth there because a Pope-blessed rosary hadn't had any effect on her, but touching the Torah might have. They hadn't even made it to that part of the service before Ruth had lost her shit.

It still wasn't proof, one way or another.

There could be a demon roosting inside her mother, rotting her from the inside out. Or Ruth could simply be an old woman descending into dementia, incapable of regulating her emotions and not caring about who she hurt. There was no way for Tamar to tell.

"You said we were going to the nail salon," Ruth said in a wavering voice. She sat up straight in her seat, clutching her handbag on her lap. "You *said*."

"I never said that."

"Take me home," her mother demanded. "I don't like it here!"

Tamar did take her mother home. The house, empty and quiet because Sally had taken the day off, was hot again. She didn't bother checking the thermostat. She simply heated up some tomato soup and made them both grilled cheeses that they ate, facing each other, at the kitchen table.

"Tell me again about the night my father died," Tamar said abruptly.

Ruth stopped with her sandwich halfway to her mouth. She put it down. "Why do you want to know that horrible story?"

"I want to know the truth."

"I told you what happened," her mother said, but she'd taken on that sly and sideways tone that only crept into her voice when she was getting ready to lie.

"Did my father try to kill me?"

Ruth tried to get up from the table, pushing up on it with both hands, but she fell back into her seat with a sigh. She shook her head. "I don't want to talk about this."

"Too bad," Tamar said. "I want to know the truth. Did he?"

"Who told you that?" Ruth cried out. "Who's been spreading rumors about me? I know, I know who it was. It was that Estrada bitch from across the street. You want to know how she looked at me when I asked her to take care of Lovey for me? How she always looked at me? Like she pitied me! Where did she get off, pitying *me*?"

"Roger Adams told me."

Ruth's jaw dropped. Her mouth worked frantically. Her throat swelled, and she clutched at it, stroking her palm downward over the rising flesh as though she was shoving something down, down, into her gut. She used both hands. Then pressed them to her belly, below the edge of the table. She leaned forward with a sneer. The woman across the table wore her mother's face, but the voice that came out of her was lower. Hard. Rasping.

"If you believe a man who'd fuck another man's wife," the mother-thing said, "well, I suppose you'd believe just about anyone about anything."

"He said you seduced him into getting you pregnant because your husband couldn't." Tamar's voice shook, but she held her ground, not flinching or retreating. There was no more than three feet of wood separating them, close enough that if Ruth lunged for her, she'd be able to get her hands on Tamar, no problem. Tamar was much faster than her mother, though. More agile, stronger. The knife block on the counter was a little farther away, but she'd still be able to get to it, if she had to.

Ruth sat back in her seat with a wave of her hand. The gesture of dismissal was familiar, as was her expression. It was like watching an old home movie, a film shown on the screen of Ruth's face, so you could see both the picture and what lay beneath it. Her mouth twisted, but her eyes were bright, her gaze focused. They looked scared, even if the rest of her face did not.

"Jake Kahan could barely keep it up long enough to fuck, much less knock anyone up."

Tamar frowned. "So it's true? Roger Adams is my biological father?"

Ruth smirked. This time the expression reached her eyes. The internal fight she'd been waging had been lost to whatever dark thing was inside her.

And still, this was not proof.

Tamar thought of what Rabbi Feldman had said about Maimonides, defining evil spirits as mental illness. "Who are you?"

"I'm your mother."

Tamar's phone rang in her purse. Shrill, bleating, insistent. She thought she'd turned the ringer off. She got to it as the call shunted to voicemail, and she checked the number but didn't recognize it. She waited for the voicemail alert to let her know someone had left a message as she turned back to face Ruth.

"So, your husband found out that he wasn't the father to either of his daughters. And he took me to a shitty motel on the outside of town, and he tried to kill me? Why not Lovey? Why not you? You're the one who betrayed him. Not me."

Ruth shrugged.

The phone beeped.

Tamar swiped to listen to the voicemail, praying it was from one of the facilities saying they had a space for her mother, that they could take her today, that she'd be able to get rid of this fucking nightmare. It wasn't from any of those places. It was from Sally Henderson's sister. Tamar listened to the entire message all the way through. Then again, certain she'd heard it wrong. When it was over the second time, she put her phone on the counter and turned to Ruth.

"What did you say to Sally this morning before she left?"

Ruth's eyebrows lifted. "Nothing."

"What," Tamar repeated through gritted teeth, "did you fucking say?"

"I told you, I didn't say anything to her. Why?" Ruth asked with a cunning grin. "Did she quit too?"

Tamar shook her head. "No. She's dead."

39

THE DARK THING that sometimes spoke out of Ruth's mouth had gone silent as she sobbed in Tamar's arms. Her grief at the news about her caregiver's suicide had seemed genuine. She'd even seemed shocked.

"I just don't understand," Ruth said as Tamar guided her to the kitchen table to sit. "She seemed so happy. I thought she was my friend!"

"I'm going to make us some tea."

Tamar filled the electric kettle and turned it on. She took down mugs from one cupboard. Her tea chest from on top of the fridge. She was trying so hard not to break down into shrieking, screaming sobs that every movement ached in her body all the way to her bones, stretching tendons and sinews and muscles. She had to put both hands on the countertop and lean, head hanging, eyes closed, just so she didn't fall down.

This morning, Sally had seemed happy to take the day off.

This afternoon, she'd gone back to her sister's house and slit her own throat so deeply she'd almost been decapitated.

Tamar's call to Karen Smith had been short and to the point.

"I found your number in her phone," Sally's sister had said. "We knew she'd gone to live somewhere else, but she hadn't told us where. My sister was deeply troubled after the death of her daughter. We tried to help her for years and years, but she'd gone into a hard decline. Very depressed. To be honest, I was so surprised to see her when she showed up at the house, because I thought for sure she was already dead. I have to ask, why was she living with you?"

Tamar had explained the meeting in the supermarket, Sally's kindness, her offer to help with Ruth. Karen had been silent for so long Tamar thought the call had been disconnected. When she finally spoke again, her voice was so thick with tears it was hard to hear what she said.

"She wasn't a nurse," Karen had said.

"I'm sorry. What?"

"My sister was not a nurse. She'd been a schoolteacher. Fourth grade. She had no medical or caregiver training. Didn't you check her background or anything?" Karen's voice had risen, shrill with disbelief, hollow and grating with grief.

The conversation had devolved after that. Tamar had disconnected while Sally's sister was still wailing. Karen called back. Tamar didn't answer, and she deleted the woman's voicemail without listening to it.

The water in the electric kettle began to bubble, ready to boil. Tamar plucked two teabags from the wooden chest and tore them free of the foil packaging, then put them in the mugs. She could not look at Ruth, whose sobs were tapering off.

"Did you know Sally had a daughter that died?" Tamar asked.

Ruth sniffled loudly. "She told me she did. Yes. When she was still a little girl."

"Did she say what happened?"

"Oh," Ruth said, "she drowned. At a birthday party, in their backyard. She said she couldn't bear to live in the house after that. She sold it. Went to live with her sister."

"She mentioned once she had a daughter, but I had the impression she was older and had moved away. I didn't know she was dead." Tamar looked over her shoulder at Ruth.

For all the sobbing she'd been doing, Ruth's face was clean of tear streaks. She sat perched on the edge of the hard-backed kitchen chair with her back hunched and her hands curled into claws on her knees. Her toes pressed the floor, her heels up. Every line of her body looked . . . wrong. She was grinning, that fucking awful grin like a slit in a slice of meat, gaping.

Behind Tamar, the kettle boiled. Ruth launched herself from the chair, both hands out. She didn't go for her daughter, though. She went for the kettle. Ruth moved fast, but Tamar moved faster. Just as her mother grabbed the glass kettle, Tamar knocked Ruth's hands upward. Boiling water spilled out. Some splashed on Tamar's arms, but most of it rained onto Ruth's face.

Ruth screamed as her flesh sizzled beneath the onslaught of the boiling water. She let go of the kettle, which smashed on the floor. She flailed, grabbing Tamar by the front of her dress and yanking her forward. Her grip on Tamar's arms loosened. She tried to step back, but she would have fallen. Tamar held her up.

"Tamar," Ruth grated out through her clenched and blood-stained teeth, "what did you do to me?"

Tamar guided Ruth to the kitchen chair and pushed her to sit. She waited to be sure her mother wasn't going to topple over before sweeping up the broken glass from the kettle. She didn't dare turn her back even for the half a minute it would take to put it into the dustpan. She left the pile near the garbage can.

The burns on Ruth's cheeks and chin were already blistering. Her eyes had been spared. Her hair, wet from the boiling water, clung in stringy lines down her face. She lowered her head, her breath coming in pants that slowed as Tamar watched with suspicion.

"We should take you to the emergency room."

"No," Ruth snapped, then, softer, "I mean, please, no. Can't you take care of it for me?"

"I don't even want to touch you," Tamar said. Her arms stung, but she'd escaped mostly unscathed.

Ruth closed her eyes. She swayed in the chair but managed to keep her balance. She spoke without opening her eyes. "You've always had such a hard time with forgiveness. I worry about you."

"You don't need to worry about me. I'm fine." This was a lie. She was nothing close to fine. She was clenching her jaw hard enough to crack a tooth to keep her teeth from chattering. She wrapped her arms around herself to stop herself from trembling. Every breath threatened to become a retch, and the only thing stopping her from bending over the sink to puke was that she didn't dare turn her back on her mother.

"Can I have something to drink?" Ruth asked plaintively.

When Tamar turned on the faucet, Ruth coughed violently. Tamar turned. Her mother's eyes pleaded.

"Not water. Something with a little more . . . kick. A nice red blend, perhaps?" Ruth's voice wheedled. "The kind you like, Tamar. The kind I like, too. Like mother, like—"

"Absolutely not." Tamar turned off the faucet and put down the plastic cup she'd reached for, too wary to give her mother something made of glass.

"What harm could a glass of wine do at this point?" Ruth cajoled.

Ah, there it was. Not gone away. Just hiding.

"If she gets drunk, you'll be able to get out again," Tamar said flatly, no longer trying to hide the fact she knew about the demon inside of her mother.

Ruth's body straightened, but it was the thing inside her that spoke. Same voice. Different inflection. "Mazel tov. It only took you half a century to figure it out. Tell you what, though, sweetie. Why not pour yourself a tall glass of something good? You look like you could use it."

Tamar leaned against the kitchen counter. Her mouth watered at the thought of a long drink of wine, but the saliva was bitter. She shook her head.

"No? Too bad." Ruth's body shifted on the chair, making it creak. Her eyes rolled. She touched the burgeoning blisters, pressing hard and letting out a cry of pain. Then a laugh in a different voice. "This hurts her, by the way. A lot."

"You want me to be drunk so you can get away."

Ruth's eyebrows rose. "No, no. You have it all wrong, girl. If you're drunk enough, or high enough, I don't care which, it will be easier for me to get *in*."

"You want to get inside me?" The moment she said it aloud, everything fell into place.

Shawn's words echoed in her head. *She told me she could make me do it. That I'd like it. No, that I'd love it. I'd love it so much that I'd want her to get inside me.*

"What are you?" Tamar asked.

Ruth's head lolled on her neck, tipping back impossibly far before snapping up straight again. A swirl of shadows turned her into the eyeless, gape-mawed thing, but only for a second before she was no more than a whimpering old lady again.

"I'm just an old lady—"

"Bullshit."

The mother-thing's smile peeled open her face. "I am the ageless, I am the void, I am the many, I am the nothing, I am the all."

"You," Tamar said, "are a weak fucking cunt."

A shriek pelted from Ruth's open mouth, but although she writhed on the chair and tried to push herself out of it with her fingers curled into claws, all she managed was to fall back and pant weakly.

"This body is dying all around me," the demon muttered.

"Does she know? That you're in there?"

The demon shrugged.

Ruth's eyes blinked, and Tamar's mother peeked out from them, like a little girl hiding behind the curtains. "Mother?"

The stink of something rotten oozed out of her. Tamar covered her nose and mouth, turning her face. She scrambled for a kitchen towel and used that instead. It did little to block the stench.

"Mother?" Ruth repeated in a little girl's voice. "What have you done to your hair?"

Automatically, Tamar touched her head and the bristles there. "I'm your daughter. Tamar."

"Oh. Yes. Of course. You always favored my mother. You really did. That dark hair. Do you know how proud she was of that hair, so thick and shining? Oh, when I was a girl, I wanted hair like my mother's." Ruth wobbled on the chair but straightened. "She never wanted me, though. She wanted a son. But instead, she got me, a daughter. And when I saw how she suffered, what else could I do but say yes?"

"Say yes to what?" Tamar demanded.

"To her."

"Her, who?" She stalked closer but stayed out of reach.

Ruth's fingers twitched on the tabletop. "I don't know her name. But she was in my mother, and my mother's mother before her, and I suppose she was in my mother's mother's mother before that, and eventually, when my mother was old and suffering and used up, she came into me. And I knew that I would have to have a daughter too, so that one day, *she* would be able to stop *my* suffering."

Tamar frowned. Her mother had always been a revisor of history, a misrepresenter of truths. A liar. This, though, had the ring of truth.

"How am I supposed to stop your suffering, Ruth?"

"Say yes to her. You have to say yes."

40

THE MEZUZAH CASE from the house on Spring Hill Drive and scroll Rabbi Feldman had given her were not where Tamar had left them. She wanted to scream, she wanted to cry, but instead she closed the drawer carefully and slowly. If they were gone forever, she would deal with that then, but for now, she was going to keep looking.

"What are you doing?" Ruth asked from her seat at the table.

Her voice drilled straight into Tamar's eardrums. She winced. "Don't worry about it."

"I worry about everything you do, Tamar. Don't you understand that? I'm your mother."

Tamar. Ruth did not call her that. Not ever.

She turned. "I don't know what you are, but you are not my mother."

"How rude."

Ruth's lips stretched over the broad expanse of her yellow-gray teeth. Her tongue slipped out, flickering like a snake's, to lick across them before slurping back between her lips. It happened so fast it would have been easy to tell herself she'd imagined it, but Tamar was finished with denial. She lifted her chin and fixed the thing wearing her mother's body with a long and steady gaze. She didn't speak.

Ruth looked uncertain. "Are we going to eat dinner soon? I'm very hungry, Tammy."

There. Whatever it was, the thing inside of Ruth was gone, at least for the moment. Or pretending it was, and Tamar would take that too for now.

"I'll get you something in a bit, okay?"

"Okay, honey. Is Sally coming back?"

Tamar eyed her mother, but the question still seemed to come from Ruth, not her internal rider. "No. She's not."

"Oh." Ruth slouched for a moment, her face falling. "She was such a good friend."

"I know."

Tamar's throat closed in sympathy for Sally. Sure, she had lied about her credentials, but she'd been good for Ruth. Without her help, Tamar wouldn't have survived the past few weeks. Sally hadn't deserved what Ruth's demon had done to her, and that was Tamar's fault. She'd known the dangers surrounding her mother, and she'd still allowed Sally to stand between them. She might as well have killed the woman herself.

"My face hurts." Ruth touched her chin with trembling fingers. "Oh, my. What happened? Did I have an accident?"

"Yes. You burned yourself. I'm going to get you something for it."

"Can I go to my room?"

Tamar's throat closed, but she managed to speak around the lump in it. "Yes. Of course. I'll bring it to you. Why don't you go rest?"

Ruth nodded and pushed herself up from the chair. Tamar took her arm to help her, ready to go to battle again at the first hint her mother might turn on her, but Ruth felt small and frail again. Steady enough on her feet, though, so Tamar let go of her. Ruth turned and shuffled down the hall toward the study. Tamar watched her go, then went back to the junk drawer and searched through it once again, carefully and slowly. She had put the case and the scroll into this drawer, and she hadn't moved them. She knew that.

Sudden inspiration struck her, and she bent to open the cabinets directly below the drawer. Using the light from her phone, she looked toward the back, behind the pots and pans. And there was the box. It must've been shoved so hard into the back of the drawer that it fell down. She was willing to bet that had not happened by accident. She imagined the demon, incapable or maybe only unwilling, of touching the holy items, simply shoving and shoving the rest of the drawer's contents until the box got lost. No matter. She had it now.

Tamar straightened. She opened the box at the kitchen table, studying the scroll that had been kept safe in its small plastic bag. The mezuzah case itself had two small holes, one at the top and one at the bottom. Two tiny nails had been taped to the inside of it.

When Tamar peeked in on her, Ruth was sitting in her recliner watching *Mary Poppins* again. Tamar brought in some first aid cream, which she dabbed onto the blisters rising on Ruth's face. Some of them had already popped, oozing clear yellow fluid down her cheeks and chin. Every now and then, her tongue snaked out to lick some of it away. Tamar's guts lurched, but she gave no outward signs of her disgust. She wasn't going to give the demon the satisfaction of seeing her affected by anything it did.

Handing her phone to Ruth, Tamar said, "Dial Lovey."

Ruth looked up. "Huh?"

"You haven't spoken to Lovey in a while. I want you to call her. Tell her you're okay. That everything is fine."

"All right." Ruth did as she was told, holding the phone with both hands.

While her mother chatted with Lovey, sounding perfectly normal, Tamar found Ruth's phone and slipped it into the pocket of her dress. She listened carefully to everything her mother said, but although it would have been natural for Ruth to tell Lovey about the "accident" with the kettle, she said nothing about it. It sounded as though she was talking to the little kids. Then back to Lovey. Her expression was blank the entire time, but her mouth moved without trouble. She handed the phone off to Tamar and turned her attention back to the television.

"How's it going over there?" Lovey asked.

"All good." Tamar's lie hurt her heart, but she wasn't going to let Lovey get dragged into any of this. "We went to services today. It was nice. Now we're settling in for the night. How's everything in sunny California?"

Her sister launched into a description of the kids' school-starting activities and how busy they all were. Mark's job prospects, and how they were going to be able to stay where they were for a few more years, maybe even until the last kiddo graduated from high school. A trip they were planning to the East Coast for Thanksgiving, if Tam was willing to host.

"Of course. I'd love to. That would be great. Plenty of room for you all," she said as she leaned against the doorframe, eyes closed, tears streaming down her cheeks. She kept her voice from giving away her sorrow by sheer force of will. "I'd love to see you."

"I miss you," Lovey said. "And I just want you to know how much I appreciate what you're doing for Mom. I know it's been hard. And I worry about you, Tam."

Ruth's head swiveled on her neck, boneless and well-greased. The rest of her body stayed facing the TV. Her fingernails scritch-scritched on the arms of the chair, over and over, wearing away at the fabric. Her tongue slithered out, impossibly long, to swipe at the oozing blisters again, then lolled from the corner of her mouth. Drool collected on the tip, dripping.

"We're fine," Tamar lied. "To be honest, Lovey, this is the closest I've ever felt to her. I think we've really managed to turn a corner."

The demon laughed with Ruth's mouth.

Lovey said more after that, words Tamar only half heard. She wrapped up the call with the excuse that she needed to make dinner. "I love you," she told her sister before disconnecting.

She thought it might be the final time she was able to say it.

"I'm hungry," her mother's body said.

"I'll get you something right now. Stay here."

"My face hurts."

"I'll bring you some ibuprofen or something. Just stay here," Tamar repeated. She backed out of the doorway, waiting for Ruth's body to spring after her, but she stayed in place.

One ear listening for footsteps in the hallway, Tamar quickly pre-pared a couple of cold cheese sandwiches, chips, some fruit. She got the bottle of pain reliever from the powder room medicine cabinet and added that to the tray. Also a few bottles of apple juice. She took all of it into Ruth's room and put it on top of the dresser. She set up a TV tray and put a plate with some food on it in front of her mother, who dug in at once, smacking and slurping.

Tamar ducked into the garage and got her hammer. While Ruth was distracted with gobbling up her food, Tamar took the small scroll from the plastic bag and fit it into the back of the mezuzah case. She set it against the study's doorframe—not straight up or down, but angled inward to the room, in the prescribed fashion. She'd already looked up the blessing to be sure she knew it by heart.

"Baruch atah Adonai, Elohaynu melech ha-olam, asher kidishanu b'mitzvotav v'tzivanu lik'boa mezuzah," she whispered.

Ruth stirred. "Huh? What?"

Quickly, Tamar hammered the first tiny nail through the hole. While her mother's body struggled with the table in front of her, Tamar hammered in the second nail. She stepped back, out of the doorway.

The TV table went flying as Ruth staggered to her feet. She fell forward, off the chair and onto her hands and knees. She turned her horrible, burned face toward Tamar.

"What did you do?"

"Do you recognize it?" Tamar pointed at the mezuzah. "It used to be yours."

Any semblance of Ruth being the one speaking disappeared as the demon grunted. The mother-thing pushed herself up onto one knee, a twisted hand gripping the tattered arm of the chair. "What do you think that's going to do?"

"It's going to keep you in this room," Tamar said.

The demon's head gave another boneless, wobbling swivel toward the room's two windows. "You think I can't bust right out of here?"

"I think you'd like to, but you're trapped inside an old woman who can barely keep herself from falling over. You used up a lot of her strength already, didn't you? You're weak."

"This body is weak," the demon spat. "Not me."

Somehow, Tamar found a laugh. "As long as you're inside that body, you're weak."

Ruth's expression twisted. She struggled to get to her feet and managed, but she was left panting and swaying. She staggered to the bed and fell onto it with a groan. She writhed, tangling the sheets beneath her.

"What are you going to do? You can't keep me a prisoner!"

Another laugh burbled its way out of Tamar's throat. "Oh, yes I can."

"For how long?"

"Until you're dead," Tamar told the demon.

Now it laughed. "I don't die."

"What happens if the body you're in dies before you can get out of it?"

Her mother's body went still.

"You don't have to answer me. I think I already know," Tamar said. "You might not die, but you'll be stuck there, won't you? Inside it? For how long?"

The demon let out a long, low and guttural growl. It writhed again, fighting against the bed like it was an enemy. It got Ruth's body up, legs over the side of the bed facing Tamar. Ruth's shoulders heaved with the demon's angry, labored breaths.

"Why couldn't you just do as you were supposed to? All the others did, from the very first one and all through time. One to the next to the next. But *you*." The demon sneered. "You just wouldn't step into line, would you? Oh, you got yourself in trouble all right. A little poke with a pin in those rubbers you thought were hidden, well . . . that happened."

"You sabotaged my birth control?" Tamar's fists clenched.

"One to one to one to one. Your grandmother waited so long to have hers, it was almost too late. Then along came Ruth, and I didn't want to risk that happening again. I wanted a young life. More fun that way. But you wouldn't let me in, and you killed what could have been mine in your place. And now, look at you. You're old, and you never did the one simple thing you needed to do to save yourself. What will you do when your time comes, Tamar? What will you do when you don't have someone to accept the gift?"

"Gift?" Tamar snorted.

Ruth's body swayed but didn't topple over. The demon's grin split the corners of Ruth's mouth, the skin tight from being burned. Blood trickled out, mixing with the drool and fluid from the blisters. The mother-thing cackled.

"Of course I am a gift. You think your mother would have ever lived the life she did if not for me?"

"If you mean a life of drinking, drugs, and reckless promiscuity," Tamar said, "it's hardly anything to be proud of. She ruined all of her relationships for her entire life."

The demon's tongue lolled out again, slick and glistening. The lengthy slice of muscle flapped as it spoke. "And what about you? You did the same thing, even without me inside of you."

For a moment, a single second, Tamar believed that to be true. She could give herself up to despair at the thought of it. How she had hurt and abandoned anyone who'd ever loved her. How much better off her life would be with someone else at the helm to guide her, to take away the emotions so she never had to feel guilt again . . .

She clapped her hands to her head. Then put one hand on the mezuzah. Those thoughts vanished, quick as a blink. She stood up straight.

"Stay out of my head. I do not invite you there. I don't invite you in anyplace at all. Ever."

The demon slurped its tongue back inside Ruth's mouth. Her body fell back onto the bed. It let out another groan.

"My face hurts," Ruth cried. The demon added, "And I'll make it hurt worse."

"I'm going to go with a nice solid, 'who gives a fuck,'" Tamar said. "Suffer."

Then she left without even bothering to shut the door behind her.

41

TAMAR MADE IT to the hardware store right before it closed for the night. She expected to see the study windows broken out when she got back, but apparently, she'd guessed correctly. At least for now, Ruth's body was too frail and weak for even the demon to use. Without going inside, she got right to work installing the window guards. She believed in the mezuzah's power to keep the demon inside Ruth's room, but she couldn't be sure that it wouldn't be strong enough in a few hours to break out of the windows. Of course, if it got really strong enough, it would be able to bend the metal bars anyway, and she'd be fucked no matter what.

It took her an hour to install the guards, and by the time she was done, her hands were so stiff and sore that she could hardly make a fist. The entire time she worked, the blue-white light from the TV flickered through the windows. Sometimes a shadow passed in front of them, but nothing tried to break through.

She'd just finished putting the ladder back in the garage when she saw Ross standing at the end of her driveway. His dog sniffed at the asphalt and tugged at the leash so she could get to the grass, where she squatted. Ross lifted a hand in greeting.

"Everything okay?" he called out.

Tamar nodded. "Absolutely."

They stared at each other. He nodded slowly and kept walking without looking back. She watched him look both ways, then again, then again, before he crossed the street, and wondered if he'd taken to walking the dog this late at night because traffic was likely to be so much lighter. He might never get over the trauma of being hit by that car, she thought. Was that her mother's fault? Or the demon's? In the end, it didn't really matter. Ruth had made this bed, and she was going to die in it.

When Tamar opened the door from the garage into the house, she paused, waiting to see if her mother's body would come hurtling down the hall. The TV light and the low murmur of singing was all that greeted her. Keeping her distance, she looked through the doorway. Her mother's body was on the bed, facing away in the familiar position. She'd covered herself with the blankets, despite the ever-present and oppressive heat in the house. The room stunk of garbage stewing in the sun, of sewage, of rot and death. Tamar choked on it.

Ruth didn't move.

Tamar didn't bother trying to talk to her. She shut the door behind her and went upstairs, where she gave herself the luxury of a cold shower that fended off the oppressive heat. For the first time since she'd woken to find her head shaved, she didn't want to cry when she looked at herself in the mirror. This face looked strong. Fierce. This was the face of a woman who'd seen some shit and got through it; she would get through whatever came next too.

After the shower, she slept.

Her ringing phone woke her. She rolled to grab it up, thinking it was her alarm, but then realized she hadn't set it. She scrolled through the messages that had come in. Miguel. Her boss. Lovey. Tamar had slept for nearly sixteen hours. It was almost seven PM.

Her phone beeped with a voicemail alert. The call was from Rabbi Feldman, checking in. She'd seen Tamar and Ruth at the Rosh Hashanah service. She hoped they were both all right.

"I'm pretty busy right now. Days of Awe, and all that. But I hope to see you both back for Yom Kippur. If there's anything I can do to make your mother feel more comfortable or welcome, Tamar, please, reach out. If you call me back and I can't answer, please leave a voicemail and I'll try to get back to you as soon as I can. I just want you to know I'm thinking about you. I'm here. Call me."

Tamar wept at the end of the message. If she'd had someone like Rabbi Feldman back when she was a kid, how much of a difference it might have made in her life. On the other hand, the rabbi didn't believe evil spirits were real. She certainly wouldn't believe Tamar if she told her about the demon that had been infesting Ruth's matriarchal line. How could Tamar ask her to come here, to help her?

It was clear from everything that had happened that Ruth's demon was fully capable of killing anyone who opposed it. She couldn't risk the rabbi's life that way. Nor her sister's. Not Miguel's either, which was why she texted him quickly that she needed some time to think about what had happened between them, and he should wait to hear from her before reaching out to her again. She didn't want to ghost him. It would hurt him to be pushed off this way, but she didn't want him showing up again, unexpected. Not while she was dealing with the thing in the room downstairs.

She would have to take care of this on her own, the way she'd always had to.

Her empty stomach rumbled with a real appetite. She made scrambled eggs with cheese, toast, butter. Hash brown patties from the freezer. She gorged on all of it until she was sated, then made another batch to feed her mother.

Ruth was in the recliner when Tamar went in. She looked up with an expectant expression. She wore the same clothes she'd worn yesterday, now rumpled and stained. Her hair hung in straggles over her forehead and cheeks, where strands stuck in the open mess of her blistered skin. Her smile seemed genuine, though, not the demon's rictus.

"Oh, honey. I thought you'd never get up. Did you sleep well?" It was her mother's voice. Her mother's words. But Tamar didn't trust that it was her mother speaking.

She set up the TV table and put the plate of food on it. She hadn't given her mother a fork or a knife but had layered the egg onto the bread for her so she could make a sandwich. Ruth looked at the food with a grimace and pushed it away.

"I don't want it."

"You should eat," Tamar said.

Ruth looked at her. "I'm not hungry."

"You should still eat. To keep your strength up."

Slowly, slowly, the corners of her lips curled up like paper being eaten by a flame. Slowly, slowly, the mother-thing pushed the plate toward the edge of the table, her eyes fixed on Tamar's the entire time. Tamar caught the plate as it tipped and before it could spill. She took it away.

The next time she came back, Ruth was pacing between the television and the bed. She'd been at it for some time, based on the wear pattern in the carpet. She shuffled from one end of the room to the other, wringing her hands and muttering. Tamar watched her from the doorway, but her mother didn't look in her direction.

In her office, Tamar began to research how to exorcise a demon. Of course, what came up first was pages and pages of Christian rhetoric, heavily Catholic but also some evangelical. She revised her search terms and found a few more sites featuring stories about Jewish demons, but the rituals for casting them out were vaguely described and slanted more toward "These are stories" rather than "Yeah, Satan's totally determined to steal your soul, here's what you do when he tries." Satan, it seemed, didn't care about Jews any more than they cared about him.

She sat back in her chair to rub her eyes. Darkness had fallen, and her office was lit only by the light of her laptop screen. From the hallway came a stealthy, sliding sound. She turned toward it, expecting to see the thing with dangling arms and red eyes standing in the kitchen doorway, but only shadows watched her. She got up and went to the hall so she could look down to the study. The door remained open. A shadow bent the flickering light from the television, but nothing came out of the room.

Tamar went back to her research.

Another hour passed, and she'd managed to dig up some useful tips. She'd need a minyan—ten men—who would read the Torah to the afflicted while prevailing upon it to cast itself out of her mother's body via her big toe, the only place it could be counted on to leave without causing permanent damage. She could find out the demon's name and say it in shorter and shorter pieces, until there was nothing left and the demon was forced to flee. There were other methods, none of which involved screaming "the power of Christ compels you," but nevertheless felt as useless and ridiculous.

She went to the study and watched Ruth pacing. "Are you hungry?"

Her mother's body turned toward her, but the demon spoke. "I'll swallow your soul!"

"Oh, fuck off," Tamar said evenly. Movie monster quotes weren't going to scare her. She was done with fear.

The demon's laugh grated out of Ruth's throat like it was shaking sand through a sieve. "Your mother is hungry."

"Then she should eat."

The demon coughed into its hand and showed Tamar its palm. A few strands of long, dark hair covered it. "Oh, yes. Feed her."

Tamar flinched in revulsion, hating herself for letting the thing get to her so easily. She straightened. "If you're so worried about her dying before you can get out of her, maybe you should take better care of her."

The thing spat a gobbet of mucus-coated hair onto the floor and ground it into the carpet with a heel. "How about this. How about you simply say yes? Ruth will get to finish out her life as an addlepated old granny, and you and I will ride out the rest of yours like it's a roller coaster. Both hands up, screaming all the way. You used to love roller coasters, Tamar."

"They make me sick to my stomach."

The demon cooed, lips pursed. "That's a shame. I have other games we can play, instead."

"Why would I ever allow it?"

"You have at least another thirty years in you. Do you really want to spend them the way you did your first fifty? You're alone. Oh, yes, I know you've got something going on again with your high school sweetie, but honey, don't you know? There's a reason why burned-out flames should never reignite. You know you're not going to be able to make it work. You know you're going to crush him again. Break his heart. It's what you do." The demon held up one crooked finger. "But I can change that. Oh, we could have such a life together, you and I. You won't be afraid to live. We can travel. We can *love*—"

"Love," Tamar scoffed. "As if something like you could ever know anything about it."

The demon stretched her mother's mouth into a terrible smile that showed off her yellowed, rotting teeth. "You'd be surprised what I know. Let me in, and you'll know too."

"And then what?" Tamar asked, truly curious. "I didn't have a daughter. Where will you go when it's my turn to die?"

"I'm very clever. I'll find a way. You don't have to bear a child to love it as your own or to make it love you. Have you ever considered adoption?"

Fury simmered low in Tamar's gut. She crossed the room so fast the demon didn't have time to react. She grabbed Ruth's body by the front of her blouse, fists curling into the stained and stinking fabric. She shook her mother's body so hard her teeth rattled. She flailed, but Tamar kept a firm grip. Beneath her hands, Ruth's muscles tensed and she got her arms up in between their bodies. She was strong enough to break free of Tamar's hold, but then she staggered back and fell onto the recliner with a mewling whine.

It looked up at her, and Tamar thought she saw a hint of her mother on its expression. Ruth was scared, tired, and hurting, but she was also angry, and that was not the thing that had been living inside her for decades but her own, true self. How much of what Tamar remembered of her mother had been what was riding her soul?

"I never made Ruth do anything she didn't really want to do," the demon said slyly. "That's what you want to know, isn't it? How different your mother might have been without me inside her? Maybe she might have loved you, if not for me. Maybe she might have been able to stop herself from the booze, the drugs, the random men. If not for me? Is that what you want to know?"

Tamar didn't answer. The demon chuckled. Ruth's body sagged into the recliner. Exhaustion etched her face. Her makeup had worn off, leaving her face lined and worn and haggard. The broken blisters were crusting over. Her lips were dry and cracked, and her tongue, when it flopped out, wore a coat of white that looked almost like fur.

"What happens if this body dies with you in it?" Tamar asked.

The demon did not answer.

"You tried to get Shawn to agree to take you in. Who else? Maybe even as far back as Gilda Roth? Ms. Carr? Did you also try with Sally? Is that why she killed herself?"

The demon muttered something Tamar couldn't make out. It writhed in the recliner, pushing back to get the footrest to pop out, then contorting Ruth's body to push it back in. It pounded on the armrests.

"*Can* you just go into anyone?" Tamar pressed.

"They have to say yes. They have to want it to happen. They have to . . ." the demon writhed again. It twisted Ruth's body in the chair. "They have to do it because they love me. I loved my daughter, and she didn't love me. So, when I died, I made sure she would always have to love me."

"You possessed your own daughter?"

"*All* the daughters," it said.

A dybbuk. The dislocated soul of a dead person that had become a malicious, possessing spirit. One related to Tamar.

"Why not Lovey?"

"Ruth wouldn't let me near Lovey. Once you were gone, she found the strength to put me in my place. Thought she could keep me there, but as you see, I can't be kept away. Not that I wanted to get inside Lovey, anyway. I need one daughter, not a litter. And I'd promised Ruth I'd leave her favorite alone."

The favorite. Tamar wasn't sure if the dybbuk was lying. It felt like truth, but she still didn't trust it.

"And she trusted you?" Tamar asked.

The dybbuk's lips skinned back with a gasp as she clutched imaginary pearls. "I gave her my *word*." A pause. "Besides, they moved away and haven't been back since."

"So . . . you need to physically be with the person you infect?"

The dybbuk hissed.

Tamar's heart thumped. She wiped her sweaty palms on her shirt, over her belly. "You made her fall and hit her head, didn't you? That's what made her weak enough for you to gain control again."

"It would have killed her, if not for me. Brain bleed," the mother-thing said. "I was barely keeping Ruth upright. I tried Gilda, but we'd never been friends. Carr, ugh. What a moron. I didn't want her beige life, but I needed her to make you take us in. Admit it, Tamar. There was a comfort in being able to find fresh reasons to hate Ruth."

The dybbuk grinned. "Like coming home."

Ruth's fist came up and socked herself in the mouth. Her knuckles came away coated with blood. More of it dribbled down her chin, wending a path through the crusting scabs. She raised her fist again, but cried out a plea, "No, please! No!"

"Mothers love their daughters, no matter what they do," the dybbuk said. "And no matter what they do, daughters love their mothers."

"Not always," Tamar said.

"If you don't love her, why are you trying so hard to save her?"

Tamar backed away. "I'm not trying to save her. I'm saving myself."

CHAPTER

42

Tamar's research hadn't turned up much more of anything she could actually use. The dybbuk refused to share her true name. Tamar didn't have time for a deep dive into her family history either. Without the real name, she couldn't call upon the dybbuk to leave of her own accord, not that Tamar though she'd do that, anyway. The thing had been possessing her matriarchal line for generations. Desperation had prompted the dybbuk to attempt seducing someone else into inviting her in, but she'd failed. She really, really wanted Tamar, the child who'd been born for her to take.

Did she have a reason? Did she need one, other than desire? Tamar didn't need to understand the dybbuk. She only needed to fight it.

There would be no minyan, no reading of seven Torah scrolls, no blowing of seven ram's horns. Tamar didn't have a single black candle, much less seven of them, and why did expulsion of this thing require the efforts of ten *men*, anyway? Especially since the dybbuk was female and had inhabited the women in Tamar's family for what had apparently been hundreds of years.

Three days had passed since Rosh Hashanah, which meant there was only a week left until Yom Kippur. This was supposed to be a time of contemplation and reflection, of apologies and making amends to those you'd harmed. It was a chance to ask for, and to receive, forgiveness so that when the final shofar sounded on Yom Kippur, and the

Book of Life was sealed and closed for another year, your name would be inscribed inside it.

In the years since their divorce, Tamar had spoken to Garrett only briefly, once or twice. She had never reached out to him to ask him to forgive her for the pain she'd caused him; she hadn't asked for or expected him to ever do the same either. If he'd been capable of that, he would've done it long before their marriage fell apart. The dybbuk had accused Tamar of ruining all of her relationships the way her mother had. She was willing to own her part in the destruction of her marriage, but it had not all been her fault.

Still, she reached out to him, thinking he might not even take her call. They spoke for thirty minutes, which didn't seem like enough time for anyone to work through twenty-some years of baggage, but somehow, it worked. He cried. She cried. He said he forgave her, and he asked for the same, and they ended the call with what felt like, at least to Tamar, genuine consideration for each other. It had been easier than she'd expected, which ought to have felt suspicious. She refused to let it. There was holding on, and there was letting go, and she was choosing the latter.

For other forgiveness, she was going to have to work a lot harder.

The dybbuk had refused to feed Ruth for an entire day before Tamar came back into the room with a bowl of oatmeal and mashed banana. Some water in a plastic tumbler. It was bland food, the kind her mother had fed her when she'd been sick, and the smell of it took her back to childhood days of being tucked up on the couch watching game shows and soap operas, a sleeve of saltines at the ready.

The room reeked of body odor, bodily fluids, and blood. Ruth's burns were infected, and each time one scabbed over the dybbuk picked it back open. Tamar had given up trying to use ointment on them.

She managed to get about half a cup of oatmeal and banana into Ruth's mouth before the dybbuk tried to force it back up. Tamar clapped a hand over her mother's mouth and kept the food inside until Ruth was forced to swallow it. The dybbuk then forced Ruth to shit herself, and Tamar cleaned her up in the shower, much the way she'd done the first night she'd woken to find her mother standing over her bed. The way this all began, she thought, but it would not be the way it ended.

She wrestled Ruth's body into clean nightclothes, even combing her hair and tying it back from her face. The dybbuk fought, but since she had also been refusing to allow Ruth to eat, the body was indeed weakening. She fell back onto the bed, whining and groaning, then went silent.

Tamar pulled up a chair. "I want to talk to my mother."

"I'm right here, honey."

"Try again," Tamar said. "I'm not stupid."

The dybbuk frothed at the mouth, tossing and turning, pulling the sheets free of the bed and rolling in them. She stopped short of throwing Ruth's body onto the floor and peeked out at Tamar from the burrito roll of blankets. So, she didn't really *want* to hurt Ruth's body, Tamar thought. Hurting Ruth would give the dybbuk more control, but she didn't want the body to die.

Not yet.

"I want to speak to my mother," Tamar repeated. "You can listen, if you want, but I want to talk to her."

The dybbuk contorted in the tangle of blankets, freeing one arm. Then the other. She got up onto a pile of pillows and leaned against the headboard. She shuddered. Ruth's mouth opened wide. Her eyes rolled back. She slumped to one side.

"I'm here," Ruth said.

Tamar's throat scratched with emotion. "We need to work some things out, Ruth."

Her mother's laugh held no humor. "You can't even call me Mom. What things do you think we are going to work out?"

"It's almost Yom Kippur. It's the time to work shit out," Tamar said. "*Mom.*"

Ruth rolled her eyes again. "You know I don't care about any of that."

"That doesn't matter. You don't have to believe in the Book of Life or God or any of that to ask someone to forgive you."

"Forgive? You want me to beg you to forgive me? For what?" Ruth pounded weakly on the mattress. "Oh, girly, you have some kind of nerve."

This was more like the woman Tamar had always known. And it *was* her mother, not the dybbuk inside her speaking with Ruth's tongue. The malicious spirit was still there, cavorting in Ruth's brain, but it was definitely Ruth who was talking now.

"I did everything for you," Ruth continued. "I kept you fed. A roof over your head. Clothes. Toys. The bills were paid and you lacked for nothing—"

Tamar shook her head. "You drank yourself into a stupor. You cut my hair while I slept. You brought strange men into our house—"

"I was a young widow! Don't tell me you, of all people, think a woman shouldn't be allowed to have a relationship! Isn't slut shaming supposed to be bad?" Ruth cried.

"I'm not shaming you for the number of men you slept with."

"You're blaming me for something, then."

"For choosing them over us," Tamar told her. "Over *me*."

Ruth frowned. "I'm not going to apologize for living my life."

Tamar stood. "I'll come back later, and we can try this again."

"What about you?" Ruth called to her back as Tamar left the room. "What about you asking me to forgive *you*?"

And then all Tamar heard was the dybbuk's grating laughter.

Every day, Tamar asked the dybbuk to let her mother speak. Every day, Ruth came forward and refused to apologize for anything she had ever done. She made excuses. She laid blame on everyone but herself. She wept and gnashed her teeth and pounded her fists on the mattress, but she would not say she was sorry.

The dybbuk did.

"I should have been a better mother," she said through clenched teeth. "I was wrong. I should have gone for therapy. I should have married a nice man who could've been a real father to you. I should have—"

"I know it's you, not her," Tamar said.

"Does it matter?"

"Yes. Of course it matters." Tamar rubbed her eyes to clear them from the grit that came from lack of sleep. She was no longer worried that the dybbuk was going to ride her mother's body out of the room or to attack her while she slept, but she still was finding it too hard to get some rest.

"If she says she's sorry, will you take her place?"

Tamar didn't answer that. Instead, she fed her mother's body, and she cleaned it, and she asked to speak to her mother every day. Every day, she hoped she'd get the answer she wanted.

The dybbuk, at least, had stopped trying to cause harm to Ruth's body. The burns healed faster than would've been normal, leaving behind pink, fresh skin. She grinned at Tamar, turning her stolen face from side to side.

"See what I can do? It's not much, I know," she said in a voice rotten with false modesty. "But it's something, isn't it?"

"If you can heal those blisters, why can't you just heal the whole body? Keep on living inside it forever?" Tamar asked.

"This body is old and decrepit, and there's nothing I can do with it! I had its best years, and then you ran away—" the dybbuk faltered.

It was the first time Tamar had seen the thing show uncertainty. "And then what?"

"She got sober."

"It was easier to control her when she was using, right?"

The dybbuk grimaced. "It was definitely more fun."

"I left, and she got her shit together. She became a real mother to Lovey and what's more, she kept *you* away from Lovey. She wouldn't let you even get close to her. But I came back, and Lovey went away, and then what happened?"

"I looked at the old woman in the mirror and saw my time was running out."

Tamar frowned. "You couldn't get her to start drinking again, so you fucked with her mind. Gave her dementia."

The dybbuk showed Ruth's awful teeth. "I was always there. I had to make her to crack open again, but I was always there."

"Too bad you made her such a shitshow to begin with," Tamar said. "I might never have left."

43

THE MORNING OF Yom Kippur, Tamar found Ruth up and dressed, her hair wet from the shower. Her face, carefully made up. She'd dressed in a crisp white blouse and black skirt and had even added hose and black pumps. She moved slowly, as though she were made of glass and afraid to break herself, but she was on her own two feet. She refused the breakfast Tamar brought.

"I'm fasting," she said.

"You don't have to. Fasting on Yom Kippur isn't necessary if you need to take care of yourself for health reasons," Tamar said.

"I'm fasting," Ruth repeated, or the dybbuk did, Tamar could not be sure. "Are you going to services?"

The hopeful tone gave it away. The dybbuk, then. Tamar shook her head.

"No. And even if I did, I wouldn't take you."

"I'd behave myself this time," the dybbuk pleaded. "I promise you."

"So, you want to go to the service?"

The dybbuk clasped Ruth's hands to her chest like a schoolgirl rhapsodizing over a crush. "Yes. Oh, yes!"

It might have fooled her in the past, but Tamar wasn't going to let it again. The dybbuk didn't want to go to services. It just wanted her to let it out of this room, beyond the protection of the mezuzah.

"Good news," Tamar said. "We can attend virtually."

Tamar had taken the day off and let her boss know she wouldn't be working because of the holiday. She texted both her sister and Miguel that she was observing Yom Kippur and would not be replying to her phone. Then she turned it off.

She brought her laptop right outside the study door and set it up out of reach. She turned up the volume. The morning service had already begun, and the sound of the rabbi and cantor joining their voices in the prayers was soon mingled with the dybbuk's wretched and gibbering howls.

"You have until they blow the shofar," Tamar said.

All pretense of Ruth being in control of her body fell away. The dybbuk flung herself to the floor, contorting. Ruth's back bowed, her head nearly touching her feet. The dybbuk shrieked, and so did she.

Tamar turned up the volume on the laptop.

Many of the prayers were still familiar enough to her that she could at least hum along with the tune, even if she wasn't sure of the words. She stayed outside of the room. Inside it, the dybbuk rallied.

Ruth's body lurched to her feet. Up, up, up she stretched, onto her toes like a ballet dancer *en pointe*. The arms dangled with an illusion of length. The dybbuk dragged Ruth's body along the carpet, still on the tips of her toes, but when she got to the doorframe, she whirled away. Back and forth, she traversed the room, Ruth's body jerking like a rag doll. The dybbuk flung her onto the floor again, where she drummed Ruth's feet and her fists into the now-filthy carpet.

A long, croaking cry reverberated up and out of Ruth's throat. The dybbuk spoke with many voices, in languages Tamar could not identify. She made a mockery of the prayers being sung, mimicking them by substituting curses and profanities into the lyrics. She forced Ruth's body up again, whirling around the room and knocking over furniture. She smashed the television with one fist and spattered blood as far as it could go across the room. None of it hit Tamar or her computer, but she moved it a little further away to be safe.

"I'll kill her!" the dybbuk threatened. "I'll fucking make her slit her throat the way I did with the other ones!"

"Do it," Tamar said calmly. The dybbuk had never answered her about what would happen if Ruth's body died with the dybbuk still inside, but Tamar had some guesses.

The dybbuk did not cut Ruth's throat. She did, however, fling her body around a bit more until finally she tossed herself onto the bed and lay there, staring at Tamar. Ruth wept, but silently. Her eyes pleaded with Tamar, but no words came out even though her mouth moved.

Ruth and her internal rider stayed that way for the next few hours. Tamar prayed.

Praying didn't change her. Her mother's repeated accusations that Tamar had "become religious" had always fallen flat because observance did not mean belief, and belief did not necessarily equate to observance. She had, at different points of her life, taken comfort from rituals that had at other times felt burdensome. She prayed now because it felt right to do it, and because it seemed in some way to hurt the dybbuk. Or her mother. Or both.

During the break in the day's services, she offered her mother lunch, only to be told once again in Ruth's petulant voice that she was fasting.

"I'm not," Tamar said. "So if you want something to eat, just let me know."

Ruth jerked and sat up. "You're supposed to fast."

"I don't feel good when I fast."

"You're not supposed to feel good on Yom Kippur. You're supposed to be *grieving*," Ruth said.

"I can grieve on a stomach that's not empty. Anyway, I need my strength to deal with you." She meant the dybbuk, but it was Ruth who answered.

"You were always so sullen, Tammy. So easily wounded. You always took everything so personally."

Tamar turned away from the argument. She ate her lunch in the kitchen to the sound of Ruth's wailing.

She went back to the bedroom doorway. Ruth was still on the bed but on her back. Her mouth worked as she stared at the ceiling.

"Just say yes," she said without looking toward Tamar. "Just say yes. Please."

"I'm not going to say yes."

"I said yes to my mother, and she said yes to hers, and my grand-mother said yes to her mother—"

"Services are starting again," Tamar said. "Let me log back in. You have until the shofar blows."

"For what?" Ruth gasped out, thrashing again on the bare mattress. She'd kicked off all the covers and pillows. "To do what?"

"To love me," Tamar said. "So I can forgive you."

44

"I'M READY. I really am," Ruth said.

Tamar had been standing outside the study door for the past hour while the closing service, Neilah, built up to the blowing of the shofar. Without a prayer book to guide her along, she wasn't sure how much longer it would be, but she knew they couldn't do it until nightfall. Darkness was pressing the windows of Ruth's room. It would have to be soon.

"Hurry," Ruth urged, the timbre of the dybbuk's voice beneath hers. "Before they blow the shofar. That's what you said, isn't it? Come in here, Tamar. I'm ready."

Tamar stepped over the threshold, past the mezuzah's protection. The temperature inside this room had dropped to a comfortable level. It didn't help the lingering stench, but at least she wasn't ready to pass out from the heat. Her mother stood in the center of the room, mindless of the crunch of glass from the smashed TV under her bare feet. She swayed a little but caught herself. She reached for Tamar.

"I'm ready," Ruth said again.

From the laptop in the hallway, the rising chorus of the final prayers began. Tamar glanced over her shoulder to see the congregants who'd be blowing the shofar gathering on the bimah. She turned back toward her mother, ready to speak although she wasn't sure what she meant to say.

Both of Ruth's fists swung. Tamar ducked the first, but the second gripped a shard of broken TV screen that sliced a burning path over Tamar's shoulder and all the way down her arm. Tamar stumbled back, but her mother launched herself against her. They both fell to the ground. Tamar blocked another blow from the fist holding the glass, knocking Ruth off her and to the side. Ruth crawled away over the metal and glass, then tottered to her feet using the recliner to pull herself along.

Tamar's head rung. She was glad she hadn't fasted, she had time to think with her muddled brain, before the dybbuk swiveled Ruth's body around and leaped at her again. She was going all out now, pushing the old woman's physical body with whatever supernatural strengths she had managed to retain.

Tamar rolled out of the way as her mother's foot came down. It landed where her face would've been. Tamar got to her feet, only to be jerked around by something gripping her hand. Ruth's hand dug in, five points of pain in Tamar's palm and wrist. Her nails embedded in Tamar's flesh. The dybbuk yanked Tamar off balance and to her knees. The dybbuk bent Tamar's fingers back, back, back.

One broke.

Tamar shrieked.

The dybbuk laughed and stumbled, and Tamar wrenched herself free. The sound of the shofar rang throughout the room. The service was over. The connection to the livestream dropped, replaced by silence and a screen thanking everyone who'd joined virtually.

Somehow, Tamar managed to get to the doorway. She'd be safe on the other side, but "safe" was an artificial construct she could no longer count on. She wrapped her unbroken fingers around the leg of the sturdy, hard-backed kitchen chair she'd been sitting on in the hallway. She dragged it into the room and used it to help herself stand. She swung it at the dybbuk dancing in her mother's body. The chair connected with Ruth's head. The dybbuk howled, but Ruth dropped like a rock.

Tamar put the chair in the middle of the room. She forced her mother's limp body into it. Blood ran down Tamar's arm and filled the also-bleeding wounds on her hand from Ruth's fingernails. It made her grip slippery, so she wiped her hand again and again on her clothes until she could hold tight to the power cord she ripped from the back of the television and the cords that had once connected the streaming box and the DVD player. She tied them tight enough to dig into the scant flesh of the old woman's wrists, lashed through the chair's slatted sides, and her ankles, fastened to the braces of the chair's legs. Ruth's head hung, blood and snot and saliva pooling in the dented fabric of her skirt.

Nausea swept over Tamar, but she forced it away. Her head spun with dizziness. Her shoulder burned from the slice there. All of those discomforts, though, could not compare with the unabated and obstinate agony in her heart.

"I knew you wouldn't be able to do it," she whispered.

Tamar heard a car pulling into her driveway.

The dybbuk heard it too. She cocked Ruth's head toward the window before turning her gaze to Tamar. "Oh, what have you done?"

"Tamar?"

They both turned toward the doorway at the sound of the soft voice that drifted down the hall. Tamar's heart choked her throat. The dybbuk growled, a sound too big for the body she had worn for decades. Too strong. Too loud. She yanked at the cords on Ruth's wrists, but no matter how big she was on the inside, the outside was still worn and weak and incapable of breaking free.

"Tamar, it's me, Rabbi Feldman."

"The front door was locked," Tamar said to the dybbuk through gritted teeth.

The dybbuk let out a withering, shuddering wail through a sly and gleeful grin. It shook its head. "Not anymore."

"Rabbi, don't come in here!" Tamara shouted.

"I'm coming in," Rabbi Feldman called out.

"Don't come in here! Please!"

Too late. Rabbi Feldman peeked around the doorway. She took a single step through it, her gaze finding Tamar first before sliding quickly to the old woman tied up in the chair. The rabbi's eyes widened, but she didn't rush to her aid, even though Ruth squirmed and grunted. Ruth's teeth chattered rapidly, like a cat when it sees a bird.

"What are you doing here?" Tamar said.

Rabbi Feldman looked strained. "When I didn't hear from you, and you didn't come to services, I worried something had happened to you. I was hoping all of this would turn out to be a misunderstanding. But it doesn't look like that's what happened. Can you tell me about it? Maybe I can help."

"Don't untie her," Tamar warned. "She's weak, but she can still hurt you. And don't listen to her. Try to block out her voice, if you can. She will try to confuse you. Please, just go."

"I'm not going to leave you, Tamar. Okay? I'm here to help you." Rabbi Feldman looked at the woman in the chair. "I'm Maya Feldman. We haven't met, but I'm—"

"The rabbi from the synagogue."

"I'm also Tamar's friend. I came to help, okay? Both of you."

The dybbuk was silent. She dropped Ruth's head, shoulders hunching. The rabbi moved a step closer to her.

"I said don't. Please, Rabbi. You have to believe me."

"I believe you," Rabbi Feldman said calmly. "I believe you are in great pain, and you need help, Tamar. Why don't you let me call someone to help you? And your mother."

"Nobody can help her," Tamar said. "Not even you. Maybe especially not you."

She was tired.

So tired.

Rabbi Feldman nodded. "I understand why you might not think so. But do you trust me, Tamar?"

She did trust the rabbi, that was the kicker of it all. Her intentions, at least, if not the possibility that she could really do anything. "I know you think you can, but Rabbi, I promise. You can't."

"Will you let me check on your mother? I won't untie her. I just want to make sure she's all right."

"She's not all right. She's possessed by a demon. A dybbuk," Tamar amended flatly, harsh on purpose, hating herself for pushing away the person who wanted to help her. Knowing she had no other choice. "You know. The thing you told me wasn't real? You were wrong."

Rabbi Feldman nodded again. "I was wrong. But dybbuks are ageless. Your mother's body is not. I know you want to help her."

Before Tamar could holler out another warning, the rabbi had taken the few final steps to the chair and the woman sitting in it. She bent close. She put a gentle hand on Ruth's arm.

"Ruth. Can you look at me?"

It took exactly three seconds for the dybbuk to lift her head. To bare her teeth. And to rip out the rabbi's throat.

Blood spouted.

Tamar recoiled at the hot splash of it on her face. Her body. She cried out but choked herself off at the last moment. Tamar dropped to her knees to cradle the rabbi, whose head fell backwards on the fragile stem of her shredded neck. The dybbuk had torn out half of it.

She used Ruth's mouth to spit onto the floor a mass of blood and flesh and gristle. The dybbuk's laughter spiraled into a cacophony of baying shrieks as she rocked the chair back and forth, slamming the front legs onto the floor so hard the feet splintered. She did it again. Again. One leg broke and sent the chair tipping forward.

Ruth landed on her face with a crunch. She cried out, voice burbling, and then eased into a long, slow, and agonized moan.

Tamar grabbed at the comforter that had been tossed onto the floor and pressed it to the rabbi's neck to stanch the bleeding. Her efforts didn't matter. The light had gone out in Rabbi Feldman's eyes, and her mouth had gone slack and loose. A sewer stink slapped at Tamar's face, nothing phantom about it this time. It came from the rabbi's body.

Ruth turned her head, cheek resting on the floor. Blood smeared her nose, bent to the side. More blood framed her mouth. "Tammy?"

"You killed her," Tamar whispered.

"What's happening? What are you doing?" Her mother's voice rose, waspish and confused.

Ruth struggled. One hand had come free of the cords when the chair fell over and broke. She slid it beneath her and pushed upward. Blood covered the front of her blouse. It dripped from her chin. Her front teeth had been broken out.

One of them was lodged in the rabbi's neck.

Tamar shuddered, rocking back and forth for only a moment before she gently laid Rabbi Feldman's body down and got to her feet. She stood over Ruth with her fists clenched.

"You killed her," she repeated. "Why? Because she was trying to help me? She was trying to help you too!"

"She didn't believe you. She wasn't going to help you." The dybbuk was in control again. She moved with jerking, shuddering movements and wobbled up onto Ruth's knees. Her hands went out for a moment before the dybbuk put them on the floor to push herself onto Ruth's feet. She held open Ruth's arms, ready for an embrace. "I'm the only one who can help you, Tamar."

"You never helped me. Not once in your life."

The dybbuk opened Ruth's arms even wider. She swayed. "All I've ever done is help you, in so many ways you never even knew."

Tamar's head hung. A long strand of bloody drool stretched from her mouth to the floor. Her hair could not fall in her face or over her eyes, of course, because her hair was gone. Her bones ached beneath the soft shell of her skin, bruised and swollen, laced with slashes. The five deep wounds in her hand throbbed and oozed clear fluid. Already, faint strands of red had begun feathering out of the holes and along her arm. Creeping toward her heart. Would they poison her? Was she already dying?

"Why couldn't you just love me enough to get your shit together? Why couldn't you just be my *mother*?" Each word stung Tamar's split lip as it left her mouth. Each one tasted of blood and bile.

"I loved you then, and I love you now," gritted out the thing that had both always and never been her mother. "I gave you life."

Tamar took a step back. "Believe me, I know how much you think I owe you for that. You never let me forget it. Not once. But mothers are supposed to—"

"How would you know," the mother-thing interrupted, "what mothers do or don't do?"

Involuntarily, Tamar pressed both her hands to her belly, but she pulled them away and stood up straight. The dybbuk noticed, of course. She noticed everything. Her smile spread across Ruth's mouth and tipped her eyes upward at the corners.

"Hurts, don't it? To know how you had your chance, and you squandered it? You threw it away just like you throw away anything that means anything to you."

"You don't know anything about me."

The dybbuk laughed. "I know everything about you, girl. I'm your fucking *mother*."

Tamar wanted to scream out that this thing was not her mother. It had taken her mother. Stolen her. Consumed her. But that was not the truth. This thing had occupied her mother for as long as Tamar could remember. This malicious spirit had been there for every childhood nightmare, every skinned knee, lost tooth, and report card. She had pushed her daughters on the swings, tucked them into bed, force-fed them meatloaf, rubbed their wounds with salt, and she had been there to wipe away the tears as she reveled in every single pain she caused.

"You know I'm right," the dybbuk said.

Tamar said nothing. She calculated the distance between her mother's body and the doorway. If she could get past it, she could run out of the house. And then what? Where would she go?

"You were already in her when she got pregnant with me."

"Yes. Because Ruthie did the right thing, unlike her serpent's tooth of a daughter," the dybbuk said. "She never wanted you. I think you know that. Why do you think she married Jake Kahan in the first place? He'd told her he couldn't make babies. But I knew I'd need one, so I made her find Roger. I'm the one who made her keep you. She was ready to get you ripped out of her. When I say you owe me your life, Tamar, that is exactly what I mean."

"You lie," Tamar whispered.

The dybbuk didn't laugh this time. She shook her head slowly, back and forth, side to side. She shrugged. "Not about this."

There'd been so many tears over the years, but now Tamar found she couldn't cry. Her eyes burned. Her throat closed. The tears fought to get out, but she couldn't let them. Her fists clenched instead.

"Roger told me about my mother asking him to get her pregnant. She did want me."

The dybbuk tilted Ruth's head to look Tamar up and down. Assessing her. "No. *I* wanted you. You were mine. You were always supposed to be mine. She was going to refuse to have children. I made her. Because *I* wanted you. And once I had mine, she was allowed to have hers. She wanted Lovey desperately. You say I never helped you? Jake Kahan wanted to kill you, but I killed him instead. If that's not helping you, if that's not *loving* you, what is?"

"*Why* did he want to kill me? Because he knew he wasn't my father?"

"The man knew he couldn't get his wife pregnant and didn't say boo when she did. He wasn't going to kill you because of that."

"Why, then?"

"Because he found out what she needed you for," the dybbuk said.

"So, he wanted to save me, and you stopped him."

Ruth spoke next, with bubbles of blood bursting on her lips. "It has to be done with love, Tammy."

"Were you horrible to me so I wouldn't love you? So I could never, never do what that bitch inside you wants me to? Were you trying to save me too?"

In the silence before Ruth answered, Tamar clutched at that balloon string of hope, trying hard to hold it tight. Watching her mother's lip curl and her eyes narrow, Tamar let go. It would have been difficult, but possible, to forgive her mother for doing terrible things for a good reason. If she'd done them out of love.

"You could lie," Tamar whispered, voice breaking. "You lie about everything else."

But Ruth, it seemed, had finally found honesty. "I forgive you, honey, for not being the daughter I wanted or needed. I forgive you."

"But do you *love* me?"

"*I* love you," the dybbuk said.

Tamar believed her. And the worst part, the thing that dug deep into her guts and twisted, twisted, until she thought she might do just about anything if only the pain would stop—being wanted by a demon was better than being rejected by her mother.

"I need you," Ruth said. "Why can't that be enough for you?"

All it would take was saying yes. Her mother would be free. Tamar would take the burden from her, and they could spend the brief remainder of Ruth's life making up for all that had been lost. They could finally have the relationship Tamar had always yearned for. All she had to do was say yes.

Tamar took a step toward the mother-thing's eager embrace. Babbling with Ruth's voice and the dybbuk's words, they drew in a shuddering breath, the two of them joined as one whole entity, no way to tell them apart. They reached for Tamar with fervid fingers. They pulled her close, breath rank and hot on the side of Tamar's face, and hotter where it touched the slick trails of blood on her skin.

"I do not forgive you," Tamar said. "And I don't love you."

Ruth and her dybbuk yowled together, a caterwauling that rose up and up until Ruth staggered back with both hands on her throat. Something inside of it popped. She fell backwards onto the bed, turning her head and spewing blood and bile and long, dark tangles of hair. The body thrashed; the soul screamed.

Tamar watched as Ruth clutched at her chest. Her fingernails raked through her blouse and into the skin beneath. Her face purpled, eyes bulging. She convulsed.

She went still.

Her eyes were open, blank and staring.

She was dead. Tamar knew it without checking her pulse or listening for a breath. She knew it because the emptiness and the sense of waiting that had haunted her for as long as she had memories was gone. She bent over her mother's body, ready to fight if the dybbuk managed to take control, but it seemed as though the thing could not manifest itself to puppeteer an empty vessel. Whatever had made Ruth *Ruth* was gone, and the glimmer of intelligence left inside her lifeless gaze also blinked out as Tamar watched. Tamar hadn't taken on her mother's demon, but she'd freed her, all the same. More than that, she was free herself. And then, because she could, she let herself bend over her mother's body, and she wept. Tamar mourned the loss of what should have been and never was.

She no longer needed to consume the bitterness of her own heart.

And finally, she forgave herself for wanting what would never come.

-End-

PLAYLIST

I COULD WRITE WITHOUT music, but I'm glad I don't have to. Here is a partial playlist of songs I listened to while working on this book:

Breathe Again—Joy Oladokun
For Rosanna—Chris de Burgh
Angels or Devils—Dishwalla
Calling All Angels—Jane Siberry feat. k.d. lang
Like It or Not—Madonna
Demon—Guster
Rev 22:20—Puscifer
Daughters of Darkness—Halestorm
Dear Daughter—Halestorm
For the Love of a Daughter—Demi Lovato

*　　*　　*